> ***"Come on, Ava."*** *He touched her hand.*
> ***"You'll love it."***

She whipped her fingers away from under his and the spark ignited in her eyes. "How do you know what I'll love?"

"A cruise through the most beautiful waters on earth. Six nights in a three-thousand-dollar suite with private valet service. The chance to whip up some crème brûlée with your hero Arnot. The opportunity to advance your cause, or at least understand it." He put his hand right back on hers, teasing her with a grin. "And I'll be there. Now, what's not to love?"

In spite of herself, she laughed. A throaty, honest laugh that was as attractive as her rare smiles. "You could lure Satan out of hell, you know that?"

ROXANNE ST. CLAIRE

for Jazz

TROPICAL GETAWAY

Enjoy the Getaway!

Roxanne St. Claire

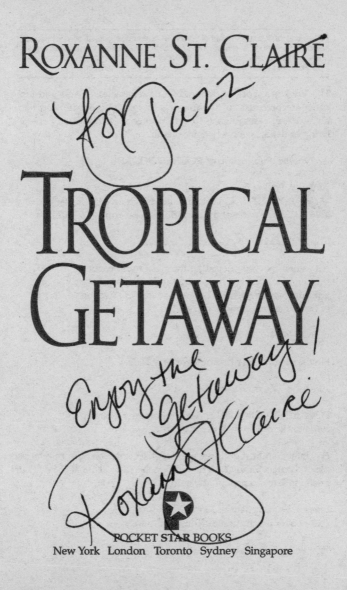

POCKET STAR BOOKS
New York London Toronto Sydney Singapore

An *Original* Publication of POCKET BOOKS

 A Pocket Star Book published by
POCKET BOOKS, a division of Simon & Schuster, Inc.
1230 Avenue of the Americas, New York, NY 10020

ISBN: 0-7434-6276-9

First Pocket Books printing February 2003

10 9 8 7 6 5 4 3 2 1

POCKET STAR BOOKS and colophon are registered trademarks of Simon & Schuster, Inc.

For information regarding special discounts for bulk purchases, please contact Simon & Schuster Special Sales at 1-800-456-6798 or business@simonandschuster.com

Interior design by Davina Mock
Front cover illustration by Tom Hallman

Printed in the U.S.A.

With special thanks to

James Clary, for the rich tales of superstitions and the sea that provided color and texture and nautical accuracy.

Anna Perrin, Sandy Moffett, and Sharon Calvin, for repeated reviews and thoughtful considerations of the manuscript.

Cecelia Zink for exceptional proofreading and cheerleading.

Roberta Brown, an excellent literary agent whose determination and enthusiasm keeps me afloat.

Micki Nuding, the ideal editorial mate in the uncharted seas of publishing.

This book is dedicated to

My husband, Rich, who nourishes my spirit and navigates our ship through the adventure of life. He is the wind in my sails and forever my captain.

and

The thirty-one men lost at sea on board the *S/V Fantome* in 1998. They lived and died with amazing grace, and inspired me to tell a happier story.

Heavenly signs of wind and rain,
Long the seafarer's weathervane.
Into the Sea of Darkness they sailed,
And with the devil's compass, prevailed.

—James Clary
Superstitions of the Sea

Prologue

The kitchen of Santori's was as raucous and spirited as the Italian family that owned the landmark restaurant in Boston's North End. Ava Santori didn't even hear the shout of her teenage cousin over the din until a hint of panic shuddered in the girl's voice.

"Ava! You have a long-distance call on three!"

Marone! Ava bit back the Italian curse and continued chopping. "Is it urgent, Mia? I'm a little swamped right now."

Surely Mia had inherited the good sense to know a packed dining room at twelve-thirty on a Friday meant take pity and take a message.

"Uh, well, yes, Ava. I'd say this is urgent."

She looked up, the knife suspended midchop.

Mia's green eyes were wide and insistent. "You need to take this call."

With a rueful glance at the remaining shallots, Ava dropped the knife. She dodged a sauté pan being passed by a sous-chef from stove to oven. Over the sizzle of a sudden flambé, she shouted, "Who is it?"

"It's"—a stock pot clattered in the prep sink—"Marco."

Every drop of blood drained from Ava's head, down through her body, down to her soul. Marco. Her brother. It had been five years since she'd heard his voice. She steadied herself by gripping the edge of the stainless steel counter.

"Go back to the front, hon. Get Nicky to cover the last few orders for me."

Ava wiped shaking hands on her chef's apron and left the chaos for the back office.

Marco. The missing piece of her life. Finally, the moment, the call. The forgiveness she'd fantasized about for so many years.

She stared at the flashing yellow light on line three with a mix of hope and fear. What could she say to her little brother? *Marco, honey, I love you and I miss you and I'm so sorry . . .*

An intense shudder shook her whole body, and she lifted the receiver, unable to wipe the smile that came from her heart.

"Marco." She savored the utter contentment of lingering over both syllables of his name. At last.

"Uh, no. This is Captain Donald Taylor with the United States Coast Guard."

The free fall of disappointment forced her to close her eyes.

"I'm trying to reach Marco Santori's closest relative," the caller continued. "Would that be you, ma'am?"

Closest relative? Mama wouldn't be back for hours, and her father was in New York, taping his TV show. She cleared her throat, her eyes still closed. "I'm Marco's sister, Ava Santori. What do you need?"

"Miss Santori, I have the unenviable task of calling to deliver some bad news."

Nicky barked an order in the kitchen and someone swore. Reaching across the tiny office, she shoved the door closed.

Please, Mary, Mother of God, not Marco. She fell into a seat, tears threatening, waiting for the words.

"You may have heard that a category five hurricane destroyed most of the island of Grenada a few days ago."

A hurricane. The Coast Guard. Where on earth was this going? She tried to think. "Yes. Yes. A storm that hit Grenada or Trinidad or some such island." A faint newsreel of destroyed shanties and flattened palm trees flashed in her mind.

"Your brother's ship was caught in that hurricane, ma'am."

"His ship?" What in God's name was Marco doing on a ship?

"The *Paradisio*, ma'am, one of Utopia Adventures' passenger sailing ships. Marco Santori was her second mate."

Marco, a sailor? It seemed preposterous. It must be a mistake. But then, five long years had gone by since a nineteen-year-old boy slipped out the back door of Santori's on a winter night amid his mother's tears and his father's angry diatribes. He could have done anything with his life.

"We've been conducting an extensive search and rescue operation for the past four days that will go on for three weeks or until we find the ship or debris," he continued in a somber tone. "But we haven't recovered any materials or men. As of this morning, we have officially classified your brother and the rest of the crew as presumed dead. I'm sorry, Miss Santori."

Presumed dead.

The sob started from deep inside her gut and swallowed her whole. Marco was gone. She would never, ever see his teasing brown eyes or hear him call her Avel Navel. Her baby brother, the risk taker, the thrill seeker, the bad-to-the-bone boy she adored had ended up on some boat in the Caribbean Sea, and her fear and cowardice had kept her from even knowing that he could sail. She wanted to scream.

"We've got about a hundred men on the search effort, ma'am. And Utopia's hired a cadre of private divers and aircraft . . ."

She didn't hear what else he said, regret filled her mouth and turned her stomach.

"How . . . how did you find us?"

"Utopia's personnel records, ma'am." He sounded surprised at the question. "Your family is listed as next of kin."

Could there be any more sickening words in the English language? *Next of kin.* It implied a closeness, a kinship. The right to mourn. Ava swallowed hard.

"I'm sure you have a lot of questions, ma'am. And you probably need some time with your family. Let me give you my number and I'll be happy to provide you with a status of the search effort."

She reached for a pen with shaking hands.

"Oh, and ma'am, you might be getting some calls from the media. The announcement of the shipwreck was just formally released and it's going to be news. Be prepared."

She had to tell her mother. Dear God, she had to tell Dominic.

"And, well, this is not really my area, but it only

seems fair to warn you," he continued. "I understand some attorneys are contacting the victims' families already. There will be settlements and the inevitable lawsuits. Sorry, ma'am. It seems harsh at a difficult time like this."

She barely heard him. She was still imagining what Dominic would say upon learning that his only son, banished by his own edict, was dead. Presumed dead.

"Excuse me, Mister—Captain. But, are you sure? Is there any chance he's alive?"

His hesitation filled Ava with hope. But hope turned to dread as the silence dragged on.

"Is there?" She heard the imploring, insisting note in her voice.

"This storm killed about four hundred people on Grenada. At sea, a two-hundred-foot ship wouldn't stand much of a chance in waves the size of six-story buildings. We're looking for bodies, Miss Santori, not survivors. I'm so sorry. Really I am. You can call me or anyone in my office with questions and, like I said, we'll be informing you if we find anything at all."

"Wait a second." Her focus started to return and reason rose to the top. Hurricanes were on the Weather Channel for days before they hit anywhere. "What was a two-hundred-foot sailboat doing in a hurricane? Didn't they know it was coming? Why would they sail right into a storm?"

"That's what we're trying to figure out, ma'am."

1

Dane Erikson stood on the weather-beaten docks of St. Barts harbor, where mourners had gathered in clusters. With them, he listened to the tributes to twenty-one men delivered from a makeshift podium. Every few minutes, his gaze returned to the ebony-haired beauty in the back, drinking in her uncanny resemblance to Marco. There could only be one reason for Ava Santori to attend the memorial service for the victims of *Paradisio*.

Money.

So, not one reason. One million reasons.

Why else, after years of estrangement, would she join the mothers, wives, and island children who gathered at the edge of a bloodred sunset to mourn the men who perished in the wreck of his ship?

In a simple black dress, she stood out among the colorful islanders who honored the dead by donning the brilliant hues of the Caribbean.

He had no doubt of her identity, although she had apparently spoken to no one. Smaller and paler than her brother, she had the same unruly curls and enor-

mous eyes the color of ripe black olives. The amazing
likeness unnerved Dane and remorse rolled through
him.

The mourners closed their eyes in prayer or
moaned in grief. A small child called out for his
mother, who scooped him up with one hand and
slung him into a natural curve on her hip. More than
a few glanced his way.

These island people understood the capricious-
ness of the sea that fed and nurtured them. But how
many, like Ava Santori, would want retribution and
vengeance and mountains of money? How many
needed a villain to blame for the deaths of the young
men who tried to sail the ship to safety? The orange
swirl on a map that became known as Hurricane Carlos was too intangible to take the blame for their loss.
Someone must pay. Someone must be held account-
able. That someone was him.

Beyond the docks, two of Utopia Adventures'
majestic sailing ships rested in the harbor of St.
Barthélemy, a row of matching masts against an in-
digo sky, listing leeward in the tropical breeze. But no
familiar sense of pride filled Dane at the sight. He'd
been numb for the last three weeks since his favorite
ship—his first ship—had thrashed and sunk under
the deadly rogue waves that few sailors live to describe.

He'd arrived from the search site last night, ill prepared to make a poignant address. Exhausted, frustrated, and as stunned as everyone else, he'd planned
to keep a typically low profile among his employees.
But Cassie had begged him to speak about Marco,
and he couldn't stand for her heart to break any further.

So he agreed to give the eulogy for the *Paradisio's* second mate. He certainly never expected a Santori in the audience. But, then, there was never such a compelling reason for any of them to show up. Money: the great reconciler.

He kept his eyes on the ships as he strode across the wide planks of the dock, purposely avoiding eye contact with the unexpected guest from Boston. He placed a set of index cards etched with furious notes on the top of the temporary pulpit created for the event and inhaled the scent of frangipani mixed with salt water.

"I consider Marco Santori my brother."

At the edge of the crowd, he saw her sway at his opening line, closing her eyes for a moment.

He shifted his focus to the familiar faces that watched him. He knew every employee, spouse, child, and parent in the crowd. Knew their troubles and their family secrets. Knew their children's ailments, their marital problems and their superstitions. That's who he needed to worry about right now.

After his three-week sojourn to the rescue site fifty miles east of Grenada, he'd returned to find suspicion. Doubt. And greed. He smelled it all around him.

He flipped the cards facedown, abandoning the prepared words of sympathy and grief. He'd better speak from the heart.

"Many of you know the story of how I met Marco. It's Utopia folklore by now." The murmur of a response rolled through the crowd, some chuckled softly.

"The folklore is true. I saved Marco's backside in a barroom brawl on St. John. I felt sorry for the kid. No family, in exile from someplace called New England, and he couldn't fight worth a damn."

Her eyes narrowed. Piercing, reproachful.

"But he wanted to sail." Dane thought of the hot-headed, emotional kid with boundless energy who came to Utopia and touched everyone with his humor and enthusiasm. "Even though we all just wanted him to cook." Knowing laughter lifted the crowd as many nodded with their own memory.

Dane smiled with them. At first, Marco had been such a passionate brat, but despite that and their disparate backgrounds—one with a boiling Mediterranean temper, the other shaped by cool and controlled Scandinavian values—they quickly found common ground. Sailing. Their mentor-student relationship developed into what both expected to be a lifelong friendship, but in Marco's case, life hadn't been long enough.

"He loved the sea as much as I do—as much as you all do—and watching Marco develop into a fine sailor, well on his way to being a captain, was a great pleasure. A very great pleasure."

Ava plucked at the silk of her dress, assaulted by the relentless humidity and the canned speech. *Then why did you send him to his death, you bastard?* A band of sweat formed under her chest, and she could feel the weight of her unrestrained hair threatening to spring into a mass of damp ringlets.

None of it mattered, she told herself. She was here, years too late, but here nonetheless.

Dominic would not let go of his stubborn pride. He wanted no part of a memorial service. He would have nothing to do with a lawsuit. He would burn the money from a settlement. He wouldn't hear of some southern lawyer's trumped-up claims that his son's ship was sent directly into the storm by the cruise company's owner. He wouldn't even talk about it.

The fire in Dominic's black eyes had burned hotter than ever, his own bitter regret consuming him. And Mama had just locked herself upstairs and cried.

But Grayson Boyd was one persistent lawyer. Every day, he faxed his legal briefs, sent articles from the newspapers, and E-mailed schedules of filings. And, by God, he'd convinced her. Not just to come to the island for the service. Ava needed to do that with every fiber of her being.

No, the lawyer had convinced her that Dane Erikson stood under a black cloud of suspicion. He had so very much to gain. A forty-million-dollar insurance settlement. The payoff from a slight navigational error.

She studied the man and tried to reconcile what she observed with the little she knew of him. He exuded a powerful self-assuredness that Ava would never, ever possess under any circumstances. She always envied it in people. Marco, for all his charm and exuberance, had it too.

Dane Erikson's arresting good looks had startled her at first. The strong lines of his Nordic heritage were obvious in his square jaw and a sculpted mouth. The handsome hollows of his cheeks and the knowledge in his piercing gaze made him look every one of his thirty-seven years, somehow both a prince and a rebel. She stared at him, trying to quell the dizzying effect it had on her. She'd been prepared for someone dark and menacing and evil. She'd expected her stomach to turn at the sight of him. Instead, her heart raced every time a smile broke across the chiseled angles of his face.

The face of an angel with the heart of a devil, her father would say.

"Marco Santori commanded respect and encouraged esprit de corps among his fellow crewmen. He touched us with his unexpected sensitivity, his dry sense of humor, and his heartfelt passion for living."

The twin sisters of regret and guilt choked Ava as she listened to the man who claimed brotherhood with the brother she had lost.

"It is impossible to imagine how many lives were touched and changed by these men." Erikson paused, the epitome of a grieving chief executive officer, displaying an appropriate amount of mourning but completely in control of his emotions. A towering figure with broad shoulders and taut muscles straining his shirt, he looked as though he could easily bear the weight of this disaster. His ramrod straight posture oozed confidence, as though through sheer strength and force, he could keep his accusers at bay. Then he smiled, and Ava imagined if all else failed, he could charm his way out of a courtroom.

His gaze locked on her, and she held her breath, like a thief caught red-handed as she stared at him. When his attention moved on, she exhaled.

"The *Paradisio* was a beautiful ship," he continued. "Graceful, elegant, majestic. Like all of our ships, her name means *heaven*, and it is certainly a fitting and poignant reminder of where our crew is today."

Marone! Ava didn't want to listen to the hypnotic words of Dane Erikson, talking of the history of the sea, ancient sailing customs, and thousands of brothers and sisters resting quietly on the ocean floor. One of them was hers.

Blessedly, he finished. In the sudden silence, she

heard someone stifle a sob, another person moan. Heartache hung over the docks as palpable as the late summer humidity and just as uncomfortable. Suddenly, a fluttering whoosh startled the crowd as twenty-one white doves were released from up front, flapping their way to freedom. At the same moment, dozens of white sails unfurled on the masts of the matching tall ships in the harbor, a symphony of crackling canvas against the wind.

A woman cried out to God in French, a young man sobbed. Ava looked up at the doves, picking one at random and watching it disappear into the golden sky. *Good-bye, Marco. I loved you, I really did. I'm so sorry.* She dug the heel of her sandal into the soft wood of the dock and felt it make a slight indentation. *Don't second-guess, Santori. Blessed are those who don't look back.*

Suddenly, a six-foot shadow darkened her view. She knew before she even looked at him, that Dane Erikson stood next to her. The auburn sunset backlit him, denying her the chance to read his expression.

"Ava Santori." His voice was low, the whisper of an English accent hidden in the syllables. "What a complete surprise."

Unnerved, she stumbled on an uneven plank. He *recognized* her? He reached out to steady her, and she flinched away from his touch.

"This is a memorial service for my brother." She repositioned her feet and squared her shoulders. "I have every right to be here."

"Of course you do." He held out a hand. "Dane Erikson."

Finally, the remaining sunlight fell on his face and lit the golden streaks of his hair that flipped arrogantly over the collar of a loose linen shirt. His aquamarine eyes matched the color of the sea behind him, fringed with thick lashes and touched by fine lines etched by the sun and salt air. Everything about him was bright and bold. And breathtaking, Ava grudgingly admitted.

She briefly touched his hand. Cool and dry. Just like the rest of him. "I know who you are."

"Marco would have been—happy you're here."

She raised a dubious eyebrow. "I doubt he would have enjoyed any aspect of his own funeral, Mr. Erikson."

A half smile crossed his face, revealing more perfection. Straight, white teeth. "How true."

She wasn't prepared to talk to him. Drawn by pain and curiosity to the service, she'd thought she could mingle anonymously with the crowd, then leave unnoticed. Then she'd go back to the tiny hotel on the hillside where she could wait to meet with the lawyer.

At her silence, he continued. "I'm sorry it took a tragedy to finally bring a member of Marco's family to his side."

The impulse to strike back tore at her, but a lifetime of controlling her temper kept her voice low and calm. "It's entirely possible that we wouldn't be standing here if it weren't for you, sir."

His own voice dropped to a menacing whisper. "I suppose I can thank the bottom-feeding attorney Grayson Boyd for your visit."

"That's correct," she hissed in response. "He makes some very compelling arguments about who is really responsible for the suicide mission that ship was sent on."

"I'm afraid you have no idea what you're talking about."

Taking another step back, she tried to regroup. Why had she come here alone? She should have insisted that Boyd accompany her. But he might have tried to talk her out of coming at all. Now she didn't know what to say, how much to give away. *Don't say too much, Santori. For once, be cool, girl.*

She took a deep breath and flipped her bag over her shoulder, hoping he'd let her escape. "The service was lovely."

He glanced around the milling crowd. "I hope it helped a little. How long are you staying?"

He's scared, she thought with a spark of power. He's guilty and he's scared.

"A few days, a few weeks. Long enough." She refused to let him draw her into the fight here, on this dock. He'd figure out soon enough what her mission was. He was smart enough to realize that Marco's sister, estranged or not, could easily persuade the confused and uneducated families of the crewmen to join the suit. "I'd like to know . . . what kind of person he had become."

His eyes narrowed in challenge. "Then you should have come sooner. It would have been a hell of a lot easier to figure it out when he was still breathing."

Her temper sizzled at a slow burn.

"Perhaps you are unaware of the situation with my family, Mr. Erikson—"

"It's Dane, and I know enough about the situation. Marco was my closest friend." The aquamarine eyes closed for a moment. "He's mentioned you."

It hit like a sucker punch. "I didn't come here to discuss Marco with you. Just to pay my last respects to my brother." The wind lifted a strand of hair across her face, and she flipped it back. "I had no intention of speaking to you."

"If you want to find out about your brother, you should talk to me." The same breeze took a pass at his sunstreaked hair, but he made no effort to move a fallen strand from his brow. "I could tell you a great deal about Marco. His zest for life and his passion for taking risks—"

"Oh, he liked to take risks, all right." She spat the words. "But he wasn't stupid and neither am I." *Stop now, Santori. Don't taunt the devil.* But the damning paragraphs of Grayson Boyd's legal brief flashed in her mind. "You were the last person to communicate with that ship and its captain. You sent them straight into that hurricane, and there are satellite phone recordings to prove it."

He leaned closer, a blue-eyed wolf ready to bite. "You really have just enough information to be dangerous."

She straightened to every inch that her five-foot-five frame could offer.

"I *am* dangerous." She stabbed a finger ineffectively at his solid chest. "You're the one with forty *more* million dollars and I'm the one who has no brother."

"That, Miss Ava Santori, has been the case for many years. And whose fault is that?"

The low hum of voices nearby brought Ava back to her senses. She looked over his shoulder to avoid those piercing eyes and regain the self-control she needed. She might have had a hand in Marco's leaving, but she had nothing to do with his death. He could *not* turn the tables and make it her fault.

"If you think that you can get away with this and not have to pay—"

"Ah." He nodded with an air of inevitability. "It all comes down to money. Why else would you be here?"

Ava took a sudden sharp breath. "Now *you* have no idea what you're talking about." She nipped his upper arm with her fingers, unable to resist emphasizing her certainty.

Dane dropped a distasteful glance at the spot where her fingers had touched him. His eyes turned the color of ice cold steel and just as sharp.

"When you calm down and decide you have time to hear facts, and not some lawyer's self-serving account of what happened, I'll be happy to provide them. And I can tell you a lot about your brother that might interest you."

"No, thank you. Save your side of the story for the courtroom and spare me your insights on Marco. I don't want them."

"Then perhaps you want mine."

A lilting foreign accent floated toward Ava, and she turned and looked straight into one of the sweetest faces she'd ever seen. Sparkling green eyes fringed with reddish lashes, a spray of soft freckles, and a halo of autumn gold waves greeted her.

"I'm Cassie Sebring. Marco's fiancée."

Marco's fiancée?

Ava could only stare at her.

"You look so much like Marco," the girl commented with a tilted head, making her own intense assessment of Ava. "The resemblance is truly remarkable. Don't you think, Dane?"

Ava felt like a horse being appraised by traders.

"She certainly has his temper." Dane smiled, a

sudden, break-your-heart smile that almost took
away the sting of his words.

Ava turned away from him to study the will-o'-
the-wisp imp in a pale peach sundress. Should she
shake hands with the person who would have been
her sister-in-law? "Hello, I'm Ava." She extended a
hand in greeting.

No such discomfort seemed to confuse Cassie. She
took Ava's hand in both of hers and gave it a squeeze.
"Marco told me about you."

Ava recognized the musical tone of an Australian
accent and thought how perfectly it suited the natural beauty of this young girl, barely in her twenties.
But then, at almost five years younger than Ava,
Marco would have been nearly twenty-five. They
must have made a striking couple.

"I—I had no idea that Marco was engaged." God,
she'd missed so much of his life.

"Then it seems we've got a lot to talk about."
Cassie kept her eyes on Ava but addressed Dane. "Do
you mind if I steal Ava for a few moments?"

Ava longed to get away from Dane Erikson, but
would Marco's fiancée be any more forgiving?

"No, Cass, your timing's perfect." He leaned
closer to Ava, assaulting her senses with his proximity. "My offer's open. I'd be happy to talk to you
about Marco. He really was like a brother to me."

The heat of his breath fired her response. "He
wasn't *like* a brother to me. He *was* a brother."

"Then you should have treated him like one." A
direct hit, shot with burning blue eyes before he
turned and left.

"Where are you staying while you're in St. Barts?"
Cassie broke the awkward silence as they walked

toward the pastel buildings of Gustavia, leaving the remaining groups of mourners on the docks.

"I'm at a small hotel in town." Grayson Boyd had made the arrangements and promised to pay all the exorbitant hotel expenses if she'd help his cause. At four hundred dollars a night, she might have to swallow her pride and let him.

"Why don't you stay with me?"

"Oh, no, thank you, I couldn't."

"Why not?" Cassie asked. "Unless you like to throw thousands away on a hotel. I know what they charge here. We—I have plenty of room."

Ava stopped and regarded Cassie closely, her nymphlike features contrasting with a daring butterfly tattoo just above her left breast.

"Are you serious?"

The younger girl laughed, a lovely, innocent sound. "I wouldn't ask if I weren't. You're Marco's sister. It's his home too. He'd want you there."

Ava suddenly thought of the lawsuit and tried to remember seeing Cassie's name on a list of family members. Maybe she wasn't considered family. She said she was engaged to Marco, not married. Maybe Cassie saw Ava as a threat to take her portion of any money earned from the lawsuit. Either way, Grayson Boyd wouldn't like it.

Cassie smiled as Ava weighed her options. "Never mind. I didn't mean to make you think so hard."

"I appreciate the offer. I'll see how things go." Ava really had no idea how long Boyd would want her to stay or what he had in mind while she was here. The decision to come had been made so quickly, so emotionally, that she hadn't thought it all through.

"Do you have a car, or can I drive you to Dane's house?"

Ava froze midstep. "Dane's house?"

"Utopia is having a private gathering after the service. His house is the only place that can hold everyone. It won't be festive, but it won't be formal, either. Didn't he mention it to you?"

"No. I'll just go back to the hotel." Her unofficial host would surely frown on a trip to the defendant's house.

"That's ridiculous. All of the Utopians will be there."

Ava considered that. It could be a good way to meet the family members, to talk privately without Boyd around. "Even the families who are suing the company?"

"Yes," Cassie answered quickly, the smile evaporating from her pretty face, replaced by a furrowed brow and questioning eyes. "But today, most of us are thinking about twenty-one friends we lost. Not how much money can be made on their deaths. Is that why you're finally here? For your piece of the legal pie that some ambulance-chasing lawyer dreamed up?"

The accusation echoed and Ava said nothing.

"Is that what you're all about, Ava?" The Australian accent deepened in anger. "I thought maybe you were different. I thought maybe you realized that you lost a brother when Marco died, and you were here to—I don't know—make amends for what happened."

So she knew too. Cassie didn't rile her as Dane did, however. For some reason, Cassie's accusations seemed justified.

"It's very confusing, Cassie. My family is compli-cated and my reasons are . . . well, they are mine." Ava knew she sounded weak and vague. "Yes, I came here at the urging of Grayson Boyd. But that's not the only reason."

How could she describe the war that raged in her heart? How could she tell this stranger that regret was her motive and that she longed for forgiveness from a dead man?

"I'm just here to figure out what happened and say good-bye to my brother."

They reached a set of stone steps that led toward the main street of Gustavia.

"Americans love closure," Cassie said softly, her smile returning. "You're so much like him, Ava. Did you know that?"

Unbidden tears surprised Ava. She shrugged gently, hoping to keep them at bay. "Well, he was my brother. We always looked a little alike. But, really, I guess I don't know anything about him anymore."

Cassie gently put her arms around Ava. Sur-rounded by the warmth and comfort of this young woman whom Marco had loved, Ava closed her eyes and tentatively returned the embrace. Balmy sea breezes mixed with the honeysuckle scent of her would-be sister. A sob caught in her throat and choked her.

"I guess you better tell me what I've missed, Cassie."

From his vantage point at the edge of the harbor, Dane watched the two women comfort each other, the impact of his encounter with Ava still clinging to his senses. He could still see the black, fiery eyes in contrast with the pale skin of someone who rarely saw the sun. Her sultry voice, tinged with the edge of a Boston accent, but so ready to attack with venom. She even had a telltale single dimple in her left cheek, poised just above her full mouth. A Santori trademark.

Hotheaded and impetuous. Like her brother. And just as vulnerable.

His gut level response to her made no sense. When he first saw his own reflection in the eyes so dark they were all pupil, he'd wanted to hold her. To comfort her and beg her forgiveness.

But there would be no forgiveness. Hot-tempered little Ava was on a mission to destroy. Of all the weapons Grayson Boyd had in his arsenal, this tempest of a sister was the most dangerous.

2

Ava held the dashboard in a death grip as the Gurgel gobbled up the narrow washboard roads of St. Barts, jostling her speechless. Cassie shoved her windblown hair out of her face. "It's so much easier to take the back roads. Especially in tourist season." Apparently noticing Ava's blanched knuckles, she mercifully tapped the brakes. "It looks worse from that side of the car."

"You call this a car?" Ava raised her shaky voice over the wind, and Cassie threw her head back and laughed.

"Bienvenue à St. Barthélemy! This is our official all-terrain vehicle."

Ava closed her eyes as the roll bar brushed a low-hanging palm frond.

"When did you and Marco plan to get married?" Ava asked, shouting over the rumbling engine that explained the car's odd name.

Cassie's smile disappeared. "Very soon. We'd been together almost from the moment I arrived."

"When was that?"

"About two years ago. When I answered the call to Utopia." Her green eyes widened at her play on words. "I read about openings for crew members. They were looking for housekeepers and cooks, and I was dying to get out of Australia and see the rest of the world. It's a Sagittarius thing, you know. We just move on and on, like tumbleweeds."

She seemed willing enough to share, so Ava pressed on. "How did you meet Marco?"

"He interviewed me. We made love before the hour was over." A sly, slow grin broke over Cassie's delicate face.

"Oh." Ava could easily imagine Marco, a consummate girl magnet, seducing the fair and wispy Cassie. Every girl fell for him. Oh, yes. Marco had every gift God could hand out.

"He was terribly flirtatious and sexy. Impossible to resist." Cassie rolled her eyes. "Not that I even tried!"

"When did you get engaged?"

"Recently. Not long before . . . before the storm. We were going to get married this month, maybe next."

It sounded so vague to Ava, foreign to a person used to full-scale productions for weddings. "This month, maybe next" was not exactly engraved on parchment invitations.

"Marco talked about getting in touch with your family before we got married. I guess he wanted them to meet me."

Ava squeezed her eyes closed. A reunion with Marco had always seemed nearly impossible. Now the dream was utterly gone. "I'm not sure that was ever in the cards," she said softly. "Nothing has changed in Boston."

"Not even you?"

The question hung unanswered as Cassie pulled the Gurgel up to the island's single stoplight, across from an open-air restaurant. A few relaxed tourists lingered over drinks, soaking up paradise.

Ava kept her eyes on the floral print of someone's shirt. "I'm sure Marco told you the circumstances of why he left."

"Yes. Once. Right after we met."

"Then you know that I'm the one who needs forgiving."

Ava swallowed hard, tears blurring the brilliant colors of the scenery. Cassie's warm hand touched her bare arm, gently, in comfort. When she turned, Ava was surprised to see Cassie's own lashes spiked with wetness.

"Marco had a good life here. He probably would thank you for getting him out from underneath his father."

Yeah, right.

"I'm sorry for what happened. I mean in Boston. Years ago," Ava said. "I can't change it now."

"You're not going to change it with a lawsuit, Ava. You'll just tear Utopia apart."

Ava grabbed Cassie's hand on the gearshift. "Cassie! Dane Erikson had a lot to gain by leading that ship astray. Forty million dollars is a pretty compelling motive, don't you think?"

Still stopped at the light, Cassie leaned her head back and closed her eyes with a sigh. "You don't know Dane."

"Then explain to me how *Paradisio* happened to go straight into a hurricane, when the captain was taking orders from Dane Erikson?"

"The captain is in charge of a ship, Ava."

"Grayson Boyd makes a very persuasive argument that if the last person to speak with the captain is in a position to influence him—"

"No one knows what happened on the *Paradisio*, Ava. Something . . ." Cassie's voice trailed off.

"What, Cassie? Something what?"

Cassie's eyes flashed open and she lifted her head. "Don't pursue this lawsuit, Ava. Don't rip our little family apart."

"These families live in abject poverty. They deserve some of Dane's millions, not a settlement of one month's pay. And as Marco's fiancée, you deserve more than that."

Cassie snorted and threw the Gurgel into first gear as the light turned green. "You've been fed a bunch of bull from that scum-sucking attorney. No Utopians live in abject poverty. They live better than most other islanders. True, that's not like middle-class Americans. But they wouldn't know what to do with a million dollars. It would ruin their lives."

"That's not up to you to decide for them." Ava felt the sweat trickle down her neck. "I, for one, don't believe *Paradisio*'s fate was an accident, and I owe it to Marco's memory to find retribution and justice."

"Find out the truth, first."

The truth of what? What happened to the ship, or how these people lived? "I intend to. And to be perfectly honest, Cassie, I'm going to try and persuade people to do the right thing."

"Fine. You just be sure you know what the right thing is, okay?"

Ava had to smile at her spunk. No wonder Marco liked her. No, loved her. "I will."

"All right, luv, here's the turn." Cassie raised her eyebrows in question. "Up to your hotel, or to Dane's house to meet all the Utopians who adored your brother?"

Dane Erikson's house was no place to start her campaign, and she had no right to join the mourners. "I think the hotel, please."

Cassie shrugged and flipped the gearshift into first to start up the hill. "You're not as much like Marco as I thought. He loved an adventure."

And died having one.

"Okay. I'll go."

The villa Dane Erikson called home looked as if it should have a name. Ava studied the rambling pale pastel stucco, graceful columns and arches reaching out from its perch over the sea. It should be called something French and grand. *La Belle Plantation*. But also inviting and imposing. *Xanadu*. Something tropical and lush. *Poinciana*. Because it was all those things.

But it had no name, Cassie informed her.

"It's just Dane's house." Cassie shook her strawberry blond curls. "The cruise business has made him wealthy, but not spoiled. Really."

Wealthy. Unspoiled. A lover of luxury, for sure. The handsome head of a family of islanders who depended upon him for their livelihood. The only son of the renowned Erikson Hill Hotel magnates, who evidently opted out of the family business for the challenge of making his own mark in the world. Reported to be aggressively building his luxury cruise business by adding the biggest, most glamorous sailing ships to his fleet.

That exhausted what she knew about Dane Erikson.

With tingling nerves, she passed through the carved wooden double doors and stepped into his private world.

He appeared immediately. He still wore the linen shirt and dress slacks, but he looked far more relaxed than on the docks in Gustavia. His feet were bare. Bare and, like the rest of him, staggeringly male.

"I thought Ava should meet the Utopia family." Cassie's firm tone deflected any objections before they were voiced.

That mesmerizing smile blinded her again, along with an unreadable expression in his eyes. "An excellent idea, Cass," he agreed.

His hand settled on her back. Ava shivered as his fingers touched the flesh of her bare shoulder.

"Allow me to introduce you." He led her through a massive entryway across polished marble and under a sweeping archway flanked by fat columns. The veranda could seat sixty in its various groupings of plush rattan furniture overlooking a panoramic water view. Ava tried to take it all in but couldn't get beyond the sensation of his self-assured touch, searing her bare skin. She stepped aside to escape it, and his open appraisal of her.

An old demon of insecurity nearly forced her to back away. Surely this physically flawless man would find her blend of Italian and Irish features less than extraordinary. Not that she gave a damn about what he thought of her, but the intense assessment made her uncomfortable.

"Mr. Erikson—"

"It's Dane."

"Is something wrong?"

"No." He said the word slowly, as though it had two syllables. "Not at all." His gaze traced a line from her eyes to her mouth and back again. What a damn cool son of a bitch he was.

An older black woman materialized by his side, resplendent in a flowered print dress. She greeted Ava with a wide smile.

"Lord above," she whispered, staring at Ava. "It's de eyes of Marco as I live and breathe."

"Close, Marj. His sister, Ava. Ava, this is Marjory Hemingway. Her son, Mitchell, was the first mate of the *Paradisio* and a good friend to your brother."

The woman radiated an inner peace in spite of the red-rimmed eyes of mourning. As Ava began to express her sympathy, another young man came over. Someone's cousin. And two more women, other crew members, both married to lost sailors.

Dane disappeared in the house and the time passed in a haze as Ava spoke to small groups of people about her brother. She couldn't keep their names and faces straight, a mix of islanders, Brits, and Frenchmen. A festival of accents and pigeon English sharing stories of Marco's sailing prowess, his renowned good looks, and his universal appeal.

Marjory put her hand on Ava's arm and pulled her closer. "Have you talked to de lawyers yet, Miss Ava?" The small group clustered tighter to hear.

"That's one of the reasons I'm here," Ava responded. "To find out what happened and to talk to all of you."

"We donno what to do," Marjory admitted, her Jamaican tones sounding more like singing than speaking. "Dis man, dis lawyer, he offer us a million dollar, maybe more. But Mr. Dane and Utopia been our life since he came to de islands."

"I think it's important that you meet with Grayson Boyd this week," Ava told them quietly. "You owe it to yourselves to hear what he has to say."

"A lot of people are getting very greedy now," said Trinia, one of the widows, shaking her beaded braids. "And no one even knows how much Utopia is planning to offer in settlements."

"Whatever it is, it won't be a million dollars apiece," said a native man. "The only people who see that kind of money work for the Colombians, huh?"

A sharp look passed among several of them and deep lines formed across Marjory Hemingway's forehead. "No money will bring my Mitchell back, Miss Ava. And I clean dis house and I work for Mr. Dane"—her chocolate eyes swept the veranda with love and familiarity—"since he come to St. Barts. We donno."

Ava studied the round face of Mitchell's mother, marveling at her open warmth despite having lost a son. It was not the time or place to push these people. "You have to do what's right."

Marjory leaned closer and whispered, "De ship was marked, Miss Ava. De *Paradisio* was marked."

Ava shuddered at the pronouncement. Marked? For what? But Marjory backed away, shaking her head. "Ill-gotten gain," she mumbled softly and quietly slipped into the house.

Shivering in the evening air, alone for the first time since she arrived, Ava wandered into the living room of the luxurious villa.

A contrast of light and dark cherry woods, eclectic antiques, and rich, colorful Oriental carpets decorated the room. Modern art and classical paintings blended side by side on the coral stucco walls, but Ava couldn't help but notice a complete lack of anything personal or sentimental. It was professional, superb decor lifted from the pages of *Architectural Digest*, with not a single clue to the inner workings of the occupant.

The sense that she was being watched drove her out of the room, back to the fresh air of the patio to take in the lights of the neighboring island and perhaps find Cassie. The feeling of being watched didn't lessen. In a moment, as though a chilly breeze blew over her skin, she felt a cool presence at her side.

"Am I the only person here who hasn't met the long-lost Santori sister?" The woman's voice was low and earthy, with the sound of money and class. Ava turned to see that the face and body matched it.

Ava had to look up several inches to meet the gray eyes and restrained smile directed at her. They definitely hadn't met. Ava wouldn't forget this country club blond.

"I'm Genevieve Giles. Executive vice president of Utopia Adventures."

Ava shook the delicate fingers extended to her, dimly aware of precious gems and well-manicured nails. "Did you know my brother well?"

"Mmm." Genevieve nodded and sipped a goblet of chardonnay. "Dane and I discovered Marco. Oh, you were at the service, you heard the story. We adored him from the day we met him." *We.* No doubt this gorgeous creature made a perfect companion for the handsome owner of Utopia Adventures.

"I didn't realize Dane had a partner."

"Unofficial partner." Her pale gray eyes narrowed,

but she smiled, revealing perfect teeth and only the tiniest laugh lines. "I've known Dane since childhood, nearly twenty years now. When can I meet the rest of the elusive Santori clan?"

"Not in the near future, I'm afraid." Once again, Ava was left to wonder who knew what about the family.

Genevieve took another sip of wine. "I understand your father is something of a celebrity."

"He has his fans," Ava said wryly. Dominic might be an unforgiving tyrant, but his well-known name, his beloved cooking show, and his best-selling cookbooks held a remarkable amount of cachet. Fans loved him. Critics adored him. Everyone else just walked softly around him.

"And what's your claim to fame?"

Ava shrugged. "No fame. Just food. I'm head chef at my father's restaurant."

"Then you must meet Maurice while you're here."

"Maurice?"

"Maurice Arnot, the head of Utopia cuisine."

"Maurice Arnot?" Surprise jolted her. "Maurice Arnot is here? On this island? I thought he never left his restaurant in Paris."

Genevieve shook her head, her blunt platinum strands dancing over bare shoulders. "Like your father's restaurant, Beausoleil is run by underlings."

The comment stung, but Ava decided to let it go, far more interested in finding out more about one of her professional idols. "How long has Arnot been here?"

"A few months. It took a few trips to Paris, but I managed to lure him here to oversee Utopia's culinary operations."

Ava tried to imagine the French master Arnot plying his trade on a cruise ship. "I've heard Utopia's cuisine is the best of any cruise line. Now it makes sense."

Genevieve's laugh turned heads in their direction. "Utopia is not just any 'cruise line,' and we like to think we're known for excellence. Maurice seals the deal in the area of cuisine."

"I'm surprised I hadn't heard of this. In the trades—"

"Oh, he's kept it very quiet." Genevieve leaned closer to Ava. "Food critics are fickle, as I'm sure you know, and might downgrade Beausoleil's five-star rating."

From the opposite end of the veranda, Dane watched Genevieve in hushed conspiracy with Ava. Genevieve had never been very good at disguising her dislike for Marco. He decided Ava might need rescuing.

"I see you've met Genevieve," he said as he approached them from behind.

Ava jumped, twisting her whole body away from him in one quick movement. For all her bravado she was a bit like a skittish kitten. What did she think, he was going to nudge her over the railing and get rid of yet another pesky Santori?

"Dane, I was just telling Ava about the coup of getting Arnot to join us."

"I've studied his work for years," Ava said. "He's a genius."

"He's a pain in the ass," Dane shot back with a smile. "Would you like to meet him?"

"Oh, yes!" And then, as though embarrassed by her enthusiasm, she asked casually, "Is he here?"

"No. He's on *Valhalla*, one of the ships we have in

port right now. Perhaps you can visit him before it
sails tomorrow evening."

She hesitated. Studying the slight shadows under
her dark eyes, he wondered just how much sleep
she'd lost in the past three weeks. Probably as much
as he had.

"You can come early, before the passengers arrive.
Watch the preparation for a sail." He realized how
much he wanted her to see it. With an inviting smile,
he added, "It's quite a memorable experience, I assure you."

"Perhaps it would be too difficult for her."
Genevieve spoke as though Ava weren't standing
there, and Dane wanted to throttle her. The thought
of getting her on the ship appealed to him. A chance
to get her alone, to convince her of his innocence.
Genevieve might scare her away with her sarcasm
and condescension.

"How do I get on board?" When she asked, he
could have sworn her dimple deepened in challenge.

"All you need is my permission," he lobbied
back, liking her spirit and the impulsive response.
Just like her brother, all wrapped up in a pretty
package.

Genevieve cleared her throat, breaking their eye
contact. "You should find Cassie, Ava. I'm sure it's
been a long day." She gently tapped Ava's shoulder
in a gesture of comfort. "Again, I'm so sorry for your
loss, dear."

Ava raised her eyebrows slightly, causing Dane to
doubt Genevieve had showered her with sympathy.
"Thank you. It was a loss for everyone," she responded gracefully and turned to retreat to the
house.

He followed her. "Would you like a ride to your hotel?"

"No. I would not."

So much for grace. He put both hands on her shoulders and deliberately turned her to face him. He could see Marco's fire in the almond-shaped eyes, although delicate arched brows topped hers. She had the same arrogant nose and deep V at the bow of her lips. Her skin tone was lighter, as though the Irish mother had thrown in just a few more genes on this one, but her eyes and the soul they reflected were pure Mediterranean. Rich and dark and full of the same passion that drove Marco. Passion for life, for music, for food, for family. Perhaps his best course of action was to tap it.

"Come with me."

She started to shake her head, but he intensified the pressure on her shoulder and drew her down the hall to his study.

He couldn't remember a woman being in this room. Maybe Genevieve, to pour over numbers and profits, but those he entertained for pleasure weren't invited into this sanctuary. He strode past a rosewood desk buried under navigational charts, files, and a partially opened laptop computer, to the far end of the room.

There, a framed five-by-seven photo stood out from the reference books and novels. The blood drained from her face as she stared at the image of her brother.

In the picture, two men stood side by side, Marco's hands on the polished and splendid helm, Dane's splayed on his own hips. The moment remained vivid in Dane's memory. Not just because it was the maiden voyage of *Valhalla* under the Utopia flag, but also because of the bone deep sense of contentment Dane had experienced that day.

Everything had come together, every plan and dream realized. The business flourished, and with *Valhalla*, he could boast ownership of six of the most magnificent clippers in the world. Utopia Adventures had become synonymous with luxury and attracted the most discriminating and adventurous travelers in the world.

On that day Marco had been promoted to second mate and assigned to *Paradisio*. He'd just graduated from the officers' program in England, and they were celebrating his twenty-fourth birthday. Dane remembered the silver compass he'd given him, engraved with his initials and the words *Find your way*. An artist had etched the word *Utopia* on it.

Find your way. The compass, and his friend, had lost their way.

Ava remained riveted on her brother's face. "He changed. A lot."

Dane gave into the temptation to look at her instead of the picture, his gaze drawn to her smooth complexion and the curve of her full lips as she almost smiled.

"Ava," he said softly, liking the way her name felt on his lips. "I have as much reason to blame you as you have to blame me—"

She stepped back from the picture, blazing dark eyes replacing the near smile she'd had a moment earlier. "Our family problems may have hurt Marco, but they didn't kill him."

"I didn't say they did."

She swept him with a demanding glance. "So,

what happened? If you didn't direct that ship into the hurricane, then how did it get there?"

He looked at the photo, away from her accusing glare. "Some ships are unlucky. Did you know that the first captain of the *Paradisio* died during her maiden voyage in 1927? Many sailors believe that's a curse."

Ava ran her hands over her bare arms. "A curse? You sound like Marjory, saying the ship was 'marked.' Next you'll tell me they're seeing ghosts where the ship went down."

"They will, I assure you."

"I'm not interested in your theories or sailors' superstitions. I'm interested in the truth. If *Paradisio* wasn't navigated into the storm, then why did they sail in that direction? Why didn't they follow orders?" Urgency strained her voice.

"The captain is the ultimate authority on a ship. Not the company owner on a satellite phone."

"I know what your defense will be, Dane. What is the *truth*?"

The truth was at the bottom of the Caribbean Sea. And she just stormed into St. Barts without a thought to the exhaustive search going on a hundred miles southeast of here, where he had spent the last grueling twenty-one days. "If you're so hell-bent on finding out what happened to Marco, why didn't you come down here sooner? Why not during the search that's been going on for three weeks? Why not, for God's sake, when he was still alive?"

She didn't withdraw from the force in his voice. Instead she leaned closer, her voice seething with restrained temper. "Don't you dare answer a question with a question. I'm not the one on trial here. You are."

She very nearly sizzled, and for one unbelievable second, Dane imagined how passionate this woman would be undressed and in his arms. Shoving the thought away, he simply smiled at her. "I'm not on trial anywhere, sister."

"Not yet."

3

Ava had dreamed of Marco. A different dream than the one she'd had so many times over the past five years. Marco had blue eyes in this dream; haunting aquamarine eyes that saw through her as she floundered uncontrollably in a black sea.

It didn't take Freud to figure that one out. Especially considering the memories of Marco churned up by this visit and, of course, the picture Dane Erikson had shown her. How different the two men were, Ava mused as she took a cup of aromatic French coffee to the tiny balcony of her hotel room. Marco had been passionate and funny, but she couldn't remember any overwhelming need to control. Dane, judging by his success, undoubtedly manipulated everything that mattered in his world. Even the loss of one of his precious ships.

From the balcony, Ava could see the rolling hills of Gustavia. Beyond the small harbor town, dozens of small boats floated in the crystalline teal water. Creamy stucco buildings topped with terra-cotta roofs dotted the curved streets and cliffs. A few bold seagulls dove past her balcony, undoubtedly accustomed to handouts of fresh croissants. Too bad she couldn't just relax and enjoy the pleasures of the island.

She closed her eyes and imagined taking in paradise on the arm of a sinfully attractive man like Dane Erikson. Women must fall at his feet and in his bed in droves. A shiver waltzed through her at the thought and Ava shook her head at her girlish musings over a man she planned to ruin. It must be island fever.

That afternoon she would finally meet Grayson Boyd. After a few brief conversations with the man, she was certain she wouldn't like him. His cocky personality had irritated her from the moment he'd contacted her in Boston to suggest the Santori family seek retribution for Marco's death. She recalled his first icy words: *your brother was murdered*.

Dominic had been furious she'd even taken the lawyer's call, and Mama had been too distraught to discuss it. Nearly as much as the negligence issue, Boyd drove home the settlement problem. He believed Utopia Adventures would offer the victims' families only the standard settlement required by law, about one thousand dollars per family. It was a crime, he insisted, saying each family should be entitled to at least a million dollars.

Grayson Boyd had posed enough questions to make Ava want the answers that a lawsuit and inquiry would provide. She wanted to do something right for Marco in death, since she had failed him in life. Marco may never have been on this island or that ship if not for her. That knowledge had given her the strength to face the demons that she might find in paradise.

She took a last sip of coffee and squinted toward the horizon, where the two giant sailing ships rested. The bigger one, she now knew, was *Valhalla*. With Maurice Arnot, of all people, on board. A genuine attraction, but also a wonderful excuse to get on one of the ships and talk to some of the crew. People might be more forthcoming and open in their own element than under the intimidating eye of their boss.

Ava turned to find her bag and caught her reflection in the mirror. She touched the fragile skin under her eyes, noting the shadows. She'd dressed in white capri pants, not at all sure what to wear on a luxury sailing ship. She tugged the cotton tweed of her sweater so that it wasn't quite so tight around her bosom and tried to smooth her willful curls, habits she'd had for so long she barely noticed the actions. A light tap on her door interrupted her self-assessment.

"Who is it?"

Cassie's cheery voice called out. "Your personal driver, luv."

Ava whisked the door open with a smile that came from her heart. "What are you doing here?"

"I couldn't let you go on board alone, so I thought I'd play escort. D'ya mind?"

The gesture touched Ava. "Not at all, I welcome the company. I've never been on any kind of cruise ship, you know."

"Well, brace yourself. This isn't *any* kind of cruise ship. And I haven't been on one since I climbed off the *Paradisio* . . ."

Ava knew from the reports she'd read that all passengers and nonessential crew had disembarked in Barbados when it became obvious that Hurricane

Carlos wasn't turning north, as most storms did, but heading east.

"Well, you're not technically sailing today." Ava closed the door behind her, and they walked out into the brilliant sunshine.

"I know." Cassie climbed easily over the half door of the vehicle while Ava opted to use the door. "But I'm on the schedule to work *Nirvana* in a few days. Quite frankly, I'm kind of dreading it."

Ava squeezed her eyes shut as they started down the first impossibly steep road toward the harbor, preparing herself to find out more about Marco's world.

From his familiar place on the grandstand sundeck overlooking the bridge of *Valhalla*, Dane watched dozens of crewmen and prep teams hustle across the main deck of the four-hundred-foot sailing ship as they equipped her for departure. Five masts stood in various states of readiness, with giant canvas sails being checked and tightened in preparation for the seven-day cruise through the Windward Islands of the Caribbean.

By sunset *Valhalla* would have motored out of the port. Her polished brightwork and brass railings would shine with a blinding finish. The first of forty-two sails would unfurl with a deafening snap accompanied by Utopia's signature orchestral performance of "Ride of the Valkyries" piped through the sound system. The intoxicating aromas of Maurice Arnot's artistry would waft from the galley of the clipper deck, and the well-heeled guests of Utopia would begin their dream vacations. Under his watch, it would all come together.

The launch approached port side, and he could see Ava and Cassie in animated conversation as the crewman secured the lines. An unfamiliar sensation of anticipation tightened his usual steel gut.

Gripping the railing and squinting against the sun, he watched a young deckhand struggle with a mizzen sail halyard. The boy, no more than eighteen, looked directly at Dane, obviously aware he was being watched by Utopia's owner. Dane read the doubt in the kid's eyes.

Grayson Boyd had gotten to most of the crew and their families, all so closely intertwined within Utopia. Nearly everyone who worked for him was related to or close to one of the victims of *Paradisio*. Men he'd known and employed for years weighed the millions Boyd was dangling against their loyalty to Dane.

It was a tough call, but loyalty could win. Unless an outsider, with no loyalty and a five-year-old guilt trip for her dead brother, really got them going. Then, he could lose.

He wished desperately that he had all the answers Ava needed. For now, he'd do everything to keep her close.

Which won't be a hardship, he thought as she crossed the main deck with Cassie. The wind caught her shoulder-length hair and whipped the long waves back from her heart-shaped face. Her hand shading her eyes, she scanned the grand ship.

He couldn't resist admiring her body. She had shapely legs shown off by white slacks that tapered to her calves. Her hips had a delicious curve, not too round but definitely not the stretched skin and bones of most of *Valhalla*'s visitors. Her generous breasts moved with every step in a natural, sexy bounce. The twinge of male response didn't surprise him, but the knock in his chest did.

"Welcome aboard." Dane greeted them as they stepped up from the main deck to the sundeck.

Ava looked around but didn't catch his eye. "It's lovely," she said coolly, her arms crossed in front of her.

"It's a *she*," he corrected, "not an *it*."

"Don't start a sailing lesson on the spot," Cassie warned. "I've just learned Ava's only been on a few motorboats. And I promised her that on a Utopia adventure—even just a visit—you don't have to do a thing but enjoy the amenities."

He watched Ava take in a towering mast and winding snakes of white lines wrapped around it.

"Don't the guests pitch in with the coming about and all that?" Ava asked.

Cassie snorted. "Not these guests and not at these prices."

"These aren't the barefoot cruises you may have heard of," Dane added. "There's very little rum swilling and absolutely no serenading the captain with pirate tunes. As you'll see, we go for a more sophisticated adventure."

"Too bad. I'd pay a lot to see Maurice Arnot belt out 'Tis a Pirate's Life.' "

Ava's dry delivery caught him by surprise, and he chuckled. "Come and meet him. You could probably talk him into anything."

Cassie moved away with a wave. "I've met the Great and Powerful Arnot, thank you very much. I'll go down to housekeeping and tell the girls what they're doing right."

The familiar lilt in Cassie's voice still hadn't returned. Dane reached out and took her hand. "You okay, Cass?"

She nodded and patted his hand. "I'm fine, luv. I've missed the sea under my legs. Thanks." She took a step toward the stairs and threw back a grin. "Don't bore her to death with legends and tales, Dane."

Dane turned to Ava. "Could I give you a quick tour before I lose you to the magic of Maurice Arnot?" He held out a hand to guide her. She preceded him toward the main deck, pointedly refusing his assistance.

"*Valhalla* is unquestionably the jewel of the fleet," he told her as they rounded the bow and stopped at the navy blue Olympic-size pool that was being cleaned and refilled by two brawny crew members. "It's our largest and newest. And the most luxurious."

"I read you started this business on a bet. Is that true?"

Her directness teased a smile from him. How much propaganda on Utopia, and him, had she been fed? "Not exactly. The *Paradisio* was my first ship. I won it in a poker game from a man in St. John named Nathaniel Giles."

"Giles? Any relation to Genevieve?"

How quickly she picked up the connection.

"Yes. Nathaniel and Elizabeth are Genevieve's grandparents. I met Nat almost twenty years ago. I was barely out of my teens, sailing around the Caribbean doing . . . whatever kids do when they drop out of college and escape the bonds of their parents."

"Playing poker, in your case."

He chuckled. "Among other things. Anyway, he was a cocky player. Had a full house and put *Paradisio* on the table. Not that he didn't have the money. I had a straight flush and Nat was good on his word." He remembered the look of satisfaction in the older man's eyes when he looked at Dane's cards. Definitely satisfaction. "I don't know what the hell I'd have done if I'd lost. Been his indentured servant, I guess. But I think he was hoping the ship would help me find that missing 'thing' in my life if I owned her."

"Did you?"

He paused to wipe a smudge off the railing as they descended another set of stairs, then glanced at her, feeling an unfamiliar desire to tell her more than he usually shared. "I found a way to make my own life, apart from my parents. I avoided the confines of the Erikson Hill Hotel business, which held no appeal to me. I prefer the open air to a boardroom, and I prefer the freedom of a private company to a public one." He pulled open a cut glass door. "Right through here is the spa—"

"I really don't need the five-dollar tour. I just wanted to meet Arnot."

"Five dollars won't get you much on this ship, I'm afraid." He let the spa door close and shook his head a little at her ineffective attempt at being bitchy. "I thought you might want a glimpse into Marco's world. Didn't you say that was one of your reasons for coming down here? To discover who he had become over the past five years?"

"In the spa?" She sighed heavily and folded her arms, deepening an enticing shadow between her breasts. "You know damn well why I came down here, so let's get on with it. All you're doing is showing me how much luxury you offer while the children of your sailors live in squalor."

"Squalor?"

"They make a thousand dollars a month. What do you call it?"

She knew nothing of island life. Should he enlighten her that his employees earned three times what other cruise lines paid? That some of his people had been with him since he had only one ship, loyal for many reasons? Most of them would be deeply involved with selling or using drugs if not for the generous salaries he paid. But her dark eyes sparked with accusation, and he knew an economics lesson would be lost on her. He'd have to show her another way. His gaze dropped to her feminine figure as she turned from him. The thought of seducing her into agreement flashed in his mind, but he knew he'd be better off with a more sensible approach. Less appealing, but sensible.

"Perhaps you'll take the time to get to know some of the Utopians while you're here. Even check out their 'squalor.' "

"I plan to."

"Good. Then let me be your guide, not Grayson Boyd." He opened a door to another hallway. "The galley's this way."

An awkward silence accompanied their footsteps and Ava stole a glance at him. He really didn't merit such a snotty response, but he was melting her resolve, and she had to fight it.

She didn't want to respond in any way to his towering presence of lean, roped muscle and his masculine scent of soap and salt. Or his tales of poker games. She didn't want her every sense to react to this man, to his cool control and subtle sense of humor. She tried to ignore his perfectly formed mouth and forced herself not to look at the few golden hairs that peeked out of his open collar and begged to be touched. But every womanly instinct was betraying her.

How easy it would be to fall under the spell of his mesmerizing eyes and silken voice, lost in the opulence of his majestic ships. She wanted to ask him where he got the slight British accent. She wanted to abandon the hostility and explore every inch of this amazing ship alone with him. *Marone!* What the hell was the matter with her?

"How many ships are there in the Utopia line?"

"There are five, now. The others, *Olympus, Celestia,* and *Utopian Dream* are all in dry dock. I decided to use the downtime to give them thorough physicals."

She remembered Grayson Boyd's claim that *Paradisio* hadn't been dry-docked for two years, and his suggestion that the ship could have weathered the storm if it had been properly maintained.

"*Nirvana* is the smaller ship that's in port right now," he told her, stopping for the second time to pick up a minuscule piece of lint from the carpet, perhaps in an effort to show her that poor maintenance could never be an issue on his ships.

"I saw it—her. Hardly small."

"Well, the other ships are only two hundred and sixty feet and carry about a hundred and fifty passengers and crew. *Valhalla* is four hundred and thirty-nine feet, and she generally holds well over two hundred people." His blue eyes sparkled with a parent's pride. "There's only one other five-masted passenger sailing ship in the world. It sails the Greek islands."

"Are you planning to steal that one too?"

He laughed a little, or tried to hide a choke of surprise.

"They say you got this for a song. From a competitor in financial trouble who was in the middle of building it when he ran out of money." One of the few articles she'd dug up had painted him as a ruthless entrepreneur determined to build a unique and highly profitable business.

He leaned closer to her and whispered, "Most definitely. At gunpoint. With an eye patch and gold earring."

Something fluttered in her stomach at the close contact. "I'm serious," she said defensively.

"So am I." He winked at her, further unraveling her nerve endings. "But that's called business. Not piracy."

Oh, he was a pirate all right. A rogue, with magnetic eyes and a heat wave of sexuality that emanated from every cell. She turned to a magnificent double staircase leading to the first level of a three-tiered dining room, refusing to succumb to his tricks. She knew better. A man like Dane Erikson wouldn't flirt with her unless he needed something. Unless he wanted her to close her mouth, drop her lawsuit, and flee his private island.

She turned her attention to the grand rooms in front of her. "This is a fitting stage for Arnot's artistry," she commented, running a hand along the curved wrought iron railings. "I'm looking forward to meeting him."

He led her down the dramatic staircase through the Euro-elegance of the darkened dining room and flipped open a swinging door to the galley. Not surprisingly, given the rest of the ship, it resembled the most active and modern kitchen of any large, high-end restaurant.

The galley's blinding fluorescent lights were a harsh contrast after the dim hallways and dining room. Ava's senses quickly adapted to the familiar environment. She recognized the scent of bay leaves and thyme simmering in an aromatic veal stock. A sea of stainless steel counters gleamed below rows of glistening salamander ovens and magnetic knife racks. The rhythmic chop of knives on wood and the clatter of pans relaxed her.

The cooks didn't notice them walk in. Four of them, dressed in classic white aprons, were gathered around one burner like kids in a science lab.

"Mon Dieu! Qu'est-ce que ce passe?" a gentle French voice questioned. *"Non, non,* Jean Paul. Do not boil this poor salmon. She must poach gently. Bring her to a slow, steamy simmer. Like you would heat up a woman, *non?"* The group chuckled like sixteen-year-old boys at that one. "Slowly, slowly build to the exquisite pink, soft and moist, *non?* Ah, *voilà!"*

A small figure in white flourished a wooden spoon at the stove and grinned with satisfaction. Ava bit back a laugh.

The chef turned, his eyes widening at the sight of Dane. Despite thinning brown hair, his youthful face revealed Maurice Arnot to be no older than his mid-forties. He tilted his head in apology as he stepped forward and wiped his hands on a spotless apron.

"Monsieur Erikson! You surprise me in my kitchen, *non?"* It might have been an apology, but a note of accusation was buried there.

A half smile lifted Dane's lips. "Next time I'll call ahead. I've brought a guest to meet you."

Maurice turned his attention to Ava with an appraisal as intense as he might give a cut of prime tenderloin, searching for flaws. She must have met with his approval, because he offered a wide smile, his front teeth charmingly misaligned, a genuine sparkle reaching his soft brown eyes.

"Bienvenue à la monde du Arnot, mademoiselle." He swept his hand to indicate a welcome to his world, then reached out and took her hand, turning it over to kiss her palm. *"Enchantée."*

Dane shifted from one foot to another and crossed his arms with an exaggerated sigh. "Ava Santori, this is Chef Arnot, but we are in St. Barts, not Paris, so feel free to call him Maurice."

Maurice Arnot lifted his head and a frown deepened the lines across his broad forehead. "Santori?"

She nodded.

"Marco?"

"My brother," she replied.

"Let me extend my deepest sympathies for the loss, mademoiselle." He squeezed her hand and pulled her imperceptibly closer. "It was devastating for all of us."

"Thank you," Ava whispered and returned his genuine smile. "It's an honor to meet you, Chef Arnot."

"Non, non. The honor is mine. You are related to two great men, so you must be a very special woman."

"Do you know my father?" They seemed such worlds apart in cooking. Arnot was the epitome of haute cuisine. Dominic appealed to everyman, the couch potato and amateur cook.

"Of course, *ma cherie,* I know of your father. And

your brother! He invaded my galley and made a mess with his pasta and anchovies. Every cruise, at least once! But Marco, he was very skilled at cooking, like your father, *non?*"

"He was skilled at everything," she responded quietly. "My father and I hold your work in the highest esteem, Chef."

He clasped his hands, as delighted as a child with the compliment. "You are a chef too?"

"Yes," she said, nodding, but held up her hands to keep his expectations at bay. "Not exactly in your league, sir. And, of course, I've done most of my work at Santori's, my family's restaurant, so I am far more schooled in Italian cooking than French."

"That is a shame," he said with a devilish grin and a wink at Dane, who stood silently observing their conversation. "And do you plan your own flashy TV show and slew of expensive cookbooks also?"

The thinly veiled sarcasm made her laugh at the little man who stood barely her height but was regarded as a legend. "No, I concentrate on the restaurant."

"Good for you, *cherie.* All that other stuff . . ." He waved his hand in dismissal. "It is marketing. Just fluff, *n'est ce pas?*"

"I'd love to look around your kitchen, Chef."

"But, of course. I would be delighted to show you everything." He stepped back and put both hands on his hips, as though struck by a brilliant idea. "Perhaps you will come and cook with me sometime. I do not know how long you are staying in St. Barts, *cherie,* but we can teach each other, *non?* Your Italian and my French, eh?"

She wasn't sure if her mission to enlist more families in the lawsuit included getting cozy with the head chef and settling in for a nice lesson on preparing a roux. "Perhaps," she answered vaguely.

Dane stepped in. "I think that's an excellent idea, Arnot."

"*Très bien.*" Maurice nodded as though it were done. "I must sail on *Valhalla* tonight. I will return by plane in three days, after I am certain the kitchen is running perfectly. Then I must prepare the next ship." He tossed an exasperated look at Dane. "The Viking is a slave driver, you know."

Dane laughed and put his hand on the smaller man's shoulder. "Not exactly slave wages you're getting, Arnot."

Maurice moved away from Dane's hand. "It might as well be slave wages when a man can't get decent white truffles—not a single one in two weeks! How am I supposed to make the demanding customers happy, eh?"

Dane rolled his eyes. "I know you need truffles. We're a thousand miles from France, and I have every contact working on it. Use a mushroom, for God's sake."

"A mushroom?" He spat the word as though it were lethal and turned to Ava to share his incredulity. She smiled in empathy. "*Mon Dieu!* He knows nothing of food, *ma cherie*. Only the water, only the boats."

Dane chuckled at the insult. "I'll leave the culinary delights to you, Arnot. Genevieve told me one of the vendors you suggested came through. You'll get the truffles delivered when you reach St. Kitts tomorrow morning. I have to go back to the bridge to meet with Captain Jack now. Would you like to stay for a while, Ava?"

Before she could respond, Maurice waved Dane away with his wooden spoon. "*Allez, allez.* You are not needed here. I will take care of the lovely lady."

"That's what I'm afraid of." His blue eyes flashed with amusement, but Ava could swear she saw something else too. Jealousy? She dismissed the impossible thought and returned her attention to Maurice.

After two hours with the disarmingly sweet Frenchman, Ava understood the "groupie" mentality of the cooks who surrounded him. A natural teacher, a hopeless flirt, and a complete genius with every ingredient, Maurice Arnot defied every stereotype of the temperamental chef.

As the activity level rose, she reluctantly prepared to leave. Nothing was more intrusive than visitors breathing down a cook's neck in the middle of a tricky deglaze. More importantly, she'd arranged to meet Grayson Boyd for lunch and it was nearly noon. Ava scanned the room for Maurice, but he had stepped away.

"Someone just grabbed him a minute ago, ma'am," a prep manager deveining a small mountain of shrimp told her. "He should be back soon. Things are getting crazy in here now."

Ava responded with a grin and a knowing nod. "I see that. Just tell him I said good-bye. By the way, can you tell me how to get to housekeeping?" She'd find Cassie and tell her she would take the launch back to Gustavia.

"Go to the port side of the clipper deck. That's up one level. The main housekeeping offices and storage are there." He held up a shrimp in one hand and a paring knife in another with an apologetic half smile. "I'd take you, but . . ."

"No, no." She waved in dismissal. "I understand. I'll find it. Thanks."

As she started toward the galley doors, they swung open, Arnot barreling through with a frown.

"Oh, Chef—"

A quick smile broke in response. "Ah, Ava. I am so sorry. Are you leaving?"

"Yes, you are busy. I promise I'll try to see you again while I am here."

"*Bien. Bien.*" He studied her thoughtfully, a small frown creasing his forehead.

"What is it?"

He took a step closer to her and spoke softly. "You are not taking part in this lawsuit against the company, are you?"

She raised her eyebrows in surprise. "I'm here to figure that out." Another kitchen worker rushed by, reminding her that this wasn't the time or place to discuss it. "Thank you for the personal attention."

"*Mais oui.* You come to see me on *Nirvana, non?*"

"I'll try." Impulsively she put her hands on his shoulders and pressed her cheek to his. "Thank you."

He grinned like a little boy.

The first floor of the dining room barely received a trickle of the natural light from the upper-level portholes. In the shadows, Ava lingered at the beautifully set tables, admiring the china and crystal already set for an elaborate dinner. As she approached the grand white marble and wrought iron staircase, she heard a man's voice coming from a room off the dining area. The angry tones made her pause. A response hissed in the distinct clipped tones of Genevieve Giles stopped her cold.

"Don't be a fool. Nothing has changed. They are expecting you at the warehouse. Make the delivery and get back to the ship."

Ava dropped into the shadows at the foot of the stairs, not wanting to be caught eavesdropping.

"They are expecting more this time, *señorita*, and you know it," a man said. "There are complaints about our service."

"I am not interested in their complaints and neither are the people we work for."

Did Genevieve talk to all the employees that way?

"You are being very foolish, *señorita*," he insisted. "That ship carried four hundred thousand dollars' worth of precious cargo. And it's a miracle it hasn't been found yet. Before it is, you better figure out how to pay for what was lost when the ship sank."

When the ship sank. They were talking about *Paradisio*. She tiptoed closer toward the voices.

"It's impossible," Genevieve responded.

"Nothing is impossible, *señorita*." Spanish. It was definitely a Spanish accent.

"That is. Anyone involved is gone and so is the profit. It's over and done with and the consequences have to be accepted. Now, get back to your station and don't talk to me again."

Anyone involved is gone. Involved in what?

"Genevieve. Surely you're smart enough to know why that ship went down," the man insisted.

A chill as cold as death itself slivered through Ava, and she froze in her spot.

"You asked a boy to do a man's job, that's why." Her voice oozed with hate and accusation.

"Is that what you think?" The Spanish man's voice stayed low and Ava strained to hear his words. "It wouldn't be the first ship to vanish without a trace. It won't be the last."

"Well, next time get your precious cargo off before it disappears. Forget it this time. It's a write-off."

"Erikson's going to get forty million dollars. You work the books. Get it."

"I can't just take four hundred thousand dollars. And don't be so sure he'll get the money. There's a lawsuit pending, you know."

The man's scornful laugh resounded through the empty dining room. "As if anyone would believe Erikson is responsible. He'll just take the insurance money and build another damn hospital in Jamaica so the papers can call him a hero."

A wave of dizziness threatened Ava's stability.

"There will be lots of settlements and lawsuits, Genevieve. Get the money. Pay it to a family member who doesn't exist. Steal it outright if you have to. Erikson trusts you."

"You're an idiot and he's not. He's already suspicious. He's been combing the logs and inventory. God, I know him. He's not going to rest until he has some answers. Just give it up. We all make plenty on every other trip. We just lost on that one."

Silence. Then a moan, a throaty wheeze of pain, made Ava's stomach roll.

"We don't *lose, señorita*. You understand what this *idiot* is saying now? Fuck Erikson. And fuck you if you think you can back out of this now."

A fresh gasp from Genevieve.

"We got a good thing going, *señorita*. And you're in too deep to get out. Unless you want to end up like the poor sailors left on that ship. Is that clear?"

Ava heard a scuffle, the sound of a chair, or something, being pushed.

"Don't you touch me again, you bastard." The acrimony was back in Genevieve's tone, but Ava's pulse banged in her ears, making it nearly impossible to hear. "Just leave me alone. I'll handle it."

"You'd better."

Ava heard footsteps and panicked—adrenaline firing her limbs. Clinging to the railing, she flew up the stairway, stumbling once as her sandals slipped on the smooth marble. She longed to know if someone saw her, but the possibility of locking onto the gray eyes of Genevieve Giles or meeting the mysterious ones of her vicious cohort kept her from looking back.

She reached the top, her heart thumping and her breath coming in quick short spurts, relieved to see the artificial light of a hallway. Breaking into a run, she saw a small brass sign. PURSER'S OFFICE. She threw open the door without thinking.

Help. God, she needed help.

The slightly balding man pouring over charts and papers and the person in the chair facing him both jumped at her unexpected entrance. Ava opened her mouth to speak, not caring that she must look like a dazed maniac. But before the first word could come out, she recognized the man in the guest chair.

"Ava!" Dane stood as he stared at her. "What's wrong?"

He's already suspicious. He's not going to rest until he has some answers. The words exploded in her brain. *I am not interested in their complaints and neither are the people we work for.*

"I—I—I got lost."

"You look frightened." He immediately came to her side, his eyes dark with concern, his strong arm reaching out to steady her. When his hand touched her arm, she jumped as though he'd burned her.

"No! No, I'm just . . . completely disoriented. And a little seasick—"

"That's unusual when we're not under way," Dane said. He nudged her into the chair. "Sit down. Let me get you some water."

She gasped for air, terror still denying her a deep breath. Should she tell him? She looked at the man behind the desk, who stared back with unabashed curiosity. Not yet. Not here. *Think, for once, Ava, before you blurt.*

"No, thank you. I just want to find Cassie. I was looking for housekeeping and got completely lost." She tried to laugh and knew it sounded false and forced.

Before either man could respond, the door opened, and Genevieve Giles, slightly flushed but still elegant in a linen suit, swept into the room.

"Ava! There you are."

Ava swallowed, certain she was suffocating. "Were you looking for me?"

"I heard you were in with Chef Arnot, dear, and I wanted to say hello. But I got distracted with an employee." She turned to Dane, who looked questioningly at her. "Nothing serious. Just a new hire a little confused about his job."

Dane seemed to accept the explanation and turned his attention back to Ava. *Don't you know what's happening on your own ships?* She bit her tongue to keep from screaming.

Dane regarded her closely. "I'll take you to the deck and you can take the launch back to Gustavia."

Genevieve looked down at Ava, tilting her head in sympathy. "Had enough heaven for one day, dear?"

An angry response bubbled up, but Ava choked it back as she saw the red finger marks just under Genevieve's chin, not quite hidden by the thick blond strands. She stood and kept her gaze on the woman, fighting the quaking inside.

"I do need to leave. I have an appointment with my lawyer." Ava took a step toward the door as Dane opened it for her.

"That should make you feel better." She heard the sarcasm in Genevieve's voice, so different from the terrified gasp of pain she'd heard earlier.

Ava spun around and faced Genevieve, her eyes flashing with the anger and fear that burned in her. "I won't feel better until I figure out who's responsible for my brother's death."

4

Grayson Boyd looked nothing like the overweight, balding older man Ava had expected. His thick head of auburn hair and compact, muscular body surprised her when he rose to greet her at the entrance of L'Hibiscus.

"Miss Santori." He flashed a quick smile and watery blue eyes peered at her from behind rimless glasses. She hated those kind of eyes.

"How do you do, Mr. Boyd."

He guided her to a corner table of the patio. "Please call me Grayson. And may I call you Ava?"

His southern charm was wasted on her. She hadn't had a moment alone since leaving the purser's office with Genevieve and Dane. The launch had been crowded with Utopia employees who chatted with her, and one had even shared her cab. She ached to analyze what she'd heard. But she still had to deal with Grayson Boyd.

"So . . ." He settled in across from her and flipped his napkin back on his lap with a quick glance around the restaurant. "You got here yesterday. Quite a place, St. Barts. Don't you think?"

"It's lovely." She bit back the temptation to tell him to get to the point. And that he might have the wrong guy. Dizzy, she leaned back in her chair.

"Would you like some iced tea? A glass of wine?" He lifted the wine list from the table and offered it to her.

She shook her head. "Have you filed anything yet?"

"Not officially. We're meeting with some of the families tomorrow and as soon as I have five or so signed up, we'll draw up the suit. I'm counting on you."

She paused in the act of opening her linen napkin. "I haven't decided for sure if I'm going to participate in the suit."

The smile went out of his liquidy eyes. "Of course you are. Not just for the memory of your dead brother or for the money. Although those are two compelling reasons," he added with a hasty smile. "Think of these poor island people, living in the depths of poverty, scraping together to live on the few pennies Erikson paid their husbands and sons."

He shook his head at the injustice of it and then leaned forward, his southern accent thickening. "He lives like a king, you know. He's worth millions and pays a paltry sum to the poor people who depend on him."

He'll just take the insurance money and build another damn hospital in Jamaica. Was that true? And if so, did he do it for the good of mankind . . . or the good of his own image?

She didn't know. There were too many contradictions surrounding Dane.

"My dear, you are key to our success. You can persuade those folks to go against him far more effectively than I can."

"How is that, Mr. Boyd?"

"You're a family member from the United States who isn't doing this for money, but for justice."

She took a sip of water and said nothing.

"I've interested *Dateline* in doing a story on this."

"What?" She choked on the drink.

"Very few people are aware that the son of a celebrity was on that ship. I know you said your father won't talk about this, but *you* can. As the Santori family spokesperson. The NBC producer loves this angle."

"No. Absolutely not. Forget it." Her fingers tightened around the water glass.

"Ava, if we can get some international press coverage about this wreck, it would really help. The Hurricane Carlos story has come and gone, but there are still some network crews lurking about Grenada, which is in ruins. I think we can get one to go with us into the slums of some of the islands and really drive home how poorly they live."

He leaned forward to drop his next bomb.

"The producer wants to film Erikson's house from a helicopter. It's a mansion on the water, I'm told. We can juxtapose that against the poor conditions these people live in, with a nice 'forty million dollar' graphic over it." He chuckled and wiped an imaginary crumb from the table, a false humility seeping into his voice. "I'm not much of a TV producer, but you know, sometimes you can just envision these things. We need to really drive home the fact that Erikson intentionally sent the ship into the storm for a fat profit—"

"You don't know that for sure."

"Ava, we have evidence. Signed affidavits from people who picked up the satellite transmissions—"

"But no recordings or transcripts of any conversation between Dane and the captain, as I understand it."

His blue eyes suddenly narrowed. "Are you in this or not, my dear?"

"I will *not* talk about this on television or to anyone else." She glared at him to ensure the message was understood. "Mr. Boyd, do you really think a man would send his own ship and twenty-one men into certain death—just for money?"

Boyd sighed, as though he had to explain the simplest concept *yet again* to a moron. "That ship was more than seventy years old. It wasn't worth that much to him anymore. It was the least glamorous of the fleet. He wants to buy another, something in keeping with the upscale image he's carefully creating. I told you *Paradisio* hadn't been in dry dock for years. Things were falling apart on it, and he knew it."

She shook her head, the Spanish voice still ringing in her ears. Dane Erikson knew nothing of what Genevieve discussed in the darkened dining room. That much was clear to her. "That's hardly a motive for mass murder. I have a hard time buying it, and maybe a jury will too."

He took a furtive glance around the restaurant before he spoke. "Let me tell you something. That man doesn't play to lose. Oh, he's fooled a lot of people with his devil-may-care barefoot sailor act. But he's ruthless, dishonorable, and cunning, and he'll do whatever is necessary to succeed."

Ruthless, dishonorable, and cunning. Who did that describe? Dane or this pushy man determined to use her for his gain?

"I want to do what's right for Marco and the men he sailed with."

"That's what I like to hear," he said with a condescending smile. "Now, about our meeting this week. I'll tell those family members about maritime law. I'll explain to them that they are entitled to more than lost income. They are actually owed hundreds of thousands of dollars for lost companionship and punitive damages for the misery suffered by those poor men as they struggled for their lives and drowned. I'll describe the negligence involved in terms so potent, they'll be ready to hang Dane Erikson when I'm done."

She closed the menu, her appetite long gone. "And what do you expect of me, Mr. Boyd?"

"You act as their leader who will help them find retribution for what they lost." He put a gentle hand on hers, a damp palm that made her want to wipe the spot with her napkin. "Emotional trauma costs a lot of money, my dear. And Dane Erikson's going to have forty million to dole out." As the waitress approached, he whispered, "Don't you want a piece of it?"

The words on the computer screen ran together, the passenger lists and purser's inventory dancing in front of Dane's fatigued eyes. Three weeks worth of E-mails and administration and virtually no sleep took its toll. He flipped off the laptop, drawn to the open window of his study. Absently rubbing the late-night beard that darkened his face, he studied the familiar celestial patterns in the night sky.

At least *Valhalla* had a marvelous send-off. A bit light on passengers due to some cancellations, since it was the first Utopia cruise in three weeks, but he'd expected that. The crew had been uneasy too, eyeing the heavens for signs and one another for support. No star-dogged moon tonight, he thought. Perhaps he should have heeded that warning when *Paradisio* set sail.

When would he stop feeling guilty? Every time he looked into the eyes of a crewman or a sad widow . . . or a grieving sister . . . he felt responsible. The thought of Ava Santori and her mission twisted his gut for the hundredth time. He was the last person on earth who would hurt Marco Santori or any of them. She might not know that, but surely the rest of the Utopians did. Unfortunately, her presence could legitimize a lawsuit that he had very little energy or time or desire to fight.

It could ruin him. This messy lawsuit and the resulting newspaper and TV stories could cripple the business, which hurt the very people he supported. Didn't they see that?

If he fought it hard—and he could, the son of a bitch Grayson had no case—it would look like he didn't care about the families. If he settled out of court, he would look guilty of murder. Not that he gave a rat's ass about how he looked. But he did care about the two hundred people who worked for him, and the hundreds of extended family members who ate and slept in comfort because of Utopia's success.

He ran a hand through his hair. The lawsuit was just a fact of life that he'd deal with. Along with the appearance of Ava Santori. He studied the vivid formation of Orion's Belt in the eastern sky, but his mind's eye envisioned the exotic features of Marco's sister. He smiled as he recalled her enthusiasm in the kitchen, then remembered how shaken she'd been when he'd seen her later. She was a bundle of emotions, a constant brewing storm that struck with no warning. For some reason he liked the idea of keeping a close watch on that storm. He liked the idea far too much.

The sound of a motor, a Moke or a Jeep, slowly coming up his half-mile-long drive interrupted his thoughts. The car door slammed just seconds before the doorbell rang.

Enough troubled sailors and lifelong employees knew that Dane's home could be a place of refuge that he didn't question the late-night visitor. He padded barefoot through the dark hallway and opened the front door.

Her black hair blended into the night. Her eyes caught the moonlight, revealing something childlike and frightened, and he put his hands on her shoulders without thinking.

"Ava? What are you doing here?"

She opened her mouth to speak, but her eyes dropped down his bare torso and boxer shorts. Then she glanced into the hall behind him before tentatively asking, "Are you alone?"

He grinned at the assumption. "All the dancing girls have left."

"I need to talk to you." Her dark eyes narrowed, as though she expected an argument.

He opened the door wider. "Come in."

She inched in, keeping her distance. He reached over and touched the switch on the wall, gentle uplighting suddenly spilling from unobtrusive wall fixtures. She still wore the pink sweater and white pants that she had on this morning, her hair windblown into a tangle of soft curls.

Her gaze darted down his chest again and lingered a moment, then flew back up to his face.

"Sit in here," he said as he guided her into the living room. "Can I get you anything?"

"No, this isn't a social visit." She crossed her arms and looked around the room, at the window, obviously avoiding him.

As intrigued as he was by the late-night call, he took pity on her obvious discomfort at his state of undress. "Then you'd probably appreciate it if I put some clothes on."

She sat on the edge of a chair. "Yes. Good idea. I mean . . . that'd be fine."

"I'll be right back." On the way to his bedroom, he stole a glance back at her. She still had her gaze determinedly set in the opposite direction, and he smiled.

Marone, this was stupid. Ava ran a hand through her unruly hair and realized she must look like a madwoman. And he looked like a Viking god. She hadn't expected him to be naked. Or nearly so. She hoped she hadn't gawked at the carved muscles of his shoulders and chest, where his hair darkened over masculine planes. How long had her gaze lingered over the sculpted stomach muscles above his boxer shorts? Oh God, *boxer* shorts. She squeezed her eyes closed to erase the sparks of arousal at the thought of what they barely covered.

She dropped her head back on the sofa, realizing that her temples had throbbed all day since she'd left the ship. She'd spent the afternoon wandering around town until she finally stumbled into a tiny shop that sold French bread and bottled water and rented cars. She bought a loaf of bread and took a chance on something called a Mini Moke, much smaller and more manageable than Cassie's Gurgel, but just as noisy and open. In it, she'd traveled the mountainsides of St. Barts, stopped at a breathtaking Anse de Gouverneur beach, and parked at the top of a rocky cliff. By sheer chance, she had a perfect view of *Valhalla* as it set sail.

During her private picnic, she replayed every nuance of the conversation she could remember, fighting for the bits that eluded her memory. She didn't know where to turn, who to trust. She kept coming back to Dane.

And, then, literally, she did. Miraculously, or at least unconsciously, she found herself at the foot of his driveway. She'd parked there for a good twenty minutes, considering what to do. Should she trust him? Would he believe her story? Did he know what was behind the conversation she'd heard? It was entirely possible that no matter what, he would protect Genevieve Giles. The granddaughter of a good friend, the man who set him up in business. An extremely beautiful woman. He could easily be in love with her.

She considered tracking down the police, but the voice of bitter experience told her to slow down. That same voice kept leading her back to Dane Erikson.

The conversation she'd overheard and nearly everything she'd observed so far conflicted with the demonic picture Grayson Boyd had painted to get her down to St. Barts. Her instinct told her Marco wouldn't become so close with a cold-blooded killer.

If she were to ever figure out what Genevieve meant and what happened to *Paradisio*, she had to take a chance and trust him.

At the sound of him clearing his throat, she opened her eyes. He still looked like a Viking god, only mercifully dressed in cotton sweatpants and a T-shirt. He stood in the arched doorway, barefoot and holding two glasses of red wine. She looked at the glasses to keep her eyes off his striking features.

"I know. Not a social call. But you look like you could use a drink." He handed her the goblet. "I'm guessing Chianti. Your brother's favorite."

She took it and tried to steady her hand, wishing her emotions weren't always written all over her face. "He was raised on my Uncle John's homemade wine from a jug. I hope he didn't have you imagining otherwise."

Dane smiled. "He was honest to a fault. Cheers."

She took a sip, barely tasting the dry wine.

"And," he added with a smile, "he had an annoying tendency to speak before he thought."

"A family trait, I'm afraid."

Dane took a seat next to her and set his glass of wine on the coffee table.

"I'm guessing this is about your meeting with the lawyer?"

She smoothed a wrinkle from her white pants. "No. Not really. It's . . . it's something else."

When she didn't say anything more, he prompted her. "Do you need some more time to think, or do you want to just get it out there, Santori fashion?"

She couldn't help smiling. "No. I've been thinking all day."

He was being extremely patient. She'd burst into

his home well beyond a reasonable hour, openly stared at his display of masculine assets, accepted some expensive wine, and hadn't yet offered an explanation. She took a deep breath.

"Okay. I have reason to believe that something . . . something really wrong happened on the *Paradisio*."

He stared at her. "It certainly did."

"I overheard an unnerving conversation today and I think you should know about it."

"Okay. Tell me." He was walking a thin line between gentle and patronizing.

"I overheard Genevieve talking to someone about money. About profits." She paused to consider how to phrase it.

"Ava, that's what she talks about. That's her whole world, profit and operations. I know she's not the most lovable person in the world, but she's really good at what she does."

She knew he'd defend her. "Embezzlement? Murder? Is she really good at that?"

He shifted imperceptibly in his seat, and a shadow of confusion crossed his face. "Start from the beginning. Please."

"Okay." Melodrama wouldn't work on him. "Remember when I saw you in the purser's office this morning?"

"Yes. You seemed upset."

She fingered the crystal stem of the wineglass. "When I left the galley, I overheard a strange conversation coming from some back room off the dining room. I was trying to find the way to go up—above deck—whatever you call it on a ship. Upstairs."

"I understand. Go on."

"I heard two people talking. One was Genevieve.

The other was a man with a Spanish accent, and they were talking about the accident. He said he wanted her to get—to take—four hundred thousand dollars from you to pay him back for what was lost on the ship. Some kind of precious cargo. He said 'you know why that ship went down.' Genevieve said, 'You sent a boy to do a man's job and now they are all dead.' "

He raised his eyebrow slightly, and she took it as doubt. She leaned forward to reinforce her certainty. "I remember her words clearly. I've heard them in my head a thousand times today."

He kept his eyes on her, searching her face before he spoke. "You said the man had a Spanish accent. Did Genevieve ever use his name?"

Ava shook her head. "I don't think so. But there's more. He said that it wouldn't be the first ship to vanish without a trace and it won't be the last."

His blue-green gaze flashed at her. "What?"

"And she said 'next time get your precious cargo off before the ship disappears.' " As he frowned in disbelief, her voice rose. "Then he . . . he threatened her. I think he . . . he hurt her. Choked her or something, it was hard to tell."

He said nothing but stood, pressing his palms together in thought. She watched him, waiting and hoping he'd respond with the same horror and determination that had wracked her all day.

"Do you believe me?"

He walked toward the veranda. She bit the well-worn spot on her lower lip and waited. Finally, he turned back to her. "Is it possible that you misunderstood—"

"I knew you wouldn't believe me!" She jumped

out of her seat and nearly lunged at him. "There's something going on and it cost a lot of lives. If you don't care, fine. Or maybe you want to protect your girlfriend. But don't you want to know what happened?" She froze as another thought planted itself. "Or perhaps you already know."

"Ava, please." He took a step toward her.

"Maybe this explains why the ship sank," she insisted. "Maybe people on the ship were involved." She narrowed her eyes, knowing that what she heard had vindicated him, but unable to let go of her nagging suspicions. "Maybe you were involved."

He gripped her shoulders, his thumbs resting on her collarbone. "Calm down. I'm trying to figure this out. I do believe what you heard, but Genevieve could have been talking about Arnot's truffles, for Christ's sake."

Ava tried to shake his hands off her. "She wasn't talking about freaking truffles, Dane. Unless they cost four hundred thousand dollars now."

Her blood was near the boiling point. Then he touched her cheek. Just grazed his finger along the side of her mouth and everything froze. Her fear, her temper. Her entire being.

"Calm. Down."

At the whispered command, she felt her breath catch in her throat, trapped between pulse beats. "Okay," she choked. "I'm calm."

"Liar."

He was so near that she could see the pale stubble on his cheeks, the dark lashes edging his eyes. His fingers were warm and the caress sweet. It should have calmed her, and in a sense, it did. It made her forget her mission. It made her imagine what it would feel like if he lowered his hand, traced a line down her neck, and touched the very spot where her heart pumped madly. For one insane instant, she wanted him to.

"What are you going to do, Dane?" she managed to ask.

He didn't say a word as his salty, soapy scent made her as dizzy as his unbroken gaze. Then he stepped back, leaving a warm spot on the skin he'd touched. "I'll look into it."

"What does that mean?"

"What would you have me do?" he asked, crossing his arms. "Demand Genevieve take a lie detector test?"

A little shaky, she dropped back into the chair and took a deep sip of wine. "That'd be a good start."

"I'll look into it," he repeated. "I have access to everyone's computer and I'll carefully—quietly, mind you—talk to some people. Okay?"

"Will you tell me what you find out?"

"Depends. How was your meeting with Boyd?"

She snapped her head up at the question. Was he trying to blackmail her into dropping the lawsuit?

"To be perfectly honest, my mind was still in that dining room with Genevieve. But he made some compelling arguments."

He ran a hand through his hair, a mussed tangle of honey-shaded streaks, long around his neck, a few strands grazing his earlobes.

"You let me know when you want to hear the other side," he said softly.

"Now would be a good time."

He sat down next to her. "I had nothing to do with Stuart's decision to sail east instead of west. We had charted a course straightaway in the opposite direction, reviewed the list of remaining crewmen and what their jobs would be, and promised to stay in touch. Two hours later, all communication with the ship was lost."

"All communication? I thought you were in constant contact with them—directing them all the way."

"That's what Boyd wants you to think, but it's not true. Ava, I've been working with the Coast Guard and investigating satellite links that may have gone down in the area before and during the storm." He stopped and sighed, a bewildered expression darkening his striking face. "It was so strange. One minute we had a satellite connection and the next it was black. There were rough waters, yes, but nothing that Stuart couldn't handle. Even though the storm had changed tracks, they were hours from any real danger. I never dreamed it would be my last conversation with any of them."

A little tremor in his voice seized her heart. "So, it's my turn," he said to her. "Do you believe me?"

She regarded him intently, trying to see past the magnificent roll of genetic dice, to get beyond his impressive mix of power and perfection. Was that guilt that darkened his expression every time he looked at her, or something else? "Maybe your crime was ignorance about your employee's extracurricular activities."

His blue-green gaze stayed locked on her just long enough to unravel the few strands of composure she had left. She remembered her own disheveled appearance, certainly not enhanced by hours of driving around in a tin can. Forcing herself to avert her eyes from him, she reached for the keys to the Mini Moke she'd set on the table.

"I should go. Thank you for hearing me out."

"I appreciate your telling me this," he said as he walked her to the door. "There may be a perfectly rational explanation—"

She turned to him, ready to blaze. "Don't you dare minimize this until we get to the bottom of it."

"We?" He stifled a laugh as he opened the door and stepped outside with her. "I'll handle it, Nancy Drew."

Ava bit her cheek to keep from arguing with him. She'd give him a day, maybe two, then start her own investigation.

"I'm sorry you missed *Valhalla*'s send-off today," he commented as he glanced up to the sky. "It was superb."

"I didn't miss it." At his surprised look, she tapped the hood of the Mini-Moke. "I took this thing to the highest peak I could find—over a gorgeous beach—and watched it from there."

Pride shone in his eyes. "What did you think?"

"Breathtaking, even from the hilltop."

"You should experience it on board. There's nothing like it, really."

She opened the driver's door of the Moke and slipped behind it, smiling as she remembered the spectacle. "I could hear Wagner in the breeze. Very stirring."

He stood just inches from her, only the thin metal door separating them. Their eyes met, and once again, she simply couldn't look away.

"This couldn't have been easy for you," he said softly. "Coming here. Trusting me."

She raised an eyebrow. "Who said I trusted you?"

Without a flicker of warning, his hand was on her chin, lifting it to his face. His lips came down on her cheek, taking every breath and thought away as he kissed a spot just to the left of her mouth. The same one he'd caressed a few minutes ago.

"I like that dimple."

Her lips parted to respond, but he kissed her again, this time directly on the mouth. She felt his breath, then the tip of his tongue touched hers. At her tiny gasp, he increased the pressure of their contact, leaving her dimly aware of the blood rushing through her weakened limbs. She gripped the metal frame of the car door for support.

As quickly as it happened, it was over, leaving only the imaginary warmth where his mouth had been. The moonlight cast a shadow on his expression, but she could see a glimmer in his eyes. "Thank you for giving me a chance," he whispered.

Her voice came out raspier than usual. "I expect you to do something. Quickly."

He touched her cheek again, next to her mouth. "The dimple must be a family trait," he whispered. "Along with impatience and hot blood."

He was so right. She managed her impatience. But his finger seared her skin, reminding her that the hot blood could be her downfall this time.

Genevieve had always thought Dane was careless not to have a gate or guard at the foot of his driveway. Everyone on St. Barts knew where he lived, and could walk right up to his house and look in the windows if they wanted. Like she so often did when she ran. It was only four miles from her own hilltop home, and Genevieve, a competitive runner since she was a teenager, could make it in less than half an hour. Especially late at night, when it was cool and there were few cars turning the bends and forcing her to the side of the road.

She made the jog at least three times a week, often stopping at the foot of his driveway and usually deciding to take the steep hill up to his house. She loved the pull on her hamstrings as she tackled the incline, always rewarding herself with a two-minute break to breathe and stretch. During those two minutes, she could easily figure out what Dane was doing by the lights, the music, the cars parked outside. Most evenings it was dark, except for the glow from the back. His study. She'd only been in the room a few times, he guarded it as carefully as his heart.

Some nights the whole place would be bathed in light. Marco's Gurgel and several others parked in front, pounding rock music and bursts of laughter echoing into the early hours. Other nights, she'd hear jazzy notes from the veranda, see a dim light in the front hall, a single rental car in front. There were a lot of those nights when that redhead was around. The one he met when some fashion magazine booked *Celestia* for a week-long photo shoot. The leggy model had come back after the shoot was over and stayed with him for nearly a month.

Genevieve pushed the thought away and counted her steps. Up, up, up to the steepest part where the driveway curved. It comforted her to know what he was doing, who he was with. Almost as if they shared a life. Then she heard voices. Soft. She recognized his voice, but not the woman.

Her feet stilled, careful not to hit a stone or branch.

She literally held her breath, not wanting the slightest pant to give her away. She took the precise number of steps she knew would be necessary to afford her a view of the front door. Two feet to her left and through a copse of hibiscus plants, she could see him. Talking to a woman leaning on the open door of a Mini Moke.

She couldn't see the face, but she could see the mass of black waves.

Dane reached down, close enough for a kiss, but she couldn't be sure from this distance. Genevieve backed down, silently, carefully, around the bend to the bottom of the driveway and started a fast jog in the direction of her home. Her feet pounded a rhythm on the concrete. What the hell was Ava Santori doing there?

Stupid question. Of course Dane couldn't wait to get his hands on her.

She hated when a new woman came into his life. Recognized and dreaded the symptoms from beginning to end, like the flu. It always started with a few late mornings and his lazy, bad-boy grin. Then he'd move into full-blown happy, so fucking happy, for three or four weeks. He'd tease her endlessly and let her make all the decisions while he holed up in his mansion and played house with his latest girlfriend. Then everything would change. He'd get a little dark, moody. And the bitch *du jour* would be on a plane—sometimes the Utopia Piper if he was in a real hurry to get rid of her. Before she left, she'd show up in the office in tears or call twenty-six times in one day hunting him down. Well, this one wouldn't last long. Marco's sister would be just a novelty. He'd tire of her after a week.

At least this got her mind off the conversation with Ricardo this afternoon, she thought bitterly. Now she could torment herself by picturing Dane and that raven-haired witch from Boston in bed together, instead of dwelling on how damn deep a hole she'd dug for herself.

It didn't matter. She was over him and her girlish fantasies. It was almost time to leave St. Barts. One more shipment and delivery, one more deposit into her rapidly growing account, and she'd be completely free. She'd spent ten years waiting for him, and that was all she'd give any man. She knew Grandy would be disappointed. Ever since she and Grandfather Giles had befriended the poor little rich boy and given him his first boat, they'd always hoped Genevieve and Dane would get married.

The lights and engine of a car approached and she dropped back into a thicket of palms until it passed. The Mini Moke. Well, little Miss Ava would learn. She'd fall for him like the others had, and he'd make a big show of not wanting to hurt her, but she'd disappear in time. They all did eventually. The line started here.

5

The night produced little sleep and a lot of questions for Dane. The next morning, he strode into the two-story building that housed Utopia Adventures with a plan in mind. Settlements, inventory, Genevieve: a simple to-do list. As he turned the corner to his office, he silently blessed Claire Shepard, already at her desk as always, while other, more laid-back Utopians still slept. Excellent French coffee would be brewing, and his desk would be uncluttered and work prioritized. With Claire on the job, a calming sense of order prevailed.

"Morning, Claire." He spoke to the back of her salt-and-pepper hair and stopped to leaf through a pile of messages picked up from the overnight answering service.

"Hi, Dane." Her gaze remained glued to the E-mail on her screen. "We have six more cancellations on *Nirvana*. That software CEO pulled out of the Owner's Suite."

He said nothing but crushed one message slip into a ball. He'd already gotten this one. Captain Donald

Taylor of the U.S. Coast Guard had called him at home last night to give him the dismal update on the search.

"A producer from NBC called again, and so did that freelance writer from *Sailing* magazine. Someone from your lawyer's office called to say don't talk to the press, and your accountant's secretary called. Said it was urgent." She exited her E-mail with a determined click and turned to face her boss for the first time. "You look like hell."

"Thanks. It matches my mood."

She shook her head and rose. "Let me get you some coffee."

As he reached his desk, he called back out to her, "Claire, could you print me out a complete purser's inventory of every item on *Paradisio?* On the last few of its cruises, actually."

She stuck her head through his office door. "More than the dry goods and crew's personals that you had me send to the search site?"

"Everything. I want everything logged in any department, including checked luggage and last-minute freight."

She gasped, looking at the balled message still squeezed in his hand. "Dane! Did they find something?"

"No. Not yet. But I want to be sure we know everything we could be looking for." *Precious cargo.* What the hell did that mean?

She followed him into his office. "But isn't the search officially over this week?"

He flipped on the computer and laid three of the messages next to his phone, in the order he would return them. "Yeah, but I've decided to keep the private divers down there awhile and extend the search area."

A moment later, Claire waved a coffee cup in his face, the rich aroma tempting him. "Don't get used to this." She winked as he took the cup. "I'm only spoiling you because you look so bad today."

"I haven't slept in weeks, Claire. I'm sure it shows."

"I'll get started on the inventory. You need a vacation, Dane."

He almost laughed at the notion. "When you have a chance, I also need a passenger list for *Nirvana*. What's left, anyway."

"Oh, there are plenty left," she called from her desk. "Some VIPs too. A U.S. senator and his wife—allegedly—and two New York Yankees. They're celebrating the World Series win, I understand. Genevieve will probably want to upgrade one of them into the newly vacated Owner's Suite."

The germ of an idea was growing, but he didn't have time to play with it now. "No. Keep it open." He'd work that out later. *Nirvana* didn't sail until Friday, three days from now. Today he wanted to concentrate on that inventory and have a long conversation with his executive vice president.

He sipped the delicious coffee. "Claire, can you let Genevieve know I need some time later this morning?"

"She left a message saying she's meeting with vendors in St. Lucia and St. Kitts and a couple of other places. She won't be back until late Thursday. You want me to try her cell?"

Damn. "Yes, please. A little later."

He'd concentrate on the settlements then, and

picked up the message from his U.S accountant, Alex Walker. The sooner they were finalized, the sooner he'd have the monkey Grayson Boyd off his back. Maybe. He dialed the New York number and while it rang, an image of Ava at his door flashed in his mind, all fired up and looking for a villain. He'd managed to avoid thinking of her all night, concentrating only on the possible explanations for the evidence she'd presented to him. But in the less menacing light of day, he let his mind wander back to more pleasurable thoughts.

Thoughts that were far too erotic, considering they focused on a woman with the mission to bury him. He shouldn't have kissed her, but he'd moved without thinking. Acted on his instinct and desire, instead of planned strategy. That was something he rarely did.

Marco had talked about his sister in vague but positive terms. Dane had the impression Ava was protective and that she'd gotten her little brother out of more than a few scrapes. So why the hell hadn't she ever come to see him?

Dane remembered asking him that once. Marco had shrugged and said she would when she was ready. He never really offered a specific reason for the estrangement from his family, other than his father's tyrannical nature. After Cassie came along, Marco talked about Boston more, as though he wanted to heal the old rift because he was about to create a family of his own.

With a will of its own, Dane's mind wandered back to Ava. He thought of her rare smile, the calming of the storm in her eyes when he touched her cheek. A distinct ache stirred in his groin as he remembered the jolt he got from their kiss. Their first kiss.

"I don't like what I read in the fax, Dane." Alex Walker's New York accent came through the line, returning him to the problems at hand.

"You're tight as a crab's ass, Walker, and just as nasty."

"Tight with your money. Seriously, Dane, are you sure you want to do this? You don't even have the insurance money yet, and that maritime personal injury lawyer's sniffing all over hell and back for dirt on you."

Dane kicked off his Docksiders and stretched back in the chair. It was his company and his money. Alex could harp all day, but Dane knew what he wanted to do. What he had to do.

Claire leaned around the corner and whispered, "It's that TV producer from NBC. He says he'll hold all day until he can talk to you. That'd be my choice, but do you want to talk to him?"

Dane held up a "one minute" finger, letting Alex finish his sentence. "Alex, I need to take a quick call. In the meantime, chill. I know what I'm doing. I'll call you back in five." He looked at the flashing light on line two and hit it hard. "This is Erikson."

"Mr. Erikson, thank you for taking my call. I'm Jeff Krawsky with NBC's *Dateline*. How are you, sir?"

Lousy. Tired. Worried. Give it a break, kid. "Fine, Jeff. What can I do for you?"

"Mr. Erikson, we are in the process of producing a segment on the disappearance of *Paradisio*. Could we get you on camera, sir?"

"No."

"But, Mr. Erikson—"

"Jeff. I've got twenty-one men dead and a couple of hundred employees in shock and mourning. I'm still running a business that's moving into the height of its season. And, as you may know, I don't do interviews under the best of circumstances. Thank you and good-bye—"

"Please!" His voice rose and Dane resisted the urge to hang up. "The son of an American television celebrity was second mate on the ship."

Something pinched in his gut. "I'm aware of that."

"Dominic Santori's daughter has agreed to be interviewed. She's speaking for all the respondents in the class action suit against Utopia and we are anxious, sir, to get both sides. It's not our policy to present a biased story and your interview would—"

The pinch in Dane's gut turned to a full-blown twist. "When did you talk to her?"

"Who? Oh, the daughter? Her lawyer confirmed it."

"When?" He spat the word into the phone.

"This morning, sir. Just before I called you."

Dane closed his eyes and took a deep breath. "My answer is still no." He dropped the phone into its cradle.

Ava knew as soon as she arrived at the elementary school that Grayson Boyd had made a tactical mistake. Although the school was close to the Utopia offices, the air-conditioning was off for the evening and the airless library offered only student-size seating. The fifty or so people who gathered looked like giants squeezed into a dollhouse. The physical discomfort only added to their already tense and miserable emotional states.

The cacophony of French, English, Spanish, and

Caribbean pigeon reached an earsplitting level in the room designed for quiet, and the posters of characters from children's books detracted from the serious nature of the meeting. Everyone knew everyone and Ava had an outsider's sensation of being invited to someone else's family reunion.

Cassie stood with Marjory Hemingway toward the back, the two women's heads together in animated discussion. Marjory's giant brown eyes widened in surprise at what Cassie had just told her.

"Oh, yes, it's time for dat! I know!" They shared a secret grin as Ava approached and greeted them.

"Cassie, I wasn't sure you'd be here."

"Neither was I," Cassie said with a smile and tilted her head toward Marjory. "Marj talked me into it."

The three of them folded themselves into seats near the back of the room.

"I gonna break dis chair!" Marjory exclaimed as she struggled with her bulk in the tiny wooden seat.

Chuckling with Cassie, Ava was suddenly aware of a presence behind her.

"Come up front and sit next to me." The demand in her ear startled her and she turned to see Grayson Boyd's pale blue eyes blinking rapidly behind his glasses.

"I'll stay here."

He wiped a drip of perspiration from his forehead and kneeled to the same height as her elementary school seat. "I need you up there."

"No, thank you. I'm just here to listen. Like everyone else." She turned back to Cassie and Marjory.

He straightened abruptly and Ava caught his quick angry look before he moved on. Marjory's brown hand dropped onto Ava's, and the women exchanged glances just as a young man reached their table and pulled out a chair to join them.

"*Bon soir, mes amies.*"

Ava remembered meeting him in Arnot's kitchen, recognizing the thinning black hair and knowing dark eyes of Philippe Basille. Cassie introduced them and Philippe offered his hand and a friendly, crooked grin.

"I was assisting in *Valhalla*'s kitchen when you visited," he reminded her.

"Yes, I remember. Hello again, Philippe. Why aren't you on the ship in an exotic port by now?"

He shook his head vehemently, his hands held up in mock protest. "Not me, ma'am. I don't usually sail. I am strictly prep in the galley. I move from ship to ship before she sets sail and am happy to sleep on dry land."

"Why are you—who did you—" Ava stumbled over the awkward question.

"My cousin Jacques," he responded, gracefully saving her. "I just got him the job not five months ago. He was a sous-chef in Paris, but came here to work for Chef Arnot." His French accent thickened with sorrow. "They kept him on as essential crew— one person to feed the other twenty. Perhaps he should have stayed on dry land too, eh?"

"I'm so sorry, Philippe," Ava said quietly.

He offered a half shrug, so French and sad. "*C'est la vie.* But we are here to collect our blood money now, are we not?"

Grayson Boyd began to speak before anyone could answer.

He launched into his opening argument as though the whole jury sat in front of him. Pacing the room, sucking even more air out of it, Grayson Boyd laid out his case that the loss suffered by every person in the room was Utopia Adventures' financial gain. And retribution was essential. He never mentioned Dane Erikson by name.

At first they listened, rapt. But his southern drawl lost a few of them and claustrophobia got the rest. Arguments and individual conversations broke out at each table, making Ava feel more at home. Santoris always interrupted one another.

"What if you are wrong, Monsieur Boyd?" An older man called out from one side. "How can you prove these accusations?"

"Our firm has signed affidavits . . . ," Boyd began, and Ava wondered how many of them actually knew what an affidavit was.

"What if we all get fired for doing this?" Another person cut him off before he could finish.

"You can't be fired. You are protected by law!" Boyd insisted, then added with a chuckle, "but who needs to work with a million in your bank account?"

Marjory moaned, low and heavy. "Not one person in dis room can count to a million."

"How much of it do you get, Mr. Boyd?" A woman's crisp American accent caught Ava's attention, but she didn't see who'd asked the question.

"A percentage. For my efforts on your behalf." Boyd leaned against a display of *Clifford the Big Red Dog* books and tapes, and Ava resisted the urge to laugh at the image. Instead, she glanced at Cassie, who raised her eyebrows and gave a tiny smile in response.

"I am a sailor myself, my friends." Boyd lowered his booming voice, perhaps deciding on a softer approach. "When I left the U.S. Navy I decided to specialize in maritime law, to protect the rights of sailors and their families. I have, in my twenty-five years of practice, recouped more than one hundred million dollars for victims' families. No one else in the country or the world, can claim that kind of success and—"

He was shut down by more questions.

"What if we've already taken money from Utopia? Is that a settlement?"

"What about the Death on the High Seas laws? How can you ignore them?"

"It's wrong to take money for the dead," a Jamaican voice called out.

"Yes it is, Violet," Marjory whispered in vehement agreement. "Yes it is."

"Ladies and gentlemen." Boyd struggled to regain order. "I ask you to speak with Miss Ava Santori. She's the sister of the poor, dead Second Mate Marco Santori. She's from a wealthy family in Boston; her father is a celebrity who makes weekly appearances on television. She is here for justice, not money. As you all should be."

Ava nearly flipped the undersize desk over as she jumped to her feet. How dare he speak for her? She sensed every eye on her, but she kept her gaze locked on Boyd as she worked to control the fire in her gut.

"I have not made up my mind about this lawsuit, Mr. Boyd." A rumble traveled through the room in response. "I'm here with everyone else to learn more about the situation."

He nodded agreeably, but she felt the daggers of anger shooting from his blue eyes.

"Dane Erikson lives in a mansion, ladies and gentlemen." He ignored her, evidently choosing to dig deeper into his bag of lawyer tricks for his trump card. "He flies a private plane to Europe. He has millions of dollars in banks around the world and grandiose plans to expand his empire. He has—"

"He built this school," Cassie said, silencing him.

"And a clinic in St. John where my mother had her first mammogram," someone added from across the room.

"He flew my papa in from Trinidad for his eightieth birthday," a man offered with a deep Caribbean cadence.

"He gave me a job after—"

"That's all part of his plan!" A young man stood up from a side table. "Everything he does is meant to keep us loyal and working for him and no one else. He's no saint and someone's gotta pay for this!"

"And a million dollars is a small price for my son!" another man shouted.

The room erupted in chaos, and Boyd started flipping papers onto desks, shoving the printed pages in front of every person. "This is the legal brief my firm has drawn up. It spells out the case against him and what you need to do to participate and win—be awarded—one million dollars for the loss of your loved one. Someone who can never be replaced."

The people in front leafed through the pages. Frustration and confusion, mixed with grief, threatened to ignite more harsh words. Boyd waved the brief in front of Ava when he reached their table.

"I know you've seen this, my dear," he said pointedly, as though they'd been meeting for weeks to discuss the subject. "I'm sure you'll want to do right by your dead brother."

"His name was Marco." She managed to keep the revulsion out of her voice. "And, yes, you can keep this. I've read it."

He'd lost most of them by then, and Ava and Cassie left together, anxious for fresh air and the opportunity to consider what had just happened.

"Marco would pronounce that man a grade A prick," Cassie announced.

"Well, he certainly left a lot of people more confused than anything," Ava said.

"I just hope people think before they jump on his bandwagon. It's a lot of money, and some people might do anything to get it legally."

"What did you think?" Ava asked as they stepped onto the grass outside the school.

"I wish I could get behind the quest for a million dollars. God knows, I need money right now. But I feel like Marj. It's blood money for the dead, and I know in my heart Marco would hate the fact that Dane's being blamed for this. Marco worshiped that man. He insisted that Dane be the—"

She stopped suddenly.

"What?"

Cassie turned to face Ava, a warm glow in her eyes. "Give me your hand," she said, reaching for Ava. Cassie guided Ava's hand to the loose material over her midriff, pressing it harder until Ava could feel . . . a hard, rounded bump.

"Oh, my God." A thrill ran through her, warming her to her toes and springing tears in her eyes.

"I was going to say that Marco insisted that Dane be the godfather."

"When are you—why didn't you—Oh my God." She threw her arms around Cassie in a big hug. Then she pulled away, impulsively taking the freckled face between her hands. "Oh Cassie, Marco will never see his baby!"

Cassie put a gentle finger on Ava's mouth. "Don't remind me. I'm trying to accept that, luv, and not lose the joy of it. As for telling you, I've been waiting for the right moment."

"Oh, what an extraordinary gift." Ava turned her face toward the sky with a wide smile. "Forget Grayson Boyd. I feel like celebrating!"

Cassie giggled, clearly pleased with Ava's response. She hooked her arm into Ava's. "Locals go to Au Port. It's an institution in Gustavia, just a few blocks from here. The only place in this rich man's paradise for a cheap beer and a nonvintage wine. And milk, for me."

"I don't believe this," Ava exclaimed as they fell into step together. "A baby. A baby Santori."

"Well." Cassie sighed. "I guess. We didn't have a chance to get married. I'm not sure what Junior's last name will be."

Ava turned with a sudden realization. The lawsuit! She wasn't Marco's immediate family anymore. "Cassie! The money—the suit. If it happens, it should all be yours. For the baby. For his future. For college."

Cassie laughed softly. "Don't worry about the baby, Ava. Dane will take care of him. Or her. I just wish my child had a real last name."

"Names don't matter," Ava assured her with a pat on the arm. "We will love this baby no matter what it's called. It's Marco's baby. And yours." She paused and inhaled the tropical evening air. "And I'm going to be an aunt!"

They grinned and gossiped like old friends until they reached the patio bar of Au Port.

Dane knew where they'd all go after the meeting and he didn't want to be hidden in his home tonight. He wanted to be right there with his people as they mulled the attorney's offer.

Violet Quindlen and Marj entered the open-air watering hole together, heads close in discussion. Deirdre and Yves Galloit, who worked in his office and mourned their oldest son, Gregoire, *Paradisio*'s chief engineer, followed a few minutes later. They nodded to him, and a few others stopped by his table and said hello, but no one sat down. Dane kept his eye on the street, refusing to admit to himself that he was waiting for Ava Santori.

A twist of desire coiled through him when he saw her, surprising him, since the NBC producer's words had rung in his head most of the day. Her wavy hair was pulled partway up tonight, showing off distinct cheekbones and a slender neck. Her nose was not perfect, but the slightest patrician bump seemed to perfectly fit her face. And her eyes. Her magical, black eyes had haunted him long after she left him alone last night, and all day when he thought of her agreeing to do an interview.

Cassie strolled right up to his table, pulled out a chair, and grinned. "You look lost, mate."

He laughed a little. "Just waiting for the verdict, Cass."

Cassie dropped into the seat across from him and Ava stood, hesitating. He pulled out the chair next to him and looked up at her expectantly. The material of her dress grazed his leg as she sat. It tickled his skin, but he made no effort to move aside.

"Jury's out," Cassie said. "But we could be swayed if you buy the drinks."

He signaled the waitress. "What would you like, Ava? Red wine?"

"The beer looks good." She lifted the collar of her dress, drawing his attention to the curve of her throat, the sheen on her skin. "A short walk here is more of a workout than the hills of the North End."

"It's the humidity." Dane averted his gaze. Why the hell were they talking about the weather?

The waitress brought beers for Dane and Ava and an ice water for Cassie. The women shared a secret smile as they toasted their drinks.

"You gonna let a man in on this?" he asked before he took a drink from his bottle.

Cassie had an inner glow about her and suddenly he knew why they'd been laughing on the way into the bar.

"Ah," he said, the beer bottle still midair. "My godchild has been announced."

Ava shivered with joy, an emotion he'd definitely not seen from her yet. "It's wonderful news. I can't wait to—" She turned to Cassie with a frown. "Can I tell my family?"

Cassie shook her head and sighed. "I don't know. I guess so. It's not due for five more months."

Dane sensed her hesitation and wanted to help. "Cassie hasn't told very many people, Ava. She and Marco were waiting . . ."

For a wedding that isn't ever going to happen now, he thought. Which reminded him of the reason they were together. "Full house at the meeting tonight, Cass?"

"Full enough," she said. "But Boyd didn't convince too many people. I don't think more than two or three are signed on. Ava threw him for a loop, though."

Dane looked questioningly at the woman to his right. She kept her eyes on the table, running a long finger over the condensation on her beer glass.

"What'd'ya do, give him the old Santori one-two?" She smiled a little. "I'd like to."

"Really? I thought you were in bed with this guy."

She squared her shoulders and aimed the fire in her eyes directly at him.

"Figuratively speaking, of course," he added hastily.

"I have not made a decision. And you know it."

He shrugged and took a sip. "That's not what they say at NBC."

"What are you talking about?" she asked.

"Jeff, the producer of *Dateline,* mentioned your interview to me today." He'd been burning to confront her since this morning, compounded by Genevieve's disappearance and the fact that the purser's inventory for *Paradisio* was no longer in the computer system. He hated roadblocks. And he hated deception.

"I repeat: what are you talking about?"

He searched her face for signs of honesty. He saw them all. Clear eyes, wide and beautiful too. No quivering lips, no shifting glances.

"I was told you were doing an interview with some TV news magazine, on behalf of the lawsuit respondents. Evidently your lawyer confirmed it."

She crossed her arms. "That bastard."

"He is a slimy one," Cassie agreed.

"I'm not doing any interviews, so don't worry." She sighed in complete exasperation. "Grayson Boyd is scum. Maybe I should drop out of the whole thing and head home."

He doubted she was serious, but he didn't want her to leave. "You can't. You're booked on *Nirvana*. We sail tomorrow night."

Her jaw dropped, and he found himself wondering when his guiding principles of *slow* and *easy* decided to take a vacation.

"She's cruising the Leeward Islands, which includes Guadeloupe, Dominica, Nevis, and Antigua. Several of the men lost on *Paradisio* are from those islands, and I'm going to visit their families. To discuss their future. I thought you should meet them."

She looked down at her beer, then up at him wordlessly.

His chest tightened at the appeal in her eyes. "You can decide for yourself what constitutes 'squalor.' You can even enlist them in your cause, if you like."

"When did you come up with this plan?" She frowned, clearly unsure of how to take the invitation.

He had made the plans to meet with the families in person this morning, after finalizing the settlements with his accountant. The idea of Ava joining him had barely been a seedling, yet here he was, presenting it as a full-grown fait accompli.

"I want you to make an informed decision before you add your name to a lawsuit or go back home. Isn't that why you came here?"

At the pointed question, she nodded.

"Then it makes sense for you to go. You can stay in the Owner's Suite."

Cassie squealed. "Oh, Dane!"

"Excuse me?" Ava's look of curiosity melted into surprise.

"It was vacated by a last-minute cancellation," he informed them.

Cassie stepped in to help him this time. "Ava, you've no idea how wonderful that is. The suite is gorgeous! It beats the crew bunks, I'll tell you. I may come and share the room."

Or I might. The thought darted through Dane's mind, along with an image of Ava in the oversize hot tub in the suite, and the king-size bed. He quashed it. He needed her trust, not her body.

"Come on, Ava." He touched her hand, unable to resist the contact. "You'll love it."

She whipped her fingers away from under his and the spark ignited in her eyes. "How do you know what I'll love?"

"A cruise through the most beautiful waters on earth. Six nights in a three-thousand-dollar suite with private valet service. The chance to whip up some crème brûlée with your hero Arnot. The opportunity to advance your cause, or at least understand it." He put his hand right back on hers, teasing her with a grin. "And I'll be there. Now, what's not to love?"

In spite of herself, she laughed. A throaty, honest laugh that was as attractive as her rare smiles. "You could lure Satan out of hell, you know that?"

He laughed right back. Damn, she made him feel good. Good and whole and happy to be alive. He'd almost forgotten what that felt like.

6

Three days later, Ava experienced *Nirvana*.

It had taken very little convincing for her to agree. While they were still at Au Port, Dane had whispered in her ear that they could do a little "investigating" on board. He hadn't found the answers he needed yet to the questions she'd posed the night before. He felt certain he could find out more—if indeed there was anything to find out—by being on a ship and examining it and the staff at work.

She wasn't certain if it was his words or the shower of sparks caused by his breath in her ear that sealed the deal. She tried not to think about it.

In the two days that passed, they had talked a few times. Dane called her at the hotel to finalize details of the trip. When she demanded to know if he'd talked to Genevieve, he said she'd flown off the island to make last-minute arrangements for the *Nirvana* cruise, but he promised he would talk to her before they left. And to some of the other Utopians on the ship. She believed him. She had no choice.

At the hotel, Grayson Boyd conveniently ran into

her twice a day. Far more disturbing, she'd found tiny clues that gave her the distinct feeling that someone had been in her room when she'd been out. Finding nothing missing, she'd tried to dismiss the unnerving sensation it caused but double-locked her door at night and checked the placement of her personal belongings every time she entered the room.

But the invasion of her privacy was just the incentive she needed to rationalize taking a cruise on *Nirvana*. Plus the fact that she could meet some more of the victims' families. One of those victims was "a boy sent to do a man's job" in Genevieve's words. The ship seemed like the most likely place to get some answers, so she agreed to go.

She had checked in with Mama and Dominic, purposely keeping her updates vague but warning her father not to talk to any media people and expressing her doubts as to the validity of the lawsuit. He had mumbled something about lawyers, and when he got off the line, Mama had whispered that he'd been having a very hard time since Ava left. Her mother's voice had sounded strained and exhausted and not too thrilled that Ava couldn't call for a few days, since she'd be leaving to meet other family members on the islands.

Nirvana, she discovered as a cabin steward escorted her to her suite, was aptly named. Thought not as large as *Valhalla*, it rivaled the other sailing ship in luxury and appointments. The decor captured the Edwardian era, with polished woods and plush fabrics. Where *Valhalla* had been contemporary and chic, *Nirvana* epitomized old European elegance. Ava loved it.

Nothing on the ship, however, prepared her for

the Owner's Suite. She didn't even try to hide her gasp when the steward opened the door. The sitting room and dining room combination opened to a private deck overlooking the endless blue water, with rich, inviting furnishings. Beyond it, she found a spacious bedroom with a four-poster bed laden with layers of lavish white-on-white bedclothes. A marble and glass bathroom with an oversize Jacuzzi tub in the middle of it offered another breathtaking view of the water out another set of sliding glass doors.

She tried to smother her guilt. She was supposed to be on a mission seeking retribution for Marco's death and instead she'd wound up on some kind of dream vacation.

"Is everything suitable, Miss Santori?" the young man asked with all the formality the rooms deserved.

Ava nearly laughed out loud. "Suitable is one way to describe it." She walked across the Oriental rug toward a huge bouquet of white roses on the coffee table, their potent fragrance drawing her. A card lay next to the vase.

Vikings believed that the color white brought calm seas and fruitful journeys. I wish you both. Dane.

She nearly swayed, but that could have been the rocking of the ship, she told herself. Thanking the steward with a generous tip, Ava wandered through the palatial rooms like a child in a candy store. She ran her fingers along the carved wood of the bedpost and fingered the feather-light silk comforter, afraid to sit on such a work of art. Why did he do this for her? He must really want to keep an eye on her. Maybe he thought he could buy her trust.

The thought was interrupted as Cassie called to her from the sitting room. "You in here, luv, or have you already drawn a bath?"

Ava came around the corner to see Cassie waving a plastic card key. "I've got access to every cabin. So I happen to know that no one else on this ship, no matter who they are, has accommodations like this."

"Cassie." Ava exhaled a breath she didn't know she was holding. "It's amazing. I'm stunned. Out of my league!"

Cassie laughed and spun a three-sixty, her arms extended. "Ah, money. Nothing like it, don't you think?" Then she nonchalantly picked up the card on the coffee table.

"Mmmmm." She fanned herself with it after glancing at the words. "Turning up the heat, isn't he?"

Ava's stomach did an unexpected flip. "What do you mean?"

"Ava. I know you're a nice Catholic girl from Boston. But, hon, I assume you've been, uh, courted before."

"I—I don't understand."

Cassie smiled and flopped onto the cream silk davenport, her right hand absently rubbing her tummy. "Once he's got a lady in his sights, very few escape unscathed."

Ava stared at her. "You can't be serious. I am hardly Dane Erikson's type."

"Not his type? Look at you! You're all breasts and hair. Gorgeous eyes and creamy skin. Sweetie, you underestimate yourself." Cassie leaned forward and set the card at a jaunty angle in the flower arrangement. "Don't underestimate *him*, though. That's free advice."

Ava dropped onto the chair across from Cassie, the swaying from the ship getting to her again.

"Stop it, Cassie. He's either being kind because I'm Marco's sister or trying to make me forget why I came here in the first place."

Cassie's frown made Ava drop the second option and focus on the first. "You both are being extremely kind to me. Considering my history with Marco . . ."

"Forget it, Ava. Marco's gone, and I don't see any good reason to carry grudges. My baby needs family, regardless of the past. You never have to question that again."

Ava studied the sweet freckled face of Cassie Sebring and wished to God that her brother had married this girl. What a breath of fresh air she'd have brought to the Santori family.

"Thank you, Cassie."

"Don't mention it. And don't mention my offering you free advice to Dane. He's never liked me poking in his personal life."

"I won't. I appreciate what you're saying. But I'm certain this"—Ava held out her hands to indicate the luxurious room—"has more to do with his need to have me on his side than attraction."

"Believe that if you want, luv. But from what I've seen, they don't know what hit 'em until it's over." She rolled her eyes. "And it's always over eventually with him."

She stood before Ava could speak.

"I've gotta go. I forgot I'm working." At the door, Cassie turned and winked at Ava, who hadn't yet found the legs to stand. "Enjoy the ride, luv. Call me if you need towels or . . . anything."

Ava could swear she heard Cassie giggle as the

door closed. Her words—*her free advice*—rang in her head. She went to the sliding doors for another view of the water and harbor but saw her own reflection in the blue glass. All breasts and hair. Yeah, but they went out in the eighties.

Ava refused to think of the remote possibility that Dane Erikson had taken an interest in her. She'd never attracted—or even tried to attract—a man like that. Her boyfriends were salt-of-the-earth North End kids, with loud families and louder kitchens. They were also few and far between, and not one could compete with the restaurant for her attention. A fact that, as she approached her thirtieth birthday, was beginning to worry her mother.

She studied the crystalline Caribbean waters and wondered again what motivated Dane. She had no doubt why he was showering her with luxury and roses. A pending lawsuit . . . and his possible involvement in the loss of that ship. Those were mighty strong motivators. He wasn't seriously attracted to her. That was out of the realm of reality.

"I can't imagine why those inventory logs are gone," Genevieve said, scrolling through the lists of documents on her computer to find something they both knew wasn't there. Dane stood behind her desk and noticed her free hand fiddle with a few strands of hair.

Genevieve was a cool liar, but he'd only realized it recently. Except for her schoolgirl crush on him, which she'd tried to hide from him since she literally *was* a schoolgirl, he'd believed her to be honest. He demanded truthfulness from everyone and she had never let him down. Then, about six months ago, light-headed from wine on a cruise they were both supervising, Genevieve had all but taken her clothes off in his suite when they were supposed to be discussing how to handle a last-minute booking change from a passenger.

He'd gently buttoned her blouse and walked her back to her own suite. From then on, she had been more distant and cool. They had put the incident behind them—at least, he had—and she continued her excellent work of handling marketing and so many aspects of operations. Until now.

"Someone in John Bronder's office must have thought we didn't need them anymore," she said. "Maybe when we started taking *Paradisio* off all the marketing materials last week."

Dane knew no one in his senior purser's department would do something so stupid, or care what marketing materials were being altered.

She abandoned the keyboard and turned her chair to meet his direct gaze. "I can check with him. Do you need them for the insurance, Dane?"

"Nope. I just want to see them." He sat down in the chair opposite her and extended his long legs, clad in his usual khaki shorts and deck shoes. "I can understand why previous records might be gone, but why would anyone destroy the inventory from the last cruise? We're still conducting an official search."

"We are?" She seemed surprised. "I thought it ended formally at the three-week mark. That's why we were able to finally hold the service. That's why we started sailing again."

"The Coast Guard search ends, that's true. But Utopia can fund a private search as long as we like."

"Dane." She shook her head and pursed her lips in pity. "It's just extending the heartache. You're not going to find anything."

Or is it that you don't want me to find anything?

"I need your opinion on something." He knew he wouldn't get anywhere with direct confrontation. He'd do better to play up her role as his confidante, his unofficial partner, as he'd overheard her say. "How do you think everyone is doing? Are they handling it? Anybody seem ready to jump ship? I know you're close with so many Utopians."

"Everything will be fine, Dane." She adeptly ignored the question, something he realized she'd done a lot lately. "I know you're worried about the lawsuit. It's a nuisance, but I think we're going to get through this. There will be a few who smell easy money. There always are in situations like this." She paused and frowned a bit. "Like Marco's sister. But she's not one of us, so she doesn't count."

Oh, she counts all right. "I'm not worried about the lawsuit, Gen. I'm worried about my people."

"I understand. I think everyone is anxious to get back to normal." She picked up a paper on her desk. "Especially Arnot. He's ordering more exotic delights. I finalized a host of new vendors at my meetings this week so we'll be able to keep him happy for a while."

He let her change the subject and rattle on about the chef's insistence on using only *fleur de sel*, the hand-harvested sea salt that cost an ungodly fifty-six dollars a pound.

"It really does add a distinct flavor to the food, Dane. You know it's hand-skimmed from the sea," she explained.

"At that price, it should be sucked out by mermaids."

She laughed, clearly relieved. "He doesn't care about cost, Dane. He's obsessed with quality."

Genevieve wasn't going to give an inch. Dane stood, anxious to study some files that Claire had located and then get to the ship. He picked up the list of new vendors she still held, their hands grazing briefly. "Can I keep this?"

The faintest rose tint brightened her prominent cheekbones. "Of course."

He hated having that effect on her. "By the way, I'm taking this next cruise, so I'll be gone awhile. You know how to reach me."

A shadow crossed her face, but she held her gray eyes steady. "Yes. I saw that you booked the Owner's Suite."

"Actually, I took a deluxe on the main deck. I put Ava Santori in the Owner's Suite."

Her smile was quick, a little too quick. She already knew that, he thought. "An excellent way to keep her away from the lawyers, the press, and the *Paradisio* families. Good idea."

He made no attempt to dissuade her from that line of thinking, and she spun her chair around to face the computer before he could respond.

"Have a good trip." Her voice was flat. He'd heard it before and always attributed it to a mild case of jealousy. But, today, he wondered if he understood Genevieve at all.

Ava decided to explore the ship as soon as she unpacked. She kept telling herself she hadn't sold out and abandoned her mission in St. Barts. She could learn more on a ship than lounging around the island. Who knew? Maybe she'd get lucky and run into Genevieve and her Spanish friend again.

She wandered the teak decks and watched the crewmen hustle about. More and more passengers were arriving by the launches, beautiful, rich people ready to start their week in paradise. Restless with all the elegance around her, Ava followed her instincts and found the galley. Maurice Arnot's welcoming hug warmed her, and he dangled an apron in front of her to convince her to tackle a tapenade for the reception.

"You would trust me? Right off the street?" She waved him off. "I'm sure you have qualified help everywhere."

"We are shorthanded. Come now, *cherie*. It's olives, garlic, oregano, and capers. Italian staples. Show me what you can do."

She took the apron and tied the strings around her waist with a laugh. "I love a challenge."

"*Bien, bien.* Philippe!" He signaled to another sous-chef who responded with lightning speed, as they all did. "Come and show Mademoiselle Santori the sidebar, *s'il vous plait*." He grinned at her. "I'll be back to check on you, my friend."

Ava remembered Philippe Basille from the attorney's meeting. He'd lost his cousin on *Paradisio*. Maybe this was a chance to chat about it.

"Hello, Ava." He put out a friendly hand. "Welcome to *Nirvana*."

"Thank you, Philippe. Looks like I've been recruited."

"Good. We need the help." He touched his clipped mustache in thought. "The tapenade, eh? Let me show you into the cold storeroom and then you can work right here."

"Sounds good."

She followed him around the galley, not nearly as spacious as *Valhalla*'s but still modern and well equipped. In a cold storage room, he showed her supplies and answered her many questions about how they prepared for each cruise.

"Philippe! *Vite!*"

At Maurice's voice, Philippe jumped. "I'll be right back."

"That's okay, I'll figure it out."

Ava found at least fifteen different kinds of rare Italian and Greek olives and took a minute to marvel at the quality and quantity. She spent five more minutes in the caper section, amazed that they had some unusual types that she hadn't seen since cooking school.

She still needed some spices. They must be in a dry goods storeroom. Ava moved naturally through the galley to the next door, far more at home here than among the jet-setters above deck. In the dim light of the storage room, she picked through the spice shelves. It was beautifully organized, alphabetically arranged the way she loved it, the way she'd been taught. But no oregano. She turned to the crates on the floor, some unopened, and she bent to examine them.

Blinding light filled the room and she jumped.

"Hey, you're supposed to be cooking." Phillipe stood near the light switch, a surprised look on his face. "What are you doing?"

"This is cooking." She grinned. "I'm finding oregano."

He took her hand and gently tugged her up. "That's why we hire galley hands, Ava. So we can do the part that takes the brains, not dig through cartons like common kitchen crew. I'll send someone for it."

He guided her back to the stainless counter where Maurice worked. "A true Italian girl. Only wants the oregano."

Maurice gave her shoulders a squeeze. "Just have fun, *cherie,* and make me a tapenade as beautiful as you are. Then you must go up to the main deck so you don't miss the party when we set sail."

She nodded. "I will, Chef. I hear it's quite the scene."

"Who knows?" He shrugged with mock misery. "The Viking keeps me down here all the time."

Ava and Philippe shared a smile at Maurice's joke and she lost the next hour chatting with him and creating her best tapenade.

The magical combination of music, wind, and laughter floated over the main deck as *Nirvana*'s elegant guests turned out to watch the ship set sail as the sun dropped into sapphire seas. Dane enjoyed letting the captain and crew show their stuff to the responsive crowd. Leaning back against a rail, he watched them work but kept an eye on the aft stairs until a brilliant, eye-catching color sent a warning flash to his brain. And other parts.

She reminded him of a child's ice-cream bar—a Creamsicle—dressed in a cool tangerine halter top that showed off well-defined arms and a short flippy skirt that revealed shapely legs. In high-heeled sandals and her hair loose and free, Ava definitely looked good enough to eat. He suddenly envisioned her on her back, ready to be tasted and taken.

His arousal was instant and strong, and he tried to will the response away, but his brain wasn't working at the moment. He couldn't stop looking at her, and their gazes met across the deck.

Her slight flush might be a little extra makeup, but he doubted it. Something told him their thoughts were traveling down the same dangerous path. She walked directly to him, undaunted by his stare. He liked that.

He stayed at the railing, resisting the urge, the constant urge, to touch her. He couldn't resist dropping his gaze over her top, though. Not tight, but not overly modest, either, it revealed more than a hint of cleavage. His grip tightened on the rail.

"How's the cabin?" he asked.

She broke into a grin. "Outrageous. I'm sure you have more than a few well-heeled guests who would pay real money for it."

"They're used to the good life." He glanced at the groups of people around them and then back to her. "I wanted to show off Utopia to you."

"Thank you." She smiled slyly. "Anyway, I've thought of a way to pay my freight." At his questioning look, she added, "Taste the tapenade. The chef put me to work in the galley."

He stepped back, surprised. "You don't have to work on this cruise."

"I know. It was fun, and I don't know any other way to repay you for the luxurious accommodations."

His gaze slipped down again to the tantalizing rise of her breasts but didn't linger. He really didn't want to seduce her, he told himself. She was still reeling from the death of her estranged brother. *His best friend.* And she was still threatening to sue the company. *His entire world.*

But he couldn't resist touching her silky shoulder. Her skin was as soft as it looked. "We'll consider you a celebrity guest chef. But don't spend too much time down there. Arnot's a wolf." He let his fingers follow the curve of her back, wanting to continue the path they were on, imagining the pleasure of melting this Creamsicle. "Let's go up to the bridge. It's the best view."

As Ava felt his warm touch on her back, Cassie's words echoed in her ears. *Don't underestimate him.* How many have done just that, she wondered as she fell into step with him across the teak deck. How many had fallen for the impossibly deep blue-green eyes and tempting face? How many had longed to explore the symmetrical muscles of his stomach and chest, and listen to him describe just how he got that hint of a British accent?

Ava swallowed hard. One meaningless kiss and a bouquet of roses and she couldn't control the direction of her thoughts. She glanced at him, determined to see the man who might have sent Marco to a watery grave, but her gaze fell on his lips, and she remembered how warm they'd been when he'd kissed her. A hot, unexpected shudder teased her, making her want to swear under her breath.

A waiter approached with crystal champagne flutes on a tray. Dane thanked him, taking two drinks and handing one to Ava.

"Champagne is part of the ritual. You'll anger the gods if you don't have a sip."

She held up the glass and offered a shaky smile, thinking the only thing godlike here was the Viking in front of her. "I certainly don't want to anger the gods."

"Captain Guy's nearly ready to get under way. Come with me." He guided her up a short set of stairs to an observation area on the sundeck. From there, she could see into the bridge and across the entire length of *Nirvana*. Brilliant colors against more than a dozen unfurled canvas sails, four towering masts, and miles of nautical white ropes wrapped around brass and wood railings. The chatter and laughter of excited passengers mingled with the sounds of a steel drum band from another part of the ship.

Dane's gaze swept the magical view and he fairly glowed. "Everything looks good. We're ready to sail. There's Captain Guy."

Ava watched an imposing man in a crisp, white uniform step onto the bridge to start the ceremony.

"Do you always set sail at sunset?" she asked, inhaling the clean, pungent salt air, and the sweet smell of champagne nearly overpowered the subtle, masculine scent of Dane.

"Generally. But never on the day of a full moon, never on the thirteenth, and never without champagne open."

"Angering the gods, again?"

"Sailors take superstitions very seriously. It's considered terrible luck to launch a ship or set sail with any of those conditions. Did you realize that the ship has turned almost a full circle since you boarded?"

She shook her head.

"A clockwise rotation is an acknowledgment of the sun. For good luck."

She tilted her head and smiled. "You are serious."

He grinned, not admitting whether he was or not. "There's usually a bit of truth to superstitions." He glanced at the sky, then back at her. "I try to appease the demons and deities."

The steel band that had played softly suddenly stopped and a hush suspended over the ship. Dane slipped behind her, trapping her between his body and the rail. His fingers touched her hair, lifting the curls to whisper in her ear. "Just listen, now. Don't think of anything else."

Captain Guy's shout echoed over the decks. "Raise the sails!"

More than a dozen crewmen, dressed in matching royal blue and white uniforms, scurried about the deck, and four massive triangular sails dropped with a whoosh and hundreds of feet of white ropes uncoiled in harmony with the canvas. The sails caught the first gust of salt-scented wind, curving gracefully with a crisp, loud snap.

The heady and inspiring opening notes of Wagner's "Ride of the Valkyries" boomed through the speakers as the remaining sails dropped in unison, a whipping, cracking of wind against canvas that shocked everyone into a spontaneous shout of delight. The majestic ship began to dance over the waves, picking up speed in time to the rising drama of Utopia's musical signature.

Tears threatened in Ava's eyes as she reveled in the spectacle. In another life, in another place, she might lean against the man behind her and lose herself to his world. The urge to nestle into his rock hard chest and arms was so compelling that she gripped the railing harder to keep from giving in to it.

She could feel his breath on her cheek, warmer and softer than the tropical wind that carried them off to their adventure. Spellbound, the pounding of her heart kept a rhythm with the music. She turned to look up at Dane. He was staring at her, his unreadable face just inches from hers. His mouth curved slightly. The rolling of the ship, the champagne, something made her feel as though warm liquid shot through her entire body.

"Bon voyage, princess."

She forced her gaze off his mouth and back to the aquamarine eyes. *Very few escape unscathed.*

7

One hand on the wheel, a firm foot on the gas pedal, and a cell phone pressed against her ear, Genevieve charged down a mountainside road, trying to keep the alarm out of her voice.

"Look, the search isn't over yet. I know the son of a bitch. He's persistent as hell. He'll stay out there six months until he finds a frigging hair dryer, okay?"

"You can't panic, Genevieve." The man's voice crackled on the line, but she could hear the force behind it. "I will negotiate more time on the payments for the loss. You just make sure everything is in order and the money goes into the right accounts. Dane will find nothing at the bottom of the sea. Nothing that can incriminate us. I'm certain of that."

"You don't know that for sure—"

"Genevieve!" he barked at her, the sound reverberating in her fearful stomach. "I've got much bigger problems. I've got to go."

He clicked off. She thrust the phone on the passenger seat, narrowly missing a Moke turning in front of her. Her heart skipped a beat and she laid on the horn full force and got the finger in return.

"Fuck you too, pal." Palpitations escalated into a pounding against her ribs. Her sweaty palms could barely hold the slippery steering wheel as she headed toward Dane's house. *Please, Marj, be there.*

She was certain Marj cleaned on Saturday mornings. Marj would let her in. She wouldn't care if Genevieve went into his precious study. She wouldn't question Dane's executive vice president searching his desk.

Damn, why had she let him take that paper? Why had she changed the subject by talking about Arnot's stupid salt? Now he had names and freaking addresses all over the Caribbean.

She'd scoured his office in Gustavia that morning, thankful that the ever-efficient Claire didn't work Saturdays. He couldn't have taken the list, could he? But his desk was clean, no list in sight. It had to be at his house. She'd handled the little vendors for years now. Why, all of a sudden, did he care where they got their fucking spices?

At the top of the familiar drive, she blew a breath of relief when she saw Marjory Hemingway's dilapidated Dodge Dart. How that thing made it up these hills, she'd never know. Or care. *Just let me in, Marjie. Let me in.*

The Jamaican woman was in the side yard beating the life out of an Oriental carpet and singing an island blues melody, off-key, at the top of her lungs.

"Marj!" She poured warmth into her greeting. "Hi, hon. How are you doing?"

"Oh! Miss Genevieve." Marj dropped a corner of the rug. "You scared me!"

"I'm sorry, dear." Genevieve looked anxiously at

the house, not wanting to spend one second more than necessary on the pleasantries.

"Mister Dane's on de *Nirvana*, Miss." Marj raised an eyebrow. "Don't you know dat?"

Of course I do, you idiot. "Oh, yes, I just talked to him." She waved her cell phone as proof. "But I have a little administrative problem and he told me you could let me into the study to find something he forgot." She smiled and reached for the fallen end of the rug. "Here, let me help you."

"Dat's all right, Miss Genevieve." She pulled back the rug and looked hard at Genevieve. "He didn't call me about it. Sometimes I fax to him on de ship."

"I know, Marj. That's precisely what he wants me to do. But I'm looking for one little piece of paper. You'd probably never find it."

Marj nodded toward the utility room door. "Go ahead, Miss Genevieve. It's open."

"Thanks, sweetie." Genevieve flashed her most genuine smile. "I'll just be a second."

"De fax is on," Marj called to her as she headed toward the door. "I can help you send it if you like."

"No, I know how to do it. Thank you."

The house was cool and dim. And silent. Genevieve paused for a moment in the kitchen, taking in the polished granite countertops and wall of windows overlooking the water. She squeezed her eyes shut against the longing that always tormented her when she stepped into his private domain. How happy she would be here. How satisfied she'd be as his partner. His legitimate partner.

Stop it, she scolded herself. *Just find the damn list. You've got to save yourself, girl. Take care of Genevieve, because he isn't going to.*

The achy feeling lingered in the hall. In the vestibule outside the study, she stopped to run a finger along the carved Botticino marble top on an antique side table. He had exquisite taste for a man who generally considered shoes and shirts optional. Exquisite and complicated. Didn't he see how much alike they were?

She picked up a delicate Baccarat crystal dolphin. She had given it to him when they acquired *Valhalla*. Sailors loved dolphins. They signified good luck and great prosperity. He had treated her to that dear little boy smile when he opened it. Her gut twisted as her fingers squeezed the crystal animal.

Just find the list and get out of here, you idiot.

As soon as Miss Genevieve's Jeep rumbled down the drive, Marj marched right into the study. She shouldn't have let her in the room.

Something troubling dat woman for sure, she thought. And now it was troubling her. Miss Genevieve had spent a long time in Mister Dane's study and nothing looked quite de same when she was gone. Papers moved all over his desk. His sea maps all piled up in a different place. And dat pretty glass fish broken in the hallway.

Marj shook her head and looked closely at the fax machine. She pressed the Redial button and bent over to peer at the number on the machine. The Utopia office fax in Gustavia. Not de long number of de ship's fax. She knew for sure, because she had all Mister Dane's important numbers memorized.

Marj didn't want nothing on her conscience. Her baby Mitchell was in heaven watching her, along with his daddy. A guilty conscience is de devil's tool.

Picking up the study phone, her thick fingers dialed another number she knew by heart: Mister Dane's cell phone number. He never minded when she called.

Ava felt a little foolish as capable hands rubbed her feet into a state of pure bliss. She looked at Cassie in the pedicure chair next to her, and the two shared a smile.

"Your guilt's written all over your face, luv. Just let Miranda do her job and enjoy it. I do this on every cruise my first afternoon off."

Ava dropped her right foot back in the bubbling warm water and lifted her left for Miranda to dry. "I've never had a pedicure in my life."

The exotic-looking woman holding her foot laughed out loud. "It is a necessity to most of Utopia's guests, not a luxury."

"Well, I'm not the usual guest." Ava leaned back into the leather chair, enjoying the gentle mechanical massage it offered as part of the service. "But I could get comfortable faking it."

Cassie's appointment was nearly over and she wiggled her red-tipped toes as they dried, examining them for imperfections. "You certainly looked like you belonged last night."

Ava popped her head up from its comfortable repose. "I didn't see you last night."

"Of course not, darlin'. The help is invisible." She leaned over and whispered, "But who could miss the lady in orange? The one dining at the captain's table?"

"I tried to keep a low profile, but Dane insisted I join them for dinner." Not that she required a lot of persuasion.

"Was it fun?" Cassie asked casually.

Ava refused to give in to the temptation of girl talk. "It was fine. Captain Guy is funny and warm and Dane was very . . . very kind to me."

"Kind again, was he?" Cassie stood, carefully stepping around the footbath so as not to smudge her ruby toenails. "Ah, this was fun. I don't get another break until Nevis. We'll be in Antigua in about an hour, and then the merry maids go into full swing while you all plunder the island."

"I'm not plundering, remember?" Ava knew she sounded defensive, determined to remind Cassie that her vacation had an important purpose. "I'm going to visit some families. Two, he said last night."

Cassie frowned. "Oh, in Antigua. That would be Michael Steele's wife and three kids. She's sweet. And . . ."

"Christa Brier," Miranda supplied. "She's pregnant with her first."

Ava marveled at how all the Utopians, as they referred to themselves, knew one another and their families. British, Creole, Jamaican, West Indian. It didn't matter in their company culture.

"Pregnant? That's a shame—" Ava stopped, remembering Cassie and looked at her guiltily.

Cassie offered only a wistful smile and reached down to ruffle Miranda's hair.

"Give her the mystic mauve, Miranda, it'll look beautiful on her sexy little feet. And tell Bree thanks for squeezing me in. I owe her." She blew a kiss to both as she reached the door of the private treatment room. "Bye, girls."

Ava dropped back into the headrest, the sadness in Cassie's green eyes still vivid. What was Cassie going to do? She couldn't go off on weeklong cruises as a housekeeper and leave a baby behind. How long could she work in this physical job before the baby was born? And then, would Dane pay her while she stayed home and raised a child? Maybe she could have a day job in the office, Ava thought. Yes, he would probably be amenable to that.

He certainly hadn't turned out to be the ogre Grayson Boyd had painted him to be. He *was* kind. He had treated her like an honored guest among the chosen few at the captain's table. He had deftly kept conversation light and animated, away from the recent tragedy and the reason for Ava's visit. And he'd walked her to her cabin in the moonlight with merely a reminder that they would meet on the deck at noon for their mission in Antigua. Although, for a moment, she had thought he was going to kiss her. When he said good night, just for one second, she thought his mouth would . . .

Her body tightened, as if she were on a roller coaster chugging up to the first drop. As it had last night when she closed her cabin door. Fear, anticipation, adrenaline pumping wildly. What was *wrong* with her?

After the topcoat was dry, Miranda pulled the white cotton from between Ava's toes, and they shared a smile. An ultrafeminine sensation tickled her right down to their mystic mauve tips. Did he know it would make her feel nothing less than completely sexy to have her toenails painted?

She had no doubt who was behind the early morning phone call from the spa informing her that she had an appointment for a massage and pedicure. Cassie seemed surprised to see her walk in, so she hadn't arranged it. Maybe it was an automatic perk for the Owner's Suite tenants. Maybe not.

It seemed she questioned his motives at every turn. Did he really want to take her to see the families today . . . or control her access to them? Did he really want her at the captain's table last night . . . or away from the kitchen crew? Did he really find her attractive . . . or was he just flirting with her to get her on his side?

Marone! She was acting like a schoolgirl. Sure, he was drop-dead gorgeous. And charming. And successful. And adored by everyone. So what? Cassie's comments left her to believe he'd had a string of women and none of them seemed to pass his test, whatever it was.

It didn't matter. All that mattered now was finding out what happened to *Paradisio* and Marco. She had to remember if it weren't for that snippet of talk she heard in the dining room, she'd be signing legal papers in Grayson Boyd's office right now.

Justice. Retribution. Reconciliation. All noble causes. So, what was she doing getting a pedicure and going gaga over the guy who was trying to charm her out of filing a lawsuit?

She wanted to see just how these poor widows lived and be certain, absolutely certain, that justice was done.

The water taxi that picked them up from the *Nirvana* left a lot to be desired in comfort and speed. Ava knew immediately that Antigua would be far different from the exclusive enclave of St. Barts.

The taxi operator's melodic English droned on about shore excursions to Nelson's Dockyard and shopping in the markets of St. John's, but Ava paid little attention to the tourist information. Dane sat next to her, dressed like the other passengers in khaki walking shorts and a T-shirt, but without the expectant look of an adventurer. He'd seemed preoccupied since they met on the main deck a few minutes ago.

"Where do we go when we dock?" she asked when the taxi operator paused for a breath.

"We'll take a cab from St. John's, the biggest city on the island. We're meeting both families together, at the Steeles' home near English Harbour. It's about a half-hour drive. Pretty, though." He wore dark wire rim sunglasses against the glare, so Ava couldn't read the expression in his eyes. But she could see a slight frown between his brows.

"Are you okay?"

He nodded slightly, still studying the water. "I'm not looking forward to the visit, as you can imagine. Each time I'm with a widow or a parent, I lose the man all over again."

A wave of sympathy hit her and she put her hand on his arm. "It's very thoughtful of you to go in person. I'm sure you could have sent a representative from the company. Even a lawyer."

The crease deepened. "I wouldn't consider it."

She lifted her hand and repositioned herself on the wooden bench. "Have you spent a lot of time in Antigua?"

"Some. I used to go every year for Sailing Week. It's a huge regatta. Marco and I raced it together a few times." He smiled at a memory. "Never won, though."

So he was a sailor before he was an entrepreneur. It explained the bare feet, the ultra relaxed dress he adopted. The anti-CEO.

"I can't imagine Marco sailing in a regatta or even living in this tropical, mellow world," she said. "He never showed any interest in sailing or this type of life. If he hadn't left—I don't know, I guess I always pictured him in a kitchen somewhere."

"Evidently no one in your family knew him very well."

At his sharp tone, she turned to him, ready to defend. But before the heated words came out, she realized he was right. "Apparently not."

They joined hands automatically to navigate the crowds on the shabby docks. Dane strode purposefully past the weather-beaten wooden houses with corrugated tin roofs and peeling louvered shutters that shielded the occupants from the relentless sun, toward a line of European cars with various colorful taxi logos and nodded to the man who leaned against the first one.

"You need a taxi, mon?" The driver dropped a cigarette on the ground without moving anything but his hand and wrist, and disengaged himself slowly from his reclining position, flipping his shoulder-length dreadlocks over a shoulder.

Inexplicably, her heart started to pound. She suddenly realized how far from Santori's she was. In another world, with this breathtaking, determined, complex man taking her into a strange land. She shivered, even though the cab felt like the inside of an oven.

"I'd have rented a car, but it requires a visit to the Inland Revenue Department in St. John's for a temporary license," he explained. "It's not a Caribbean experience you want to have, believe me."

"This is fine." She turned to the open window.

"The scenery will improve, I promise." Dane bent over her to study the building on her side. "St. John's has seen better days and the crime rate is soaring here. But before you know it, we'll go over the main mountain range to get to English Harbour and you'll think you've landed in the rain forest."

Leaving the town, they passed a massive stone cathedral and a freshly painted museum, then skirted the iron fence of a botanical garden. With each mile away from the city, the landscape became lusher and Dane seemed to relax a little. He told her about the history of the island and the influence of the British Navy when it turned Antigua into a powerful naval base.

"How do you know all this?" she asked as he described how British men-of-war chose the coves and harbors to hide from hurricanes and pirates.

"I never paid attention to any subject but history, as a boy. Ten years in British schools, and I picked up a lot of nonessential trivia. And I always loved sailing and sea stories."

"Ten years? Did you grow up in England?"

"My parents moved there right after I was born, when my father took over the European operations of Erikson Hill Hotels. We lived in London until I was about eleven and then moved back to New York when he assumed control of the entire company."

That explained the faint British accent.

"Then did you live in New York City?"

"After that, I never *lived* anywhere. I grew up in boarding schools in various places. I never spent more than a week at a time at home—or whatever hotel my parents called home, once we moved to the

States. The business was their life. I even did some time up in your area at Andover."

"Did some time?" She chuckled at the expression and tried to imagine him among the elite of that rich kid's academy.

"School was like jail to me. I never stayed in one for too terribly long, though." She suspected why and he confirmed it. "Expulsion was my favorite extracurricular activity."

"You were a bad boy?"

He grinned at her. "Were?"

She laughed to cover the zing that shot through her with the single word. "Seriously, how'd you get through college?"

"I didn't." He rubbed his hand over nonexistent stubble on his chin, then studied the scenery. "Did you think I was kidding when I said I dropped out?"

She remembered him referring to it when they toured *Valhalla*. "I assumed you got back in somehow."

"Nope." He turned to her, dropped his sunglasses, and shot a deliberate, challenging stare over their rims. "Still like me?"

That roller coaster dipped again. She wanted to take his arm to steady herself but gripped the edge of the seat instead.

"I don't judge people on their education. It certainly hasn't hindered your success." She paused for a moment. "I guess Marco never finished school, either. He was only a freshman at Boston College when he . . . he left."

Dane nodded. "Marco and I had a lot in common."

She watched a filthy goat eating the grass of a run-down churchyard.

"How about you? Harvard or MIT?"

Ava gave an incredulous laugh. "CIA. There was never anywhere else for me."

"The Culinary Institute? Whoa. You really are serious about cooking."

"I had no desire to study sociology and calculus. I knew what I would be doing for the rest of my life. Even though Marco would have gotten the 'real' degree *and* the restaurant, had he stayed."

"So what would you have done? If he had taken over the restaurant?"

Heat and humidity closed in on her and the foliage thickened to a wall of green along the mountainside. "I really don't know, Dane. I never had to figure it out."

"This is Fig Tree Drive," he said, pointing out the window.

Ava suppressed a sigh. "What a pathetic change of subject."

He dropped his hand to her arm and lowered his voice. "Look, we'll have enough grief in a few minutes. I didn't mean to make it worse by bringing up Marco and what might have been. I'm sorry."

Did he know how appealing he was when he relinquished his constant control and slipped into kindness for a moment? Was that part of his scheme to confuse and unnerve her? Or was he genuine? She wished she knew.

She purposely didn't respond to the apology but turned toward the car window. "I hate to tell you, these aren't figs. They're bananas."

The cabdriver twisted around, laughing. "Fig means banana. In Antiguan."

"Oh, that explains it." Ava realized he'd been listening to every word. "So where are we now?"

"Here's the island." Dane drew an imaginary map in the air. "We're going to this area." He indicated the southeastern corner. "Be prepared, though. It's a fishing village, not much more."

He saw it through her eyes, and it did indeed look shabby. Still, Dane knew that Delia Steele and her three children lived much better than most of their island neighbors. They had running water, electricity, an indoor bathroom, a separate bedroom for the children, and plenty of food on the table in their tiny whitewashed home. The same was true of Christa Brier, who would have a doctor deliver her baby at the hospital in St. John's. They had a lot more than most Antiguans.

He just wished they still had their husbands.

Delia's oldest boy, Thomas, burst through the screen door as the cab pulled up. "It's Mr. Dane!" he yelled into the house, his skinny, boyish legs hopping in excitement. "Mama, come on!"

Soon they were all out there, three boisterous children under seven who seemed oblivious to the tragedy they had just experienced. They weren't, he knew. Delia had just been doing a good job of holding it together.

The tall, graceful black woman embraced him and apologized for not being at the memorial service.

"I could not bring these children," she whispered, wiping a wayward tear from her big, dark eyes. "Too much sorrow for them."

Christa lumbered out to the patio, looking as

though she could give birth then and there. "Hello, Mr. Dane." He kissed her on the cheek and she clutched him. She too had missed the service. He touched her lovely brown face.

"I'm sorry you weren't there, Christa. Everyone missed you."

Ava had scooped up the baby and bent over to say hello to young Thomas. Dane made the introductions and watched the women react with warmth and sympathy to the news that she was Marco's sister.

Marco had told almost no one about his estrangement with his family. Whether it was from embarrassment or a deep sense of privacy, Dane never knew. But his decision saved Ava from having to be anything but the grieving sister. They hugged and held her. A wellspring of pride in the Utopians and their families burst in him.

The two women bustled about to set up lemonade and sandwiches on the veranda, and baby Angelique climbed on Ava's lap to play a finger game. Ava giggled with the child, the sweet, charming sound of someone enamored with the innocence of a little one. Looking at her in the high-backed wooden chair, the sun revealing reddish highlights in her curls, she looked so appealing. As beautiful in this shabby setting as on the deck of *Nirvana* at a cocktail party. He swallowed against the unfamiliar sense of protectiveness she seemed to ignite in him. He didn't want protectiveness or desire to cloud his thinking where Ava was concerned. He had a reason for bringing her here.

She looked up and caught him staring at her. The baby smacked a tiny hand on Ava's cheek, demanding her attention back.

"Again! Again!"

But Ava held his gaze, wordlessly. Then her smile faded and she looked at the child self-consciously. He was starting to read her wonderfully unfiltered expressions, and what he read rattled him. The attraction was mutual . . . and strong.

Ava stayed discretely in the background, focused on the children, while he talked to the widows about the settlement. He knew from their reaction they were astonished by the amount but, he hoped, not surprised at the offer.

"It is my promise that you will never have to leave your children to work, or worry about money," he said quietly, leaning his elbows on his knees as he spoke to them. "I can never give you back Michael or Quincy. I'm so sorry. I truly am." He looked from one to the other as they squeezed each other's hands.

"Mr. Dane," Christa said quietly. "This is generous. This is good. But, we don't know what to do about this lawyer. One of his people, a woman, came here yesterday. They keep telling us that you—you are responsible for the shipwreck and that you are going to get millions of dollars . . . I am so sorry to say these words, Mr. Dane . . . I . . . this lawyer . . . he wants us to get . . . more . . ."

Dane nodded. "I understand that, Christa. I know what he's saying. I'm sure you know I had nothing to do with this accident."

"It's not that we don't believe you, Mr. Dane," Delia broke in, beads of sweat darkening her brow. "It's just that a million dollars . . . we . . . well . . . we would be very rich."

"Delia, I know he wants you to think that. But he will get at least half of it. And then I will not be legally allowed to give you the payments I want to make."

Ava sat a few feet away, quietly cooing in the baby's ear but still, he suspected, listening to the conversation. "Ava will talk to you about that. She is in the same situation as you are regarding that lawsuit. I don't want to discourage you. I want you to do what's right. I want to take care of you and your families."

He stood and saw Thomas sitting in the corner, bouncing a tattered tennis ball against the floorboards.

"Tom?" The boy looked up, black eyes expectant and excited. "Go over to the cab and grab the black bag in the back. I've got something for you." He reached down and lifted the baby from Ava's lap. "Come on, darlin'. Let's find your sister and go open some presents." He nuzzled the irresistible folds of baby fat and looked at Ava.

"Would you talk to Christa and Delia for a few minutes? They have some questions for you."

She watched his strong hands stroke the baby's head and then glanced over to the two women. "Of course I would."

Dane took a long time to set up the plastic construction site and show Tom how to move the trucks through their paces. Angelique chewed on the toy foreman's head while the middle child, Devinia, lay on the bed asking a million questions. When he finally left the children, he found Ava in the small kitchen with Delia and Christa holding up tiny green fronds.

Ava brightened when he came in. "Look at this, Dane! Lemongrass grows right here in their yard. It's native to the area!"

He couldn't quite capture her enthusiasm over lemongrass but ambled over to join the group. "You don't say." Whatever they'd talked about on the patio was behind them.

"I never knew it grew anywhere but Thailand and some Asian countries. It's very expensive, you know." She held up a stem and inhaled the fragrance. "It's exactly like Asian lemongrass."

"We call it King Edward's mint," Delia said, wrapping a thick bundle of it in wax paper. "You take it with you. For your tea. No more headaches."

Ava took the package and nodded. "Yes, I've heard that. And it's in several Eastern dishes I love to make, but it's so hard to find. I usually have to wait weeks to get my orders from Thailand." She leaned over and hugged Delia. "Thank you. For your hospitality and your honesty."

After they left amid a flurry of kisses and thanks and a few last tears, Ava and Dane got into the waiting cab. An idea took form as he remembered that in his pocket was the piece of paper listing new vendors that Genevieve had located for Arnot's outrageous food requests. One was in Antigua, not far from St. John's. He smiled, imagining how Ava would light up with infectious enthusiasm at whatever rare spices and foods they'd find.

"Let's make one more stop. I think you'll like this one." Dane leaned forward and gave the address to the driver.

The braided head spun around, and he shot Dane a wide-eyed look. "You sure, mon? With a lady?"

"It's a rough area?" That didn't make sense. He'd expected a marketplace, somewhere women could shop comfortably and alone. "Not a spice market?"

"Spices? There?" The driver raised his eyebrows and laughed. "Not for the food. For the crack pipe, mon."

A sudden trickle of sweat dripped down his back. "Just drive by it, then. I want to check it out."

The driver shrugged and dirt kicked up behind the cab as they left the tiny home of Delia Steele. Thomas and Devinia waved from the porch, and as they drove away, Dane studied the paper in his hand.

"We're going to a spice store?" Ava asked, a questioning look at the exchange she just heard.

"I'm not sure." Suddenly Marj's strange call this morning started to make sense.

There was no spice vendor on the eastern outskirts of St. John's. Just a dusty road with broken-down shanties and sullen native men eyeing the cab with curiosity and malice. At the address from Genevieve's list stood a two-story apartment building with missing window shutters and a blackened hallway for an entrance. Dane wanted to go in, he wanted to know just what he was up against. But he couldn't take Ava in there and wouldn't risk leaving her alone in the cab.

"No spices here, mon," the driver said nervously.

"What's goin' on in there, bro?" Dane asked.

The driver shook his dreadlocks and ran an uncomfortable hand over his beard. After a long look in the rearview mirror, openly assessing Dane, he said, "Just the smackers, mon. It's a halfway point to the U.S., eh?"

"Let's go." Dane reached over to pat Ava's hand, sensing her unease and amazed that she hadn't yet demanded an explanation. "We need to get back to the ship anyway."

Back in town, they walked toward the water taxis, too busy dodging tourists and street vendors to talk. Another cruise ship had just landed, and the piers rocked with the noise and pressure of humanity. He held her hand again, an unnecessary protective gesture that he liked too much to stop.

As they waited to board, she finally crossed her arms defiantly. "Okay. I can't stand this anymore. Are you going to tell me why the side trip to Hell's Kitchen?"

"At the right time and place." He resisted the urge to take her hand back. "But you can't fly into action and accusation, Ava. Let me figure this out my way."

"Figure what out?"

This was no topic to discuss in the open air of Antigua's piers. He stepped close to her and lowered his voice. "I can only think of one type of 'precious cargo' worth four hundred thousand dollars. And we may have just seen its last stop before it gets brought on board."

8

They fought all the way back to the ship. Not the loud voices, hands-flying kind of arguing that Ava had mastered by age nine. Dane's voice never rose a decibel and he was still as stone. But, to Ava, it was a fight.

"Would you please tell me what in God's name this is about and what it has to do with the wreck?" Ava insisted as they squeezed next to each other on a water taxi crowded with cruise ship passengers.

"Shhh. Relax. Don't jump to conclusions." He put his arm around her shoulders. Naturally, casually. Romantically. Then he whispered discretely in her ear, "I have some theories and suspicions. But this is no place to discuss it."

Ava tried to match his composure with a calm and steady voice. It was anything but. "What are those theories, may I ask? I take it this isn't about spices. Is it illegal trade of some sort?"

He pulled her head a little closer into the crook of his neck. "Be quiet, Ava."

She felt the blood running through her veins at a steady boil.

"Nobody can hear me," she said through clenched teeth, stiffening her neck against his arm. "What is that piece of paper you have? Is that a cargo list? Have you some—"

"Stop talking, please." His arm tightened imperceptibly.

"What did he say—crack cocaine?"

His kiss was hard, sudden, and demanding. In the instant his lips covered hers, she felt an intense, addictive bolt of pleasure ricochet through her body. She stared at him in shock, then shut her eyes to block out any sense other than the taste and heat of his kiss.

"Shut the hell up, Ava." He moved his lips against hers, his voice rough.

She staggered back to attention, escaping his kiss just enough to see her own stunned reflection in his sunglasses. "Was that necessary?"

"It was effective." His breathy whisper tickled her ear. "Any one of these people could be in on this. Any one of these passengers could have seen us there. Anyone could have made a delivery or pickup. Even him."

He tilted his head toward a round, marshmallow-skinned man, telltale tourist signs blaring from his dress, right down to the sleek digital camera around his neck. Before she could fully assess the possibility, Dane took her chin and turned her face back to him. His mouth was centimeters from hers. To the casual observer, he whispered affectionate, secret words. But his voice was hard and demanding.

"This isn't a game, Ava. And I'm not going to argue with you now."

In the cramped space, she couldn't retreat from the

heat of his legs next to hers, his powerful arm gripping her shoulder. She sat completely still and picked a spot on the horizon to stare at. She shimmied her shoulders under his immobile arm.

"You can unhook me anytime," she whispered without looking at him.

His arm never moved as they rode back to the ship.

Her mind whirled with questions. And repeated reenactments of his mind-blowing kiss.

It was effective.

That's for sure.

Back on board, he walked with her to the Owner's Suite. She was trembling a little as she concentrated on keeping her thoughts and questions in check, as ordered.

"I have some calls to make, some things to do," he said vaguely. "I'll arrange for dinner in your suite tonight."

As she reached for her card key, her fingers froze in her bag. "In my suite? Am I being grounded?"

"My cabin doesn't have a dining room, princess. I'll come up around seven-thirty. You can bombard me with questions and poke me with your accusing fingers then. Anything. But don't yell."

Maybe he'd have to shut her up again, she thought as the door closed and she stepped into the air-conditioned comfort of her luxury suite.

"Oh my God," she whispered and numbly walked to the marble bathroom and flipped the hot water faucet on the tub. "What am I getting into?"

The tap on her door came at seven and Ava cursed him for being early. Well, he could damn well wait.

She had put on makeup and dried her hair, but she wouldn't answer in her bra and underpants.

"Cabin service. I have your dinner," the cabin steward called.

Oh. The food. "Just a minute." She grabbed a short cotton skirt and slipped a tank top over her head before opening the door.

He took nearly ten minutes clanging plates and chafing dishes to set up the feast, complete with hors d'oeuvres, wine, salad, and a selection of several small entrées. From the sitting room, she watched him set the table for one. For one. The steward asked if he could pour the wine. She numbly agreed as he removed a single crystal goblet from the small china cabinet. Dane must not be coming. The stab of disappointment annoyed her more than anything.

Alone with her over-the-top room service, she picked up the wineglass and stepped out onto the balcony, abandoning the idea of changing into something nicer for dinner. She'd been worried about what to wear, and he'd opted out altogether. It didn't matter, she told herself as she looked back at the lone china place setting. Lenox, no doubt. The chardonnay was cold and welcome on her throat.

She heard a light tap at the cabin door. Had the steward forgotten something?

She opened the door, the wineglass still in her hand. Dane stood holding her wax paper of lemongrass, smelling of shower and soap, a few damp strands touching the collar of his shirt. His gaze dropped from the glass and down to her bare feet.

"I didn't think you were coming." She stepped aside for him to enter and tilted her head toward the table. "The cabin steward set it for one."

He handed her the package of herbs, its sweet, lemony smell momentarily tickling her nose.

"I decided to let them deliver dinner before I arrived. Gossip blows harder than the wind around here. I thought you might want to protect your privacy and reputation."

"Is my reputation at risk if you dine in my room?"

He smiled self-consciously. "Lets just say *my* reputation has taken on a life that far exceeds reality."

"I doubt that." The words were out before she could think.

He laughed and chucked her chin before going into the dining area. He opened a cabinet and removed another wineglass, without so much as a glance at what was in there. He moved as though he were home, obviously familiar with the suite.

He studied the chardonnay label for a moment before pouring. "I'm sorry if I startled you on the water taxi today." He gave her a teasing wink. "I had to be creative. You wouldn't—"

"I know!" She felt herself flush at the memory. "But I have a right to know what's going on. You wouldn't have suspected anything if I hadn't heard that conversation."

"I would after what I saw today." He held up his glass to toast, and reluctantly she did the same. "Cheers, princess. Let's sit down and I'll tell you what I know."

He was so frustratingly cool and in control. Loosening her grip on the glass to avoid breaking the delicate stem, she followed him into the sitting room and chose a chair. Across from him. Away from him.

As he sat on the sofa, she saw him eye her bare

feet again. "I forgot to ask you. Did you like Miranda?"

So, he *was* behind the pedicure. Heat dropped through her body as he studied her pink-tipped bare feet and his gaze traveled up her legs where the very short skirt climbed higher. She tugged ineffectively at the hem, then curled her legs up under her.

"Yes. Thank you. It was a real treat."

He sipped the wine.

Her patience strained. "Dane. Please."

"Okay, okay." He put the glass on the coffee table and settled back into the sofa. "I don't know exactly what this has to do with *Paradisio*'s accident, but perhaps, based on what you heard, there's some connection. Lots of islands around here are transshipment points for drugs, mostly cocaine, on route to the U.S."

She crossed her arms and listened to him.

"The eastern Caribbean is a hotbed of drug trafficking and it's not too difficult to figure out why. It's close to the U.S. ports of entry, easily navigated, with inadequately patrolled waters and not enough money for law enforcement. Add to it fragile economies and poor, hungry islanders. It adds up to a huge drug trafficking problem." He leaned forward. "The drug cartels from South America get more and more creative every year. I think that it's possible someone is arranging transshipments that come on board my ships and then go to St. Barts. And vice versa. St. Barts is not really drug country, but it is full of wealthy tourists who are rarely checked closely at customs and can bring it in relatively easily."

She raised an eyebrow. "What's Genevieve's role?"

"I don't know." He stood and walked to the sliding glass doors, and stared at the darkening sky. "She handles all of the passenger and employee arrangements—visas, passports, tickets, everything. I did notice that in the past few months, we've had a lot of last-minute guests that she quietly rushed through the red tape. It's not unusual for us to do that for a VIP, so I didn't question it. But she might be helping it all along. Perhaps unknowingly."

Ava jumped up. "Not unknowingly, Dane. I heard her! She said 'we sent a boy to do a man's job' and then agreed with her friend that it could happen again." Her voice rose but she didn't care. "We have to alert the authorities. She has to be brought in for questioning."

He said nothing, which only infuriated her more.

"What? *What?* You just want to protect her, don't you? Are you—are you in love with her or something?" She hated herself for asking that question. For sounding like she cared.

He just shook his head. "No, Ava. I've known Genevieve for twenty years. I met her when she was in high school, being raised by her grandparents after her parents were killed in Chicago in the crash of their private plane. I've always felt sorry for her, even admired her strength. But I'm not in love with her."

"Then who do we call? The FBI? Interpol? Who runs these islands?"

He spun around. "Wait! Will you just wait? We have nothing to go on, and an investigation would turn this company upside down. I will do—"

"That's all you care about! Your precious company! Your money!" She flicked at his arm in anger and he grabbed her hand and held it tight.

"No, Ava. I care about the people who work for

me. They've been through hell this past month. Every single person is in mourning right now. Plus, you can't just go running off accusing people without any kind of proof." He still held her hand, but his grip had softened, along with his voice. "I'll get to the bottom of it and I'll stop it. Anyone involved in any way will be punished. Legally. I promise. But if I don't move cautiously, someone could get badly hurt."

She remembered the grunting sound of pain she'd heard from Genevieve. She stepped back, sat, and pretended to be calm and serene. He definitely did not respond well to hysteria.

"So, now what?" she asked.

"I know where to start looking for clues. Tomorrow we get to Guadeloupe. This time you don't come with me." At her look, he shook his head vehemently. "I need to go alone. It's dangerous. I have to look at passenger logs and check out the names of the last-minute guests that Gen has handled, and then I need to talk to her. I think I can get her to give me enough information to figure out their system. And stop it."

"She's in love with you." Ava squeezed the wineglass again, oddly certain of her feminine intuition on the subject.

He ran his hand through his hair. "I know she has . . . feelings for me, but she's almost like a sister. Her grandparents would probably prefer if she weren't." He sighed, lifting his shoulders in an apologetic shrug. "But you can't manufacture chemistry where there isn't any."

Chemistry. That was one way to describe it.

"One thing I know for sure, Ava," he said as he

returned to the dining area and pulled out a place mat and plate from the china cabinet. "I'm not stopping the search for the ship. I don't care what it costs or how long it takes. We're going to find something."

"Assuming there's something there to find."

He looked questioningly at her.

"What if, oh, I don't know, the captain or some of the crew were in on this? What if they had so much cocaine on that ship that he had to sail it somewhere else and they're on an island somewhere, waiting for . . . I don't know . . . the heat to be off."

She knew it was far-fetched and stupid. But it gave her hope that Marco was still alive.

He stepped in front of her and set his hands on her shoulders. Tenderly, he realigned the narrow straps of her top with his fingers, his gaze traveling over her neck, her face, her eyes. "Ava. If anyone on that ship were alive, I'd know about it. Please don't do that to yourself."

The force of his command, as gently as it was delivered, rocked her. So did his intoxicating presence just inches away from her body. His face, so close she could almost feel his breath. His hands stayed near her neck, the pressure of his fingers on her collarbone. Every cell was dancing where he touched.

"You can stop me from talking," she said softly. "But you can't stop me from dreaming."

His gaze dropped to her mouth and the ship shifted gently in the water. *Dear God, he's going to kiss me again.* Her legs weakened with the rolling ship.

"Come on, princess. We've had a long day. Aren't you hungry?"

* * *

Dane let her talk about the food, the ingredients, the presentation. He noticed she talked more than she ate. She barely touched the shrimp and nervously poked at the sea bass. He let her chatter and purposely kept his attention on her face, never once lingering on her body, even though it looked particularly appealing in the tiny skirt and skimpy top.

"So, what exactly did you say to Christa and Delia this afternoon?" he asked when she finally took a breath.

She looked up from her plate and smiled. "It's secret."

A spark flickered in her eyes, igniting his gut, then traveling lower. "I don't like secrets."

"Too bad." She laid down her fork. "I have a lot."

A smile tipped the corner of his mouth. He wanted to play games with her, wanted to touch the part of her that laughed from the heart. He wiped his mouth with a linen napkin and leaned back in his chair. "Oh, really? Secret recipes? Family secrets? Tell me one."

"The recipes would bore you." She looked down at her plate. "And the family secrets . . . well, I guess they're no secret."

He pushed his plate away, done with dinner but not with the conversation. "I don't know why Marco left your family."

She shot a surprised and dubious look at him. "You don't?"

He shook his head. "No. He never told me."

"Are you finished?" She glanced at his plate.

She clearly had no intention of exploring this subject. But he had no desire to leave yet. He wanted to stay and talk to her, to curl up on that sofa and listen to her melodic voice and watch her get animated and passionate. Especially passionate.

"Well. *Have* you?" The edge in her voice told him he completely missed the question.

"Uh, have I what?"

She narrowed her dark eyes accusingly. "You weren't listening."

"I was looking." His gaze dropped down to the rise of her breasts and back to her face. "Not listening."

She stood abruptly. "Don't do this, Dane."

"Do what?" He couldn't help teasing her.

"You know." She walked toward the balcony and out the sliding doors.

He followed her, and she spun around to face him. The balcony railing kept her from backing away. She sidestepped him. "Don't flirt with me. It's ridiculous. I'm not in your league."

The moonlight backlit her face, eyes, and lucious mouth. A mouth he'd tasted and wanted again. He chuckled and maneuvered back in front of her.

"You're right, princess." At her shocked look, he touched her dimple again. "You're in a league of your own."

She opened her mouth to say something and he kissed her. She tasted sweet and tangy from the food and every bit as delicious. He opened his mouth to explore her teeth and find her tongue. His hands dropped from her cheek to her neck, into her hair, and he pulled her into him.

The control she'd been clinging to evaporated and her mouth opened in hungry response. Through the thin top she wore, he could feel her heart pound. Her breasts, her provocative, tempting breasts pressed against his chest. He had no power over his hand. It moved on pure animal instinct. He had to touch her, just for a moment, just to run his thumb over her to feel her react.

She moaned, low and breathless. A fire singed him and he grew furiously hard, pressing her into the balcony railing. One hand was wrapped in her luscious hair, the other rubbed the flimsy material, savoring the raised nipple underneath.

She grabbed his hand. Pulled it hard. Down. Away. He found the strength to lift his mouth from the spot on her neck where it had ended up.

"Ava," he groaned. He rested his hand near the hem of her short dress. Another gold mine beckoned. His fingers brushed the skin of her thigh and stroked it lightly, lifting the skirt just a little to touch the delicate flesh.

Panic flashed in her eyes, and something else. Passion, maybe? Something that she was fighting with every ounce of strength she had. He knew he had to stop.

He took a step back, ending the contact. But not the burn that he'd started. "I'm sorry," he whispered, hearing the husky frustration in his own voice.

Her breath was ragged, but her inky eyes stayed steady. "I didn't ask for that."

"I know." He took another step back. Damn, she turned him on. Hot and sexy, but definitely not to be tampered with. "You're a very attractive woman."

Distrust and disbelief showed in her eyes.

"You think I'm lying?" He glanced down to the vicinity of his pants. "I'm not faking this."

"I think your reputation, as you put it, precedes you."

He ran his hand through his hair, wondering exactly what she'd heard. "I'm a normal red-blooded man, Ava, and if the feeling is mutual . . ."

She shook her head. "I think you'd better go."

He backed into the sitting room. "Okay. I'm leaving." He hadn't meant to come on so hard, so fast. Damn his hands. Damn his mouth. Damn every womanly, mouth-watering inch of her. She didn't trust him and maybe she was right. She was no pet he could adopt for a few weeks and wrestle around with until he got bored. And he didn't really know any other way.

"G'night, princess."

Ava stayed on the balcony after the door shut into place behind him. The ship rocked from left to right, lights from islands danced in the distance, a sliver of a new moon hung sleepily on its side. The rich sea air worked like smelling salts, calming her, clearing her head.

She took deep breaths to stop the quivering that started in the most feminine part of her and electrified every cell in her body.

Why was he doing this to her? To distract her from the lawsuit? Or from the drug-running, shipwrecking, life-threatening problems they'd uncovered? He couldn't just want to seduce her.

Oh, but he nearly did, she thought with a shiver. With one kiss. One astounding, earth-shattering kiss. She could still feel the weight of his hand on her breast. The pressure shot hot signals down her body, making her weak and damp and sinfully excited. She nearly melted at the thought of how hard he'd been against her. Her thigh still burned where his hand had been, where his fingers had started a brief jour-

ney up her leg. She closed her eyes as the quiver
started again.

The phone in her cabin rang, sharp and demanding. She knew it would be him.

"Hello?" She tried to sound in control, not breathless and full of lust.

"Bon soir, cherie. I hope it is not too late to call to see
how your dinner was?"

Maurice Arnot. Not the man she'd been expecting.
Wanting.

"Chef! No, it's not too late. It was delicious." *Except I was almost dessert.*

"I heard you ate in, and I hope everything was just
right."

"Yes. Perfect. Thank you." She couldn't think of
anything to say; small talk was too far from where
her thoughts had been.

"Did you have a lovely day in Antigua?" he asked.

Oh, yeah. Especially the visit to the local crack
house. "It was fine. It's a colorful island. Did you stay
on board all day?"

"For the most part. Can I get you to join me in the
kitchen again tomorrow, *cherie?* I enjoyed your help
and had many compliments on the tapenade."

She had seriously considered doing some of her
own investigation of the island, but common sense
prevailed. And there was plenty to learn on board
that didn't involve the menacing underworld of the
Caribbean. "That would be lovely," she agreed. "I'll
come down tomorrow afternoon."

"Bien, cherie. Sweet dreams. *Bon soir."*

"Bon soir, Chef."

She set the receiver down gently, relieved for the
distraction and touched by his thoughtfulness. Sweet

dreams, he'd said. Well, they wouldn't be sweet tonight. She fluffed the white silk comforter on the bed and thought of how Dane's blue eyes and honey-colored hair would look against it. Sweet dreams? Not a chance. Hot, sweaty, lusty dreams were the only thing on the menu.

9

There was nothing Dane liked about Guadeloupe.
The port city, Pointe-à-Pitre, offered none of the Old
World charm of most Caribbean capitals. Just narrow
streets filled with slow traffic, and rows of shacks
awash with lavender and canary yellow paint that
couldn't disguise the poverty within. The smell of
pungent outdoor cooking mixed with the stench of
sewage permeated the whole town. If it weren't for
the impressive volcano, La Soufrière, tropical forests
and crescent-shaped white beaches, he'd have taken
it off the Utopia itinerary long ago.

   He rented a car from a local who refused to speak
anything but thick, unintelligible Creole until Dane
showed a willingness to part with cash. No special
license necessary in Guadeloupe. Just currency, and
he'd brought plenty of that, anticipating that it
would be the only way he'd get what he wanted. In
the rusty twenty-year-old Peugeot, he managed to
navigate the rugged terrain to the tiny fishing village
of Le Moule, buried on the coast of one of Guadeloupe's two main islands.

After spending an awkward and unpleasant hour speaking halting Creole to a bitter *Paradisio* widow who'd already met with Boyd, Dane left Le Moule. He wrapped a bandana around his head and straightened his sunglasses. He didn't think he'd be recognized by the locals, but he didn't want to take any chances of running into *Nirvana*'s passengers or crew, unlikely as that would be in the seedy sections of Guadeloupe.

In Pointe des Châteaux, Genevieve's list led him to ramshackle huts where an intrepid visitor could snag dope. But he had a hard time finding someone as willing to talk as they were anxious to sell. He bought nothing, preferring to tempt someone high enough in the food chain to discuss major shipments. He judiciously slipped cash to a few who might know anything about the connection to Utopia, but he got nothing in return.

As he put the key in the ignition to leave, a skinny, scared kid who had tried desperately to unload some ganja suddenly stood next to the rented car. He stuck his head in Dane's open window.

Dane held up his hand. "No, man. I told you. I don't want it."

"You wan a name, missur? Thas wha' you wan?" His frightened gaze darted across the street to where a few others sat on barrels, watching the man in the rental car trying to score dope.

Dane nodded.

" 'spensive."

Dane knew it would be. Two United States hundred-dollar bills passed through the open window.

The kid didn't count it, just stuffed it into his

pocket and wiped his nose on his arm with another
furtive glance across the street. "You wan' Estaphan
Calliope. At La Soufrière."

"The volcano?"

"A bar. In Point-à-Pitre. You find him."

The kid disappeared as quickly as he had mater-
ialized. Dane started the car and drove back to
Guadeloupe's capital to find Estaphan Calliope.
There was no such name or location on his list.

He stopped at a shop filled with French scarves,
perfumes, and quality crystal that catered to the
tourists looking for the well-known discounts on
brand names. On a whim, Dane picked up an exquisite peach and black Hermès scarf, the colors reminding him of Ava's skin and eyes, the material as soft as
a breath in his hand. He asked the shopkeeper where
he could find a bar called La Soufrière.

Her eyebrow shot up at the question, but once he
paid in cash for the scarf without negotiating the
price, she told him in flawless French where he'd find
the place.

When he arrived, he suspected very few tourists
buying Hermès and Chanel asked how to get to this
particular joint. He kept his sunglasses on despite the
darkness and sat at the bar, drinking a beer. It took
less than ten minutes for a young native to approach
him.

"You wan' something, mon?" The question came
in thick island Creole.

"Yeah. Estaphan Calliope."

"Wha for?"

"Business. Shipping business."

He looked Dane up and down, deliberately and
slow. "*Venez.*"

Dane knocked back the rest of the beer and followed the man out of the room.

When Dane laid eyes on Estaphan Calliope, his gut lurched, and he blessed the bandana and sunglasses. They were his only hope that the fat Frenchman wouldn't recognize him. Damn, the man had been on a Utopia cruise. On *Paradisio*, if he remembered correctly. Dane struggled to remember the date, the circumstances. He stood stone still against the wall of a filthy office as Calliope eyed him suspiciously.

"*Oui?*"

Dane took a chance. He knew he only had one. "Genevieve sent me."

Calliope narrowed his eyes. "You're too late. Her man just left."

"*Bien! Merci! C'est parfait!*" Maurice Arnot's squinty brown eyes twinkled with genuine delight as his musical French compliments warmed Ava. He took another taste of the *jambon* Mornay sauce. "*Parfait!*"

"Thank you." She smiled proudly, secretly certain that it *was* perfect.

He put his arm on her shoulder. "Come and see my pastries. They are a delight today."

"Tell me, Chef, why don't you write cookbooks?" she ventured as they crossed to the other side of the galley. "You could make so many people happy. And you could make a fortune."

He waved his hand in dismissal. "I leave the books to your daddy, *cherie*. I am not a writer, not a publisher. I do not want any business but food and my restaurant."

"Then why did you come here?"

The hint of a shadow crossed his face. Damn, why

couldn't she keep her mouth shut? It was none of her business. But it was out now.

"The weather. The *naturel* beaches with glorious women." He winked at her. "And the Viking pays me lots and lots of money."

Before she could change the subject, his gaze fell on the door as Philippe Basille walked in, looking hot and tired from his travels to the island.

"Ah, *merci, mon ami*," Maurice said as Philippe approached and handed one of his heavy paper bags to Maurice. "How did you do? Did you score, as the Americans say?"

Ava's stomach fluttered and she stifled a surprised gasp at the expression. Score? As in drugs? Could these two be drug runners?

Philippe grinned. "Blazing hot, Chef. You'll love them."

"Ah, *bien*." Maurice turned to Ava. "Tonight we treat the passengers to island heat. Guadeloupe's *guajillo* is hotter than the house of the devil. We need to soak the peppers for half an hour in boiling hot water. Would you like to help?"

She nodded, relief flooding through her. "Absolutely."

"Let's get your packages into the back and we will start *immédiatement*." The little man led Philippe away and Ava returned to her *jambon* Mornay. She was too jumpy, too quick to conclude. She wasn't going to find the bad guy in the kitchen while Dane was off . . . wherever he was.

Philippe approached her, adjusting his toque blanche and apron, a friendly grin on his face. "We can work on this one together, Ava. Do you mind?"

"Love it." She grabbed the stockpot he handed

her and went to the oversized stainless sinks. "I'm surprised to see you, Philippe. I thought you said you only did prep and hated to sail."

"*C'est vrai*, yes. I do not like to sail. But the seas are calm and Arnot needed help. He is missing the help of my cousin, I'm afraid. And schedules have been juggled, calling some galley hands to *Valhalla* for the last cruise. So, I agreed to come." With a colander full of deep red peppers, he joined her at the sink. "And I am likewise surprised to see you, I must admit. Have you made a decision about the lawsuit?"

She flipped the faucet toward his peppers after filling her stockpot. "It's complicated, Philippe. I came on this cruise to meet some of the families on the islands so that I could talk to them personally."

He raised both eyebrows. "Really?"

"Dane wanted to give me an opportunity to see how they really live. To see if Boyd's claims are true." She hoisted the heavy pot. "And if I still believe Utopia should be sued, he told me to go ahead and enlist them."

"I saw him on the launch to Guadeloupe. Why didn't you go to meet Monique Jaillet?" He shook his colander with a grunt, the last of the rinsing water falling out of the holes.

She knew Dane wouldn't want her talking about their suspicions, even to another cook who'd lost a cousin on *Paradisio*. "Dane had some other business on Guadeloupe, so I decided to stay and take the chef up on his offer to visit the galley." She sensed he was testing her about the lawsuit. "I'm not convinced that Utopia was responsible for the shipwreck, Philippe, and it seems to me the settlements he's offering are generous and sympathetic."

He said nothing as he loaded up another colander with peppers.

"How about you? What have you decided?"

He walked over to the iron cooktop where she'd started the water and looked directly at her, his smile gone. "I'd like to see the whole chapter closed. Stop the search, stop the lawsuits. I want to bury my cousin and move on."

She wondered what he'd say if he knew the shipwreck could be the result of drug running, and his cousin could be a murder victim.

"Philippe," she whispered, ignoring a voice that told her to shut up. "It may not be that simple."

He shot her a sharp look, confusion and curiosity on his face. "What do you mean?"

"I mean . . ." She looked around the galley. "There might be more to the accident than bad navigation."

Philippe opened his mouth to say something, but before he could, Maurice appeared behind them, wooden spoons flying, his usual entourage of three cooks in tow.

As Maurice launched into a lecture in mixed English and French on who should handle the grilled lamb with *guajillo* peppers, Ava's conscience berated her. She tried to tell herself she hadn't revealed anything, but she knew she'd planted questions in Philippe's mind. In a few minutes, the activity level soared and everyone was too busy to talk. She was relieved not to have to finish her conversation with Philippe but got lost in the dizzying pace and physical labor of cooking for over a hundred people.

The dishes clanged against stainless steel; the aromas of seafood and vegetables and savory sauces filled the galley. Maurice stood beside her, arranging a marinated white bean and *chipotle* chili salad that was in keeping with the evening's hot pepper island theme.

"Magnifique!" He kissed his hands like a cartoon character French chef. "And you did not break the beans with overcooking! A common error."

"But I'm not common," she teased flirtatiously, wiping a damp spot on her temple with her wrist.

"That would be obvious to a blind man." Dane's voice came from right behind her, and she whirled around.

"Oh! You're . . . you're back." His hair was sweaty and stuck to his head. His T-shirt was filthy and he . . . well, he smelled. Bad. "You look like you had a rough day."

No smile curled his lips in response. His gaze darkened and he lifted a sardonic eyebrow. "Can you tear yourself away from here for a few minutes?"

"Of course. I'm just helping out."

"Come on." He reached for her hand and then seemed to notice the dirt on his own. He just tilted his head toward the back door. "Let's go."

Maurice stopped cooking long enough to shoot an unfriendly look at Dane. "She is quite talented, you know." His eyes softened as he looked at Ava. "But he is right. You should not be working, *cherie*. Go upstairs and dine. You've done enough."

"Thank you." She reached behind her to untie the apron. "I've had fun. I'll come back tomorrow."

She dropped the apron onto a pile of soiled linens and followed Dane out of the galley. Without a word, he strode down a hallway to a set of stairs that led up two levels, to a deserted corner of the main deck where they sat on a cushion meant for sunbathing. Her heart thumped at his silence.

"Have you said anything to anyone?" he demanded.

His sharp tone grated on her. "For God's sake, Dane. How about 'how are you' and 'hello.' Or do you just think you can grab me from whatever I'm doing and tear me away like I'm some kind of wayward child—"

"Have you talked to anyone at all? Ava, I need to know."

"No. I've been in the galley." Just a few words to a sous-chef. Nothing he needed to know. "Do you suspect the cooks?"

"I suspect everyone until I know differently," he said. "Did you tell anyone in there about what we saw yesterday? About what you heard on *Valhalla?*"

"No." It wasn't a lie. She watched him run a hand through his hair, which didn't help how disheveled it looked. She knew the sign by now; he was troubled. "What did you find in Guadeloupe?"

"More than I bargained for. I have to talk to Genevieve right away. I've called to have the Utopia plane in Nevis tomorrow. I hope it's not too late."

She cursed the disappointment that tugged at her. They weren't on vacation together, so why did his leaving make her feel cheated? Then she realized what he'd said.

"Too late? Too late for what?"

"I'm certain my poking around the drug lords of Guadeloupe is going to get out. I'm worried about her—"

"About *her?* She *is* the drug lord, for crying out loud! She knows what happened on that ship and is letting you take the rap for it. Go to the freaking police, Dane!"

"I will, Ava. But not here. The police have probably been bought. This kind of corruption can go up to the highest level."

He stared at her, but she could tell his mind was far away. Processing. Planning.

"I'll start with the constable in St. Barts. I think that's safe. If there are Americans involved, it will go to the FBI. Europeans will be Scotland Yard or Interpol. And certainly the DEA." He sighed heavily. "What a mess."

"You're a mess too," she said. "What happened?"

He plucked at his ragged T-shirt and grinned. "Well, I got out before anyone shot me."

Her gaze widened at the words. "What did you find out?"

"Nothing concrete."

She rapped her knuckles on his arm. "Damn it, quit being vague and protective. I have a right to know."

He gripped her wrist and held it in midair. "Do you mind not hitting me?"

She shook off his hand. "I'm sorry. It's just that . . . I want you to take action, Dane."

"I think I took a little too much this afternoon." His expression softened. "Look, I don't want anyone else to get hurt. Genevieve is like family to me, and I think she's in a little over her head. If there's any way I can help her get out—gracefully and with her pride—I will. Not at the expense of the law, but not with any more risks to the people who work for me, either. Whatever's being done on these ships can be stopped. And I will stop it. Believe me."

"What about *Paradisio*? What about those twenty-one men who died because she is in 'a little over her head'? Don't they matter?"

A deep and agonizing shade of blue darkened his eyes. "How could you say that?"

"I don't like to ponder and worry about someone's *pride* when lives were lost. Just attack the problem. "

"I am. In my own way."

She shook her head, unwilling to be quieted. "I don't know why you don't march right into the police and tell them what's going on."

"There aren't police. It's a constable. And you have no idea what could happen if I do that. First of all, there's a U.S. senator on this ship. There's also a cargo of illegal drugs, I'm guessing, in some passenger's or crewman's cabin."

Her jaw dropped. "There is?"

"And the constable could be in the chain of command from a cartel, for all I know. You can't mess around like some kind of vigilante with these guys. Someone could get killed."

A sickening wave of déjà vu rolled through her. Of all people, she should know he was so right. "Please tell me what you found out today."

"I found a transshipment location, and a Frenchman named Estaphan Calliope who runs it. He recognized Genevieve's name but, I hope, didn't recognize me."

"Do you think he might have?" she asked, frowning.

"Maybe. I've seen him before. He's been on a cruise, believe it or not. I have to check the back passenger logs, which I can probably access from my computer tonight." He squinted in thought. "I can't remember which cruise he was on, but it wasn't too long ago. But word travels fast around there. By now he might have figured out who I am and he may even get in touch with his contact on this ship."

"What did he say to you?"

He smiled wryly. "I didn't stay for tea. Once I found out that the shipment had already been picked up, I told him Genevieve had sent me to check things out, that she was worried about their man. But he wouldn't budge, wouldn't give me a name or description. I had to rush out of there, if you know what I mean."

She didn't, and she wasn't sure she wanted to. "When are you leaving?"

"We're leaving early in the morning."

"We? Do you want me to go?"

"Are you kidding? You're not staying on this ship with drugs on board and God knows who trying to get them delivered."

She crossed her arms, determined not to let any emotion show. "I don't need a baby-sitter, Dane. I could still find some things out—"

"That's precisely what I'm worried about. You'll be digging through the cargo bay for clues tomorrow morning." He shook his head. "No. You go with me."

"What will you do when you—we—get back?"

"Once I talk to Gen and get a feel for how deeply she's involved and how willing she is to come clean, I'll decide. It could mean stopping all the cruises for a while. It could mean a lot of cancellations. It could be the end of my business."

"Completely? I hadn't thought of it like that."

"Oh?" He narrowed his blue-green eyes. "You came down here to pin the wreck on me and you succeeded."

"I don't believe that anymore," she said softly.

"But I am responsible."

She looked sharply at him. Was he admitting it?

He leaned over the railing, watching the waves below, a pained look on his face. "I should have been more vigilant. Drug deliveries are happening in my company, under my watch, on this very ship tonight. If it had anything to do with why *Paradisio* went down, then I'm as guilty as if I sat in my office and deliberately sent them into the hurricane."

She was no stranger to the anguish of guilt, and a sudden surge of sympathy filled her. "We don't know that for sure, Dane. It could have been conjecture, even from Genevieve."

He sighed deeply, from the heart. "I don't know what to believe anymore. I'm going to go take a shower and get on my computer. It could be a long night."

Genevieve ran to Dane's house every night when he was out of town. It was comforting to see it, dark and quiet. It helped her sleep, helped her dream of him. But tonight the mantra she'd spoken since he'd been in her office continued to deafen her. *He has the list. He has the entire list.* It was only a matter of time until he figured it out. Then he'd send her away, like all the rest. Even though she wasn't like all the rest. Ten years, and it all came down to this.

She pounded up the driveway and wondered for the millionth time about the ship. How did the kid manage to get the captain to turn *Paradisio* around and sail toward Grenada and into the storm? She didn't think he had it in him. Such a greenhorn. He must have been determined to prove he could get to Grenada, come hell or high water. She choked back a laugh at her bad joke. Come hell *and* high water.

The still night hung over Dane's house with none

of the familiar clues to his activities. She bent over, leaning into her cramped stomach and taking shallow runner's breaths after the steep hill. She knew what he was doing, though. Rumpling the silken sheets of the Owner's Suite. The sheets that *she'd* handpicked in Paris.

The image of Dane thrusting himself into the dark-haired witch squeezed the breath out of her. Bastard. Bitch. Laughing and fucking. Her gut twisted, and for a moment, she thought she might throw up. *More breaths, Gen, take more breaths.*

No, Ava Santori was not the problem. He'd be tired of her before *Nirvana* dropped anchor back at St. Barts. Her problem was getting out of this hole before she got caught. Before she had to look him in the eyes and admit what she'd done.

She stood straight, sucked in air, and threw her head back to find the sliver of the moon. What would he think when he learned the truth? Would he feel betrayed? Would he understand that without her he would be nothing, absolutely nothing?

Of course not. He had no idea what Genevieve Giles did for his business. Or what she could do for his life, if only he'd let her. Then she wouldn't have been forced to find another way, to use him the way he'd used her.

He thought he was so damn cool, so smart, but they wouldn't let him stop them. They wouldn't let him undo the whole ring; too many millions were at stake. Dane Erikson would be just like that former diplomat in St. Kitts. Disappeared in the night. And the son of the deputy prime minister in Nevis. Burned in a sugar field. Maybe they'd take his new girlfriend along for the fun of it.

She turned down the driveway. Her heart thumped in rhythm with her pounding feet. Home, home, home. She must get home and as far away as possible. When they realized he'd found the trans-shipment points, they'd be certain she gave the names to him. They'd never let him live. And they'd kill her too, if she didn't get out fast enough.

Let him die, let him die. It doesn't matter. He deserved to die. But she could get out tomorrow, far away and safe.

No, no. The pavement punched her feet in disagreement. *He's too perfect to die.*

She shook her head. *Yes. Yes. He deserves to die. He's never known how to love anyone but himself.*

Yellow fog lights preceded the rumble of an engine, signaling a car coming around the hairpin turn. She stepped off the road, out of the way. But the lights didn't speed by. They caught her, blinded her, and then the engine screamed in acceleration toward her. She stumbled into the bushes on shaking legs and fell, desperately praying for the screech of the brakes and the wheels to turn away from her. But they kept coming.

I don't deserve to die!

It was her last thought.

10

"I miss you." Dane's voice on the phone was soft, low, and, dear God, he sounded genuine.

"It's ten P.M."

"On a cruise ship, that's early. Come and meet me for a drink."

Ava laid down the magazine she was holding but not reading. Why was he doing this to her?

"I've been ordered off the ship tomorrow. I'm packing," she lied.

"Do it in the morning. I have a present for you."

The roller coaster in her stomach inched up, toward the inevitable free fall. "Give it to me tomorrow."

"Nope. I want to bring it over. Are you dressed?"

"Would it matter?"

"Good point." She knew he was smiling. Damn him. "I'll be there in five minutes."

For one second, she gave into the temptation to lay back on the pillows and savor the flirtatious conversation. Then female instinct took over and she scrambled off the billowing bed to the cabin closet, pausing in front of the dressing table mirror to see herself as he did. Exotic, not ethnic. She smoothed her hands over the soft cotton T-shirt she wore. Sexy, not overendowed. How did he make her feel that way? Passionate, not impetuous. She sighed and smiled ruefully at her reflection. *Just one drink, Santori.* No harm in that.

He knocked at her cabin door six minutes later, holding a flat package and wearing a deadly smile.

"This is for you, princess."

She took the feather-light tissue he handed her. "You were supposed to be hunting down criminals, Dane, not shopping." She lifted a piece of tape and pulled out a long, silky scarf. "Wow. It's gorgeous. Hermès. *Merci beaucoup!*"

"De rien." He grinned back.

The silk tickled her fingers, the contrasting colors appealed to her taste. She looked up at him questioningly. How did he know?

"I was thinking of you." With his words, she plummeted down the first drop. "And I had to buy something to get the information I wanted."

She had no doubt which of the two explanations was the truth.

He took the scarf from her hand and fanned it against the back of a chair. "Come on. I'll show you my favorite place on this ship." He picked up her card key from the table next to the door and dropped it in his pocket. "And I'll give you the latest on Calliope."

He could lure anybody into anything, she thought, closing the door behind her and trying to quell her butterflies. But she wouldn't be lured into anything except one drink.

At the end of the main deck, they went down a side stairway and walked toward the pounding rhythm of a dance beat coming from Captain Nemo's lounge.

"*This* is your favorite place on the ship?" She didn't take him for the disco type.

He laughed and gave a nod to the steward at the entrance. "Just getting refreshments."

She waited with him at the noisy bar, packed with passengers and some off-duty crew, nodding to a few people she recognized from the kitchen. She looked around for Cassie but realized the poor woman was probably sleeping when she wasn't working. She would have to find her tomorrow morning to tell her they were leaving in Nevis. She wasn't sure how she'd explain it.

Dane handed her a crystal snifter and whispered over the music into her ear, "Follow me."

They retraced their steps back to the main deck, up to the sundeck, past the bridge, to the bowsprit. It was a tight space, a two-foot-wide finger that hung over the water at the very bow of the ship, accessible to one or two passengers at a time. Tonight there were none. He easily took the oversize step up, then reached for her hand and brought her into the narrow opening with him. A railing on either side locked their bodies into a tight fit. He eased her in front of him, so that she stood at the very farthest point over the water. He kept one hand on her shoulder.

"This is it," he said. "The best place to study the night sky."

She tilted her head back, inhaling the humid salt air and letting her eyes adjust to the darkness. Every second, more stars appeared. With each movement of the ship she swayed slightly and gripped the handrail to keep from pressing against him.

"This reminds me of *Titanic*. You know, the movie? 'I'm king of the world!' "

"*Titanic?*" He choked back a laugh. "Don't even say the name at sea. A doomed ship if there ever was one."

"Doomed?" She was surprised at the force of his words. "That's just folklore."

He took a sip of cognac and shook his head. "First of all, she was never christened. Very bad luck for a ship. Years ago, you couldn't even find a crew for a boat that wasn't formally christened."

"How do you know? About the *Titanic?*"

"Oh, it's common knowledge. Moments before the ship would have been launched with the official crash of a champagne bottle, a worker was pinned beneath a support beam he'd been cutting. His leg was crushed, and in the effort to free him, the ship went in the water without a formal breaking of spirits on the bow. He died the next day. And the *Titanic*, well, you know . . ."

"Any such superstitions for *Paradisio?* Didn't you tell me the captain died on its maiden voyage?"

"She was an old ship, about eighty years at sea, although she'd been rebuilt and restored several times. She had a pretty colorful history." He paused for a moment. "There was a star-dogged moon the evening they set sail. That sort of bothered me."

"A star-dogged moon?"

"One star ahead and one towing the moon. It's an old Irish sign of deadly storms." He paused and regarded their own moon, a thin crescent that shed little light. "We knew there was a big storm brewing off the coast of Africa, but all indications were that it would turn north. When it kept heading southeast, toward Grenada . . ." His voice trailed off as the water slapped against the hulls and the winds moaned against the massive sails.

"Was Marco superstitious?" She shifted her position to see his face in the moonlight.

"Not at all," he said. "He was pragmatic. He believed you controlled your own fate and no one had a hand in it but you."

"Did he . . . did he tell you about the hand I had in his fate?" she asked, her voice barely loud enough to hear over the wind.

"He never said why he left home, only that he did." At her silence, he continued. "He did say your father was pretty demanding and your mother was sweet and passive."

She still said nothing.

"And that you got him out of trouble a lot."

She took a deep sip of the cognac, which burned down her throat.

"Easy on the firewater, princess. You don't need it."

"Then why'd you give it to me?"

"An excuse to bring you out into the moonlight and make out with you."

She tried to shrug casually and not let him know that the idea made her dizzy. "So, what did you find out tonight that you wanted to tell me?"

He swirled the amber liquid in his glass and studied it. "I found the cruise Estaphan Calliope was on."

"Really? Did he travel under his own name?"

"He did. And he booked passage about five hours before we sailed. Genevieve pushed his paperwork through without the usual checks of passports and identification. There's no official record of his travel around the islands. But he stayed in a cabin under that name."

"Which ship? When?"

"About four months ago, on *Paradisio*. It was a Grenadine Island trip through Barbados, Martinique, St. Lucia, and, of course, Grenada. We've removed that itinerary since the hurricane. There's not much in southern Grenada these days." He took a sip of his drink. "But I have something to take to the authorities, you'll be happy to know. They can run checks on every crewman and passenger on that ship."

"And they can bring Calliope in for questioning."

He shrugged. "Hard to say. If the DEA's involved, they may already know him, but not have enough to bring him in. The local law enforcement probably gets paid plenty to ignore him. Or protect him, more likely."

"Was Marco on that ship?"

"Yes. So was Genevieve. We had a few celebrities on board, a movie producer and some musicians. We often go on those cruises to supervise events."

We. Dane and Genevieve.

The breeze blew a strand of hair across her face and he lifted it away, gently running his hand through her curls as he put it back in place.

"So, why don't you tell me the story?"

She shook her head. She wasn't ready for his disappointment. "You might not like me anymore."

He laughed, deep and honest. "I doubt that very much."

The comment warmed her whole body.

"Come on." He absently ran a finger over her hand that grasped the railing. He was always touching her, always making some contact with her skin. Each time, it took her breath away. "I want to hear the story. And you want to tell me."

A heavy sigh escaped her lips, and she picked a random star to watch while she confessed.

"I did look out for Marco a lot, like he said. And I guess that was at the root of the whole thing. He was always getting into situations. Nothing major; boyish scrapes. Cutting school, getting in fights, driving recklessly without a license. Nothing I couldn't help him hide, or at least sway Dominic or Mama into reduced punishments."

"Big sister stuff, huh?"

"I guess so. Marco started college, but a lot of his neighborhood buddies, the guys he'd hung around with since he was a little boy, didn't go anywhere after high school. They were going the way a lot of Italian boys go in communities like the North End."

"Organized crime."

She nodded. "More like disorganized, at that age. But yes."

"And Marco?"

Ava tilted her head and regarded Dane. "First you need to understand something. In the ninety-some years that Santoris have had the restaurant, no one has ever, ever, worked with or for the mob or any families."

She paused and smiled. "Well, during Prohibition, the Ciprianis next door made their own wine and pumped it through basement hoses into our saloon, but even that was outside of the Mafia."

Dane sipped his drink, listening to her.

"It was a law, handed down each generation. A guiding, unbending family principle. The Mafia was the reason Italians had such a bad reputation in this country. The mob was a scourge on good people with ethics. Never, ever give them an inch. This was ingrained into us our whole lives. But not all of the neighbors felt the same way. Especially the young boys who didn't have such a bright future and could be tempted by the money and power."

He nodded and studied her as she talked, but his scrutiny no longer unnerved her. In fact, she was beginning to like it.

"A couple of Marco's childhood friends became small-time crooks. Not very high up in the pecking order, but runners, or gofers."

"I get the picture."

"Well, one of them was in a jam. There was a little war going on between two families and one of the kids, Angelo Ferrisi, was playing both sides. In name, he was associated with his uncle, Anthony Ferrisi, who'd grown to be pretty powerful. But Angelo was also secretly working for another family."

"So Angelo was stupid *and* greedy."

"Very much so." She remembered the beady green eyes and fat cheeks of the kid Marco had always felt sorry for. She'd never liked him as a boy, and he grew into a surly, scary teenager, who leered at her chest and made every excuse to brush up against her when Marco wasn't around. A snotty kid she had hated. But that didn't matter anymore, because Angelo Ferrisi had been dead for five years. Ava shuddered at the memory of his battered body, the blood in the snow, drops spattered on the gleaming glass door of Santori's.

"Angelo needed to hide a stash of illegal guns somewhere clean, somewhere the police and his own family would never check. He talked Marco into letting him use a storage room at the restaurant."

She remembered the morning she was digging around the storeroom to start the tedious task of monthly inventory, when she found the boxes of hard black guns. Shaking in fear and anger, she'd marched upstairs to the apartment and found Marco asleep. He'd been cavalier and dismissive, telling her to just forget it. Everything was cool.

"But everything *wasn't* cool," she said, unaware that she hadn't spoken her thoughts out loud for a few moments.

"What happened?"

"Oh, you know Ava. Woman of action. Takes matters into her own hands."

"Yeah." He smiled and took her hand, but she barely noticed. "I know her."

"Well, I stewed over it all day. I was really worried about Marco, not anything else. I knew from local gossip what was going on between these two families, and I knew Dominic would kill him if he found out."

"So what did you do?"

"I ratted on them all." She said the statement with the same disgust that grabbed at her gut when she thought of the consequences.

"But you just said Dominic would kill him."

Ava squeezed her eyes shut. "Better Dominic figuratively kill him, than the Ferrisis or Galuccis literally kill him." She opened her eyes and looked directly at Dane. "I really did want to protect him, Dane. But in retrospect, I may have had other, far more selfish motives. It wasn't always easy living in the shadow of the amazing and gorgeous Marco Santori. Even if he was five years younger."

"Is that why your father sent him away?"

"No. It gets worse." Damn the crack in her voice. He stroked her arm gently. "Go ahead."

"I told Dominic, called the police, and set up Angelo. Only it didn't unfold quite the way I thought it would. The family who Angelo was working for thought he'd turned them in, and cost them thousands. So, they killed him. Beat the life out of him and left him bloody and dead. In front of our restaurant." She closed her eyes again. "I found him."

He squeezed her hand.

"Angelo's family blamed Marco. They threatened to kill him. And they would have, Dane. Dominic said that the only way for Marco to stay alive was for him to leave. For good. With no contact with us, so that he was safe." She couldn't stop her tears and didn't try. "I did it, Dane. I got them in trouble and I got Angelo killed and I am the reason Marco had to leave and give up his family."

She pulled her hand out of his firm grip and wiped away a tear. "The police wouldn't put him in witness protection or anything so formal, and there was no way he could be safe in Boston. He had to disappear. So he did."

"But why the estrangement?" Dane sounded confused. "Why not letters or secret family visits?"

"Well, he didn't exactly leave on the best of terms. Dominic was furious that Marco had broken our personal family code. And Marco and I . . . He didn't want to see me, Dane. He hated me for what I did. When he left, he said horrible, horrible things . . ." She turned away. "He swore he'd never speak to me again, I was not his sister, I was a mean, jealous bitch . . ."

"Ava." He took her face in his hand to bring her back. "He was nineteen. Just a kid. You were trying to help him. You knew he was in with the wrong crowd. You were young yourself."

She shook her head at the hollow defense.

"Didn't your parents want to forgive him and have a relationship with their son?"

"They believed if they had any contact with him, he could be found. Dominic made an edict. No one could ever have contact with Marco. Dominic was so angry at him that he wouldn't even allow us to say his name for years. Only my mother could get away with it. She worshipped Marco. I think she did exchange letters with him; she didn't seem at all surprised to find out he was on a ship in the Caribbean." She closed her eyes. Not a day went by that she didn't question her own motives. And bitterly regret the results. "But I—I obeyed Dominic. I thought someday, he'd call me. But he never did, and now . . ."

He bowed his head so close to hers that his hair touched her forehead. "He never told me, Ava. He never said a thing against you. Except that you were a great big sister."

It couldn't be true. Marco couldn't have forgiven her. If he had, wouldn't he have called her or written to her?

"He may not have told you, but he didn't forgive me. He died hating me." The lump in her throat threatened to make her sob.

"I think you're wrong about that. He was very happy here. I don't think he regretted how his life turned out."

Ava's gaze flashed at him. "Short, Dane. His life turned out to be very short."

He winced.

"What *did* he tell you?" she asked. "Why did he say he left?"

"He said he fought with his father because he didn't want to go into the family business."

"And you believed that? Didn't you wonder why he never talked to us?"

"No. It's precisely the reason I rarely see or speak to my parents. It made sense to me."

She turned toward the sky, trying to find her star again.

"I always had a fantasy that someday I'd pick up the phone and it would be Marco. He'd say, 'Hey, Avel Navel.' And I'd say 'Hi, Marco Polo.'" A sob broke through. "That's what we called each other. When we were little."

"Instead you got a call from the Coast Guard telling you he's dead." His voice was flat, pained.

"Presumed dead, Dane. I thought there was hope." She turned to face him, blinking back a tear. "I'm sorry I've been so pushy about what you should do. Apparently, I didn't learn my lesson about taking the law into my own hands."

Gently, he outlined her face with his fingers. Her cheeks, her chin. His feather touch skimmed over her lips. A smile tipped the corners of his mouth. "You can't help it, princess. You're a woman of action."

He set their glasses on a ledge next to him, then he put both arms around her and tucked her head under his chin.

"The lesson to learn is that you can't change history." He kissed her hair gently. "If I could bring your brother back, I would."

She looked up and saw the determination mixed with pain in his aquamarine eyes, and it squeezed her heart. "It wasn't your fault," she told him.

"And it wasn't yours." His gaze locked on hers, straight and steady. "I promise you this: I will do everything possible to find out whose fault it was. Not that it will change history, but perhaps it will help you understand it."

She held his gaze. And her breath. And then he closed the few inches between them and his mouth nearly met hers. Almost. So close, she could taste the cognac on his lips.

"Not here," he whispered, his breath on her mouth. He stepped off the bowsprit and put his hands on her waist to bring her down. Grabbing the empty snifters, he held her hand as they walked down the deck. He set the glasses on a cocktail table and then put his arm around her, sliding her naturally into the solid and comforting length of his body.

As he slipped the card key into her cabin lock, Ava shuddered, anticipation igniting every cell in her body. Just a kiss, she told herself as the door opened. Just one kiss. That didn't make her a statistic. Just one kiss. He hadn't judged her harshly. He'd made her feel whole again.

He stepped into the darkened room and gently tugged her with him. She heard the resounding click of the door behind her. *Just one kiss*. Like one sweet taste of chocolate to fill the ache of craving. She nearly swayed from dizzy expectation, closing her eyes for a second. But before they opened, she tasted his mouth, tasted the almonds and vanilla of the cognac. As he parted his lips, she reached for his tongue with hers, a fire building low inside her as she instinctively pressed her body toward him in a reflex so natural she couldn't have even thought to stop herself.

Just this kiss.

"I've thought about this all day," he whispered.

"When you weren't fighting the bad guys."

He smiled. "Even when I was." He pulled her closer, letting her feel his response to her. Her knees weakened at the sensation. He lowered his head and his tongue barely touched her lower lip, tracing it from one side to the other. His tongue skipped along her upper lip. Tasting her, tempting her.

He flicked down the warm skin of her throat, sending electrical shocks through her body. She moaned in response. *This is more than one kiss.*

An urgent need to push her hips against him silenced the warning voice. The force of his erection pressed against her stomach, making her want to stand on her toes and clasp him between her legs. She took his head in her hands, cupping his face and bringing it back to her mouth. He moaned softly as he kissed her and his fingers moved along her collarbone, along the line of her blouse, lower to the deep indentation between her breasts.

"You're beautiful, Ava," he murmured between kisses. "I want to touch you. Every time you're anywhere near me, I want to touch you."

His fingers grazed her nipple, a contact she'd fantasized about a thousand times that day. Dear God, did she just say *yes?* His hands moved down her back, over her hips, around the curve of her backside.

His hardness and her softness and his hands on her body.

"Come here, princess." He pulled her farther into the room, still kissing, still touching, still pressing. She followed him, unable to stop the throbbing in her body, wanting more and more of his solid, sexy body and what it was doing to her.

She wouldn't open her eyes; then she didn't have to face it. Didn't have to admit she was attached to his mouth, his hands, his legs, in a sensual dance toward the bedroom. That she was falling onto her lovely, delicious white silk bed, and the entire male length of him was on top of her. She heard her sandals drop to the floor.

They don't know what hit 'em until it's over.

She forced her eyes open and watched him kissing her breasts, her stomach. He whispered words of abandon, of pleasure, throaty prayers using her name. *This is what hits them.*

But his hands were full of her breasts, torturing her with pleasure. Nothing mattered but his hands and mouth and the desire overtaking every sense. She arched against him and her head fell back with a moan of arousal and ecstasy that came from deep inside her, a place she didn't even know she had, a sound she didn't know she could make.

Then she saw the knife.

Stabbed into the headboard, viciously gouging the antique oak. A stream of knotted peach and black material hung from its glinting blade.

The air rushed out of her and she choked, fought for air, and then screamed.

* * *

"What the hell—" Dane gasped for breath. "What's the—"

Ava rolled off the bed in one movement and stood with her hands over her mouth, staring. Then he saw it. He leaped and seized her shoulders, pulling her into him.

"Oh, Christ." He peered into the shadows around the room, possessed by an animal instinct to pounce on the intruder and use his own weapon on him. But the intruder was long gone, leaving only his evil calling card.

Ava started to shake with fear and shock.

"What *is* it?" she gasped in horror.

He guided her toward the door, as far from the bed and its ominous symbol as possible.

"It's a message."

"What . . . what kind of message?"

Still holding her, he flipped on the light. The white-handled knife looked no less menacing bathed in brightness. It meant one thing to sailors: death. The symbol of imminent death at sea. And the scarf; the silky peach and black fabric repeatedly bound and brutally stabbed. He didn't need to count the knots. There were thirteen.

"Come here, baby. Come with me." He walked her into the sitting room and sat her on the sofa. Terror darkened her eyes and her skin was alabaster even in the dim light.

"What in God's name does it mean?" Ava demanded. "And my scarf! Who would do this? How did they get in here? Why?"

He could sense her getting angry as the shock wore off. "Stay here," he ordered. "I want to look at it."

Her huge eyes stayed steady on his, but her mouth, still red from his passionate kisses, quivered. One last shiver and she seemed to regain some semblance of control.

He turned into the bedroom. The crystal clear warning sickened him. Who was in this room while they were on the deck?

The scarf really turned his stomach. At the end of the thirteenth double knot was the hangman's noose. Thirteen knots for the devil to untie before he owned the victim's soul, the old legend said.

She wouldn't be safe alone tonight. He took in the rumpled bedding, her sandals on the floor. Maybe she wouldn't be safe with him, either.

"Can you save it for fingerprints?" Her voice startled him.

Of course she couldn't stay in the other room.

"I doubt it." With a jerk, he yanked the butcher knife out of the wood and gently removed the torn material from its blade. He rolled the silk into a ball and stuck it in his pocket.

Hesitantly, she approached. "That's a cheap knife, nothing of the quality you have in the galley. That thing wouldn't cut a vegetable."

"I don't think its owner was threatening to slice tomatoes with it," he said bitterly. "Anyway, no one would keep a white-handled knife on a ship."

Her jaw dropped. "Is this some kind of ridiculous superstition?"

"Someone wanted to deliver a message, Ava. To threaten you. Or me. The cabin's registered in my name." He set the knife gingerly on the nightstand. "Get some things. You aren't sleeping here tonight."

He heard her slight intake of breath. "I'll be fine."

"You've got to be kidding. I won't let you stay here."

"Excuse me?" Temper flared in her voice. "You won't *let* me?"

"Ava," he sighed, knowing what was at the bottom of her anger. "It would be stupid. I'm not leaving you until we are off this ship."

She took a step back, her gaze burning into him. "Where are you suggesting I sleep, Romeo?"

"Romeo?" He choked on the word. "That wasn't exactly a solo act, princess."

Her cheeks darkened and the flush slipped down over her throat, to her chest. Where he'd caressed her so intimately.

"It won't happen again." Unmistakable resolve rang in her voice and determination flashed in her dark eyes. She was having some big, fat second thoughts.

"It's entirely up to you."

"Good." She pointed to the door. "Then leave."

He shook his head and looked around for what she might need. He'd pack her up and carry her if he had to, but she wasn't staying in this room. A hint of fear crossed her face and he damned himself. Why hadn't he taken that slower? He'd acted like a teenager, for Christ's sake, he wanted her so much.

"Look, I have a small suite. There's a sofa in it. You'll be safe."

"It's not you I don't trust, Dane." She looked away from him and whispered, "It's me."

He took the three steps to her in an instant. "Ava. It's not you. It's not me. It's us."

"A bad combination?" she asked warily.

"A highly combustible combination." He kissed her forehead, as brotherly as he could. "Please come with me. I'll sleep on the sofa. You'll be completely safe. I couldn't live with myself if anything happened to you in here."

She sighed. "Okay." Her eyes moved to the knife on the nightstand. "This is really serious, isn't it?"

"It could be. I need to figure out how big it is. I'll close the business and deal with the consequences. Tomorrow, I'll talk to Genevieve and start the process."

"What are you waiting for? Call her now."

He smiled at her overpowering need to act. "I tried all night. Can't find her." He smoothed her hair and inched her toward the bathroom. "Come on, get what you need. Let's get out of here."

He took the knife into the sitting room and wrapped it in the tissue paper he'd brought the scarf in.

He closed his eyes, grabbing onto the memory of the ecstasy they'd very nearly shared. God, he ached for her, literally. But his hard-on for Ava Santori was the least of his problems now.

Yet it didn't feel like pure physical craving. It didn't feel like something that could be satisfied with the kind of sex they were headed toward on that bed. But there was something else bothering him. Talking to her, looking at her. Son of a bitch, just being in the same room with her made him feel something. Whole. That's what it was. She made him feel whole.

He jerked the sliding glass door open and stepped onto the balcony to erase the ridiculous thought with fresh sea air. Whatever was going on in his head, and other places, would wear off and the inevitable would happen. His walls would come up and his alarm would go off. She deserved more than that. All her spunk and determination, all her hot-wired passion. Those enigmatic eyes and that soul-wrenching mouth. She deserved a guy worthy of it all. Not him.

Impossible as it seemed ten minutes ago, he'd have to keep his hands off her. Then, she'd leave the islands. And once she did, the memory of her would fade before the next full cycle of the moon.

11

The shrill tones of his pager yanked Max Roper from an icy dream of shoveling snow uphill, on the steeply angled driveway of his childhood home. His arms ached from scraping metal against the frozen mountain, the white flakes turning gray as they danced through the polluted air of Billy Buck Hill in Pittsburgh. Bitter cold burned his lungs. Shoveling snow uphill, he thought as his mind cleared. A perfect metaphor for his life.

He tossed back the sheet and reached for his pager. Or maybe the dream was due to the fact that he'd set his air conditioner to "freeze your balls off" so he could sleep in the miserable heat and humidity of Trinidad. A dismal attempt to stay cool and dry so that mold didn't grow in his ears before he ever got the hell home, to the USA.

He peered at the orange glow of his digital pager's display. Nine-one-one followed the familiar digits of his office. Good. Things had been pretty damn dull down here, and he hadn't accepted the assignment for the pure fun of sweating in Satan's playground.

No way, man. Special Agent Maximillan P. Roper III wanted to kick some scum-sucking drug-dealing ass. But, so far, the only ass getting kicked since the Drug Enforcement Administration moved him to this inferno six months ago was his own.

He reached his desk in one swift movement and picked up the secure phone line to call his office. *Come on, man, gimme something good.* He hit the speed dial.

The line was answered instantly by the poor schmuck who pulled the unenviable overnight duty at the DEA's office in Port of Spain, Trinidad. Someone even more desperate than Max Roper.

There were no niceties exchanged.

"Pack, Roper. We just opened up a warehouse in Grenada and hit a mother lode."

"Grenada? Is there anything left up there?" He frowned in the dark and scratched his crotch with his free hand. "I thought everything was wiped out by the hurricane."

"Somebody got sloppy when they had to move about nine hundred kilos of coke out of St. George's after the storm hit. It ended up in some dumpy town called Sauteurs about twenty-five miles north. Wilson and Dombrowsky tracked them over the last couple of days and they finished the raid about two hours ago. We got about nine kilos of smack, a miniarsenal, and the makings of a fine science lab. They made six arrests. You definitely want to talk to these morons."

Max's heart skipped a beat. There was only one reason to bring him in to grill some drug flunkies in Grenada after the undercover agents had handled the raid: Operation Carib. It was finally going to start.

"Port Salines still closed?" Grenada's airport, located in the southernmost tip of the island, had been mowed down by the vicious winds of Hurricane Carlos. He doubted that those slow-as-molasses islanders had it up and running yet, even though legions of Red Cross and disaster volunteers had descended after the storm.

"Oh, yeah. And St. George's is done in for months too," the agent told him, referring to Grenada's capital city. "Nothing but dead and dying left around there. The place is a mess. They opened up the old Pearls Airport on the northeastern shore and you can drive through the mountains to Sauteurs. Wilson or Dombrowsky will meet you. They smell the link you've been looking for, Roper."

Max hoped so. He spent six months doing housekeeping after his predecessor had racked up twenty-three hundred arrests and seized enough coke, heroine, morphine base, and marijuana to keep every junkie east of the Mississippi high for three months. Operation Conquistador was one of the most successful campaigns in the history of the DEA, and he had done a lousy job of maintenance after the cleaning crew went home.

Those shrewd Colombian bastards had pulled the whole system back together as fast as lightning and Max hadn't even been able to find a single new trans-shipment point. This was only the second respectable bust on his watch. Resources were fewer than white women down here, and no decent agents wanted to pull this duty, even with the incentives the DEA had packaged up for them.

And he was never going to get back to snow and blessed cold and Steelers games if he didn't figure out how these mothers were shipping the shit and who was behind it.

The DEA had not officially sanctioned Operation Carib. It was his baby, named for the bloodthirsty warriors who controlled the Caribbean for more than three hundred years before old Chris Columbus made a wrong turn into paradise. Fierce and vicious, Caribs preferred eating their enemies to fishing. Just like the animals who did the dirty work for the Cali Mafia all over the Caribbean.

He packed in the dark, like he had a million times. He knew better than to bring any attention to his tiny apartment by turning on the light. The locals knew he was the head guy for the DEA in the Caribbean. They respected him and kept their distance. Still, he didn't need to broadcast his middle-of-the-night departures.

He slapped a clip in his forty-caliber Baby Glock and checked the safety. Probably wouldn't need it for interrogation, but he never left home without it.

He hadn't focused too much on Grenada lately. His mistake, maybe. Wilson and Dombrowsky had been awfully quiet, and he'd assumed the hurricane had slowed down their undercover work on the Island of Spice. Instead, it had led them to a sting. *Good work, boys.*

Over the last sixty days, DEA and the Coast Guard had picked up two dozen go-fasts tearing through the Caribbean. All empty. Somehow, they were getting shipments moved. In the last six months, they'd changed their typical delivery patterns. The sons of bitches created new transshipment points overnight, bribed the longshoreman and ticket counter agents, and corrupted every law enforcement officer. They were unstoppable and hiding in every corner of every island. Like cockroaches that just wouldn't die.

Someone in the Caribbean was masterminding this, but none of the suspects they'd been watching for months checked out.

Maybe these new jokers would give them a clue.

He threw his bag over his shoulder, quietly closed the door behind him, and headed for the airport.

The faint aroma of salt and soap clung to everything in Dane Erikson's cabin. The sheets were fresh, but Ava could still pick up his scent. It made her want him. It made her restless and hungry and confused.

They hadn't spoken much once inside his L-shaped cabin. In the bathroom, she put on a T-shirt and running shorts and then climbed tentatively into his bed while he settled on a love seat around the corner. She doubted he slept much more than she did. She heard the click of keys on a laptop, then paper rustling, and eventually, silence. Plotting and planning, scheming and strategizing. That was Dane Erikson.

She took a deep breath and the scent conjured up the taste of his mouth and the power of his hands, forcing her to bite her lips to keep from moaning at the memory. That took her back to the gruesome image of the knife stuck in her headboard.

She turned over quietly, not wanting to draw his attention. But the potent sensations assaulted her again at the thought of him just a few yards away. By dawn, the weight of sleep deprivation made her body ache. She got out of bed, brushed her teeth, and prepared to face him.

In the early morning light, she could see the dusting of golden hair on his long, tan legs and his bare feet hanging over the side of the love seat. His arms embraced his own chest, probably to keep from flopping off the undersize sofa. A tangle of honey-streaked hair fell softly around a not so cleanly shaven face. She turned away, unwilling to wake him.

"How'd'ya sleep, princess?"

She started. *Like a caged animal in heat.* "Fine."

He opened his eyes and shot her a grin far too pronounced for a man who'd really been sleeping. As he dropped his legs to the floor to sit up, she noticed he still wore last night's khaki shorts and pullover shirt. She wondered if the scarf was still in his pocket.

"Want some coffee?"

She shook her head. "Am I allowed to go back to my room?"

His gaze darkened into a cobalt blue that matched the water behind him. "You're not a prisoner, Ava. I'm just trying to make sure you're safe."

"Fine. Can I go pack or do you want to do that for me?"

Evidently, he chose to ignore her sarcasm. "You'll need to meet me on deck at ten. After we drop anchor in Nevis, we're going straight to the airport. The Utopia plane will be waiting for us."

"And when we get to St. Barts?"

"You can stay with me." At her reaction, he added, "I have a separate guesthouse on the property, Ava. And guest rooms in the house."

More of his scent to assail her. "All right. I'd like to go back now."

He slowly stood, his gaze never leaving her face. "Ava, I'm not fooling around with your personal safety. Believe me, you're better off with me than in a hotel somewhere."

She bit her lip and avoided looking directly at him.

"Hey." He reached across the space that separated them and nudged her chin up. "Did I come anywhere near you last night? I *can* control myself."

She felt her cheeks heat but managed to glare at him. "I don't want to be under constant surveillance and protection, Dane."

"That's not what's bothering you, Ava," he said softly.

"It certainly is," she lied.

"It's a mutual attraction. Very natural." He moved to a small wet bar and began making coffee. "You're fairly easy to read."

She stared at his back. She didn't want to be easy to read. She wanted to be fascinating. Mysterious. The kind of alluring, worldly woman he no doubt entertained regularly in the mornings. She sighed. Not in this lifetime.

The coffeemaker bubbled, starting up its task.

"That's a fact, Dane. What you see is what you get. I'm a cook. A daughter of a chef, a granddaughter of a chef, the great-niece of a chef, and maybe, someday, I'll be the mother of a chef."

He turned toward her, but she didn't let him speak.

"I'm not here to have some kind of island fling. I came here because I had a hand in screwing up my brother's life and then found out he was dead. I got on the plane to put some sort of closure on a very painful chapter of my life. I'm going to stay until you or I or the FBI or the CIA or *someone* figures out what the hell happened on that ship. Then I'm going back home to be a cook again."

"So, why aren't you married?"

"Why aren't you?" she shot back.

"You're the one making speeches about baby chefs." A sparkle danced in his eyes. "I am well known as a solitary man."

"Solitary, but not celibate." The words were out before she could swallow them.

He raised an eyebrow and leaned on the counter. "At this particular moment I am."

She said nothing, consciously silencing the questions and retorts that rang in her head.

"And you?" He frowned a little, as though he didn't want to ask and, maybe, didn't want to know. Would her response make any difference to him?

"Both. Solitary and celibate." *At this particular moment*.

"I'm surprised you haven't found a nice Italian boy to help make baby chefs."

She smiled. "They're all scared of me."

"You hit them, no doubt." He laughed a little and held her gaze, then turned back to the hissing coffeemaker. "And while I'm sure you'd be able to *swat* your way out of any danger, I do believe you'll be safer at my house when we get back." He flipped a white mug over to pour. "Sure you don't want a cup?"

"No, I don't." She did, but she wanted to get away from him more. "I'm going to get my things."

She dressed in less than five minutes, refusing to look at her face in the mirror or consider a drop of makeup. This wasn't a romantic morning after, and she didn't want to mull over his *solitude* or *celibacy* one minute longer. Finger combing her curls, she gathered her cosmetic bag and the clothes she'd slept in and found him in the sitting area, finishing his coffee.

Ava held up her hands in protest as he stood to join her. "No, please. I can find my way back. Not even knife-carrying criminals are up this early."

"I'm going to the cabin with you to make sure no one has been in there overnight." Despite her exasperated sigh, he angled his head toward the bathroom. "Give me one minute. I'll be right back."

"Can I at least wait outside?"

"Don't run away."

Like hers, Dane's cabin opened to a passageway along the main deck. Stepping out, she heard a soft rumble to her left, and she snapped her head toward the sound. Cassie grinned from behind a rolling cart of linens and towels. Immediately, Ava realized how she must look. *Guilty.*

"Well, well. That didn't take long, luv."

"No, Cassie." An unwelcome heat wave rushed to Ava's face. "It's not what you think. I had to . . . someone . . . it's not what you think."

Cassie's smile broadened. "I don't care, sweetie. It's the ship. Happens all the time."

"No, it's not how it looks," Ava said lamely. "It's . . . not fun."

"Well that's a pity." Cassie shook her head. "It's *supposed* to be fun."

There would be no convincing Cassie that she and Dane hadn't just shared every imaginable intimacy. And she didn't feel like trying.

"Listen, Cassie. I'm going back to St. Barts with Dane. Today. From Nevis."

Cassie stopped the cart in front of Dane's door and frowned. "Why?"

"Long story. But I'll stay with him—in his guesthouse—until you return from this cruise. Is your offer still good? Could I stay with you when you get back?"

Cassie's penetrating green eyes swept over Ava's face, ignoring the question. "You don't look so great. Not like you should after a night with him."

Ava shook her head. "I'm fine and it really isn't what you think. Trust me."

"I do, luv." Cassie rubbed Ava's arm with reassuring warmth. "We'll be home in a couple of days. Of course you can stay with me."

How much could she tell Cassie without terrifying her? "Cassie, listen. A lot is going on. It's too complicated to explain, but it will all come out eventually. Then you'll understand."

Cassie leaned on her cart, a rare serious expression on her face. "Just be careful, luv. He's a heartbreaker."

The cabin door opened and Dane came out. He lifted his eyebrows in surprise at Cassie. "Good to see housekeeping's up and at it early," he said.

"And management too." She winked at him and pushed the cart away.

Before he left for the deck, Dane tried Genevieve's cell phone again. Voice mail. Where the hell was she? He didn't want to go to the constable or alert anyone to the situation until he'd had a chance to talk to her; he owed her that much. Hell, he owed her grandfather a whole lot more. He called his secretary, Claire, who hadn't heard from Genevieve either, and then he tried her home phone repeatedly. Nothing.

Ava waited for him near the tender embarkation, in intimate conversation with that dog Arnot, who obviously wanted more from her than a little assistance in the galley. They stopped talking as soon as he approached.

"It is a disappointment that my new sous-chef is leaving, Monsieur Erikson." Arnot peered at him with his beady brown eyes. The bon vivant French chef act really annoyed Dane. Especially when it worked so well on Ava, who all but melted into a puddle around the little twerp.

"I'm sure you two have had a chance to exchange recipes," he said dryly and turned to her. "You all set?"

She hugged Arnot. "*Merci beaucoup*, Chef. I'll see you on dry land, I promise."

"Ah, *cherie*, I leave this ship and go right back to *Valhalla*, then *Celestia*. Eventually, I will get a holiday. Hopefully before you leave for home."

Ignoring Dane's watchful eye, Arnot air kissed both Ava's cheeks and then planted one right on her lips. The little son of a bitch.

"Okay, kids. You'll only be separated for two days." Dane put his arm around her with a deliberate squeeze and guided her toward the platform. "We need to go."

They hadn't settled on the seats of the launch before she attacked. "Why are you so rude to him? He's a—"

"Genius. I know."

She tapped his forearm. "Yes, as a matter of fact, he is. And a very nice man. Unusual for great chefs, you know."

"I wouldn't know. I've never met any." Dane pulled his sunglasses out of his pocket and polished the lenses with his shirt before putting them on. "Present company excluded, of course."

She stewed for a minute, blessedly quiet, letting

him think. But all he could envision was Arnot and Ava together on the deck, whispering and serious. She couldn't be attracted to that little geek, could she? Or perhaps they were talking about something other than ingredients.

"You didn't tell him anything, did you?" he demanded.

She kept her gaze on the water. "No."

"Why did you tell him we were leaving? What reason did you give him?"

"I told him it was personal." She turned to him with an accusing eye. "And like everyone else on the ship, he probably assumes it's . . . we . . . I'm . . . romantically involved with you."

No doubt they did assume just that, and frankly, that was fine with him. They'd stopped in the lounge together, late at night. They'd traveled to Antigua and kissed on the water taxi, if only because of her persistent questions. By now the entire crew undoubtedly knew he had dined in her cabin and that she'd spent last night in his.

He tried Genevieve on his cell phone one more time when they reached the metal hut terminal, knowing his phone wouldn't work on the plane. He stabbed the Power Off button as soon as he got her voice mail again and muttered a curse.

"What's the matter?" Ava asked.

"I was trying to get Genevieve. Nobody has heard from her."

"What are you planning to do, Dane? Give her a one-way ticket to hide out before you call the police?"

Dane watched his pilot deplane and stride toward them. "I know what I'm doing, Ava."

"You're just going to give her enough warning to skip town," Ava said. "If she hasn't already."

He wouldn't admit that the same thought had occurred to him.

At his lack of response, she flipped her hair over her shoulder, a sure sign of an impending temper flare-up, but Captain Galbraith reached them before she could blow. They exchanged greetings, got the luggage stored, and took seats. They were the only passengers on the six-seater, a purely functional plane that Dane and his staff used to hop islands and change ships.

Ava shouted over the noise of the engine, apparently not ready to give up her argument. "I just don't understand why you want to protect her."

With his most menacing frown, he pointed to the cockpit, reminding her of the pilot's presence. "I only know one way to shut you up, Miss Ava Santori. Shall I employ it?"

She buckled her seat belt and crossed her arms, seething with unspoken thoughts. After they took off, she studied the scenery below. Dozens of dark emerald islands dropped like jewels into liquid sapphire settings, each wrapped in palm-fringed beaches of white sand and azure water. Jagged mountain peaks broke through low hanging mist, giving an unreal aura to the vista.

Feeling Dane's stare, she turned to him. His mesmerizing aquamarine eyes offered no hint to what he was thinking. He simply watched her. Sometimes, she imagined he could read her mind.

"We're coming to St. Barts," he said, his gaze still on her. He reached over and ran a light finger over her white knuckles. "Are you all right?"

She nodded and turned back to the window. Dane's gentleness got to her more than anything.

The single engine changed speed, and she felt the plane drop gradually, then quickly. They practically kissed the peak of a mountain and then flew so close to the tree line that the palm fronds bent in response. The landing strip appeared from nowhere at the base of the mountain and ended, abruptly, at the edge of the sea. She closed her eyes and felt her stomach dip as they descended. With a jolt, they touched the runway with a deafening screech. Like every other plane that landed in St. Barts, they came to a stop within a few hundred yards of the water.

She exhaled with relief when the engine quieted down.

"You either like that drop or hate it," he said as they unhooked their seat belts.

"I hate it. I hate feeling like I've lost control."

"No, you don't." He shot her a sly grin. "You love it."

Her stomach repeated the sensation of descent. With ease, he released the door and dropped the metal stairs, and in a few moments, they gathered their luggage and walked the short distance to the tiny terminal.

Then Ava saw the pack of people, hustling toward them with purpose. A handheld television camera with the NBC logo at the center of the group brought her to a standstill.

"Holy hell," Dane muttered. "Is this your friend Boyd's doing?"

A man holding a microphone signaled to the cameraman, and they ran toward Dane and Ava. "Mr. Erikson! Mr. Erikson!"

Ava's heart thumped as she grabbed Dane's arm, steadying herself against the urge to run back to the plane.

Dane held up his hand and continued at his same deliberate pace. "I'm not doing an interview," he said firmly.

"But do you have any theories, sir? Do you think it was a hit-and-run?"

Dane stopped midstep. "What the hell are you talking about?"

"The accident, sir. Miss Giles. Your executive VP."

Dane took off his sunglasses and stared at the man.

"Haven't you heard? She was struck by a car, Mr. Erikson. She was jogging near Morne Rouge late last night."

His face blanched. "Is she . . . what condition is she in?"

The reporter's arms fell to his sides, the bite gone from his attack. "She's dead."

12

Ava longed to be alone. More than that, she longed to be with Dane. But neither was possible.

He'd left her at his home, after a whirlwind trip in a Jeep with a fifty-ish woman named Claire at the wheel. Around the hairpin turns, he alternately barked orders and suddenly went silent, closing his eyes and wincing like someone had punched him in the stomach. Then he'd focus on the road ahead and throw more instructions at Claire. Call all the ships into port, notify employees, and dear God, had someone called Nat and Elizabeth Giles? Then he squeezed his eyes again with a quiet grunt as the invisible blow landed.

He told Claire to get Ava to his house, drive him to the constable's office in Gustavia, and then round up some people for various tasks he enumerated like a computer. For a man who liked to think things through, he sure acted with an admirable amount of purpose.

Claire had virtually no details on the accident, as she called it. Genevieve's body had been found by a tourist early that morning, crumpled in roadside shrubbery not too far from Dane's house.

"What the hell was NBC doing at the airport?" Dane asked.

"They've been poking around the offices for a day or two, working on some stupid story that lawyer put them onto. As soon as word about Genevieve hit, it flew like fire. They literally followed me to the airport." Claire had looked at him regretfully. "I'm so sorry, Dane. I didn't want to radio the plane. I wanted to tell you in person."

He put his hand on her arm. "I know, Claire."

Evidently Genevieve was a runner who had often been seen jogging along the dangerous, narrow roads at night. She could have easily been hit by one of the many drivers unfamiliar with the treacherous, narrow roads of St. Barts.

But Ava knew better. And she was certain Dane did too. She sat quietly in the backseat with one thought pounding in her head.

They are killers. Whoever they are, whatever they sell and wherever they do it, they kill.

She closed her eyes, and images of Angelo Ferrisi dead on Salem Street flashed in her brain. She tried to concentrate on what Dane was saying, but she could only hear Genevieve's strangled sound of pain in *Valhalla*'s dining room the day she overheard her conversation.

They are killers.

Before she got to talk privately to Dane, he'd ensconced her behind the palace walls and left. She stood on the veranda, looking at the mountains of St. Martin against the horizon and listening to the house noises. People spoke in hushed tones, the phone rang over and over again, the front door opened and closed. More Utopians.

Marj had been put in charge of her, she could tell. The woman continually ambled over, put her arm around Ava, and asked her what she needed.

"I need to cook," Ava announced. If she couldn't be alone with her thoughts and she couldn't corner Dane to demand answers he didn't have anyway, Ava knew only one escape.

"Well, darlin', you do just dat. Come to da kitchen, sweets. Dere's lotsa folks comin' and goin' and we should feed dem."

Dane's kitchen was glorious. Built for entertaining, with top-of-the-line appliances and utensils. Ava dug around the walk-in pantry, then spent a few minutes perusing the oversize Sub-Zero refrigerator for ingredients. Marj sent her nephew to the market while Ava busied herself with prep for several dishes. A few more unexpected guests arrived, and Ava realized they would be gathering here all day. It didn't matter that he had left. They were simply drawn to his home for support and shelter in their storm.

She found a box of semolina and silently blessed whoever bought such a lovely ingredient, then quickly began boiling the water to mix it into gnocchi alla romano. The perfect comfort food. As she listened to the hushed tones of French, British, and other less recognizable accents around her, something felt oddly familiar.

It certainly wasn't the Italian kitchen of her childhood. The voices weren't as loud or insistent as those of the aunts and uncles and cousins she loved. And the faces surrounding her came in every imaginable skin color. But it felt exactly like home. A gathering of clan, brought together in consolation or celebration. From baptisms to funerals and every sacrament and holiday in between.

Ava added a dash of salt and oil to the water and smiled for the first time in hours. Dane Erikson had created a family all his own. She suspected he didn't even realize that in the process, he'd become the classic patriarch.

No one around her seemed to suspect foul play in Genevieve's death. Accusations were made against an unknown hit-and-run driver, probably a tourist, lost or drunk. They blamed Genevieve herself for foolishly running at night. No one gave any indication that she might have been bumped off for knowing too much about the drug trafficking that was going on under their noses. And no one, she noticed, mentioned the lawsuit.

As she glanced up from the cooktop at the people around her, she wondered what they thought about her being there. Had rumors about Dane and her already spread?

"What is de matter, Miss Ava? Do you need something?"

"What have you heard from Grayson Boyd over the last few days, Marj?"

Marj shook her head. "Dere are only tree or four of de families dat want any part of de lawsuit, Miss Ava. Not too many folks want dat blood money."

"The settlements are fair and generous, aren't they?"

Marj nodded. "Oh, yeah. Mister Dane, he take care of all of us."

Ava slammed a wooden spoon on the granite counter. "I want to call Grayson Boyd right now. I want no part of his lawsuit. Can I use a phone some-where?"

"Come with me to Mister Dane's study, Miss Ava. He won't mind you being in dere for dat call."

When Marj left her and closed the door, Ava couldn't resist wrapping herself in the aura of Dane that lingered in his private surroundings. Sitting at his massive desk, she traced its polished rosewood edge and gently caressed the leather armrest of his chair. She imagined him working here, doing his planning and strategizing. Thinking . . . of her.

Ah, what a *gibroni*, her grandmother would say. What a fool.

She picked up the phone and struggled with a French operator to get connected to Grayson Boyd's hotel in town, studying the comfortable, masculine room.

A slow southern drawl interrupted her reverie. "Well, well, Ava, my dear. Where *have* you been?"

He knew damn well where she'd been.

"I don't believe Utopia or Dane Erikson was responsible for the loss of *Paradisio*." Her heart knocked with each word. "I've talked to the families of the victims and visited their homes. The com-pany's offering a fair settlement, and I will not par-ticipate in the lawsuit or any action that will further this situation."

"Uh-huh. I heard you two were gettin' real cozy. He's quite the ladies' man, I imagine."

She squeezed the receiver. "Mr. Erikson con-vinced me of his innocence, and the victims' families have confirmed that he's shown every indication of responsibly caring for them."

"So he screwed you right into submission."

"I have no further business with you." With shaking hands, she hung up the phone.

It's what everyone would think. Dane had seduced Marco's sister to convince her to drop the lawsuit. Why else? What else would he see in her? And she, like every other woman he'd targeted, had fallen for it. *Face the truth, Santori.* If it hadn't been for some knife-wielding maniac on that ship, Grayson Boyd would be completely correct.

A hard lump formed in her throat. Maybe the lawsuit *was* the reason he was so attentive. She laughed bitterly at what a cliché she'd nearly become.

She pushed herself away from his desk and swallowed the ache in her throat. She'd better get back to the kitchen before the semolina boiled over.

They were idiots. Lazy French idiots wrapped up in their tiny ministration of justice for crimes no worse than the occasional tourist mugging. Dane patiently told his story to the official gatekeepers, two local policemen. They listened politely and explained that they believed a drunken tourist had killed Genevieve. An impaired driver could have veered around that tight corner and crashed right into the bushes, not even realizing they'd hit someone. Disgusted with them, Dane finally forced his way into the airless office of Georges DeLuque. St. Barts' constable had a condescending attitude and an air of self-importance that far exceeded his meager amount of power. He also weighed about three hundred pounds and struggled with every movement and breath.

In his position, he explained to Dane, he supervised a security force of six policemen and thirteen gendarmes who were sent from France on a two-year tour of duty.

"You see that we do not have an army of law enforcement at our disposal, Monsieur Erikson. This type of investigation will take some time. I will demand it is done properly." DeLuque leaned his girth forward and smiled. "You must understand that."

He needed to go over this fool's head, but nothing was more convoluted than St. Barts' government. The island laws were administered through some half-assed tribunal called a subprefecture on St. Martin, and that rolled up into the government of Guadeloupe, which in turn was run as an overseas department of France. The constable and his band of merry men all answered to the mayor of St. Barts, who was conveniently unavailable.

Dane pleaded his case succinctly, in French. He had reason to believe his ships were involved in transshipments of illegal substances. He suspected Genevieve's death was somehow connected, and he needed the proper drug enforcement authorities to handle an immediate investigation.

"We are blessed to be in a pristine enclave here on St. Barts. Drugs are not a problem," the indolent French bureaucrat insisted.

Dane wanted to kick the desk that separated them. Oh, it was true enough. The enormous sums of money brought in by the world's wealthiest travelers meant St. Barts had virtually none of the drug-related crimes and violence that plagued its poorer neighbors. Until now.

"Was Ms. Giles an addict, perhaps?" the constable asked, as though he already knew the answer.

Dane cut the fat man with a stare.

"Then why do you think there are drugs involved, Monsieur Erikson?"

"I have done some preliminary investigating. I believe my ships are being used to transport drugs. As a result, I'm ceasing all cruises." He refused to tie *Paradisio* to this situation. Not until he had an audience with someone who had a brain.

"Preliminary investigating?" DeLuque chuckled and leaned back, dangerously far, in his swivel chair. "It sounds exciting."

Dane ignored the sarcasm. He'd already explained this to two other morons and no one seemed to appreciate the impact of it. It represented too much goddamned work for them. "I recommend that you contact the U.S. Drug Enforcement Administration—"

DeLuque waved him off. "*Non! Non!* They are cowboys, wild animals with Uzis who raid and kill. *Non.*"

"They are trying to stop drug trafficking in the Caribbean islands." Dane leaned forward, controlling the urge to throttle the bureaucrat's folded neck. He wouldn't get anywhere by ticking this guy off.

"We do not want the world to think we have a drug problem on St. Barts, Monsieur Erikson."

Ah, another motive for doing nothing.

"At least one woman is dead. We do not want the world to think we have a *murder* problem on St. Barts," Dane said. "Especially under your watch as constable."

DeLuque's face reddened. "You have your own 'murders' to deal with, Mr. Erikson. I understand you are being held responsible for the tragic loss of your ship. This is a convenient distraction, is it not? An excellent way to redirect attention away from the charges being made against you."

He should have expected this. DeLuque was either lazy, scared, or already on some Colombian's payroll. Dane rose slowly.

"It would be much easier to expose the bribery and incompetence that seems to have taken over so many of the island law enforcement offices," he said casually. "Perhaps you have very compelling reasons *not* to contact the DEA."

DeLuque lifted his bulk from his seat, straining from the effort. "We will handle an investigation, Monsieur Erikson. We will inspect your ships and interview your employees."

"And the investigation into Genevieve Giles's death?"

"We have alerted all of the car rental vendors to check for damage on returned vehicles. We are carefully examining the scene of the crime. We will interview anyone who may have seen anything."

"Are you searching her home, her office? Looking for clues to the names of contacts she might have within the drug underground?"

DeLuque shook his head as he waddled around his desk and opened the door for Dane. "Don't you worry about how we do our work, Monsieur. I will be in touch with you."

Dane balled his hands into frustrated fists. When he left the constable's office, he found the SUV that Claire had arranged to leave for him. He stuck the key in the ignition and knew exactly where he had to go. He had no idea how he'd enter Genevieve's house without a key but decided he'd figure it out when he got there. At her front door, he realized he'd have no problem entering. Whoever had been there before him conveniently left the door unlocked.

They'd been neat. There were no overturned tables or slashed pillows, just a slight disorder that he knew the efficient and organized Genevieve would never allow.

Looking around the sparse, contemporary rooms, grief hit him again. He couldn't believe she was dead. The guilt that had barely begun to diminish from *Paradisio* flared into an ugly burn in his chest.

Damn, he shouldn't have gone back to the ship for one more night. He should have left Guadeloupe and come straight here. She might still be alive. He walked toward her bedroom, starkly decorated in pure black and white. Beyond the sleeping and dressing areas, he saw the windowed alcove with a sleek black desk, her computer and file cabinets.

Whoever had searched her home made no effort to hide his handiwork in here. All of the file cabinets were open with papers strewn about, her calendar left askew and desk drawers hanging open. What were they looking for? He remembered the computer printout that he'd taken off her desk. Perhaps her reaction that day had less to do with his accidental touch and far more to do with how much she didn't want him to have that paper.

In the files, everything seemed to be related to Utopia. Marketing materials, sales brochures, ad campaigns, Web site updates. He gathered up as much as he could to take home and examine. For a moment the weight of grief, deepened by her invisible presence, pushed down on his shoulders. God, how did this happen?

He had to face the inevitable. He had to call Nat

and Elizabeth Giles. Now, before another moment passed. He didn't know their number, but surely Genevieve had an address book here. He opened a few more desk drawers, then scanned the desktop for a Rolodex, but found nothing. In the top drawer of the nightstand, under a box of tissues and a magazine, he found a slim black leather book. With one glance inside, he realized that it was not an address book but a journal. He closed it immediately. It seemed like such an invasion of privacy.

But perhaps it held answers. Names. Explanations. The privacy of a murdered woman had to be invaded.

He leafed through the pages and began reading. Some entries were curled and feminine in their style, and others were scratched in anger as though written with poisoned ink. But one word appeared in every line, on every page, buried in heated, passionate prose.

Dane. Dane. Dane.

He snapped the cover closed. Genevieve had been obsessively in love with him, and he'd treated it like a schoolgirl crush.

When Dane finally came home, he briefly acknowledged the guests milling about his house, then locked himself in his study for two hours. When he came out, he seemed pensive and angry. Ava longed to confront him and to find out what had happened with the constable, but he'd erected an invisible barrier. He softened only when comforting someone who seemed to be falling apart. He barely spoke to her.

By sunset, nearly everyone had left. They'd been fed, Ava had seen to that. A steady rain added to the dark depression that hung over the house. Dane returned to the study, so she and Marj cleaned the kitchen, put away the food, and restored order throughout the house. The domestic tasks and the sound of Marj's soft humming soothed Ava. But when Marj left, Ava was alone in the house with Dane, and every cell in her body went on alert, waiting for him to find her.

But he didn't. She wanted to wait for the rain to stop before she made her way to the guesthouse that she could see up the hill, but it showed no sign of letting up. Marj had said the keys to the tiny cottage were in the study.

She finally walked the length of the hallway toward the closed door. Taking a deep breath, she knocked lightly.

At his grunted reply, she nudged the door open. A desk lamp provided the only light. She glanced around and found him sprawled on a sofa under an open window, his eyes closed.

"Everyone's gone. I need to get into the guesthouse," she said quietly.

With a slow sigh, he sat up and opened his eyes. He stared at her for a second, a regretful look darkening his face. Then he tapped the seat next to him. "C'mere. I'm sorry."

The leather crunched as she took a seat on the edge of the sofa and frowned at him. "For what?"

"For one thing, leaving you to play hostess to a bunch of people you don't know."

"I just fed them. That was easy." His face looked weary and beat. Still striking, but worry and grief had taken their toll around his eyes and mouth. Her fingers tingled with the urge to touch the tiny lines and soothe them away. She clasped her hands on her lap. "When are you going to tell me what happened today?"

He fell back and rubbed his eyes. "I hit a few more brick walls."

"I'd really like to hear about them."

"The constable's an asshole—pardon my French. And then I spent hours tangled in DEA red tape, only to learn that the guy I need is based in Trinidad and on some special assignment right now." He finally looked directly at her. "I'm beginning to wonder if anyone really cares about drug running around here."

The apathy in his voice jarred her. "These people are killers, Dane."

"And they probably know I have more information than I ought to. I'm rethinking your being here at all, frankly."

A sharp breath caught in her throat. "Do you think they'll just show up here and come in and kill us?"

He smiled a little. "They'll ring the doorbell first."

He must have sensed her horror, since he immediately sat up and reached for her. He put his hands on her shoulders and pulled her toward him on the sofa. "Don't worry, princess."

Electrical shocks jolted her and she stiffened, backing away with a little more force than she needed. No, no. She would not fall into his arms on this sofa, in this study.

He smiled apologetically. "You looked so terrified."

Of you. "Well, it's not a pretty thought. Murder."

"Nothing's pretty right now, I'm afraid." He dropped his head back and closed his eyes. "I just had to tell the man who's the closest thing I had to a father that his granddaughter is dead."

Heartache crossed his face again, as it had on the way back from the airport. The poor man had been kicked hard lately.

"I feel completely lousy," he admitted. His powerful tan hands ran through his hair, tousling it into disarray. "Completely empty."

Here it comes, she thought. *I need you. I want you.* She had to stop it before he got her. Before those hands were working on her. "Empty? You're hungry."

He chuckled at the statement, eyes still closed.

"I bet you haven't eaten all day," she added, certain of her tack now.

"No, I haven't." He opened his eyes and smiled sheepishly at her. "But not everything can be cured with food, I'm afraid."

"Everything is better on a full stomach. That's what Grandma Rose says." She stood and took his hand. She'd be safer on her own turf. At the stove, in front of a cutting board. This darker Dane in a rare moment of vulnerability could be her undoing.

He let her pull him up. "I did smell something quite good when I walked in. Like a real Italian kitchen."

She nodded knowingly. "That's the basil. Come on. Let me feed you."

In the kitchen, Dane settled on the bar stool with a glass of wine and suppressed the guilty sensations that teased him. At a time like this, it felt sinfully wrong to be so comforted by this woman. He should be mourning, researching, tearing his world apart for answers. Instead, he watched Ava Santori move gracefully around his kitchen, her cropped yellow top revealing her tight waist when she reached for something, a kitchen towel hanging from the pocket of her shorts.

He couldn't resist the blanket of warmth she threw over his whole house with tempting aromas of food and the gentle, feminine act of cooking. It eased the ache in his chest.

And Arnot was right. She *was* talented. She chopped scallions with lightning speed and sautéed them as the flames danced around a pan he didn't even know he had. She deglazed and blackened and seasoned and stirred without a pause between each step, all confidence and concentration. Desire stirred low and strong as he absently ran a finger along the crystal rim and let the fruit and oak aroma of the cabernet tickle his nose.

"I went to Genevieve's house after I left the constable's," he said without thinking. He hadn't realized how much he needed to share it with her.

She looked up from the pan. "What did you find?"

"That someone else had already been there." He took a sip of wine. "And I guess I confirmed what you told me a while ago."

Her hands froze as she waited for him to finish.

"That she was . . . in love with me."

Silently, she designed a plate, artistically laying a piece of blackened fish over greens and angling vegetables around the dish. She finished the work and set it down in front of him.

"Her feelings can't come as a great revelation to you, Dane," she said, pushing the plate closer. "*Mangia.*"

"Aren't you going to eat?" he asked.

She shook her head. "I already did. I'll just watch. You're not an unattractive man."

He raised an eyebrow and a faint flush covered her cheeks.

"I meant to Genevieve. You two would have made a great couple."

He took a bite, savoring the flavor and considering how to respond. "God, this is fantastic. I can't believe you just pulled this together."

She smiled and leaned against the island behind her, looking the closest thing to cocky he'd seen since the day he met her on the docks. "So. How long is the string?"

"Excuse me?"

"Of broken hearts you leave behind."

It was his turn to feel the heat of a flush. "Not that long—honestly. I've never intentionally hurt anyone, Ava. I just don't get into long-term relationships." He took another bite, not wanting to talk about his failed love affairs, but she deserved some explanation.

He wiped his mouth with a napkin. "I get bored quickly. Probably some deep psychological response to my pathetic rich kid childhood, raised by parents who were never around and shuffled me off to boarding schools."

Her dubious look said she wasn't buying it.

"Or I'm just a cynical, selfish son of a bitch who can't make a commitment." Her dimple deepened with the hint of a smile and he took heart in it. "Which do you think?"

"Probably a combination of both." She turned to busy herself with the pans on the stove while he ate the delicate fish and fresh vegetables, liberally complimenting her between bites.

She wiped a counter thoroughly before she picked

up the subject again. "Do you think that's why Genevieve did it? The drug running, I mean. To get back at you for not . . . for not wanting her?"

He set his fork down and nodded, having already thought of that. "Possibly. Probably."

"Did she ever tell you how she felt?"

"Sort of. Not too long ago." He finished the last bites and stood to take his plate to the sink. He didn't want to share Genevieve's clumsy attempt at seduction. "I wasn't too responsive."

They cleaned up together in silence, then he picked up his unfinished glass of wine and dimmed the kitchen lights.

"Great dinner, maestro. Do you want me to get you settled in your room now? It's the first one on the left down that hall." At her look of surprise, he added, "It's too wet to trudge up the hill. Or perhaps I could convince you to sit in the living room and talk to me some more."

She put both hands on the counter and stared at him. "Talk. Only."

He smiled and nodded. "Deal."

She curled into a collection of throw pillows in the corner of a long sofa. He toyed with the thought of lying down next to her and just holding her, for the pure solace she offered. But he didn't want to scare her away. He knew he wouldn't sleep tonight, and the longer she stayed up with him, the less lonely he'd be throughout the night.

He touched the remote for his sound system and added some soft classical music to the room, then settled in across from her in an overstuffed chair. He thought of all the things that he wanted to ask her, all the subjects that would keep his mind off the sad places it wanted to go.

"Tell me about Dominic," he said. "And why you never call him Daddy."

She gave a surprised laugh. "*Daddy*. Gee, I haven't called him that since I was about nine. Dominic is Dominic. He's not the 'daddy' type. Plus, in the kitchen, I like to be professional and not his little girl. What do you want to know about him?"

"Is he a tyrant?"

She smiled. "No. He's not a tyrant. He's a control freak and a creative genius. Combined with a volatile temper and passionate nature."

"So, you take after him."

She laughed a little at the tease. "He's my dad. I have to defend him, right? Really, he's not a bad guy. He runs a great restaurant and an amazing add-on business with the show and books. I guess he heads up a fairly good family. We've . . . got our problems, like all families."

"Have you ever thought of leaving the restaurant?" He crossed his ankles as he watched her nervously toy with the fringe of the pillow.

"Sometimes. I have a bit of the wanderlust that Marco had, but I keep those desires in check. Santori's will be my life, I expect." She sounded less than enthusiastic about it.

"Is that what you want?"

"Sometimes family tradition is just the burden you bear. Or the privilege you inherit." She smoothed the fabric of the pillow. "Depends on how you look at it."

"Definitely a burden for me," he said. "One I didn't want."

"Why not?"

He shook his head. "My father is also a control freak, but with none of your Italian passion. He's ice cold like the country his ancestors came from, and my mother isn't much better. Our household was all about business and money and social climbing. I couldn't get away from that world fast enough."

"So you made a family here."

He nearly choked on the idea. "Hardly. I think we've already covered my problems with commitments."

She put the pillow aside and leaned toward him, a spark in her eyes. "You're so wrong, Dane. I stood among your family today. Black and brown and white. French and Anguillan and Jamaican. They all came to you. You're the head of the family."

A rush of pure, warm pleasure shot through him at her insight.

"You have no problem with commitments," she added softly. "You just have problems with women."

And maybe he just hadn't met the right one. An overpowering desire to fold her into his arms and wrap himself in her black curls twisted his gut. With a will he didn't know he could muster, he leaned back and set his chin in his hand. "Now tell me about your mother. You call *her* Mama."

"I had no idea you noticed all these things," she said, kicking off her shoes and gracefully extending her lovely legs on his sofa.

"I notice everything." He let his gaze sweep the length of her body, and he reached deep down for the fortitude to remain in his seat. He couldn't wrap his legs around the curve of her hips. He couldn't run his hands inside that little top and touch what had already teased him. He couldn't sink his mouth into the valley between her luscious breasts and inhale the gentle musky fragrance of her. Holy hell. He shifted in his seat and willed his arousal away.

"You'd better keep talking, princess. It's going to be a long night."

She shot him a dimpled grin. "Okay. I'll tell you about Mama."

"And Grandma," he prompted. "Rose, is it?"

"Oh, yes. I'm named after her," she said with obvious pride. "Ava Rose. I love her to pieces."

Into the night, they shared their stories. Ava described the saintlike Maggie Santori and her subtle Irish influence over the colorful Italian clan she'd married into. She told him about wise Grandma Rose, who kept peanuts in her apron pocket and actually held the title of Grand Cinderella in something called the Order Sons of Italy. He choked in laughter as her animated, feminine hands flew in gestures, describing her family in Boston and the history of the restaurant that the Santoris had owned for nearly a century.

In return, he offered a rare glimpse into the world of the dysfunctional Eriksons, which was so different from her childhood. He'd known only a series of changing hotel suites, nannies, and boarding schools. They hadn't even wanted a child, and he knew from the time he was a little boy that there would be no brothers or sisters for him to take under his wing. Only Nat and Elizabeth Giles, who were really just strangers who'd befriended him as a young man, had provided anything like a family life.

That seemed to sadden her, so he changed the subject, and they talked about sailing and cooking and the highs and lows of owning a business. And of course, they shared their memories of Marco, which brought her tears but also smiles.

About an hour before sunrise, she fell asleep, her arms wrapped tightly around the throw pillow.

He was still in his chair.

13

Max Roper wanted to spit on the French scum who sat across from him in the tiny interrogation room, puffing on a cigarette and refusing to speak the English he certainly knew. Dombrowsky had been browbeating the kid for two hours, and he was scared shitless but still not talking. In any language.

The raid had been even better than Max had imagined.

The quantity and quality of what they found confirmed the site as a central transshipment point. Deliveries had come from all over the Caribbean, earmarked for Haiti, Puerto Rico, and Miami. Some of it had been stored in containerized cargo from freighters, other cartons had been air-dropped. Multikilo quantities had been hidden in secret compartments of expensive luggage. Several shipments, his personal favorites, had been creatively concealed in cases of food and spices.

Since the Grenadians still loved Americans for saving their asses from Castro back in the 1980s, the locals offered some space in their pathetic little precinct station to use as jail cells and interrogation rooms. The poor slobs didn't even have concrete on all the floors, but they spoke English and made coffee and had a working phone system. It was all Max and his little crew needed to get the job done.

Max spent all day and all night with four of the six goons they found baby-sitting the warehouse, but they told him little that he didn't already know. This French kid, though, he was hiding something. This one had potential.

"You ever been in jail, kid?" Max spun the used ashtray in circles, not looking directly at his target.

"Je ne comprends pas."

He didn't understand. Max would bet a bunch that he did.

"You're going to rot in one, my man. You are going today. No one's going to fly up from Colombia and save your French butt."

A shadow crossed the young, tough face. He definitely spoke English.

"Of course," Max said slowly, still twirling the ashtray. "We might be able to arrange something else for you."

Their gazes locked.

Jack Wilson stuck his head in the door and signaled for Max, who leaned closer to the stinky kid. "Think about it, *garçon.*"

Max closed the door to the room and spat on the dirt floor. Little French bastard. " 'Sup?"

"We ran an ID on this one. He's been picked up twice in Paris for dealing and left the country about four months ago to work on some cruise ship."

Max nodded. Could be something there. Who would hire a known dealer to work on a cruise ship, but someone who wanted to use him to do what he did best? It was a clue to the high-quality luggage and possibly the crates of spices.

"But there's something else."

"What?" A flicker of anticipation burned in Max's belly at the look on Wilson's face.

"The owner of that very same cruise line called every damn DEA office in the Caribbean and Miami yesterday to report some illegal drug deliveries being made from his ships."

Max scratched his day-old beard. "He called to report *what?*"

"According to the Port of Spain office, he's left urgent messages for you."

"Who is he?"

Wilson nodded, as if expecting the question. "Erikson. Dane Erikson. Owns a bunch of fancy passenger sailing ships out of St. Barts. Utopia Adventures."

"Utopia?" Max frowned. "Didn't they just lose a ship in the hurricane? I read about it. Twenty-some crewmen died in the storm."

"Want us to call the guy?"

Max glanced at the door to the interrogation room. His gut was on fire and it wasn't the lousy coffee he'd been drinking. It was intuition. "No. Could scare him into hiding. He could be a missing link, a mole, a decoy. Who knows? Get some agents to pick him up and get him here. Maybe PePe LePuke will talk to his boss."

Dane covered Ava with a blanket just as he heard the engine in his driveway. She stirred and turned into the wool with a soft moan. He tucked back a strand of long, dark hair that had fallen over her cheek.

Before someone could ring the bell and wake her, he went to the door and peered out the glass side-light. Two clean-cut white men in oxford shirts and long pants were getting out of a Gurgel. They didn't look like drug mafia. They looked like preppies with an attitude. He walked out to meet them.

"Can I help you?"

"Are you Dane Erikson?" The taller one looked directly at him while the other one surreptitiously checked out the house. At Dane's nod, they both reached into their jackets, and for a millisecond Dane wondered if he'd made a mistake and was about to be shot. ID badges with giant red letters came out instead of guns. DEA.

"Special Agent Quinn MacPherson," one of them identified himself.

"It's about time," Dane said, looking from one to the other. "Do you have men at the ships already?"

They ignored the question, and the agent named MacPherson stepped closer to him. "Mr. Erikson, do you know a man by the name of Jacques Basille?"

A body. They must have found Basille's body. "I did."

MacPherson lifted his brows. "Did?"

"He's dead." Dane closed his arms across his chest. "He went down in a shipwreck off the coast of Grenada in the hurricane last month. What's this about? Are you here for an investigation of my ships?"

With a deepening frown, MacPherson shook his head. "He's not dead. He's in a jail cell in Sauteurs, Grenada."

Dane felt every ounce of blood drain from his head.

"That's impossible," he choked. "He was on a ship

that went down in Hurricane Carlos. He was one of twenty-one men who died."

"Maybe only twenty," MacPherson said with a shrug. "We need you to come with us, Mr. Erikson. Now."

A spark of hope ignited. "Is he by himself? Were there others . . . others from Utopia with Basille?"

"Others, but not with the same background checks." The agent looked down at Dane's feet. "You probably want to get some shoes on, Mr. Erikson. We're leaving in five minutes for Grenada." A piercing gaze sent his message. "With you."

"Do you realize I've been trying to reach you guys for twelve hours?" he barked at them. "I'm on your side, for Christ's sake."

The other agent finally spoke in a gruff tone. "Let's go, Mr. Erikson."

Ava. He couldn't leave her here alone, and she certainly wasn't going to some town in Grenada. "I want someone to watch the house. I've got a houseguest and I think we might be in danger."

"We're not bodyguards, Mr. Erikson." MacPherson's words were delivered with more than a hint of malice. "We're here to get you to Grenada. You have five minutes."

The other agent took a step to follow Dane into the house.

"Look." Dane turned on him and pointed his finger in his chest. "I'm coming with you. You don't need to coerce me. Let me take care of something in here and I'll be out with three minutes to spare."

Without a word, the agents backed up and Dane went into his house. From the study, he telephoned Claire to get people to the house to stay with Ava.

Then, he crouched on the floor next to the sofa and set a gentle hand on her shoulder. "Wake up, princess."

Her dark lashes fluttered and lifted.

"I have to leave."

A flash of fear crossed her face, but she hid it immediately. "Okay. Where are you going?"

He couldn't possibly give her hope that might be dashed so badly that she'd have to start mourning Marco all over again. Anyway, he had no idea where he was going.

"To the *Paradisio* search and rescue command center." It wasn't too far from Grenada, he rationalized. Just twenty miles off the coast.

She started to sit up. "Did they find something?"

"No, yes. Maybe." He tugged the blanket up to her shoulders. "You just stay here. Some people from Utopia will be here any minute. You'll never be alone."

"What did they find?"

He looked away, hating to lie right into her gorgeous, trusting eyes. "A body."

She sucked in air. "Was it—"

"We don't know who it is," he said hurriedly. "I'm going to make an identification. I'll call you."

"What about the ships? The investigation?"

"Just stay here, *please*." He cupped her delicate jaw. "Ava, please don't leave. Don't try to take matters into your own hands."

A slight frown deepened her eyebrows. "Sometimes I can't help it."

He leaned across the small space between them and kissed her cheek softly, willing her to listen to him. "My woman of action. Please stay put until I call you."

She touched the spot on her cheek where his lips had been. "I'll try," she whispered.

"Promise?"

She just smiled and closed her eyes.

She couldn't have broken the promise if she'd wanted to. Within minutes, Utopians started to arrive. Ava found the guest room with her bag in it, then she showered and dressed for another day of waiting and wondering. Two sleepless nights had taken their toll. The shadows under her eyes were nearly black and her skin looked drawn and pale. Some vacation in paradise, she thought wryly as she brushed her hair.

"Hello, luv. You in there?"

"Cassie!" Ava threw the brush on the bathroom counter and flung open the door into the bedroom. "What are you doing here?" She embraced the tiny woman with a flood of relief.

"The ships have been called back, don't you know?"

"Yes, of course," Ava answered. "But it was so fast."

Cassie sat down on the queen-size bed. "No kidding. We spun around and motored back like a race was on. We've got some very unhappy passengers in Gustavia, I can tell you that. They're still trying to sort it all out, but I came to find Dane as soon as I heard."

"He's gone to the search site. He said they found a body."

"Oh, God." Cassie put her head in her hands and sighed from her heart.

Ava sat next to her and wrapped a comforting arm around her. "Are you okay? Do you feel all right?"

Cassie smiled and put her hand on her tummy. "Yes. But Junior's moving, Ava. I thought it was a bit of gas, then I realized it must be a wee foot or hand!"

"Oh!" Ava brightened and put her hand on Cassie's stomach as well.

"He evidently doesn't like solid ground, since I've felt it about six times since I got off the ship."

They laughed at the marvel of it, but the mood disappeared quickly. "Dear Lord, it's so horrible about Genevieve," Cassie groaned. "What is going on in our little company? Are we cursed?"

"Evidently, quite a lot is going on in your little company," Ava ventured. She needed to talk to someone. That didn't break her promise.

Cassie frowned. "What are you talking about?"

"Drugs."

"What?"

"Someone's been shipping drugs on Utopia cruises, Cassie. I . . . we . . . think it might have had something to do with *Paradisio*. And Genevieve."

Cassie froze; her jaw dropped in complete shock. "What? What are you talking about?"

Ava told Cassie everything she knew. It was sheer relief to unburden herself to a willing and attentive audience. She relayed the conversation she'd overheard, described the trip to the crack house, and highlighted Dane's discoveries in Guadeloupe. She even told her of the knife in her bed.

"I had no idea anything was going on. I'm sure if Marco suspected, he would have told me." Cassie began to pace the room. "Who could it be, Ava? Who are the drug runners within Utopia? I know and trust everyone."

"Cassie, who could have gotten into my cabin to stick that knife in the headboard?"

Cassie crossed her arms. "Just about anyone, luv. It's a well-kept secret in the business, but master keys are frightfully simple to come by. Even the Owner's Suite, I'm afraid. You've got to keep the chain lock on while you're in there, and when you're gone . . . who knows?"

"How about Spanish-speaking crewmen? On *Valhalla?*"

"Dozens of them." She leaned back against an antique dresser, deep in thought. "I don't want to say anything bad about the dead, but Genevieve always hated Marco. She was as jealous as a mad cat of anyone who spent time with Dane. Consequently, she had it in for Marco. She'd have done anything to see him leave this company."

"Really? Was she that bad?" Ava tucked her legs under her and studied Cassie. "She seemed so self-assured and, I don't know, poised."

"Raised with money, yes. But self-assured?" Cassie shook her head. "I always thought she was a bit touched, if you know what I mean. And Dane was blind to it."

"Why?"

"Well, she did an awesome job of marketing the company and managing the details when it got too big for one person to handle. And he's always felt he owed his entire success to her grandfather. I suppose it was best for him to try to ignore her . . . eccentricities."

"He wouldn't ignore suspicions of drug running," Ava said, defending him.

"No. But he refused to face the fact that she followed him around like a lovesick puppy and turned into an evil witch every time he took up with another woman."

Ava's heart sank at the comment. "How often was that?" she asked casually.

"Oh, I guess not that often. But enough to make life hell for the staff of Utopia where Genevieve was concerned."

"How . . . how long did they last? These women?"

Cassie's face softened as she looked at Ava and then pointedly at the bed that had obviously not been slept in. "Oh, boy. Too late for you, huh?"

Ava fought a guilty smile. "No, it's not like that."

"Oh, darlin'. You are so wrong. It *is* like that."

Ava shook her head in a denial she didn't know how to voice.

"He is an attractive man." Cassie dropped next to Ava on the bed, taking her hands. "And he's good as gold, really. It's just that . . ."

"What?" She wasn't at all sure she wanted to know.

"I don't want to see you fall for him and get hurt."

It had been a long night in the living room. During it, she began to understand the influences that had shaped him as he let her peek into his heart and head. She began to appreciate his deliberate and method-ical approach to situations. And the entire time, she saw him fight the same overwhelming physical urges that plagued her.

"Too late, luv?"

Ava just smiled wistfully, unwilling to admit that she was in danger of falling hard for Dane Erikson.

The discomfort of a turbulent two-hour flight in a rickety government plane followed by a forty-five-minute drive through the mud and mountains of Grenada numbed Dane's sleep-deprived body. He tried to let it do the same to his mind, but it wouldn't stop. He could think of nothing but the remote and outrageous possibility that *Paradisio* had survivors.

His traveling companions said little to him. He couldn't shake the feeling that MacPherson and Dombrowsky were treating him as a suspect, albeit with kid gloves. Dane concentrated on the sunrise over the Caribbean and thought through every imaginable scenario. How the hell did Jacques Basille get to Grenada?

He remembered the moment he and Stuart O'Rourke made the decision to keep the cook onboard. Every single crewman left on *Paradisio* had a critical role. Feeding them while they got back to safety was critical too, he'd argued with the captain. In the end, when the list of twenty-one was complete, Basille had made the cut. Since then, Dane had a hard time looking at Philippe Basille, sensing the anger from Jacques's cousin.

Maybe not anger, Dane thought with a start. Maybe fear. Maybe guilt.

The truck rumbled into a quiet village and stopped at one of the rundown buildings on the main street. Wordlessly, they got out, and the agents took a position on either side of Dane. He fought the urge to shove them each away, keeping his arms at his sides as they entered what appeared to be a police headquarters, jail, and courthouse combination. His gut tightened.

In a dimly lit entranceway, a solid bull of a man leaned against a worn metal desk, handling a Glock as though the weapon were a toy. His deep brown eyes met Dane's, and the two assessed each other silently. He was easily Dane's own height of six feet, maybe a little more, with broad, square shoulders and a muscular neck. His clean-cut black hair revealed a few salted strands. A fierce shadow from a couple

days' growth of whiskers toughened what would probably be a passably good-looking face. His square jaw
was set tightly as his gaze traveled over Dane.

"Mr. Erikson." He stuck the gun into his shoulder
holster. "I'm Max Roper. Nice of you to come on such
short notice."

"I tried calling first," Dane said dryly. "I want to
see Basille."

Roper nodded but made no move. "Why were you
calling me?"

"Does the name Estaphan Calliope mean anything
to you?"

Roper rubbed his whiskers, his dark brown gaze
steady and clear. "It could."

"Let's not play games, Roper. I'm not your man.
I don't deal in drugs; I run a cruise business. But I
seem to have let a few of the wrong people work for
me, and I'd like to help you stop it."

"That's fine, Mr. Erikson. But I have a few questions for you."

Dane felt the muscles in his neck tense. He inhaled
a calming breath before he spoke. "I want to go see
the son of a bitch who I thought was dead with
twenty other of my men, and find out what the hell
happened to them. Then I will answer all of your
goddamn questions."

"Why'd you think he was dead?"

"We lost contact with the ship when it was close to
a hurricane. We never found so much as a piece of
wood from it after weeks of searching the area. The
U.S. Coast Guard has classified all remaining crew as
presumed dead."

Roper grinned. "Those guys have been known to
presume wrong."

Dane shot a look that matched Roper's sarcastic tone. "That's what I'm hoping to find out."

"Are you?" Roper crossed his arms. "I understand some people think you navigated the ship into the storm. Perhaps you wanted it lost for some reason? Insurance money? To pay off drug debts?"

If he hadn't been so anxious to get to Basille, Dane would have laughed. "Roper, you got the wrong goddamned man. I don't know who you're looking for, but I might be able to help. Want to let me?"

Roper's solid block of shoulders relaxed a little. "I want to know where the rest of the transshipment points are and who's the top guy in the Caribbean behind this. If you can get him to tell you what happened to your ship, that's fine. But the first two things are what I really care about."

Dane reached into his pocket and handed Genevieve's list to the agent. "Here are your transshipment points. Let me talk to him and I'll find out the rest."

After Cassie left, Ava was too emotionally drained to make small talk with the few Utopians who wandered about. Marj showed up early and busied herself with chores. She didn't seem to mind Ava's browsing through the bookshelves in Dane's study.

His reading collection was eclectic. Very little fiction, but a vast range of biographies, history books, and a full shelf of world geography. There were literally dozens of books on legends and superstitions, maritime history and tall ships.

On his desk, she saw papers that hadn't been there when she called Grayson Boyd the day before, and she glanced at the typewritten labels on a precarious stack of files. *Celestia Sales Brochure/Euro Version. Ad Copy/Nirvana. Personnel/Valhalla.* The last one grabbed her attention and she gingerly slid it from the pile.

The file contained job descriptions and the names of all crewmen. She perused the list, looking for a clue. An idea. Anything. There were none. She set the folder on top of the others and started fanning through the next one. With a whoosh, the entire stack fluttered off his desk.

"Damn." She knelt to pick them up when she noticed that on the desk, under one folder that had not fallen, lay a sleek leather book. Without thinking, Ava lifted it up and opened it. A twinge of guilt tickled her, but she stifled it as soon as she recognized a woman's handwriting.

Dane's acting like nothing happened. I'll pretend I was drunk. He thought I was a little tipsy. Drunk with lust. He didn't even touch me. He wouldn't put his hands on my breasts. I practically stuck his face there. He never stopped talking. Even when I touched him. He wasn't hard. He can't even get a fucking hard-on for me. He buttoned my blouse and walked me out. I hate Dane Erikson. I hate Dane Erikson. I love him so much that I hate him.

A sickening wave rolled through Ava. Nothing, no power on earth could make her close the book. She flipped through more pages. The handwriting changed. It was curved and sweet, almost as though a teenager had written it.

* * *

He laughed with me today. We stayed late to finish the final cuts for the TV commercials and he made jokes about the models and we just laughed until we cried. I must run to him now. I hope he's alone. I love him more than ever.

The next page was scratched, written with hate. Uneven and shaky, like a drunk.

That whore redhead model is back. She arrived today. No wonder he made jokes about the models. He knew he'd be fucking one. They are locked in his castle. I saw the lights. In his bedroom. He will be inside the bitch. In her red fucking hair. I hate her.

Ava's hands shook as much as Genevieve's must have when she wrote the words. The ink blurred in front of her eyes. She leafed to the last few entries, afraid of what she'd find but unable to stop.

This is the last one. The last one I have to watch. The black-eyed bitch from Boston. That stupid jerk's sister. I'm glad he's dead. I'm glad they're all dead. Even though it brought her here. Now he has to fuck her, too. To shut her up and get rid of her smarmy lawyer. I saw her there tonight. Laughing in the driveway, getting his playful kisses. Then she drove right past me. Too bad I won't get to watch little miss Ava whimper home after he's done with her. I'll be long gone by then.

She slammed the book shut and dropped it on the desk as though it burned her. Genevieve had watched her. Had seen her in his driveway. Laughed at her. Hated her.

An uncontrollable shiver shook her body, and Ava just stood in the middle of the study and let it knock her to the bones.

Max Roper couldn't decide who had the more shocked look on his face. The pretty boy Erikson, who looked at Basille like he was a ghost, or poor little Jacques. *His* expression was one for the books. Clearly, he hadn't expected this visitor.

Max grudgingly gave Dane Erikson credit. He didn't lunge at the kid or demand the information he wanted; he let it happen slowly. He was a cool son of a bitch. Max wondered if he was cool enough to be the Cali middleman. His gut said no, but he wasn't completely ready to rule it out.

"We buried you, Basille," Dane said with no preliminaries. "It was a really nice service."

Jacques cringed and glanced guiltily at Max before he answered in excellent English. "I'm . . . I'm sorry, Dane."

"Yeah, me too." Dane took a chair across from the kid. "Your mother came from France. And, of course, your cousin Philippe. They were real broken up."

"Yeah."

"What the hell is going on, Jacques?" Dane leaned forward. "How'd you manage to jump ship?"

Jacques inhaled slowly, looking for his pack of cigarettes. Dane grabbed them and tossed them to the opposite end of the table. The kid trembled, and Max bit back a smile of mild respect.

"Don't lie to me," he warned.

Jacques looked squarely at Dane but said nothing.

Max stayed standing in the corner, waiting for one of them to make the next move.

"What happened to the ship?" Dane asked softly.

Max cleared his throat. *Remember our agreement, Erikson. Names first, confessions later.*

Jacques leaned forward and whispered, "Do you think I can make some kind of deal, Mr. Erikson?"

"Depends, Jacques. How much can you tell these guys?"

"A little, I guess. Only what Philippe told me. I don't know who he worked for. I know some of the other runners. I know where we picked stuff up and hid the stash. I just got paid to make deliveries."

Max knew it was probably true. One of the hallmarks of the traffickers was to keep walls between the layers of people so that they couldn't reveal the names of the higher-ups. They didn't know them.

"Were you going to make the delivery in Grenada?" Dane asked quietly.

"Yeah. I had to. That's why . . . that's why . . ."

"What?" Dane urged him.

"I got off the ship before it exploded."

"What?" Max watched Dane jerk back in his chair as though he'd been hit. "Before it *what?*"

"It exploded." Jacques choked, his eyes filling as he fought frightened tears. "Can I make some kind of deal. Now, sir?"

Max stepped in and sat beside the stunned cruise line owner. "We can make a deal, Basille. Who were you working for?"

"How did the ship explode?" Dane demanded.

"Gimme a name, Basille."

"Did anyone else get off with you?"

Jacques looked from one to the other.

Dane leaned across the table and grabbed Jacques's shirt, spitting venom as he repeated his question. "Did anyone else get off the ship, Jacques?"

Jacques nodded, then shook his head, and Dane yanked the kid's collar again.

"Y—yes. But he's dead. He was . . . shot. I left him passed out in some alley in St. George's as the hurricane hit."

"Who was it?"

"The second mate. Santori."

They practically had to tie Dane down. He'd looked at the other men they'd arrested and recognized none of them, dashing his hopes that more crewmen had survived. Now all he wanted to do was get to St. George's.

"You're done with me, for Christ's sake," Dane growled at the two burly DEA agents who held him like some kind of criminal. "You got what you want. I want to get the hell out of here."

"Just wait for Agent Roper," MacPherson said. "He'll be out in a few minutes."

Marco was in St. George's.

Dead or alive. Shot in the leg, Jacques admitted, in a tussle they had on board. But *not* at the bottom of the Caribbean Sea. Dane almost burst with the knowledge; a tiny spark of hope kept flaring up inside of him. But if Marco were alive, he would have called or come home by now. Unless he was in on the drug trafficking?

No. Dane rejected the possibility immediately. Jacques's story about the explosion was rife with lies. The punk knew a lot more than he was telling, but Dane doubted that anyone else had gotten off the ship. He suspected there was more to Jacques's story of leaving Marco in St. George's. Maybe he'd killed Marco before he left him. Or just figured the storm would kill Marco, who couldn't walk from the "accidental" gunshot. Four hundred people had died in the destruction of Hurricane Carlos; he had to accept that Marco might be among them.

But *Paradisio*, it seemed, would never be found.

An explosion, for Christ's sake. What could have caused it to explode? Lightning, fire, dynamite, a bomb—Jacques knew, but wasn't saying. He claimed that once he learned the ship would not sail to Grenada, he'd held Marco at gunpoint and forced him onto a launch to help get him to the island. Then, after they got off, *Paradisio* had mysteriously exploded. That part of the story sounded like bullshit. No doubt Jacques thought he'd get off easier without adding mass murder to his rap sheet.

No wonder the search team hadn't found anything. The crew had been subjected to a completely different kind of hell. Blown apart and burned. Maybe, Dane prayed, it was faster than being crushed by mountains of waves and strangled by the wind and sea.

He erased the image. "When is he going to be finished in there?" It ticked him off that Roper hadn't let him stay in the room. He wanted to know who, beyond Philippe Basille, was in on this. Then he wanted to find the bastard and kill him with his own bare hands.

Finally, Roper opened the door.

"Let me outta here, Roper," Dane demanded. "You're done with me. I've got to find someone."

Roper stared at him. "How you plannin' to do that? You don't have a car or a clue, Erikson."

"I'll figure it out. Just let me go." Dane's body burned with the need to go, to find out the truth. To tear what was left of St. George's apart until he found Marco and took him—or his body—home.

Roper smiled and gave him a skeptical once-over. "What are you going to do, charm your way around?" He touched his holster. "You won't get far without help."

Dane's fists balled up, along with the knot in his stomach.

Roper leaned over to the two agents. "Get a team in St. Barts prepped for a full search and sting. We don't have time to go under. But don't alert the locals yet, or the crew. Just surround the ships quietly."

"I've already alerted the locals, Roper," Dane interjected. "You don't have to worry about them beating you to the punch; they're asleep. And by now there are no passengers or crew left on the ships. Just their baggage."

Roper looked up to meet Dane's piercing gaze. "Seems you've been very busy, Mr. Erikson."

"I wanted to be ready for your visit."

They continued to stare at each other, then Roper turned back to the other agent. "Have a plane ready for me at Pearls by noon to fly to St. Barts. First, I gotta make a quick trip down south."

"I don't need an escort, Roper. Just let me out of here."

"It'll take the better part of an hour to get there. You've got two hours in St. George's and then we turn around and leave." Roper grinned at Dane as he kicked open the flimsy door of the precinct. "So, we'll have a little time to get to know each other."

14

Ava fell into a chair, and picked up the journal, willing herself to stop shaking. *Calm. Down. Ava.* She could hear Dane's voice say the words.

Or would he shrug and say he couldn't be held responsible for some nutty stalker who thought she loved him? Would he remind her with his sexy grin that he couldn't be crucified for romancing redhead models, as the entries had detailed? Oh, he'd be right, she admitted grudgingly. He was young, single, and virile, God knows. And he clearly hadn't done anything to encourage Genevieve.

She picked up the journal again, compelled to read more. Who was this woman who'd loved and hated Dane with such passion, and why had she betrayed him? Ava wanted to know her, to understand her. She opened the cover and ran her hand over the first page. How many times had Genevieve held this book, aching for emotional relief and finding solace in her own words? Ava closed her eyes and pictured the cool blond with haunting gray eyes and porcelain skin. Icy and cold. Perhaps that's why Dane wasn't attracted to her. He'd described his parents that way.

Ava ran her fingers along the cover, connecting to the woman who bared her broken dreams on these pages. She should hate Genevieve, but pity was all she could muster.

She pressed her hand hard against the little book, knowing that, in a weird way, she sympathized with the woman more than condemned her. But something felt . . .

She jerked the journal up for closer inspection. The first page was glued to the inside cover, and underneath it, she felt a round, flat disk slightly larger than her palm, artfully concealed inside. She switched on the desk lamp and held the open book under it, her fingernail digging at the raised paper, tracing the circular shape beneath it.

In Dane's top drawer she found a letter opener. Sliding it along the glued edge, she broke the seal between the paper and the leather. She tore at the paper carefully, then turned the book upside down with a little shake. A silver compact disc slid onto the desk.

Ava stared at it, then picked it up with two fingers. A computer disk. There was no label or identification. Her heart started to pound. *Calm. Down. Ava.* It might hold anything. For all she knew, it could be music Genevieve played when she wrote in her journal.

But something told Ava it wasn't. She found his laptop on the floor, leaning against the desk, and prayed Dane would own one advanced enough to have a CD drive. Flipping it open, she felt around the sides. Yes. A long, thin drive. Power on. A flash of confirmation. *Please enter password.* She tapped the desk in frustration. *Mother of God!*

She jammed the CD in the side slot anyway. After a quick whispered whir, the password screen disappeared and a block of file names came up. One for every island—St. Kitts, St. Lucia, Antigua, Guadeloupe, Nevis, Anguilla, Barbados, Dominica, and more. With her fingertip, Ava guided a spongy red button to the word *Guadeloupe* and hit Enter.

A spreadsheet. At the top it read "E. Calliope" and then listed random words: *duckweed, piedmont, greyhound.* Code names? Throughout the grid of the spreadsheet, she saw numbers and dates. They meant nothing to her. She closed the file and went back to the main screen of island names. She tried St. Kitts. At the top was the name O. Molinet. The rest looked exactly the same as the first. She tried two more files, similar but with different names and numbers. Nothing recognizable except Calliope, the contact Dane had "met" in Guadeloupe.

Going back to the program file one more time, she scrolled to the bottom. There was one unnamed file. Just a square icon, indicating a "Word" document. Ava clicked on it, hoping for something enlightening.

And that's exactly what she got. The document was an orderly schedule of times, dates, cruises, addresses, and names of couriers. She scanned the list, her hands shaking as adrenaline pumped through her body.

The first name she recognized was Jacques Basille. That was Philippe's cousin, she remembered, killed on *Paradisio.* His name appeared five times next to the word *Paradisio* and an island, date and time. *Jacques Basille . . . Paradisio . . . October 6, Grenada,*

6:00 P.M. . . . The last communication with *Paradisio* was October 4.

Then a new name came into the rotation. *Philippe Basille.*

Lovely, kind, warm, friendly Philippe? With a start, she remembered the moment she eyed him warily in the galley. *Did you score,* Maurice had asked. Of course, he had no idea what he was asking Philippe. He'd wanted peppers. Didn't he?

The other four names were vaguely familiar; she'd seen them in the personnel list or heard them. She was fairly certain she'd never met them. On a hunch, she picked up a *Valhalla* personnel file to cross check. Ricardo Salazar was listed on both; also a cook, she noticed. The Spanish voice?

At least two of these men worked for Maurice Arnot. Could he be involved? Could the famous little chef be a drug dealer? She examined every file again, but his name was nowhere on any list.

Once again, she studied the names she recognized. They were all connected to the kitchen. She thought of Arnot's crooked smile, his talented hands. He wouldn't risk a world-famous reputation with drug trafficking. No. He could be just the person to help. He had every reason to help identify the culprits and clear his name.

This was surely what the local law enforcement officers needed to move past the brick wall that Dane referred to. Names. She shook her head and stared at the list, focusing on Philippe Basille. She would never, ever have suspected him.

She closed the file, removed the disk, and turned off the computer. She couldn't wait for Dane to come back from the search site. This was too urgent.

In the open desk drawer, she saw a set of car keys. She wouldn't have to let anyone here know she was leaving. She'd just go straight to the Utopia offices to find Maurice. He would help her explain the situation to the constable. In French.

My woman of action. She winced at the words. She wasn't *his* anything.

To Dane's satisfaction, Roper drove like a maniac through the mountains and mud of Grenada. He was a skilled and smooth driver, unafraid of what might be coming around the bend. As the forest gave way to drier woodlands and blue sky, Roper kept shooting questions at Dane.

"Howd' ya meet Calliope?"

Dane told him. He explained how he got the list of transshipment points and gave him the highlights of the "accident" that killed Genevieve.

The agent zeroed in on it, wanting to know everything about Genevieve, her background, her habits, her friends.

It made Dane realize how little he knew about a woman he'd known for twenty years and worked with for the last ten. "Her work was her life," he explained.

"No boyfriends? Lovers?"

"Not that I'm aware of." Was that his fault? Did he prevent her from having a social life?

"Did she travel much?"

"She went to New York, Miami, and London at least twice a year to market the ships to a select group of travel agents, and she spent some time in France a few months ago when we hired Arnot."

"Who?"

"Our chef from France."

"Aren't Jacques and the other guy, Philippe, galley workers on your ships too?"

Dane nodded, thinking about the connection. And the white-handled knife. A puzzle piece Roper didn't need to have, he decided.

"Who is this Arnot guy?"

"A French cook with a big-time restaurant in Paris. Very well regarded among the type of clientele Utopia attracts."

"Did he hire the Basilles?"

Dane studied a handmade wooden sign directing tourists to Annandale Falls and tried to remember. "I think he did. Philippe first, then he brought in his cousin."

"Did you do a background check on them?" Roper asked, not hiding his disdain.

Dane deserved the dig. "Genevieve did."

"What about this Arnot character?"

"The guy's an internationally famous chef, Roper."

Roper's smirk showed he didn't trust anyone. "So no background check, huh?"

Dane said nothing. Damn, he felt like an idiot for having trusted Genevieve so much. But she'd never shown him anything except loyalty. Or what he interpreted as loyalty.

"And what about you, Mr. Erikson? You're certain to come in contact with a great many wealthy individuals who could be interested in using your ships for more than an exotic cruise through the islands."

Dane kept his gaze on the scenery. "Remember that I'm the one who called you yesterday to report this business. Sorry to disappoint you, Roper. I'm clean."

"What about the dead man we're trying to find?" Roper was relentless. "What's his name, Santori?"

An image of Marco flashed in his mind. No, it was not possible that Marco would betray him that way.

Of course, he would have said the same thing about Genevieve a few days ago.

"Does he have a background, or didn't you check that either?"

Dane remembered Ava's story about the Mafia in Boston. Was anything on record? He was certain he'd done some kind of check five years ago. He'd had to have, for Marco to take the seamanship courses in England that he'd arranged.

"He's been with me for five years. He is . . . was . . . my closest friend."

"No wonder you're so hell-bent on finding him."

Dane nodded, willing the drive to go even faster.

But Mother Nature had other ideas as they navigated a few fallen trees that still jutted into the road, slowing their pace and frustrating Dane. Hurricane Carlos had been one of the fiercest storms in Caribbean history. Small and tightly packed into an eight-mile diameter, the deadly storm had left the northern sections of Grenada untouched. As they approached the hills of St. George's, however, the brutal handprint of Carlos could be seen everywhere. Even the protective shoulders of mountains that encircled the harbor city hadn't stopped the fury of the storm.

Trees were flattened or uprooted and naked. As they rounded the top of the hill looking down into what used to be one of the Caribbean's most pictur-esque towns, Dane's breath caught in his throat. He couldn't imagine anyone surviving the winds that caused this destruction. Unsheltered and shot in the leg.

They rumbled down toward the Carenage, as the locals called the heart of the town with its achingly sweet Georgian buildings, painted in Victorian hues of pink and purple. As they approached from the hills above town, an area that had always reminded him of the rustic Mediterranean countryside, he and Roper saw roofs that had been ripped off like they were made of paper and windowpanes that were nothing but jagged glass edges. A few of the nicer homes had been boarded up, with all signs of life long gone from the uninhabitable ones. The once lush and flamboyant foliage was stripped of its greenery, devoid of the brilliant blooms of bougainvillea and hibiscus that had charmed the tourists. Arriving at the Carenage, Dane thought "carnage" would be more appropriate. Nothing, absolutely nothing, had survived.

The docks were broken, beaten by the relentless surf the storm had brought with it, making Dane wonder again how Jacques and Marco had ever reached dry land. The landmark statue of a welcoming Jesus Christ that greeted arriving ships at the head of the harbor stood broken at the knees. There were no indications of reconstruction anywhere. One month after the disaster and St. George's was still reeling from it.

"I expect the National Museum is where they've set up some kind of command post or information center," Dane said as they abandoned the Jeep at the first clearing on the side of the road. "It's two hundred years old and probably survived this, as it has a few other hurricanes in its time. I want to go there first."

"You know your way around here, Erikson?" Roper asked, eyeing the remnants of a cluster of cafés and shops.

"It's been on our itinerary for years. I've spent a lot of time here."

"Bet it's off your *itinerary* now," Roper said, playing with the word, making Dane wonder if the agent was scoffing at the destruction or the cruise business in general.

Dane shot him a look as they walked. "Yeah. But since I know my way around and you don't seem to, why don't you shut up and follow me."

Roper grinned. "Until you need a badge or a gun to get you where you want to go, Erikson, you're welcome to take the lead."

"I wonder if the Sendall Tunnel is open." Dane stopped for a minute and rubbed his face. "It's an underground route across town to Granby Street, where the museum is and Market Square . . . was." He looked back to the mountains on their right. "Fort George is up there, by the way. I think that's where police headquarters is. Wouldn't you feel more at home comparing guns with your buddies?"

Roper climbed over a metal street sign lying along the roadside like a corpse. "And miss this? Not a chance. We'll drop in on them later and see if anyone reported a gunshot victim. Though I doubt it, in this mess. You've got two hours, Erikson. Then we leave. With or without your friend."

Dane started off toward the tunnel. He dodged small packs of homeless island natives, ignoring the smell of death and rank human odors. The trademark aroma of nutmeg and spice that hung over the rest of Grenada was eerily missing from St. George's.

The brick tunnel had been built through a mountain in the late 1800s for transporting goods from the harbor to the market without having to make the poor donkeys climb the rough terrain. Taking the few steps down into the cool darkness of the tunnel opening, the two men shouldered past dozens of people and said nothing to each other as they strode single file.

They exited the tunnel and Dane walked toward what he thought was the corner of Young and Monckton Streets, where the Grenada National Museum was located. But everything looked so different. Buildings were nearly leveled. All of the delicate colors had a green cast to them. From the chlorophyll, he imagined, as millions of leaves had whipped against them in the storm. Street signs were completely gone, and Dane moved from memory and pure determination toward his destination.

He finally saw the Red Cross symbol on the side of a stone building and broke into a full run, his heartbeat drowning out the sound of his footsteps.

He had to arrange his chaotic thoughts into a coherent request. *I'm looking for a man who's probably dead.* Someone left with a gunshot wound in an alley hours before the hurricane hit. Jesus, this wasn't going to be easy.

The Red Cross worker he finally reached looked tapped out of goodwill and kindness. She listened to Dane, then shot him a look of incredulity. St. George's General Hospital had been destroyed, she told him, and critical patients who survived the storm had been moved to temporary medical clinics set in the older buildings around town.

"Where are they? How do I find them?" he urged.

The woman pursed her lips, no doubt having heard the same plea until she'd been worn to sheer apathy. "You could try Fort Frederick or Fort Matthew. There were ICUs set up in those locations right after the storm. But, someone who was caught in the . . ." She sighed and looked at Dane as though she was seeing him for the first time. "The storm was a month ago. Didn't you miss this person any sooner?"

He ignored her accusing tone. "Are those the only two medical centers?"

She started shuffling through a stack of papers. "Yes, for the seriously injured. We've got ambulatory centers set up in the Methodist Church on Green Street and Marryshow House. Do you know where they are?" She grabbed one of her papers. "You might want this too." A list of graveyards. "Sites for unidentified victims are noted with an asterisk."

Dane turned and came face-to-face with Roper, who clicked his cell phone shut.

"It's a fool's errand, Erikson," he said, grabbing the paper. "What do you want to see? Forts or graveyards?"

The only vehicle parked in Dane's garage was a freaking red Ferrari. *Marone!* Ava could have cried. He drove a race car around a mountainous island? In bare feet, no doubt. Well, too damn bad. She wasn't going to let a damn gearshift stop her from getting to Gustavia. She'd driven a stick. Once.

She slipped into the inclined driver's seat and inhaled the scent of brand-new leather. Dane had con-

veniently backed into the garage, so she wouldn't
have to find reverse. The engine turned over with
a spine-tingling rumble. She pressed the clutch and
maneuvered the gearshift into what she figured was
first gear, then released the clutch. The car shot out of
the garage before she'd even applied pressure to the
gas. *Facime de Mama!* She hit the brake pedal and
jerked to a stop with a sharp screech.

Ava started and stopped her way down the winding driveway, certain that Marj or someone must
have seen the jerky motions of the red sports car
inching its way toward the main road.

A breath of déjà vu played at her conscious. What
did this remind her of? Certainly she'd never driven
a car like this. Maybe in her dreams.

She drove slowly to Gustavia, creeping along the
turns, cursing the horns from impatient drivers behind her. She hit stride close to town, smoothly sailing into third gear and sensing that the incredible
machine could almost drive itself. At a light, she
stuck the shift in neutral and finally had the nerve
to take her eyes off the road and study the sleek
dashboard. Next to the Ferrari logo was the word
Testarosa. Redhead.

With unnecessary force, she popped the gearshift
into place, and she cringed at the grinding response
under the hood. In town, she opened the driver's
window and took a deep breath of salty tropical air.
Maybe she should try to find Cassie. No, Cassie
didn't speak French well enough to deal with authorities. Anyway, they'd probably respond better to a
man.

With a squeeze of the steering wheel and a prayer
of gratitude, she saw a parking spot she could drive

straight into next to the Utopia offices. No reversing necessary until she wanted to leave. Good. She had no idea how to back this thing up.

Several people she recognized as *Nirvana* passengers stood outside the office entrance. She entered the lobby and navigated through the groups gathered around the receptionist's desk, the room reverberating with arguments in an array of languages between passengers and several Utopian staff. A few others complained into cell phones.

As she reached the desk, she caught the eye of a cruise director she'd met at Dane's yesterday. He held up a finger to interrupt the long-winded diatribe of the irate French passenger in front of him. *"Un moment, s'il vous plaît."* He leaned across the desk to her. "What do you need, Ava?"

"I'm looking for Maurice Arnot."

"I haven't seen him, but that doesn't mean anything." He rolled his eyes at the commotion around him. "He might still be on *Nirvana*, closing things up. Employees are registering in the back. I'm pretty sure I haven't seen him walk in, though."

Ava frowned. "Can I get on the ship?"

"I think one more launch is going to pick up the last batch of passengers and crew. You might be able to take it over and back."

She held up a hand of thanks. "Good luck."

She burned with purpose, nearly running through the charming and narrow streets, ignoring the blasting midday sun and the alluring shops and restaurants. She arrived breathless and damp with perspiration at the stone steps that dropped down to the main docks of the harbor. At one end, she saw a small crowd disembarking from a launch bearing the Utopia logo.

Chaos reigned here, just like at the Utopia offices.

"This is ridiculous!" she heard someone cry.

"Fine. Take us back to the island," another spat. "But at least let me get my shaving kit!"

In the confusion, it was easy to slip onto the launch.

"Have you brought Maurice Arnot back yet?" she asked the driver.

"No. We've got one, maybe two trips left. There's only crew left, now."

"I need to see him. Do you mind taking me to the ship on your next run?"

A passenger barked in his face and someone else started swearing. Ava slipped to the front of the little boat and knew he'd forget all about her.

Nirvana was virtually deserted. A crewman waiting at the tender embarkation platform frowned at Ava as he took her hand and lifted her on board.

"All passengers are supposed to be registering at the Utopia offices, ma'am. You'll need to go back."

She held her hands up. "Dane sent me. I'm Ava Santori."

"Oh—" She knew he wasn't sure what to say.

"I need to find Maurice Arnot. I'll take the next launch back." She squared her shoulders and climbed up the two-step ladder with purpose.

"Wait. Miss Santori!" He tried to follow her, but someone grabbed his arm to ask him a question.

"I'll be right back," she called back as she hurried toward the stairs she knew would take her right to the galley.

With the fluorescent lights off, an eerie darkness

hung over the stainless steel counters and black-topped Viking stoves. Silence reigned in the kitchen that never slept.

"Is anyone here?" Her voice echoed throughout the steel and tile galley. There was no response.

She went toward the storerooms and a small office where she knew Maurice often escaped to create menus and order ingredients. The doors to the three rooms were closed. Before she could decide whether to leave or knock, she heard a voice, soft but urgent, from the dry storage room.

She put her hand on the brass knob and thwack! It opened with a burst from the other side. She gasped and stumbled backward in surprise.

Philippe Basille stood staring at her.

"Ava! What the hell are you doing here?"

From behind him another man emerged, a huge, dark figure carrying a crate. Ava stared at it and back to Philippe.

"What do you *want?*" Philippe insisted.

"I . . . I . . ." Before she could come up with an answer, the other man spoke.

"You better get out of here, *señorita*. There are no passengers allowed on the ship now." The Spanish accent rocked her.

"Who are you?" she blurted out.

Philippe stepped forward, his forehead creased. "Ava, I'm sorry but you must leave. We are very busy."

She glanced at the crates. "Where's Maurice?"

Philippe's gaze burned in warning. "Leave. *Now.*"

A trickle of sweat slipped between her shoulder blades. *They are killers.* She turned on her heel without a word and started back toward the galley, walking swiftly.

She heard a bark from the Spanish voice. Philippe responded with rapid-fire French and then *"Non, non, non."* She slipped on the tile floor, grabbing the edge of a counter to keep from falling, her breath so loud in her own ears she couldn't hear if they were following her or not. The Spanish voice shouted again, and Ava threw herself at the double doors into a utility hallway that separated the kitchen from the main dining area. Dashing around the corner, her body banged squarely into a man. Maurice Arnot.

"Oh—Maurice! Thank God!" She grabbed his narrow shoulders.

"Ava, what are you doing here?"

She pulled back and searched his kind face. She had to trust him. Had to. Panting, she pointed behind her toward the kitchen. "Philippe. Back in the kitchen. And another guy . . ."

"What is it?" he urged.

"They're . . . they're . . . They worked for Genevieve running drugs. I have proof . . . we have to go to the constable. Come with me, now!"

He put his arm around her shoulders. "What kind of proof?"

"The Spanish guy in the kitchen. I heard him threaten Genevieve on *Valhalla* and talk about—oh, never mind. Let's go!" She pulled at his arm, willing him to follow her, but just then the double doors parted and the Spanish giant filled the space between them and the kitchen.

"Ricardo," Maurice said softly, his arm tightening around her shoulders. "You've upset Mademoiselle Santori."

* * *

To get to either of the forts, they had to pass the Methodist Church, which now housed a Red Cross ambulatory center, so Dane decided to check it first. Pews had been transformed into beds, and hurricane victims on crutches and in wheelchairs filled the main aisle. The wails of children from cribs surrounding the altar resonated through the centuries-old rafters.

Dane scanned the church as he blocked out the echoes and the ever-present odors caused by human misery. He moved up one aisle and down the other, looking into the faces of those sleeping under blankets on the pews, pausing only a fraction of a second to stare at each person.

"There are more in the back," Roper said to him.

Dane shook his head. "Let's go to the ICUs at the forts. If he was well enough to get to this place, he'd have called me."

"And if he's been in intensive care for a month, he's probably dead," Roper added matter of factly.

Dane shot him a dirty look and nudged him toward the exit. "I've got an hour and a half left, Roper."

"If your buddy's alive, he's deep in hiding under Cali cover. That's my guess."

Dane kept walking. "Shut up or get lost."

They climbed Richmond Hill toward Fort Frederick, another battlement from the eighteenth century, the sun pounding unremittingly from a clear blue sky. When they reached the top of the hill, Roper paused to wipe his face and take in the panoramic view of the harbor.

"We're not sightseeing, Roper." Dane grabbed his arm. "Don't waste my time."

The fort was dark and blessedly cool inside. The ticket office had been transformed into a triage desk, and several Red Cross nurses stood in a group, talking. One of them looked up. *Come on, Florence Nightingale. Help me.*

Dane explained who he was looking for and the expected dubious look crossed her plain features. She explained that they had about twenty patients in their ICU and none of them fit the description. But she'd take him there to look.

He flashed an appreciative smile. "Thanks."

"Did you say he was shot?" she asked Dane as they started down the hallway.

"Yes, I think so."

She looked up at him warily. "I don't remember any bullet wounds, and I've been here almost since the storm." They arrived at what was probably the soldier's dining area more than two hundred years earlier. "But let's look. Then I can check the deceased files for you too, for unidentified gunshot victims."

Dane scanned the rows of beds surrounded by IVs and machines. The modern hospital equipment clashed with the old, giant, white stone walls with narrow slits for windows. Walls originally built to house and protect armies of men, not a sea of ravaged hurricane victims.

Dane walked past every bed. At every man, at every dark head, he stopped and studied the face. They slumbered and moaned, injured, maimed, broken, and nearly dead.

When he finished, he turned to his escort. "Is that it?"

"I'm afraid so." She laid her gentle nurse's hand

on his arm. "You ought to try Fort Matthew. The worst cases are there." At his pained look, she added, "And the best doctors."

Near the makeshift triage center, Roper was on his cell phone.

"Come on," Dane urged him. "Fort Matthew is next."

Roper continued talking into the phone. "Don't go on the ship," he said steadily. "Get every man around it, call in what we need. Stay low and open communication. I'll be there in a few hours. Keep me posted." He flipped the phone closed and turned to Dane. "Sorry, pal. We're going back."

"No!" Dane nearly seized the muscles of Roper's thick neck. "One more fucking hospital, Roper."

"The DEA has one of your ships surrounded. Some assholes were dumping crates off the back."

"So tell your men to go in and get 'em, for Christ's sake. What do they need you for?"

"They've got a hostage. A passenger. A woman."

Fear danced up his spine. "What do they want?"

"A free ride out of there. Otherwise, they'll kill her."

15

"You cannot leave us, *cherie*." The pressure of Maurice's arm propelled Ava back into the galley. The words didn't scare her, Arnot's tone did. Beneath the gentle French accent she could hear a ruthless command of the situation.

"Chef . . . Maurice—"

"And you cannot talk."

He moved her toward the work area in the back where Philippe stood and watched them, his gaze darting from Maurice to Ava.

"Is everything gone?" Maurice asked him.

Philippe nodded and angrily muttered something in French as he stared at Ava.

"*Non, non.*" He looked at Ava and gave her a squeeze and a smile. "We need her company."

A band of terror gripped her chest. "For what?"

Maurice's gaze flashed with a menacing spark she'd never seen before, but it disappeared as quickly as it came. "You must not ask questions, *cherie*. You must do exactly as you are told."

She had to know. "Or what?"

The darkness returned to his expression, and this time it didn't go away. He dropped his arm and stepped away from her, as though to focus more clearly on her face.

"What proof were you talking about in the hall?" Maurice asked.

The CD-ROM was slipped into the zipper pocket of her handbag, which hung over her shoulder. Could it give her negotiating power? Should she offer to give it to them in exchange for freedom? Or maybe she should leave it in its hiding place, so it could lead the authorities to Maurice . . . *after they found her body.*

The band around her chest squeezed tighter, cutting her breath and ability to speak. "I told you," she said in a strangled voice. "I overheard a conversation. I heard Genevieve talking."

A silent look passed between Maurice and Philippe. They didn't believe her. She opened her mouth to elaborate, but shut it. Philippe made a demand in French.

"*Non,*" Maurice growled with growing impatience, and spat something indecipherable back at him.

Ricardo returned, pounding the tile floor with his bulk as he approached. He threw a hateful glance at Ava. "The fucking DEA is all over the harbor."

All three of them stabbed her with accusing stares. Her legs felt as though they were turning to water. "Please . . . please," she choked, her gaze locked on Maurice. "Let me go."

Maurice ignored her and spoke to Salazar. "Did you succeed?"

Salazar nodded. "It's crazy over there, but I registered for you. You are officially off this ship with the rest of the crew. The prick on the launch knows me, though. He saw me get back on board."

"And her?" Maurice glanced at Ava.

Salazar's stare accompanied his strained, thickly accented voice. "Who knows? But we may never get off now."

"You won't. But I must." Maurice put a hand on the Spaniard's arm. "And you know I'll take care of you." Then he turned to Philippe. "Put her in the back. Securely."

Philippe grabbed her arm and pulled Ava toward the dry storage room. She stumbled and shook off his grip, a familiar boiling of her blood starting to mix with the fear that ricocheted through her. "Wait a second!" she heard her voice go shrill and she grabbed the material of Maurice's sleeve. He couldn't be that ruthless. He had to have some sort of soft spot. "Maurice! Please, let me go!"

He shook off her grip and spoke directly to Salazar. "Get them on the phone and tell them we want a helicopter. After it's dark. One pilot." Then he turned to Ava. "Be sure to remind them we have a guest."

"Maurice!" Panic pounded in her chest.

Philippe pushed her into the storeroom. "Don't make a sound, Ava," he said roughly as he shut the door behind him, eliminating all outside light. The spark of anger simmered back to sheer terror as she blinked to adjust her eyes to the darkness.

"Why can't you let me go?" she implored Philippe. "I can't hurt any of you."

"No. You can help us." He pushed her onto the only crate left on the floor.

"H—How?" She grabbed the rough wood edges to keep from falling.

Something glinted in the dark as he leaned close to her. "You can be our escort through unfriendly waters." A cold sliver of steel touched her bare shoulder and lightly traveled down her arm.

She shivered, staring at the blade.

He straightened and opened the door, momentarily bathing the tiny room in light as he dangled the knife by its white handle.

"I'm not superstitious," he whispered as their gaze met over the knife. In the glimmer of light, she could see his eyes blazing. "Are you?" He slammed the door and left her buried in darkness again.

She dropped her head into her hands and gave in to the shivering that overtook her body.

In the unmarked DEA Cessna, Dane could only hear one side of the conversation as Max Roper barked orders into a satellite phone from the copilot's seat, and it didn't sound good. Max hung up and said something quietly to the pilot, then he hunched over and climbed into the seat next to Dane.

"Who's Ricardo Salazar?" Max asked, raising his voice over the engines.

"A cook on *Valhalla*," Dane answered, digging for a mental personnel file of the big man he barely knew. He had a heavy Spanish accent and he had only recently been hired—by Arnot. "Do you have an ID on the hostage?"

Max shook his head. "Salazar's on the ship."

"No idea at all who the hostage could be?" Dane pushed.

"All of the passengers are accounted for, although

it seems your offices aren't exactly the picture of effi-
ciency today."

"We don't often have a few hundred hostile passengers who aren't allowed to take their luggage.
And no senior management on the ground to supervise the whole thing."

"Well, my men in your office said it was pretty
damn confusing, but they got things straightened
out. That's how we ID'd the two on board."

"Then why do you think the hostage is a passenger?" Dane felt a nagging suspicion he just didn't
want to face.

"Frankly, we don't know for sure. But I expect
Salazar and company will call us before we have to
call them. By the time we land, we'll have established
contact with them."

"Very few people cruise alone, Roper," Dane informed him. "If there's one woman on board, someone would miss her."

Max nodded thoughtfully. "It doesn't matter who
it is. She's a hostage."

The nagging fear nipped at his gut. "Can you
reach my house on that phone?"

"You can get the goddamn White House on that
phone, Erikson. And it's scrambled, in case you're
hoping to send a secret message somewhere."

Dane swallowed the curse he wanted to spit in
Roper's arrogant face as he climbed into the copilot's
seat. He had to hear her voice. Just to be sure.

Marj's familiar voice greeted him. "Mister Dane!
Where are you? It's like de dams of hell have broken
here!"

"I'm on my way, Marj. Let me talk to Ava."

A long silence. *Son of a bitch.*

"Marj?"

"She ain't here, Mister Dane."

He squeezed his eyes against the truth.

"She, uh, well, she left a couple of hours ago."

"Who took her? Where did she go?"

"She left by herself."

"She walked?" Maybe she just got lost on the hillside or went to a beach.

"No, Mister Dane. She drive dat red car, sir. De one de pretty Miss Charlotte gave you."

The *Ferrari?* Jesus H. Christ—if he hadn't been so scared, he would have laughed. Even *he* never attempted to take that low-slung machine around the S curves of St. Barts. He cursed himself for not shipping it back to the redhead who'd sent it as a reminder of their brief time together.

Marj tried to explain that she never saw Miss Ava leave the study, but she did see the red car sputtering in the driveway. Oh, he bet it did just that. Marj's voice cracked like a little child admitting she'd done wrong. "I'm sorry, Mister Dane."

"It's okay, Marj," he assured her. "I'm sure she couldn't be stopped anyway."

"Well, somebody did see her at de office, so you should try to call dere now."

As he spoke, he glanced back at Roper. How much care would he take with a hostage in his effort to seize the day? Dane's heart twisted and he clung to the rapidly diminishing hope that Ava sat in some quiet office commiserating with Cassie or other Utopians.

"Thanks, Marj. I gotta go, sweetheart. Don't worry. Everything will be fine."

He thought he heard her moan a little before the connection broke.

"Whatd'ya find out?" Roper was right behind him, breathing down his neck.

"Nothing."

"Liar."

"Bastard."

Max grinned. "Need to call any more girlfriends, Erikson?"

"You worry about the bad guys, Roper. I'll worry about the innocent victims." Dane glanced at the satellite phone keypad. "And, yeah, I got a few more friends to track down."

When he connected with the Utopia offices, his worst suspicions were confirmed. No one had seen her.

"God *damn* that woman. Why couldn't she just stay home and cook?"

He heard Roper choke back a laugh and Dane hung up the phone. He hadn't meant to say that out loud.

"I think I might have an ID on the hostage."

Roper raised an eyebrow. "Don't tell me. One of your girlfriends."

Dane yanked the seat belt around his waist. "This may be a fun day at the office for you, Roper, but there are a lot of real live people down there that I care about. And I have a feeling you're going to need my help, whether you want it or not."

"We've made plenty of busts without the owner of the real estate present, Erikson. You'll stay on the dock and be quiet." Roper glared at Dane, all humor gone from his eyes. "Don't try to be a hero, pal. And none of the real, live people will die."

The sound of an airplane interrupted Ava's anxious thoughts. Still perched on the crate, she had no idea how much time had passed. At least a few hours, maybe more. She'd heard their voices raised in anger occasionally, a mix of French and Spanish, and sometimes English when all three of them had to understand one another.

Every interaction with Arnot replayed in her mind. Had there ever been a clue? She cursed herself for being so charmed by the little Frenchman, for rushing to judgment just because he teased her and lavished her with praise.

Her eyes had adjusted somewhat and she could make out certain items in the darkness. She remembered the day she'd explored this room looking for oregano, and how quickly Philippe had shooed her back to the galley. But Arnot had been so kind, so warm. She bit back a curse and the next batch of tears that threatened.

Her bag still hung on her shoulder and she considered the disk inside. It didn't implicate Arnot. Nothing did. Salazar said he'd registered Arnot at Utopia, so no one knew he was on this ship. No one except Ava.

She opened her thin, envelope-style purse. The disk was still folded in a protective sheet of white paper. The bastard should at least get caught if she died. In the dark, her fingers traveled over each item in her bag in search of a pen. Lipstick, a small wallet, a roll of mints, the Ferrari key—no goddamn pen. She reached into the zipper compartment. Something long and thin. A pencil? She held it up in the dim light. Lip liner! That would work.

She opened the piece of paper and thought for a minute. What if this was her last communication with anyone before she died? What would she want to say? To Dominic? *I'm sorry you lost both your children.* To Mama? *Thank you, sweet Mama; I love you so.* And Dane. What would she say to Dane? *You're gorgeous and good and I want you more than you could ever want me? I'm so sorry I died without making love to you.*

The doorknob rattled and she jumped and stuffed the disk and paper back in her purse. She heard the lip liner hit the floor and she cursed her time-wasting dramatics. She jammed the purse behind the crate just as the door burst open. Blinding light from the galley flooded the storeroom, and Ava blinked.

"Come here." Arnot's voice was gruff and edged with impatience. "You have a phone call."

She stood, trying to steady her cramped legs. A phone call? Was this a hoax?

As she stepped into the galley, she saw that a thin band of sweat flattened Maurice's thinning hair and his usually smiling mouth was set in a hard grimace, his eyes darting and wary. And he had taken ownership of the white-handled knife.

He lifted it to her face. "They need to confirm that you are alive. Talk to this man. This Max Roper. You will tell them only that you are alive." The blade settled into the soft hollow under her jaw and she held his threatening gaze. "If you mention my name, this will end up on the other side of your neck, *cherie.*" He intensified the pressure.

She nodded and tried to back away, but Ricardo Salazar blocked her, easily grabbing her wrists behind her with one hand and thrusting a cell phone up to her ear with the other.

"Yes?" she rasped, then cleared her throat. "Hello?"

"You okay, princess?"

Every drop of composure threatened to melt away

as she fought a sob. *Dane*. No words would come to her and she gasped for air.

"Ava? Are you there?"

"Yes," she choked. "I'm fine." She felt the cold steel pressure on her throat and kept her gaze locked on Maurice.

"We're going to try to get you out of there."

Arnot and Salazar had her sandwiched so tightly enough that they might be able to hear both sides of the conversation. Did they know it was Dane?

"That would be good," she whispered, feeling the tip of the knife with every pulse beat in her neck.

"Have they . . . have they hurt you, baby?"

The endearment, spoken so softly only she could have heard it, made tears burn again. Her gaze shifted to the white handle of the knife. "N—no. Not yet."

She heard him take a short breath. "Do everything they tell you to do, Ava. Do you understand?"

Terror released its grip ever so slightly. If there were a God in heaven, Maurice Arnot would not get away with this. How could she tell Dane that the chef was on board and behind everything? She took a chance. "When this is over, buddy, I'm going to *cook* for you."

Arnot glared at her, and she felt the knife's edge press. She could only pray Dane knew her well enough that the comment and its emphasis would resonate with him. *Please, Dane. Please.*

"On the ship?"

Did that mean he got it? "Yes."

"Please don't argue with them, Ava."

"I won't." Oh, God, she wanted to hold him again and kiss him one more time and tell him . . . "I'm sorry."

"I just want you back." She heard the crack in his whispered words. "I don't want to lose you."

Maurice jerked his head toward Salazar, who yanked the phone away from her ear.

"A helicopter," Salazar barked in the phone. "In one hour. On the deck. No one but the pilot, and no searchlights. When we're on the chopper, we'll let her go."

They'd never let her go. Arnot knew she'd reveal his identity. She had one hour left to live.

Dane stared at Max as the connection broke. He had to trust the guy now. Had to tell him what he knew. Dane had suspected Arnot, since at least three of the drug runners worked in the galley. And though he knew the chef had registered with the Utopia offices and was believed to be off the ship, he also knew Arnot was the one other person Ava might think she could trust.

Now Dane had something that Max wanted more than anything—the identity of the person behind all this. His gut told him they would want Maurice Arnot alive. Which might increase the chances of Ava staying alive.

He knew Roper wouldn't entertain the idea of replacing Ava with Dane as a hostage. There was only one reason the agent didn't shove him out the harbormaster's office on his ass: his intimate knowledge of the ship.

He looked hard at Max. "There's someone else on that ship. The one you really want."

Max frowned at him. "Who is it?"

"The chef. Arnot. That's what she meant when she said she'd cook for me."

To his credit, Max didn't question the statement. "Spell it."

One of the other agents started punching the letters into a laptop computer.

"Tell me everything you know about him," Max ordered.

"Obviously, it's not enough." Dane sighed and ran a hand over his unshaven face. "Let me call and get his personnel file pulled up."

"We got it right here," the agent with the laptop told him. Then he hooted. "Maurice *Chevalier* Arnot? You kiddin' me?"

An agent was pouring over the massive diagram of the ship. "There are only two entrances to the galley, Agent Roper, and we know from the satellite that's where they are. They're bound to have both entrances covered."

Dane's heart jumped. He grabbed the blueprint and yanked it toward Max.

"Look at this." He dropped his finger over a small square on the commodore deck. "There's an inside cabin right here that abuts the galley. You can't see it from the blueprint, because it was a recent modification. You could cut right through and land smack in the middle of the galley. I'm not sure where on the wall of that cabin you would cut, but I'd know it"— he looked up and held Max's interested gaze—"if I saw it."

"Forget it, Erikson."

"Listen to me!" Dane banged his hand on the blueprint. "You *need* me, Roper. They've got every light off and I can guide you through that ship blind. I'm sure your guys are pros, but I can get you in there faster. You've got less than an hour, for Christ's sake."

No one breathed as the two men stared at each other.

"Okay. You go. In safety gear. Get them to that cabin, Erikson, and then don't leave it. I don't care if the Virgin Mary is on board. You don't move. You got that?"

Dane finally exhaled. Someone threw him a bullet-proof vest while Max spewed orders to his men. Code words and plans were communicated to the DEA and Coast Guard in the harbor. The operation would start in seven minutes. They'd travel silently by rowboat to the bow of the ship, and climb up the tender embarkation on the port side of the bowsprit.

Instinctively, Dane looked toward the sky for a sign as he walked in the moonlight down the wooden planks. A golden haze ringed the quarter moon, re-minding him of the Viking god who sent the Valkyrie into battlefields to choose which fallen warriors would be taken to heaven. To light their way, Odin provided a gold moon and the strange glimmering lights known as the aurora borealis. Dane prayed to that god and any other one who would listen. *Please don't let this be a Ride of the Valkyrie. Please let her be safe.*

Maurice shoved Ava against the galley doors, push-ing her ahead of him. Behind them, Ricardo stood with an ominous-looking gun and a nasty expression on his face. They'd left Philippe in the far end of the galley, guarding the other entrance with his own menacing weapon.

She stumbled on the carpet of the dark dining room and grabbed a chair for support.

"Vite! N'arrêtez pas!" he shouted at her. "Do not stop!"

He pushed her forward and she banged her knuckles against the corner of a table, but ignored the pain. Her stomach rolled as Arnot propelled her up four flights of stairs. Her sweating palms slipped off the handrail.

On the moon-drenched upper deck, she saw a crazed and driven look in his eyes. He urged her toward the Zodiac that hung on the side, then whipped a small handgun out of his waistband and pointed it at her face.

"I'm not afraid to use this."

She had no doubt of that.

He nodded toward the motorized rubber raft. "We're taking a cruise, *cherie*. Take this down. Now. Do it fast and quietly or I will shoot you. *Comprendez?*"

"I—I thought you were going on a helicopter," she stammered.

"They are." He angled his head in the direction they'd come from. "They won't get far and everyone knows it. But no one has missed me in St. Barts yet."

"You don't need me. Why don't you just go?"

He glanced toward the small crafts surrounding the ship and laughed. "Swim right into the sharks, eh? *Non, cherie*. You are my insurance."

"Then you will kill me like you killed Genevieve."

He shrugged. "Ricardo killed her. I suspected her affection for her boss would eventually override her loyalty to us."

Her affection for her boss? "What do you mean?"

"We set her up with false addresses, and sure enough, he showed up at one of them two hours after we hit Antigua."

"You mean . . . that wasn't really a transshipment point?"

He tapped the gun on the side of the raft. "Quickly! Get the pins out."

Her heart dropped. The computer disk might be useless.

"I tried to warn you." He sounded almost contrite.

Her fingers felt for the pin release as her gaze stayed on the gun. "The knife?"

"Philippe's idea. He'd been following Dane all day in Guadeloupe. He knew he bought you a present, and of course, Monsieur Erikson's fondness for sailing superstitions is well known. His other well-known fondness—pretty women—made me fairly certain where he'd end up sleeping that night." He abruptly waved the gun. "Take the Zodiac down *now*. Pull the pins, it's not difficult."

Her hands shaking, Ava found the first pin that held the raft. She needed to slide it out of a metal clamp, but if she lifted the clamp itself, the Zodiac would unhook from its cable entirely and fall four stories to the water below

"Don't even think about it," he warned as though he could read her thoughts. "Release it and lower it down to the clipper deck and we'll go down and get in."

She could see the green and red lights of the boats bobbing around the harbor, all too far away to see them on the upper deck. Where was Dane? Was he out there?

"Are you going to jump, *cherie*? You'll die if you do."

She turned to him as she tugged hard on the release pin. His brown eyes looked sad and tired. "I'll die if I don't, won't I, Maurice?"

He sighed. "You know, it is ironic, I suppose, that you will die the very same way your brother did."

The pin clattered to the floor of the deck. "What?"

"On a launch. Escaping a doomed ship."

She held on to the rubber raft for support. "What are you talking about? What happened on that ship?"

"It exploded, thanks to the complete stupidity of Jacques Basille. An idiot, I always—"

"It exploded? Then how will I die like Marco did?" It didn't make sense. Nothing made sense. Standing in the dark having a conversation with a madman didn't make sense.

"He got on a Zodiac with Jacques." At her gasp, he smiled sadly. "But, alas, he didn't make it, *cherie*. Died in the hurricane when it hit Grenada."

A bang shook the entire ship and she gasped and spun around. A series of loud explosions echoed through the night and Maurice viciously grabbed her hair and wrenched her toward the stairs. She stumbled and fell against him as he dragged her down the metal stairs, her shins crashing against the edges of each step. She frantically grabbed for the rail and prayed Arnot didn't shoot her in panic.

He muttered something in French and yanked her down the length of the main deck. She couldn't jerk away, his grip was so close to her skull. The only thing she could do was keep her head down and try to stay on her feet as he pulled her toward the diving platform at the stern.

Another series of shots exploded in her ears, and she heard blood rushing in her head. For a split second she thought she'd been hit, but it was just the noise and the pain and the terror that burned a hole in her. He threw her onto the diving ramp and wrenched the small raft that hung there with his free hand.

"Take this down!" he demanded, waving the gun three inches from her face.

Her trembling hands were useless as the ropes slipped through her fingers. "I can't do it!" she screamed.

He slapped the raft with the gun in anger, making Ava jump in terror, a shriek escaping her as she thought he'd fired.

"Shut up!" he hissed and whacked the gun again, his finger on the trigger. Then he stuck the barrel into her neck.

She squeezed her eyes closed, bracing for death.

Dane left his shoes in the rowboat, preferring to feel his way through his darkened ship. Crouched on bare feet, ready to leap, he watched five men pile through the hole they had just cut into the galley. They separated like a starburst, hunched and low, weapons drawn as they moved in twos to hunt their targets.

The last one out turned back to him.

"Don't move," he commanded Dane.

Dane nodded, aching to follow, needing to find her.

The last set of bold black letters that identified them as DEA disappeared and he closed his eyes and tucked his chin into his neck to listen, his own breath and heartbeat the only sounds he heard. Where was she? Where would Arnot hide her?

He flinched at the first gunshot and the shout that followed. He gripped either side of the makeshift opening and leaned his head toward the galley to hear. Another shot, then another.

"Perp down!" he heard one of the agents holler.

His shoulders touched the jagged drywall of the opening, his body battling with his brain, willing him toward her.

Three sharp gunshots rang through the galley and he heard a man cry out.

"No hostage here!" he heard Dombrowsky yell.

Screw Max Roper. He flung himself forward and felt the cool tile under his feet. Instinct took him to the back of the galley, to the storerooms. He ran, keeping his head down against the threat of a stray bullet until he saw the closed doors of the office and food storage. He threw his body at Arnot's office door and it fell open.

"Ava!" he called into the dark.

Nothing.

The refrigerator door of cold storage popped open under his demanding pull. Nothing.

At the third door he kicked at the flimsy wood with his bare foot and the door practically flew off as he stumbled into the empty room, sweat nearly blinding him. He took a step forward, his gaze darting over the shelving units and an empty crate and suddenly something hard dug into his foot.

He bent down and picked up the pencillike thing. Makeup. It was some kind of makeup. He squeezed the pink stick so hard it snapped between his fingers.

Silently, he sprinted down the darkened hallway toward the aft stairs, mentally reviewing and dismissing every possible escape route from the ship. He had to find her. He had to save her.

He would not lose her.

Arnot's only escape would be a raft. Unless he'd already gotten off on a Zodiac. He froze at a sudden sharp sound.

Slipping from shadow to shadow, he followed the path of the sound. Toward the stern, pausing every few steps to listen, he heard only the rigging clang and the soft lapping waves against the hull.

Then a thump and knock carried distinctly over the empty ship . . . from the diving ramp, he realized.

He moved toward it and heard a sharp smack that cracked through the night and a panicked shriek. *Ava.*

Arnot yanked the cold steel of the gun out from under her neck, a watery sensation of impending death running through Ava's veins.

"Untie it!" he demanded, panic shaking his voice as he tugged at the rope on his side. He was going to kill her. This was it. She had nothing to lose by trying to escape. No, she corrected, she had *everything* to lose.

In the moonlight, she could see the water dancing about fifteen feet below. She remembered watching passengers dive merrily from this platform, enjoying the free fall sensation into the welcoming salty sea. The lock to the railing was just a foot behind her. It would just take a few seconds to reach back, flip the metal bolt, and slip out onto the diving platform. But if she turned to unlatch it, he'd see her. A few seconds would be too long.

"Vite! Vite!"

She made a show of working the rope. Who was on the receiving end of the gunshots she'd heard? Were they dead? Would someone come for her? The rope burned her fingers and she knew it was impossible. She'd never untie it.

One more time she glanced at the railing lock. She

only needed to take three steps backward, reach for the bolt, and give it one good jerk. If she could just distract him. She stole a quick look at Maurice. He had stuck the gun under his arm to use both hands on his end. This was her chance.

She inched along the rail to the gate and looked down. A gasp caught in her throat as the gate swung open, her door to freedom.

"Jump, princess. Now." Before she could even turn to look at Dane, he'd pushed her through the opening. Breath whooshed out of her as she spun in the air and slid into the warm waters of the Caribbean Sea.

She willed herself up, back up to the light, kicking her legs as hard and fast as possible. She was alive! Alive! Was that the moon that washed the water with light? What was so bright? Just as she was certain her lungs would explode, she broke the surface and saw the brilliant lights of *Nirvana* coming on one after another. Pools of white and yellow spilled around her as every light on the ship was turned on and spotlights from every craft in the harbor illuminated the majestic vessel. She sank beneath the surface and kicked harder to stay above the water. Rubbing her eyes, she searched the towering masts and combed each deck until she saw a rope ladder snap into place from the diving platform she'd just escaped. Bathed in the brilliant artificial light, Dane attacked each rung with speed and breathtaking determination. Before he reached the bottom, he turned and dove in the water toward her.

She pushed at the sea with matching determination. Water smacked her face and she spit it out with each forceful stroke. By the time they found each other, she could only cling to his powerful shoulders and wrap her legs around his waist. Salty kisses covered her neck, her face, her panting mouth. Gasping for air, she gave into his will and let him swim for both of them.

16

Dane didn't need a clock to tell him it was nearly midnight. The moon hung in the midnight quadrant of the sky, and his body ached from sleep deprivation. Still, he knew he'd never close his eyes until Ava slept soundly. He'd slipped on jeans and a T-shirt after a hot shower and when he'd passed her room, he heard her bathwater still running.

He considered a cognac, but decided he'd rather inhale the night air on the veranda and study his sky. Arnot was in custody and Basille would be as well, as soon as he got out of the hospital. Salazar was dead. He closed his eyes to relive the moments before he'd pushed Ava toward safety. The surprise kick in Arnot's gut had been downright pleasurable. Maybe Roper's job had its merits after all.

After he helped her back to the ship, Roper and company had poured over the CD Ava had found. Dane had been able to identify two other Utopia employees, both new and hired by Arnot. Genevieve's list may have been bogus, but the disk contained enough information to keep Roper busy for the next few weeks.

All the way home in the backseat of a government-owned Moke, with Roper at the wheel, Ava kept up her refrain: *Marco didn't die on the ship.* Dane hadn't yet told her of his trip to Grenada, and Roper kept his mouth shut for once. He'd finally tell her now, and they could go back tomorrow morning and continue the quest together. If he had given her that option even two hours ago, she would have pestered him to leave immediately—soaking wet and bedraggled. He knew her that well.

"Hey, sailor. You all alone?" The throaty, sexy voice seized his gut as he turned to her. Backlit by the soft light of the living room, with a white robe hugging her body and wet black waves falling around her face, she looked anything but bedraggled now. In fact, she looked amazing. Sultry. Beautiful.

He gripped the railing behind him and smiled. "Feel better?"

She nodded and took a few steps in his direction. "Can I join you?"

Erotic responses flooded his mind. She could join him anywhere and anyway she wanted. "Please do."

He thought of his favorite corner, where an oversize rattan chaise lounge waited. He wanted to lay her under the stars and untie that robe and kiss her incredible body from top to bottom. *Can I have you, Ava Santori? Can I love every inch of you?*

"Would you like anything? A glass of wine?" he asked instead.

She shook her head. "No, it would kill me, I think." With a sigh, she studied the stars while he drank in the beauty of her face. Fresh and clean, her ivory skin glowed in the soft light. She looked so pretty and feminine, yet so very strong. He stayed rooted to his spot at the railing, aching for her.

Then she looked at him, obviously aware of his scrutiny.

"Okay," she said softly. "Let's get this over with."

His heart twisted. Get it over with? Is that what she thought of the possibility of making love?

"I want to go to St. George's."

He had to laugh. "I suspected as much." Their minds were running on totally different tracks, and it was far safer to travel along hers than his. "I've already been there, though, and you shouldn't harbor any hopes that Marco's still alive."

Her mouth opened in surprise. "You've been there? I thought that DEA guy said you were up in another part of the island."

"When Jacques admitted that he'd left Marco in St. George's, we went there briefly. I tried to find out . . . anything . . . but we had to come back to the ship."

"What *did* you find out?"

"Jacques said he left him, shot in the leg—"

She gasped. "You didn't tell me that!"

"Ava." He fought back a smile, despite her blazing eyes. Next she would demand they fire up the plane and leave this minute. "We haven't exactly had time to talk about it. Jacques said that he left Marco on a street in Grenada just before the storm hit. You'll see the place. Four hundred people died—and I assume he did too."

In a flash, she was in front of him, gripping his forearm. "But what if he didn't, Dane. What if he didn't?"

Until they knew Marco was dead, they would both fan the flame of hope.

He held her gaze, warmed by its sheer intensity. "If he didn't die, baby, we'll find him." He reached across the few inches that separated them to touch her lovely face. He couldn't help it. He let his fingers graze her cheek and lift her chin toward his mouth. "We'll go tomorrow morning. I promise."

He closed the remaining space. Slipping his hand behind her head, he raked the damp tendrils at the nape of her neck as he kissed her softly and slowly. A tiny taste. A quick touch of tongues. He wanted to devour her, but kept the kiss as chaste as he could manage.

Her lips quivered under his, her breath tickled his mouth and chin.

She pulled away, and he could see the moon reflected in her midnight black eyes, the fringe of her lashes nearly touching her arched eyebrows. Unfamiliar words caught in his throat. So he said nothing but pulled her into his chest and let their pounding heartbeats fill the silence.

Finally, she spoke. "I thought I was going to die today," she whispered as she nestled her head into his neck.

He didn't want her dwelling on what might have happened. He didn't want to remember how the possibility of losing her nearly drove him insane. He pressed gently into her, knowing she had to feel the effect she was having on him.

"That's funny," he whispered huskily. "I think I'm going to die right now."

He heard the tiny breath she sucked in just as she leaned back enough to meet his gaze.

"Your reputation, as you have pointed out, is daunting."

He shook his head in denial. "It's all propaganda to sell cruises, really."

She narrowed her eyes in doubt.

"But I understand," he admitted. His relationships were high profile and short-lived. A woman like Ava Santori would want something lasting . . . something he could never offer. Good sex, good fun, yes. But he knew from experience that nothing lasted forever.

He ran his hands over her shoulders, then followed the line of the robe down to her cleavage. He slipped his hands under the material to caress her body. Heat shot through him at the touch of her satin smooth skin. Their gazes stayed locked as his hands moved over the curves of her shoulders, under the edge of her collarbone, and down to the rounded rise of her breasts. One touch of her nipples, one delicious skimming of their hard and eager surface, and it would all be over. She would be his.

He swallowed hard, hearing the thump in his chest, the rush of the blood through his veins.

Seduction. That was what it was, plain and simple. And he didn't want her on those terms. Not Ava.

He cupped her face in his hands. "Baby, the last thing I want to do is take advantage of . . . of what you've been through."

She exhaled, her warm breath caressing his face. Her head fell back slightly as she looked at him, exposing a throat so enticing that he burned just imagining the taste of its delicate skin.

"And we still have a lot to talk about . . . first," he added feebly. It would be too easy now, he warned himself. She was weakened by the day and probably looking at him like some kind of hero. And that wasn't what he wanted. He closed the V of her robe.

"Are you sending me to my room, Mr. Erikson?" she asked, her eyes narrowing.

He kissed her forehead, a ragged breath escaping his lips. "Against every instinct that makes me a man, princess, I am doing just that."

"Why?" Her smoky gaze held both desire and uncertainty.

"To prove everyone wrong." It was a lie, but he didn't want to goad her into a challenge over something she might regret letter.

A shadow crossed her features. Disappointment or relief? She took a step backward, her jaw quivering for a second.

"You don't have to prove anything to anyone, honey." She turned toward the house, her shoulders squared and tight. As she left the veranda, she tossed him a parting shot. "Thanks . . . for everything."

Oh, for Christ's sake. Could she possibly think he didn't want her? He watched the white robe disappear from view and had never felt more alone in his whole life.

She didn't slam the door—that would be too dramatic—but she twisted the lock in defiance. Damn him. Damn her for falling right into it every time he kissed her. He hadn't even wanted to make her one of his conquests. He wanted to *talk*.

Fighting back tears, she threw off the robe and grabbed the first item of dry clothing she could find in the top of her bag, a T-shirt that barely covered her backside. She flung back the bedspread and fell on top of the sheets. The pillow blessedly muffled the sob she couldn't keep in any longer.

What had just happened out there? What was she feeling for him? Lust, certainly. Gratitude, sure. *Who could resist a man who saved your life?* But there was something more, something powerful and irresistible pulling at her. Could she have done the most idiotic of all impetuous things, and fallen in love with Dane Erikson?

She finally found the strength to climb under the top sheet. She ached. The trip down the ship's stairs had battered her body. The last few moments with Dane had battered her heart. And the very most feminine core of her throbbed with desire.

She'd almost died today, and she didn't want to die with any more regrets. That she'd never had the courage to leave the Santori nest. That she'd never tracked down Marco to reconcile. And now this. That she never experienced complete and utter abandon with the man she loved.

"Marone!" She flipped over and bunched the pillow underneath her. She didn't love him. She battled the thought with sound reasoning. She was just grateful to the gorgeous, godlike creature who'd saved her from the monster.

No. The truth tugged at her heart. It might be temporary, it might be wrong and it might be foolish. But it was real. She flung back the sheet and stood in the dark. Nothing else mattered. She tiptoed to the door and quietly untwisted the lock.

Her bare feet made no sound on the tile floor. She stopped at the open doorway of the master suite. The spacious room was bathed in moonlight from the open windows along one wall. She could see him in profile at the end of his bed, his elbows propped on his knees, holding his head in his hands. She could almost feel the waves of frustration and confusion rolling off him. It was a shame to interrupt this poor man's misery, she thought, biting back a sneaky smile.

"The thing is," she said softly, "I don't *want* to talk."

At the sound of her voice, he lifted his head. He just stared at her, all tousled blond hair and questioning blue eyes.

As she approached him, she watched his gaze travel down her T-shirt, linger on her bare legs, and wander back up at his usual maddeningly deliberate pace. His chest heaved as he appeared to work for each breath.

"I don't want to talk," she repeated as she knelt on the bed next to him and tucked her bruised shins under her.

"I heard you the first time," he said softly, still staring at her.

He reached toward her bare legs and ran his thumb over her thigh. Lightly. Reverently. She leaned forward to bring her mouth close to his. Without a word, she let her tongue touch his lips slowly, savoring the sensation. She heard his whispered groan over the pounding of her own heart and the tropical breeze that sang though the screens.

He intensified the kiss, taking her tongue with his teeth and covering her mouth with the hard pressure of his own. His soapy, salty scent drifted over her like a kiss of its own.

When he broke their contact, his hand stayed on her leg, his fingers burning the skin. "You better be damn sure you know what you're doing, princess, because you've got less than two seconds to change your mind."

"Then what?" she asked, her lips curling into a seductive smile.

He narrowed his blue wolf eyes. "Then I'm going to eat you alive."

She moaned softly in anticipation. *"Mangia, mi amore."*

His teeth flashed in a wicked grin just before he untucked her legs to lay her back. He brought his mouth down on hers in a long, lazy exchange. She wrapped her legs around him instinctively, feeling him grow aroused, the soft denim of his worn jeans rubbing her bare skin as the T-shirt moved up around her waist. He lowered his kiss to her neck and breasts, his mouth finding the outline of her pointed nipple, the cotton teasingly separating her skin from his tongue and teeth.

The heat of his hand seared her back and he murmured her name as he pushed her shirt higher. Fire danced between her legs, and she pressed her hips against him and began to move. He caressed the exposed flesh of her stomach, then under her breasts, stroking the soft skin around her nipples, and finally circling each with his thumb until the bud simply had to be tasted. When his mouth closed over the point, an electrical charge shot through her and she bit her lip against the sounds she wanted to make. Against the words she wanted to say.

"You're an angel, Ava," he whispered, his tongue flicking her, teasing her, biting her, licking the dusky circle until she thought she would scream.

She explored his own beautiful chest, then yanked up his shirt. She wanted skin against skin. She ached to feel that solid chest against hers, to be tickled by his golden hair, to be dampened by his flesh. He sat up and pulled his shirt over his head, the erotic striptease dramatized by the moonlight.

His stomach muscles tightened with each breath. Kneeling over her, he locked her hips between his knees with a low growl of desire, his gaze smoky with lust.

Her T-shirt was bunched above her chest, and he slipped the material over her head, leaving her completely naked for him to devour with his eyes and hands. He played with the long curls that spread on her pillow and then his gaze traveled over every inch, his hands gently skimming the curve of her breasts, the indentation of her tummy, down to the dark mound between her legs.

"Sweet Jesus, you're gorgeous," he said in a raspy, unfamiliar voice as his fingers lingered over her navel and traced her rib cage. "I don't know where to start, baby."

She breathed in short pants with each searing contact, each erotic word. That was his gift, she realized. That was his magic. His genuine appreciation for the very things Ava wished she could love about herself. His appraisal was so honest that real and imagined flaws evaporated, leaving her feeling utterly feminine and lovely.

He leaned forward, his arms on either side of her as he kissed her mouth again, making her sit up to press her breasts against him. "I hoped you'd come to me," he said between kisses. "I wished on my lucky star."

She smiled and held his face in her hands. "I couldn't stop myself."

"How unlike you." He laughed softly, the sound warming the room even more.

Without taking his eyes off her, he sat over her again and opened the snap of his jeans, then slowly slid the zipper down. Her gaze dropped to his narrow hips, the sexy act of his undressing dampening her, exciting her. She propped herself up on one elbow and put her free hand in the waistband of his boxers, tugging slightly, her palm grazing the bulge inside.

"Could I help?" she offered, her tone husky with emotion.

With a moan, he rolled off her and she removed the last cotton barrier between them. She wanted to grab him and attack his beauty, to own it and taste it, but instead, she slowly moved her hands down his perfect body. Over his defined muscles, around his sinewy lower back, and then to the part of him that she longed to touch. When she did, he groaned. She reveled in the power of making him hard and weak and demanding all at the same time. She wrapped her hands around him, sharing her own arousal with throaty sounds that made him pulse even more.

With probing fingers, he found the swollen flesh between her legs, and she arched in shock and delight.

"I have to be inside you, Ava. I need to be inside you." He licked her ear and neck as he spoke the words.

Instinctively she spread her legs a little, still stroking him and inhaling the mixture of his scent and the sexy sweat that they produced together.

"Wait," he whispered, pulling away. She sighed in disappointment as he rolled from her embrace. She heard the drawer of the nightstand and a shuffle among its contents.

"You can look tomorrow, princess. It's pretty well stocked." She heard the foil tear. "I don't use them as often as you have yourself believing."

She stared hard at him, shaken by the depths of her feelings for him. "No, honey. I only have myself believing that I'm making love to the most amazing man I ever met."

He pulled back, a dark and wondrous look in his eyes. "Do you mean that?"

She stroked his cheek. "Do you think I came in here just because you risked your life to save mine?" *I'm in love with you, Dane Erikson.*

She helped him, their hands shaking as together they prepared him for her. With demanding, anxious kisses, he rolled her on her back and climbed on top, his erection edging into its natural place between her legs.

"So we're even," he whispered into her open mouth, the tip of him easing into her folds. "Because *you* are the most amazing woman *I've* ever met." He kissed the dimple on her cheek. "Infuriating." He lightly licked the valley between her breasts. "Sexy." He sucked a nipple. "Delicious." He nipped the other one with his teeth. "And you can cook."

Her soft laughter was lost in a gasp of pleasure as he entered her. She breathed his name as he filled her and they began to rock in a natural, slow cadence of ecstasy. She lost track of time and space and could only experience the complete joy of taking him inside her and gripping him with her legs and arms and hands. She was vaguely aware of the musky scent of sex, the music of his voice, and the salty flavor of his wet skin. As their rhythm reached a frantic intensity, she couldn't think beyond Dane. Dane in her arms. Dane in her body. Dane in her heart. She arched with each powerful thrust, burning and aching with no line between pain and pleasure.

She might have said she loved him. She might have cried. The searing heat of his body wound her so tight that she thought she'd snap. And then she did. With waves of delight that throbbed around him as she spun and pulsed and shuddered with no control. His fingers dug into her back and his teeth pressed against her flesh. He choked out her name with a sob, like a prayer, like a confession, and for the second time in one day, they clung to each other, gasping for air.

Dane floated in and out of awareness, dimly conscious of the deep sense of satisfaction that comes with sleeping soundly after many restless nights. His inner clock told him the first hint of rising sun would soon color the edges of his room. A soft puff of air tickled his bare shoulder, a gentle pressure fell across his chest.

Ava. Sweet, wild, wonderful Ava. Her gentle breath, her loving arm. She lay next to him in the still of predawn, spent from their night of exploration and discovery.

Oh, God. He had no idea it could feel like this.

He imagined a rogue wave, the kind that can't be negotiated, the kind that sailors see only once in a lifetime; the kind that breaks the back of the ship because the bow simply cannot navigate and rise over the powerful curl. Although few people lived to describe the experience, he'd heard stories of huge gray monsters with no curling crest, just walls of water that freakishly arise in otherwise unremarkable seas. They swallowed ships whole, crumpling steel and snapping beams built to last a hundred years.

Ava.

Why didn't this rogue wave scare him? Why did he feel the need to ride it, to free-fall over its steep and dangerous peak, and find whatever heaven or hell might exist on the other side? Why, when he knew damn well that the violent mix of kinetic energy and displacement of matter would end his life . . . as he knew it?

The pace of her breathing changed and one of her glorious thighs shifted between his legs, immediately arousing him. He wanted her again. Now. He needed her tasty body wrapped around him, her luscious mouth pressed anywhere, absolutely anywhere, on his body. He saw no end to that desire. As he grew harder, her leg instinctively wound around him and she moaned.

He moved his hand, trapped in the tangles of her hair, and turned her slightly to enjoy the moment when she awakened and remembered what they'd shared.

Would those expressive eyes flash in horror, or delight?

Her blue-black lashes fluttered as her moan turned to a smile and she opened her eyes. For a long moment, their gazes locked, silent and lost in each other. This was no impending death from a rogue wave, he thought as he saw his own reflection in the early morning light. This was about as far from death as he'd ever felt.

"Hello, Ava Rose."

She pressed her lips on his shoulder in silent greeting. Then she lifted one eyebrow ever so slightly and asked, "When are we leaving for Grenada?"

The laugh escaped him. He turned on his side to line up their bodies and let her feel the full force of his desire.

"When the sun is above the horizon, you little witch." He pressed into her. "When you can't walk, think or, please dear God, talk. Okay?"

She nodded, pressing her hips against him in response. Wordlessly, they started the dance, each step becoming more and more familiar but no less thrilling. She moved on top of him to straddle his body and let her hair fall over his face and chest and they found their perfect synchronization again, broken only by affectionate whispers and her throaty laugh of sheer delight.

By the time she collapsed on top of him, sweaty and satisfied, blades of sunshine pierced the shutters. Her hair tangled in his neck, their legs remained intertwined. Dane floated on the surface of contentment.

The jangling phone broke their silence. With a sigh of disappointment and a tender good-bye kiss, she rolled off of him and curled into his side. He finally picked up on the fifth ring.

"Yeah?" Dane didn't try to hide the impatience in his voice.

"Morning, Erikson."

He sighed. "Roper. What *is* it?"

"Gee, I hate to interrupt what I'm sure is a most cozy scene, but I gotta tell you something."

"Now what?" When would he be done with this guy?

"After watching your performance last night, illegal and outside of procedural boundaries as it might have been, I made a few calls to some buddies in Grenada."

The flame of hope sparked. "And?" He caught Ava's glance and held it while he listened.

"Just a little payback for your help, even though you did not follow orders."

"I follow instinct, Roper." Dane eased the sheet off Ava's naked body.

"Right. Anyway, I asked them to start a search for a man—dead or alive—who may have been reported as shot the night of the hurricane."

So Roper had a little heart beating in his tough-guy chest, after all.

"Thanks. We're going down to the island this morning." He watched Ava's eyes as she realized he was talking about Grenada and Marco. He followed a trail with his fingers, up her arm, over the rise of her little bicep, across the curves of her throat and down the intoxicating valley between her breasts. The diversion didn't pull his attention from Roper's words, however.

"Go straight to the police," the agent instructed. "We've pretty much ruled your friend out as part of Arnot's ring, and they agreed to spend the morning doing some research with the morgues and checking records. You know it was like hell down there, but maybe, just maybe, a smart doctor took the time to report a gunshot victim. At least this'll grease the skids for you." As Roper gave him the name of a contact, Dane's sense of hope began to intensify. A chance. There had to be a chance.

"I really appreciate this, Max," Dane said. "I'll keep you posted."

He got a grunt in return. "Sure. And take care of that little girl you got, Erikson."

"I'm trying, pal."

Roper chuckled a little. "You better. Bet it's not too often you manage to find somebody prettier than you are." Roper was still laughing when Dane hung up.

Ava had pulled the sheet back up to her neck, ready for an explanation. He kept the optimism out of his voice when he told her the reason for Roper's call. She started to ask a million questions, so he put his hand on her mouth and tried to distract her.

"Stop talking. We have a starting place, that's all. Now, if you will relinquish the keys to the *car* you so boldly helped yourself to, I can arrange to have it picked up. Then we can pack and take a trip to the Island of Spice."

She leaped from the bed, her delicious figure disappearing from sight. He got up and opened the shutters to check the skies for their flight. When she came back into the room, she wore the white robe and dangled the key in front of him.

"*Testarosa.*" She let the Italian word tumble out slowly with a perfect accent. "Know what that means?"

He snapped the key out of her hand. "Give that to me."

She put her hands on her hips and shot him a haughty glare. "It's not very practical, you know."

He tugged at her bathrobe tie and hungrily eyed her exposed body. "Neither are you." Still holding the ties, he pulled her toward him. "Come on, let's take a shower. Before I turn you into breakfast."

As he bent to kiss her, she leaned back, a tiny frown etched between her eyebrows. "I . . . I really want to get to Grenada, Dane. I need to know. I need to find out."

He closed his eyes in silent agreement. They both knew the day ahead of them would be far less pleasant than the night they'd left behind.

"We'll find out together, baby." He wrapped both arms around her and held her close to him. "It'll be easier that way."

17

Dane rarely broke their physical contact. He held Ava's hand across the aisle of the Piper Apache during the flight to Grenada. He kept his arm around her while they purchased a local driving permit and rented a Moke in the closest town, Grenville. He let his fingers rest on her thigh as they negotiated a mountain pass that took them right through the crater of an extinct volcano. With no apology and no apparent motivation, he just *touched*. It had a dizzying effect.

She dropped her head back on the seat, holding the seat belt with one hand and covering his strong, possessive fingers with the other. From behind her sunglasses, she stole a long look at him as the Moke bounced along the Grand Etang Road. It had no roof, just a roll bar and windshield, allowing the rays of sunshine that broke through the lush foliage to highlight the captivating angles of his face and the corded muscles of his tanned arms. He made her weak.

She steadied herself with a deep breath. "Now I know why they call it the Island of Spice. Nutmeg and cloves and cinnamon."

"There are spice factories and perfume distilleries everywhere here," he told her. "And over that hill there's a trail that takes you to two unbelievable waterfalls . . ."

She let him ramble like a tour guide, appreciating his effort to keep her mind off their mission, but it didn't erase the hope she hung on to as they made their way toward St. George's.

"Do you think he's in jail?" she blurted out, interrupting his description of his favorite beach.

"No," he responded without missing a beat.

"But you hear stories about foreigners getting thrown in jail and never being heard from again."

He shook his head. "Not here. In Turkey and Afghanistan, maybe. Not in Grenada."

"Roper said Arnot was working for Colombians. Do you think they kidnapped him?"

"I doubt it." He slowed down around a tight curve, taking his hand off her only for the moment he needed to downshift.

"Do you think he's just hiding? Maybe he thinks he'd get blamed for the explosion and—"

Dane shot her an incredulous glance. "Not a chance, Ava." He squeezed her leg. "Stop theorizing. We'll be there soon. Enjoy the scenery because it's going to disappear as we get farther south."

She continued with a silent exploration of possibilities, all ending with Marco alive and well and happy to see them. But those hopes diminished with each mile, as the deadly damage from Hurricane Carlos obliterated all beauty and life. If he really had been shot and left in the street, he couldn't have survived. He couldn't have.

They parked among the rubble of the old town

square. From there, they walked through a long underground tunnel to the opposite end of town and climbed up a short, steep hill to the historic stone structure that housed the new police headquarters. The previous one had apparently been wiped out with the storm.

Within moments they had an audience with Captain Thomas Burke, an imposing black man whose lilting English accent was peppered with the island dialect. With a wide white smile, he assured them that Max Roper had requested he do everything possible to help the couple on their quest.

"However, Mr. Erikson, I don't think there's much we can do," Captain Burke said softly after they took seats in his office. "We are still in a crisis situation here and not as organized as we used to be."

Dane nodded. "Do you have any reports of gunshot victims on file?"

"We had a few." The captain opened a file folder and slid the metal bracket to release some papers. "This is what I've found."

Ava leaned forward expectantly, wanting to seize the papers for herself, but Dane stayed still, waiting for Burke. She took his cue and clasped her hands together.

Burke read from the paper. "A domestic dispute. Wife shot the husband a few hours before the storm hit." He scanned down the page. "A barroom brawl in St. George's. A tourist attacked the owner because they were closing for the storm. Then one of the patrons shot the guy, wounded him."

Dane and Ava shared a glance as her mind spun a new scenario. Could that have been Marco? Could the "patron" have been Jacques? "What happened to him? The tourist who got shot? What was his name?" her questions tumbled out.

"Hold on there, miss." Captain Burke held up his hand to quiet her and study the page in front of him. "Just a second. Gave him a John Doe for some reason and a number. He was treated at St. George's General, but moved after the storm. He may have been sent to a jail in Grenville."

Ava looked sharply at Dane and raised an I-told-you-so eyebrow.

"I'm sorry we can't be more certain." Captain Burke furrowed his brow as he reviewed the page. "We haven't had phone service, let alone working computers, the last few weeks."

Dane reached over and took her hand.

"We have two more in the file," Captain Burke continued. "Both apparent victims of muggings who ended up in the temporary hospitals after the storm. Both gunshot wounds." At his matter-of-fact tone, Ava started to gnaw her lip. "One is dead and buried, but we had a positive ID on him. The other was a John Doe shot in the head and sent to Fort Frederick."

"I've been to Frederick," Dane said. "He's not there. There were no gunshot victims there."

"Well, this John Doe may have been moved. He was not conscious," Burke said as he set the paper on his desk. "That's it, I'm afraid."

Ava stared at the captain, willing him to say more, waiting for any other idea or suggestion.

He simply shook his head. "You can try the guy up in Grenville, he might still be in custody. Or you can go back to Fort Frederick to see what happened to that John Doe. Where they buried him."

"Or moved him," Dane said hopefully.

The captain smiled sympathetically. "I'm sorry we couldn't help you any more. Max is a good man and God knows I owe him a favor, after the cleanup job his men did in Sauteurs. But, other than what I've told you, we've had no reports that would fit the situation he described."

The dazzling sun clashed with their mood as they left the police headquarters. They found shade next to the building to plan their next move.

"The nurse at Fort Frederick said she didn't remember any gunshot victims," Dane told her. "But she did say to try Fort Matthew. She said the worst cases went there. Let's go there first."

"What about the guy in jail in Grenville?"

Dane put his hand on her back to guide her down the stone steps. "Marco wouldn't attack a bar owner."

"You don't know what happened that night, Dane. But it would make sense if he's stuck in a jail and he can't reach us," she insisted. "Maybe he didn't attack the guy. Maybe he was begging to use the phone or something and they got into a fight. Maybe . . ." A miserable lump formed in her throat, a black cloud of despair starting to descend over her.

"Let's go, princess." He nudged her forward, his voice tender but determined. "We'll look in every jail cell in Grenada if you want. But Fort Matthew is a mile up the hill, so let's just see what we can find here before we go all the way back to Grenville."

"The captain said that guy was shot in the head," Ava said softly, unwilling to go down the steps as all embers of hope started to cool. "And you said Jacques shot him in the leg. You've been to Fort Frederick, where the captain said he was sent. It's a waste of time."

"Come on. We don't know unless we look."

Tears welled up in her eyes, making Dane's face blur. "This is useless, Dane. We're never going to find him . . . or his body."

He said nothing for a moment. She was sure he'd just fold her in his arms any second so that she could cry hard into his shoulder and let herself lose hope.

She saw the square bone of his jaw set firmly as his gaze turned to dark blue steel. "You're not giving up, are you?"

She blinked, clearing the tears. He stepped back and grabbed both her hands.

"You want to quit, Ava Santori? Just give up, go home, and wonder for the rest of your life if you searched every corner?"

He hit his intended target with his direct words and sharp tone. Straight aim for her heart. It occurred to her, as she stood blinded by the midday sun and his impossibly handsome face, that Dane understood her better than anyone she'd ever met.

She jerked her hands away to wipe the dampness from her eyes while she continued to stare at him, to consider the challenge and the man who made it.

"I am not a quitter," she finally whispered.

"No. You are not." He curved his lips just enough to take the sting out and reached for her hand. "You're my woman of action."

The muscles in her thighs burned as they climbed the hill, and the tendrils that had fallen out of her hastily tied ponytail curled around her neck in the humidity. A steady trickle of sweat ran down the small of her back. But the ever-present touch of Dane Erikson propelled her up to where the white stone arms of the fort reached out for them.

He found the triage center and spoke in hushed tones to an elderly nurse who listened, nodding and sympathetic.

"Well, sweetie, I'm still new here," she explained with a distinct Carolina drawl and a generous smile. "Just shipped over last week. Let me find one of the other girls who might be able to help y'all."

The wait was interminable. Dane bought them bottled water at a gift shop. Ava prayed to every saint she knew. Anthony, for lost treasures. Jude, for lost causes. Joseph, for lost families. Anyone who would listen to the pleas of a bereaved sister searching for her lost brother.

Marco Polo, Marco Polo. She could hear her own little-girl voice as she played hide-and-seek under empty tables in the restaurant. Entertaining her baby brother after school, a favor to Mama while they prepped for the evening rush. *Where are you, Marco Polo?* She could smell the fresh basil and hear Dominic's demands when the kitchen door would swing open. Then she'd find him, a giggle spilling from his dimpled face, all wild wavy hair and chubby little toddler legs. *I found you, Marco Polo.* He'd been her living, breathing baby doll.

"Hey." His soft touch on her cheek, wiping a tear she didn't know was there, pulled her from the memory.

Just then, a tall, bald man in turquoise scrubs came through the triage doors carrying a clipboard.

"I'm Doctor Graham Whitaker." He spoke with an elegant British accent, cultured and cool. "I understand you're looking for a gunshot victim."

Dane shook the doctor's outstretched hand and offered a terse explanation. Dr. Whitaker listened intently, his gaze shifting to Ava repeatedly as Dane spoke.

"I had someone with a gunshot wound in the thigh," he said with a slight frown. "Came from the hospital, then ended up in jail up in Grenville, I believe."

Dane nodded. "We'll be tracking that lead also."

The doctor shook his head in thought. "Are you sure he was shot in the leg?"

"We're not really sure of anything," Dane admitted.

"Because . . ." He looked hard at Ava again. "I did have one young man who . . . was he related to you?"

Ava's heart jumped, and she gasped at the pointed question. "Yes. My brother."

The doctor nodded vigorously. "I treated a man several weeks ago. A bullet had apparently grazed his head, left side. Comatose with a possible herniation to the brain. Without an MRI, we had no way of knowing if the coma was caused by swelling or where the affected areas were. He never woke up."

Ava knew she was squeezing Dane's hand hard, but couldn't stop.

"Is he . . . is he here?" she asked anxiously.

"No, he's long gone."

A tiny moan of disappointment escaped her lips.

"Is he dead?" Dane asked.

"I have no idea. I move between the two ICUs and don't necessarily follow every patient. I do remember he nearly flatlined twice, but recovered. And a man of his size would need a stomach tube after several weeks. We gave him steroids to reduce subdural swelling and I ordered an MRI, but of course, we've had no access to equipment like that since the storm. If the bleeding was around the brain stem, he couldn't have survived. If not"—he shrugged—"hard to say. If he lived, he would have been sent to another island, I imagine."

"How do we find out?" Dane asked.

He aimed his clipboard toward the triage center. "With luck, someone kept a record. Come with me."

As they entered the tiny office, Dane and Ava shared a hopeful glance.

"Did you see how he looked at me?" she whispered. "He asked if we were related. It must be Marco."

Dane nodded and Ava could see him swallow hard, no doubt fighting his own rising hope.

Dr. Whitaker disappeared into a back room and Ava counted the rhythmic clumping of her heart. *Where are you, Marco Polo?*

"This has to be him," she insisted, to herself as much as to Dane. "This patient. It *has* to be Marco."

Dane ran a calming thumb over her knuckles. "We'll see, baby."

Finally, the doctor emerged with the first nurse they'd spoken to at his side.

"He was airlifted to Trinidad," he said with finality. "He stabilized enough to be transported along with several other patients about three weeks ago. To either the Port-of-Spain General Hospital in Trinidad or, if that was full, they would have taken him to Scarborough Hospital in Tobago."

Ava started to pull Dane toward the door. "Let's go."

"Wait." The nurse held up a small bag. "This was left in his file. He must have been wearing it or carrying it when he was brought in."

She handed the white plastic bag to Dane. Reaching inside, he froze, his eyes widening, then squeezing shut as though he'd been punched. Slowly, he pulled out a long metal chain. At the end dangled a glistening silver compass, a single word embedded into the face. *Utopia*.

Ava gripped it like a talisman, a rosary, a lucky charm. *Utopia*. *Utopia*. Over the mountains, back to the airport, soaring above the cobalt and teal waters, the compass told her they were headed south, to the last island in the Lesser Antilles. On the smooth silver back of the compass, a jeweler had engraved a monogram and a simple message. *MDS*. *Find your way*.

MDS. Marco Dominic Santori.

Dane called the hospital from the plane. They lost contact three times with the abysmal connection and finally gave up.

"Let's just get there," he said over and over. "Let's just get there."

As they landed at Port-of-Spain in Trinidad, Dane explained that this would be the city most likely to have sophisticated medical facilities. The maddeningly long wait through customs and the taxi line confirmed that they were truly back in civilization.

She clung to the compass as an astute East Indian taxi driver sensed their urgency and took them for a wild ride into the city. Through a complicated series of one-way streets, past a massive park lined with colonial mansions and gingerbread Victorian homes, Ava rubbed the compass with one hand and grasped Dane's hand with the other. They barely spoke, knowing they had him. They had him. Only one question remained: was he alive? It hung, unasked, between them.

Ava ran her fingers over the engraved letters.

"I gave that to Marco," Dane whispered, and she looked up, surprised that he hadn't told her sooner. "When he graduated from his last maritime training program in England. It happened to be his twenty-fourth birthday. The day we launched *Valhalla*."

"It's beautiful," she said softly.

"He wanted to captain *Valhalla*. That was his dream. The big one—the five-masted monster." Dane smiled wistfully. "He would have, too, in another five years."

"He still might."

He squeezed her hand as the taxi screeched in front of the multistory, contemporary building.

They started at the information desk, where they were politely sent to Intensive Care. There, they talked to three different nurses and an intern who suggested the Trauma Unit. A doctor listened patiently and a nurse carefully checked records, but no patient from Grenada matched the description. Based on the type of injury, they were directed to the Neurology Center.

There they were told to wait for the doctor on duty, who appeared within a few minutes.

He introduced himself as Dr. Valentino Sanchez and spoke rapid English with a lyrical lilt. He took them to a waiting area, sat down, and offered them his undivided attention.

Dane repeated his story. Ava waited for the doubtful frown, the shake of the head, the slow start of a disappointing speech.

But Dr. Sanchez lit up like a Christmas tree and jumped to his feet.

"Adonis!"

"What?" Dane stood and Ava followed. "What did you say?"

"The nurses call him Adonis. The Greek god."

Ava felt her jaw drop and clamped her hand over her mouth to keep from screaming. "You . . . you know him? You have him?"

He nodded enthusiastically. "As you describe him, yes. A bullet grazed the left temporal lobe, and he's been unconscious since he arrived from Grenada. A few weeks after the storm. We have waited for . . . for his family."

"That's us!" Ava burst out. "We're his family!"

"Come with me."

They couldn't walk fast enough to suit her. Dane tried to hold Ava back, his arm wrapped around her, calming her with a "shush." But she couldn't be contained.

"He is stable. Not conscious," the doctor told them as they hustled through double doors into a hallway. "The bullet fractured the skull but didn't penetrate. The impact caused rather severe subdural bleeding and swelling."

"Did it affect the brain stem?" Dane asked, remembering the ominous words of the doctor in Grenada.

"No. We did an MRI, shortly after he came here. There's been some damage to the eighth nerve and the inner ear, which could affect hearing and his equilibrium."

The halls smelled of medicine and antiseptic. Ava's feet hardly hit the shiny linoleum floor.

"When do you expect him to regain consciousness, Doctor?" Dane asked.

"There's no guarantee he will, quite honestly. Although there's no visible deficit shown on the MRI and no reason for him not to. We are treating him with steroids, massive doses at first and now a main-

tenance level. When the swelling is completely eliminated—if it is eliminated—then he should awaken.
I'd like to do another MRI very soon. If swelling isn't
reduced, then I'd recommend a burr hole. Drilling, if
you will, to drain blood from around the brain."

Ava cringed at the thought.

"We've been waiting and hoping for family,
frankly. At some point, he'll have to be moved. And if
he doesn't regain consciousness, then, of course, you
have a difficult decision to make."

She felt Dane's arm tighten around her shoulder.

A nurse came down the hall toward them, and the
doctor held up his hands toward Dane and Ava.
"Adonis's family," he told her.

She stopped midstep, widened her eyes in surprise. "We've been waiting for you."

Dane and Ava looked at each other. She ached at
the thought of Marco, alone all these weeks with no
one to love him, no one to speak to him and urge him
to wake up.

Was it too good to hope? Would the door open and
someone else's brother turn out to be the mysterious
Adonis? She squeezed the compass in her pocket.

At the end of the hall, they stopped and the doctor
opened the door. Tightly closed blinds darkened the
room. In the shadows, a man lay still on an elevated
hospital bed, dozens of tubes connected to various IV
and feeding units. From the door, she could only see
the bandage on the left side of his face and what
looked like an exceedingly thin body under the blue
and white hospital gown. Too thin to be Marco. But
dark hair and soft curls beckoned her. She took a step
farther. She could see a straight Roman nose, prominent and masculine.

She took one final step toward the bed and saw the face, the cheeks hollow and pale, his lips cracked. Her lungs locked up and cut off her air. Blood rushed in her ears, her hands started to shake, and she thought she felt her legs buckling under her. She looked up at Dane to speak, but the words caught in her throat. His eyes were closed, his cheeks wet, and she watched his powerful shoulders shudder with a sob.

I found you, Marco Polo.

The woman of action could take none. Ava sat at her brother's bedside, held his hand, stroked his cheek, and murmured words of comfort and love. She would not leave his side.

She heard Dane softly talking on the phone, using expressions like "acute injury" and "involuntary responses" and "herniation," calling doctors around the world, making arrangements. Quietly handling every imaginable detail.

When he hung up, he stood behind her and placed his hands on her shoulders. She dropped her head back against him and smiled up at him.

"Thank you, darling," she whispered.

He squeezed her shoulders. "I'm flying in a good friend from New York, Sebastian Young. He's a brain injury specialist, one of the best in the world, who cruises every year on Utopia. He'll be here tomorrow. He thinks we might be able to move him to St. Barts, but he wants to look at him first and do another MRI. They're sending the first test results to him now. I've arranged for a special plane to transport Marco home—if we can take him. We'll need round-the-clock nurses. There's not much of a hospital in—"

She tugged his arms, pulling his upper body close to her head. "That's not what I meant." She reached up and kissed him, upside down and backward from her seat. "I meant thank you for not letting me quit."

He crouched next to her and continued a long, sweet kiss. "You're welcome."

"I'm so happy, Dane."

"Me too, baby."

Then she gasped. "Oh my God! Cassie! I have to call Cassie! Did you call her yet?"

He shook his head, standing up with her and wrapping both arms around her waist. "No. I figured you'd want to."

As an operator connected her to the Utopia offices, Ava's heart thumped with the excitement of delivering the news.

"My God, luv," Cassie exclaimed breathlessly when she got on the line. "Where are you? I must see you! You scared us to death, getting on that ship with those madmen. Where on earth did you two *go?*"

"Cassie, honey, sit down."

"Why?"

"Sit down and put your hand on the baby. I don't want to shock you."

"Good lord, luv. You didn't run off and get married, did you?"

Ava nearly reeled at the notion and the mixed thrill of telling Cassie about Marco. "I'm looking at Marco, Cassie. He's alive." She heard a tiny gasp in response. "We're in a hospital in Trinidad. He survived, Cass, he's alive. Asleep, but alive."

The gasp had turned into a moan, a cry, and then a scream as Ava tried to explain what happened. Then they both cried so much that Dane had to take the phone and promise Cassie the Utopia plane would be back in St. Barts, ready to bring her to Trinidad tomorrow morning.

By the time he finished the conversation, Ava had returned to her spot on Marco's right side to hold his hand. She took the compass from her pocket and set it in his palm, then closed his fingers around it. Not realizing Dane was next to her, she was surprised when his hand came down on top of hers and Marco's.

"Find your way, my man," he whispered to the serene, sleeping face as their three hands connected. "Find your way."

They stayed that way for a long time. "I have to call home, Dane," Ava finally said softly. "I have to tell Mama and Dominic."

"Do you want me to leave?" he asked. "Do you want privacy?"

She smiled at his thoughtfulness. "No, that's all right. You know it all now."

The hospital operator made the connection to Boston. Ava recognized her cousin Mia's voice immediately.

"Ava! Where are you? How are you?"

"I'm fine, hon. I need Dominic. Or Mama. Are they there?"

"We're in the middle of a lunch rush, Ava," Mia shouted over the noise. Ava hadn't even looked at her watch or calculated the time difference. And she had no earthly idea what day it was.

"Trust me, Mia. They want this call." For a moment, she remembered the urgent call she'd taken from the Coast Guard so many weeks ago. *Presumed dead.* She smiled at Dane, whose gaze traveled from

Marco to Ava. She wanted to laugh out loud, to dance and sing and scream for joy while she waited for her father.

"Ava? What's the matter?" Dominic's typical greeting didn't surprise her.

"I'm in a hospital in Trinidad—"

"What's wrong?" His gruff demand couldn't hide the father's concern in his voice.

"Nothing." She looked at Marco's sleeping face and tears burned again as her voice cracked. "I'm with Marco. He's alive. He's in a coma, but he's alive."

The line was silent.

"Dominic?"

Still silent.

"Are you there?"

"I'm here," he said, his thick voice choked with emotion. He sniffed hard and Ava closed her eyes to imagine his face. His black eyes rimmed red with tears.

"He survived the wreck, which turned out to be an explosion, and he lived through a hurricane and two hospitals and he made it and I—we—found him today."

She heard him try to speak, and finally, he choked out a sound. "Thank you, sweetheart. Thank you."

She wiped her tears as they fell freely, laughing and sobbing at the same time. "Come on, now, get Mama on the phone. We can all have a good cry together."

18

Dane's whole world had shifted. Lukewarm water fell with maddeningly little pressure from the second-rate hotel showerhead as he considered the phenomenon. When had it happened, he wondered, soaping his body to remove the antiseptic odors of the hospital. When he lost the ship? When Ava Santori turned him upside down? When he saw Marco and decided to believe in miracles?

His equilibrium had been listing way off kilter for a while, but during the past forty-eight hours in Trinidad, he'd nearly capsized. And yet, he made no attempt to right himself. Toweling off and slipping on a pair of workout shorts over his naked body, he ran a hand over his freshly shaved chin.

Perfect example, he thought ruefully, staring at his clean-shaven reflection in the mirror. Since when did he use a razor at midnight after a twenty-hour day in the waiting room of a hospital? Since that woman, that sexy, funny, complicated, hand-waving, delectable *woman* had waltzed into his bedroom and set him on fire. And now she waited for him on the other side of the bathroom door. He grinned at his reflection. Shaving was a good choice.

She'd left a dim light on the dresser and appeared to be asleep in the king-size bed, a sheet pulled up to her neck. He sat next to her and ran his fingers through her still-damp curls.

She opened her eyes and their gazes locked. For a moment, he couldn't decide if he should kiss her or just look at her. Both gave him so much pleasure.

"I'm exhausted," she said softly.

"Then go to sleep, princess."

She smiled, her dimple beckoning him. "Not that exhausted."

He slid beside her, gently tugging at the white cotton sheet. "What do you have on under here?"

"Not much," she said coyly.

"That's my girl." He slipped in under the sheet, anticipation already tightening his stomach, desire making him throb before he even started his slow examination of her body. She wore some tiny cotton sleeveless thing that might have been a pajama top. He reached under it and sucked in air at the sensation of touching her bare skin. He walked his fingers down her tummy, over her hip bones, inside the tiny triangle of underpants she wore.

He forced himself to slow down, to feel and taste every curve. He lifted the little slip of silk between her legs and watched her stretch like a cat at the gentle pressure of his fingers. She closed her eyes and reached up to nip his chin with her teeth.

"Mmmm. You shaved," she whispered. "How nice."

"I didn't want to scratch this delicate skin." He

rubbed the soft skin of her thighs, then the warm and damp flesh higher to make his point.

She opened her eyes and flashed a look some-where between terror and wanton desire.

He brought his hand up to rest on her tight stom-ach and dropped his head on his other arm, his face just inches from hers. Needy and hard, he forced himself to stop and look at her for a moment.

She ran a finger down his cheek, as though to examine how thorough a job his razor had done. "Dane, tell me the truth."

He took a little breath in. If he wasn't careful, he might just do that. "What, baby? What do you want to know?"

"Do you think he's going to wake up?"

He closed his eyes. A safe question. "I don't know. He seems so deep, you know? Like he's way, way down there."

"They say some coma patients can hear. Do you think he knows we're there? Do you think he can hear us?"

Dane turned on his back, finding her hand and holding it under the covers. "I can't tell, Ava. Sebas-tian is very optimistic. The MRI looks good, and he thinks tomorrow's surgery has a very good chance for success. Young's done this burr hole operation a thousand times, but there's no guarantee. You're right, though, he's a good surgeon. That's what we need." He turned back on his side and slid his leg over her hips. "And this. We need this."

He found her mouth and kissed her hungrily, part-ing her lips with his tongue, anxious to start his jour-ney south. But something was wrong. She wasn't kissing back.

He opened his eyes and saw her troubled look. "What's the matter?"

She bit the lower corner of her mouth, her first sign of nervousness.

"What is it, Ava?" he urged softly. Then he understood. "Oh, honey, I won't do anything you're not comfortable with."

"That's not it," she said softly.

"Then what's wrong?"

She stared into his eyes, her lips pursed and a frown deepening a tiny crease between her eyebrows. She attempted a smile. "Just thanks for shaving."

She was holding back, and he refused to let her. If he had to hang on, out of balance and close to the edge, then she was coming right there with him. "Nope. I want the truth."

"Really." She tried to kiss him. "Please."

He took her face in both of his hands. "I'm willing to bet that in your whole life, you've never stopped yourself from saying what you're thinking. Don't start now."

She took a deep breath and fell back on her pillow. His heart started to beat faster, instinct telling him he might not like what was coming. "Come on. What's on your mind, princess?"

"The statute of limitations."

"What?" His gut twisted. "On that lawsuit?"

"On your attention. When does it end? When do I . . . become a statistic?"

Now it was his turn to feel a little terror. "Oh."

She turned on the pillow to face him. "I'm only wondering, Dane. I want to be prepared."

A tiny vein pounded at the base of her neck. Not with desire, like he'd made it do the other night. Not with joy, like when she saw Marco. But with fear and trepidation.

He stayed propped on his elbow, considering what to say. How to be honest but not paint some romantic forever picture for her, only to have it thrown back in his face someday.

"I can tell you this. I'm crazy about you. I am hanging by a thread of sanity for how badly I want you." He traced her mouth with his finger, dallying in the bow that dipped her upper lip. "I have no idea how long something like this lasts, because I've never felt like this before."

He felt her lips curl under the pressure of his fingers. "Neither have I."

"Good." He inched lower in the bed. "And you never felt anything like *this* before either." With a sudden whoosh, he threw the sheet over her head and heard her gasp as his mouth made contact with her stomach. Then she moaned as he began to kiss down her body, moving toward his destination with hot, driving licks that promised to thrill her and satisfy her and hang her out on the same precipice that he clung to.

When they arrived at Marco's room at seven the next morning, Cassie was already sitting at his bedside. It didn't surprise Ava that she'd beaten them to the hospital. Since Cassie had arrived the day before, she'd been no farther than a foot from Marco's side. They had to beg her to go to the hotel for sleep the night before.

"What time did you get here?" Ava asked as she set her purse on the table and looked at her brother's sleeping form.

"Three." Cassie's eyes twinkled a little guiltily. "I really appreciate your getting me the room and I needed to shower, but I couldn't sleep, knowing he was here. I've just been talking to him about the surgery."

Dane walked over to her chair to ruffle her burnished curls and drop a kiss on her head. "And what did he say? He needs it like he needs another hole in his head?"

Cassie rolled her eyes. "Very funny." Her face turned serious as she looked at Marco. "The nurse was just here. They will be back to take him in a few minutes for his surgery."

"I'll get us some coffee," Dane offered. "What do you want, Cass? A great big glass of milk for my soccer star godson?"

"Sounds divine, luv. Thank you."

Ava pulled a vinyl chair next to Cassie's to assume their positions from the day before. It felt familiar already. "Any change?"

"Nope." She ran a finger down his still, limp hand. "He always did love to sleep, though."

Ava laughed. "Absolutely. Like a rock, till eleven in the morning."

"Well, he should have that out of his system when this is over." She smiled sadly, then the smile disappeared altogether. "*If* this is over."

"Cassie, don't say that." Ava reached across and wrapped both arms around her. "You can't stop hoping. The doctors are optimistic. Dane says this Dr. Young is the best in the world."

Cassie nodded, letting her head fall on Ava's shoulder. "I know all that. I just . . . I just can't go through losing him all over again."

They sat wordlessly, Ava's arm around Cassie and both their hands on Marco until Dane came back with the coffee.

"They're right behind me." He signaled to the door as he entered. "Ready to take him down."

A nurse and an orderly followed him into the room with a gurney. "Let's go, Adonis," the nurse said cheerily as they started unhooking IVs and unsnapping straps on the gurney. "It's your big day."

The three of them stood to one side as the professionals moved his limp body with trained precision and careful timing. When they finally wheeled him out, the loss of the sleeping man's presence seemed unbearable.

"I have an idea," Ava said brightly, taking Cassie's hand. "Let's go visit maternity. I'd like to see what kind of babies they make in Trinidad."

Cassie smiled. "Oh, yes. We'll get ideas for names."

Dane grinned at the two of them and held an American newspaper up as a mock shield. "I think I'll wait here." He winked at Ava. "Sounds like a girl thing."

Ava picked up her purse and started out of the room, but heard Cassie whisper a parting shot to Dane. "Chicken."

There were sixteen babies in the Birthing Suites, mostly tiny chocolate faces of African descent and creamy East Indians with thick mops of soft, dark baby hair. For nearly an hour, Ava and Cassie cooed at them, chatted with nurses, and forgot their grief and fear in the wonder of the newborns.

"I can't believe it, Ava," Cassie whispered as she stroked the cheek of a girl named Jacinta, inhaling what they agreed was the most appealing fragrance in the world—new baby. "I can't believe that in five months I will be holding my own child."

They looked at each other and Ava knew what they were both thinking: would the father be there too?

Cassie's green eyes filled with tears. "I'm so damn scared, Ava. I'm so, so scared."

Ava stroked the buttery soft cheek of a baby being taken to its mother. "*Non ti spagnare.*"

"Don't be afraid," Cassie responded with a smile. "Marco used to say that too."

"They're Grandma Rose's favorite soothing words. Whatever the trouble: a thunderstorm, Dominic's temper, a bad spill on a bike, nerves before a test in school. She'd hand us a peanut and say '*Non ti spagnare.*'"

Cassie nodded. "I won't be afraid. As long as he's breathing, we have hope, right?"

They locked arms and headed back to the floor that had become so familiar to them. As they rounded the corner, Ava swore she heard a conversation from the room. Dane's voice and another male voice in return. They looked at each other and Cassie broke into a run, pulling Ava along, their sandals clicking on the linoleum. Cassie burst into the room first, obviously hoping for the impossible.

But Ava recognized the familiar voice, and it filled her with a deep sense of happiness. She saw Dominic before she saw her mother, leaning against the windowsill, dark and tall and imposing. It felt so right. So completely right and so important and so damn wonderful. For a moment, history didn't matter. If just for a little time, they could be a whole family again.

* * *

Dane noticed immediately that the presence of Dominic and Maggie Santori changed everything. The room was louder, happier, more intense and, somehow, complete. Even with Marco gone in surgery, the Santori family exuded unity.

Maggie, who brought light blue eyes and the pale skin of Irish genes into the mix, held her own with her dynamic and animated husband. And they laughed. Considering the solemnity of the situation, they kept finding things to laugh about. Cassie somehow blended in, looking more like Maggie Santori's daughter than Ava did. Dominic made sweeping statements and Ava argued with them. Sparks flew, and then they were drenched with humor.

Dane felt himself pushed even further off kilter as the impact of the Santori family hit him hard. He'd never known anything like it.

It was obvious where Ava and Marco got their dramatic Mediterranean coloring, Dane thought as he looked at the older man. But Maggie intrigued him even more. Her contribution had been fine bone structure and sinfully flawless skin. And, son of a gun, she had the dimple.

From across the room she caught Dane's eye, obviously aware he'd been looking at her, and she moved close to him.

"I've had a few letters from Marco," she said, her voice much quieter than the discussion Ava and Dominic had launched into over what was being fed to Marco through the tube. "He spoke very highly of you."

Dane smiled. "He spoke highly of you too."

"He told me you saved his life when you met him."

He nodded. "He's been a good friend."

"Well, thank you." She put a gentle hand on his arm. "For saving his life more than once."

Dane lifted an eyebrow and covered her hand with his own. "Don't give me all the credit this time around. Ava is a very determined and driven woman when she wants something."

Maggie grinned, and it reminded him so much of Ava that his heart tripped a little. "Yes, she is that." She glanced at her daughter, who watched the two of them talk. "She's a dear girl."

Dane smiled at Ava, enjoying the fact that she surely wondered what he was talking to her mother about. "Yes. She is that too."

A nurse came into the room and they all immediately quieted in anticipation.

"He's in recovery," she announced. "You can go down and wait. Dr. Young will speak to you there."

An ominous silence replaced the noise and they remained that way until they'd all reconvened in the postop waiting room. There, Dr. Young and Dr. Sanchez greeted them with matching optimistic smiles.

"He did very well," Sebastian Young said, glancing at the new faces of Marco's parents. "We drained a significant amount of blood, and I expect the swelling to decrease dramatically in the next twenty-four hours."

"How did he look?" Dane asked.

The doctor paused to consider his answer. Dane knew Sebastian wouldn't exaggerate just to make them feel better.

"There was significant swelling, but he was fortunate in the way the bullet grazed his skull. If he . . . when he regains consciousness, he may never hear out of his left ear. And he'll stumble like a drunk for a while. In fact, his equilibrium may never fully return."

"He'll never sail again," Dane said quietly.

Dr. Young put his hand on Dane's shoulder. "Let's just get him awake first. Therapy can do wonders, but not unless he comes out of this." He looked around the group and smiled. "He can hear fine out of his right ear though. So the more you all talk to him and coax him out, the faster he'll come back to you."

Ava and Dominic started firing questions at the same time, their voices raised over each other. Dane smiled to himself. Marco ought to hear those two easily enough.

They fell into a natural schedule of watches. Ava and Dane sat through the night, then Maggie and Dominic took over in the morning. Cassie rarely left the room, only to sleep for two or three hours and shower, then return to her chair. The twenty-four-hour mark came and went without change, and the mood among the keepers of the vigil darkened.

Ava tried to be cheerful, warmed by Dane's presence and his obvious attention and affection toward her in front of her parents. She didn't once give in to the temptation to brood about her feelings for him, but she longed to run away from the bitter smells of the hospital, from the tubes and softly beeping machines, from the stubbornly unchanged atmosphere of Marco's room to somewhere safe, and lovely and fresh. To examine the amazing sensations that teased her, to fantasize about him and *them*.

For some reason, though, she thought it would be wrong. A sin, somehow, to concentrate on anything other than Marco's recovery. Then, she promised herself, she would ride the roller coaster and delight in the thrill of the love that had captured her heart.

By the time her first night shift at Marco's bed was over, she could barely stumble into the little hotel room, take a shower, and climb under the covers. Even then, even curled into Dane's warm body before sleep overtook her, she didn't give in to any temptation, mental or physical. Just the overwhelming need to sleep.

The second day, the pulsing excitement of Port-of-Spain and the tropical beauty of Trinidad didn't exist for any of them as each hour slipped by and he didn't move. Ava counted up the hours in her head as she took the elevator back to Marco's floor. He'd been out of surgery nearly thirty hours.

Max Roper had returned to Port-of-Spain and called Dane on his cell phone, asking for a meeting to discuss the raid and the fate of Maurice Arnot. The Frenchman, desperate not to lose his restaurant and reputation, wanted to negotiate a deal that would lead the DEA to a kingpin of the Cali mafia that they'd been trying to nail for years.

Waiting for the taxi to take him there, she and Dane had kissed in the middle of Charlotte Street and Dane reminded her that it would be the first time they'd be apart since the night on the ship.

"You must need a break from Santoris," she commented as he opened the back door of the taxi.

He winked and kissed her cheek quickly. "Not yet, princess."

As the cab drove off, she stood silently, the hole left by his absence threatening to swallow her. Inside the elevator, she repeatedly stabbed the button for the fourth floor, even though it was already lit.

Not yet, princess.

The thought of going back to Boston and leaving him forever further darkened her mood. She wouldn't let her mind go there. As she turned the corner into the room, she saw Dominic sitting alone next to Marco. Spears of late-afternoon sunshine broke through the hospital blinds, particles of dust dancing around her father's weary face.

The ordeal had aged him, she thought with a start. He'd always been so handsome and striking. When salted strands had started showing around his temples, he'd grown even more distinguished and appealing to the camera. But this afternoon, he looked every one of his fifty-eight years. As their gazes locked Ava noticed that the fire was gone from his black eyes, and the creases around them and across his forehead had deepened to permanent wrinkles. Oh God, she thought as her heart dropped, he's giving up.

"Where's Mama?" she asked casually.

"She and Cassie went to get something to eat," he answered.

Ava sat in the chair on Marco's left side, across from Dominic. "Cassie's sweet, don't you think?"

Dominic nodded. "Nice girl. Your mother likes her a lot."

"And what about Dane?" she ventured carefully as she tucked the sheet around Marco's chest, as though someone else hadn't done that same thing twenty times already. "Do you like him?"

"Not as much as you do." Ava flushed at his quick response but relaxed when Dominic's face broke into a rare smile. "He's obviously very fond of Marco. And you."

"I guess you know I dropped out of that lawsuit," she said, watching her father's face carefully for the response. "Cassie said the lawyer left St. Barts anyway, after the whole drug cartel business was revealed."

He shrugged. "It got you here. If you hadn't come, you wouldn't have found my son."

Enjoying her rare quiet moment with her father, Ava sat in silence for a while. But thoughts swirled in her mind and she finally spoke. "I guess it kind of makes up for my role in getting him sent away in the first place, don't you think?"

Her father's sharp black look flashed at her, but it wasn't accusing or angry, just vehement. "Ava Rose, don't you carry that guilt around for one more day. I was as responsible as you were. And frankly, Marco was the most responsible of all. Anyway, it's all history now. He can come home."

"What?" She grabbed onto the vinyl cushion of her little hospital chair. "What do you mean?"

"I had a . . . I met with Anthony Ferrisi."

Ava felt her jaw drop. He met with a mobster? He broke his own code? "What—what did he say?"

"I told him that Marco was still alive. That he had escaped the shipwreck he read about." Dominic looked up to meet Ava's shocked gaze. "He said 'Nobody should have to bury his son twice.' "

The air rushed out of her lungs. "We can bring him home?"

"If he wants to come home, he can." Dominic took Marco's limp hand in his, tears filling his dark eyes. "If he'll forgive me. If he'll understand that I . . . I only wanted to protect him. Not punish him."

Ava watched the tears fall down Dominic's cheeks. Giant, anguished drops that fell onto Marco's hand as he held it. She stood and came around the foot of the bed to put her arms around him.

"Of course he'll forgive you. He'll forgive us both. We're family." Her own eyes burned with unshed tears. "Please, don't cry. Don't cry, Daddy."

His sob shook her as she clung to his wide, sagging shoulders. "I know he will, sweetheart. I just want to hear his voice. I just want him to come back to us. I want another chance to be his father."

Wrapped in years of love and guilt and invisible, unbreakable bonds, they held each other and cried from the depths of their hearts.

The freight train stopped. It just stopped. It had been so loud, deafening and screaming in the darkness, racing at breakneck speed, but never actually making contact. Never crashing, never stopping. Then, suddenly, silence.

Only blackness remained. A blanket of thick, suffocating blackness that fell over him, covering him, smothering him. Nothing moved. Nothing felt. Nothing. Just blackness.

Inside the blackness, water rushed. Black water that gurgled like blood out of a wound. A stream. There must be a rushing stream nearby. It was too steady to be the ocean. It whooshed, unstopping, un-wavering and steady through the blackness.

Then the thick, unforgiving blanket of black started to change color. It turned golden. Amber. The water continued, but there were other sounds. A pinging around the stream. A tree branch, perhaps. Was he in a forest? The dark orange light paled to a shade of yellow.

A voice. No, not a voice. A cry. A child crying in the forest. *Find the child.* He had to find the child, but he couldn't move. He could hear the child's sobs, hard and terrified. He had to help. Had to find the child. But the blanket, hot and impossibly heavy, trapped him.

He listened for the child. It stopped. The water had stopped rushing. Silence. He wanted to call out. Perhaps if he called to the child, it would respond. Maybe they could find each other.

He tried to open his mouth, but the blanket was over his face. *Move,* he wanted to scream. Move the blanket.

Something smelled. Was that the blanket? It stunk. Bitter and pungent, assaulting his nostrils. It didn't smell like a forest. With a stream. And a crying child.

Another sound came through, muffled by the heavy blanket. He had to lift the goddamn blanket so he could hear. A voice. A high-pitched, screaming voice. The child's mother? Was she looking for him? What was she saying? He listened hard, willing the wet, smelly blanket off his face and head.

The voice was so far away. She must be wander-ing the forest, searching, calling for her lost, crying child. *Over here,* he wanted to yell. No sound would come, but he felt something. Something moved under the blanket. His stomach tightened with the effort to make noise, but the blanket pressed so hard. He had to move his arms. If he could just raise his arms, the blanket would lift, freeing him. So he could find the mother of that crying child. He could still hear her. He could hear her screaming miles and miles away.

He could feel the weight of his own hands and arms. And shoulders. Lift, lift, *lift* it up.

He heard her yell, louder now, but still not clear, still so far away.

She sounded frantic. Could she see him? Could she see him under the blanket?

A low, long sound filled his head. What was that? The train? Was the train coming back? He heard it again. A rumble, a moan. It filled his head. It burned his throat. It was *his* voice, *his* rumble. Calling the mother. But, oh, God, it burned so bad, like knives scraping the flesh of his throat. Had he been in a fire? Was he under a fireman's blanket? Was he alive?

The scream again, but this time a man's voice. The father of the child? Were they looking for that crying baby? It was louder, they were getting closer. A man and a woman, shrieking through the golden forest. They were looking for that sobbing child and he *had* to get rid of the blanket.

The man hollered. It was so familiar. He knew the voice, he recognized the voice.

"Marco! Marco!"

The child's name must be Marco. Then the blanket lifted. Gone. Someone had finally taken it off. The pale yellow light was blinding him.

"Marco!"

That voice. *That voice. Don't go away,* he wanted to

scream, but the burn in his throat stopped him. *I've got your child*.

I am your child.

"Marco, wake up!"

Through the blinding light, he saw a face. Black, desperate eyes. Demanding. Pleading. Crying.

The father. The father.

His own father had come to the forest to find him.

19

The group of six who'd clung together in their storm reluctantly parted at the American Airlines ticket counter in Trinidad's airport. Dane watched as Maggie and Dominic bent down to kiss Marco in his wheelchair. Again and again. Then they gave Dane bear hugs too, Maggie kissing his cheek tenderly and holding his face in her hands.

"I'd tell you to take care of my babies, but you've already proven that you know how."

He grinned into the smiling blue eyes and reached over to touch her cheek. It felt so natural. "I promise to do my best."

"And we'll see you again?" she asked hopefully. "You'll come to Boston? For the wedding, maybe?"

He was painfully aware of Ava standing just a few feet away, by Dominic. The *wedding*.

"We'll see, Maggie. We need to get Marco up and running, then we'll send him up so he can dance with you at his wedding. And I've got a company to put back together." He held Maggie's gaze, knowing words were unspoken and wishing he could make a firmer commitment. He glanced at Ava. "I certainly hope to see you and Dominic again."

"Come on, Mama." Ava took her mother's arm. "Your flight is leaving in fifteen minutes." She turned her attention to Dane. "Cassie and I will make sure they get on board, then we'll meet you and Marco at the Utopia plane."

She would come back with them but hadn't committed to how long she'd stay. It terrified him to let her out of his sight. She had a habit of disappearing. "Don't get on the wrong plane, princess. You're not going to Boston."

She deliberately widened her eyes and her lips curled in a slight smile. "Not yet."

The four of them disappeared toward the gate, leaving Dane to guide Marco's wheelchair. Dane watched Ava's dark curls bounce with each step. Marco shifted and looked up at Dane over his shoulder. His face had filled out a little in the past ten days, but he still looked gaunt and drawn from his weeks without solid food.

He said nothing, but his expressive eyes got his message across.

"What?" Dane said defensively. "What's the matter?"

Marco shook his head. "Take a picture. It lasts longer."

Dane gave the chair a little shove. "You're ready to fly, bucko. You're starting to get your attitude back."

"You got that right, Erikson. Bigger and badder than ever." Marco's shoulders shook in a spurt of laughter, and it made Dane smile, something he'd done a lot of since Marco woke up. Except for the day that he had to go to St. John to attend a service for Genevieve and spend some time with the Gileses, the last week and a half had been rich with laughter and hope and an unbelievable amount of love.

The day that Marco regained consciousness and finally told his story of survival, Dane wallowed in the joy of having his friend back and marveled at the strength of the family unit. The Santoris insisted that it was Saint Anthony himself who had found Marco in the street and dragged him to the Sendall Tunnel, where St. George's homeless had holed up during the storm. Whoever it was, he had saved Marco's life because the tunnel turned out to be the safest place in the entire city. Protected from the fury of the storm, Marco only remembered the noise and described it like a moving train blasting in his ears for hours. The noise and the searing pain in his head were the last things he remembered. During the cleanup the next day, rescue workers must have found him and sent him to the temporary ICU.

He did remember the nightmare of escaping the ship. After the captain announced their course to the skeleton crew, Jacques Basille had turned into a madman. Jacques fought with Captain Stuart, screaming and threatening and then pulling a gun and shooting him in the face. Fleeing from the witnesses, Jacques disappeared into the galley, and Marco managed to break in and found him turning on every gas jet on every stove, apparently having set an oven timer so it would spark in a prescribed amount of time.

With a gun to Marco's head, Jacques dragged him through the emergency exit of the galley to a Zodiac life raft. They struggled, but Jacques won the fight with the threat of his gun, paddling away with Marco and knapsacks full of what must have been drugs. In less than five minutes, the *Paradisio* exploded, burning and burying nineteen men. They battled their way into the harbor of St. George's and Marco nearly escaped, but Jacques shot at him as he ran into an alley. Except for the noise, that was the last thing he remembered.

As Marco grew stronger, they told him their story. Ava embellished Dane's role as a hero, so he, in turn, downplayed what he still considered her impetuous act of foolishness in trying to hunt down Arnot. He only let Marco see Ava's determination to figure out what happened to her brother. The two of them may have old wounds that needed to be healed, but Dane could see the genuine love between them.

The Santori reconciliation allowed him to witness Ava's capacity for love and the incredible foundation that her family gave her. Raw emotions ripped at him when, alone in their hotel room, she showered that same love on him. Over and over, she took him to a physical ecstasy he hadn't known was possible, and washed him with her own vibrant, dynamic form of affection.

In the back of his mind, he knew something had to happen. It couldn't go on this way forever. It simply wasn't possible to stay in a permanent state of infatuation. And yet, he couldn't see an end to his feelings for her. When they danced around the subject, she just closed up and used words like *inevitable* and *affair*. Words he hated in the context of his feelings for her.

He pushed Marco out into the sunshine, where the Utopia Piper sat waiting for them. A physical therapist that Dane had hired waited by the plane with

Captain Galbraith, ready to begin his month of treatment for Marco. Although he occasionally stumbled a bit, Marco had already made great strides toward recovery. His equilibrium was still way off—as were his sailing days—but he could get across a room now, and with the constant personal therapy Dane had arranged, he really would dance at his own wedding.

Dane didn't question the wisdom of Cassie and Marco's decision to go to Boston once he was well enough to fly, and get married there. It was right, he knew. Long-term treatment would be better in the States, and Marco ached to finally go home. They promised to come back after the baby arrived, but Dane sincerely wondered if they would. If Marco couldn't sail . . .

"What are you scheming about up there?" Marco asked, breaking his reverie.

"Just thinking things through. Got a lot to go back to, Marc. Our little company is in shambles."

"You planning to replace *Paradisio?*"

"It's a long way off, I'm afraid. We've got some shocked and battered people and a whole bunch of ticked-off customers and a big fat public relations nightmare. I think we'll get the other ships sailing slowly and build up to it." Dane put a hand on Marco's shoulder. "And I need to get you back eventually. *Valhalla* will need a first mate in the not too distant future."

Marco sighed. "I don't know yet. Gimme some time."

"All you want."

With the help of the physical therapist, Dane got Marco on board the Piper Apache. He took a seat next to Marco and peered through the window to-

ward the terminal, nursing the little nag that she
might not come back.

"Don't worry," Marco said quietly. "Cassie won't
let her bolt."

Dane smiled and looked at his friend. "You never
know with that girl. She's unpredictable."

Marco shrugged. "I wouldn't know. She's so different now."

"Well, it's been five years. What was she—twenty-
four when you left? Wait till you're thirty. A lot
changes."

Marco shook his head. "No. I don't think these
changes happened until recently. I talked about it
with my mother."

"How is she different?" Dane asked, hoping his
effect on her was positive.

"She's confident. Secure. A little cocky, even."
Marco looked out the window beyond Dane. "Look
at her. She even walks like a babe now."

Dane turned his head, letting out a small sigh of
relief at the sight of her. "She *is* a babe," he said with
a smile. *My babe.*

Marco cleared his throat, forcing Dane's attention
back to him. "Listen, I know you're pretty tight with
her. I can see that." Marco leaned forward, his old
passion showing in eyes still dimmed by pain and
injury, "But she's my sister, Dane. She's not some
model or debutante that you picked up on a cruise
who goes gaga over your blue eyes and big house.
She's my sister."

"I know that," he responded softly.

"You can't just treat her like those other girls."

Dane said nothing. He turned away from Marco to
watch her approach the plane, her head tilted toward

Cassie, a sudden laugh lighting up her pretty face. He knew every inch of her body intimately. He watched her breasts move with her sexy walk and thought of how much pleasure she gave him. And he gave her.

But it had gone so far beyond pleasure that he didn't know how to describe what he felt. He was no Santori, raised in a loud, loving, lusty family. He was from the icy cold Erikson clan. He had no idea how to love as much as she did.

Maybe it was just an affair, with the inevitable outcome. Maybe not.

"Well?" Marco was waiting for his response. He deserved one.

"This is different," Dane said seriously. "This is really different."

But he had no idea what to do about it.

Dane's kitchen was getting frighteningly familiar. Over the course of just a few weeks, Ava had identified her favorite pans and had reorganized a drawer next to the stove to hold key utensils. Then she enhanced his pathetic collection of spices and arranged them alphabetically from allspice to white pepper. As Dane struggled with the problems of his business, even agreeing to media interviews to assuage nervous customers, she made herself at home in his magnificent house and felt guiltier about it each day. She shouldn't get so comfortable. She couldn't stay forever.

Cassie had ceased her warnings. Marco just whispered "be careful," and the Utopians seemed to adopt her as one of their own. Even Marj treated her like the lady of the house, asking permission before cleaning something in the kitchen, or mentioning things they needed so Ava could add them to her shopping list.

But I don't live here. Tonight, she'd tell him. She placed a batch of lemon chicken in the oven and closed the door with a sense of finality. She had to go home.

Just after sunset, he came home while she sat on the veranda nursing a cold glass of chardonnay. She'd mentally rehearsed her speech, knowing he'd try to talk her out of it. He'd try to buy more time. How long would it be until she'd overstayed her welcome? Cassie and Marco were going back in a few weeks. She would fly back with them.

He bent down to greet her with a kiss.

"Hello, princess."

Oh, this was getting far too good. Too comfortable, too right. Which meant it would hurt that much more when it was over. She clenched her jaw to keep from announcing her intention. If she'd learned anything from him, it was how to wait for the right moment.

He glanced at the wine. "Great idea." He crouched down next to her chaise and kissed her again, with meaning and intention. As always, a tingling reaction shot straight through her. "I'll be back in a minute," he promised. "I have to talk to you about something. Something important."

His blue-green eyes danced a little, making her shiver. What could it be, she wondered as he left. And should she tell him her decision first, or let him talk? She was still undecided when he returned.

"You look pensive," he said as he dropped into a chair next to her and held a matching glass toward her for a quick toast. "You okay?"

She clinked his glass with her own. *"Salud.* Yes. I'm fine."

He held the wine to his mouth but didn't drink. "Liar."

"What did you want to talk to me about?" She crossed her legs and tried to offer her most casual smile.

"Anything." With his left hand, he reached over and took her fingers. "I could talk to you about anything and it would be fun. I never get bored."

Her heart flipped a little and she took a shaky sip of wine. "But you said you had something to tell me. What's it about?" A tingling sense of anticipation teased her tummy.

"Food. It's about food."

She coughed back a laugh. So much for secret fantasies. "Food? Well, I can probably help you there."

"You can." He leaned forward, a serious look on his face. He rubbed his hand across his stubble, grown from the long day but sure to be shaved before they got in bed together. "And I want you to consider this very seriously."

Her heart started to knock her ribs. Where was he going?

"I want you to stay and take over Arnot's job." He broke into an expectant smile. "Isn't it perfect? You'd be awesome, Ava. Head of Culinary Operations."

A black wave of disappointment rolled over her and left her dumbstruck. Ava stared at him. He was serious. He wanted her to stay and work for him.

"Isn't it a great idea? You're so talented and you'd love the work . . . and . . ." His voice trailed off a bit as he studied her reaction. "And you could stay. Here. With me."

"Until when?" she finally asked. "Until I get fired?"

"Ava. It's not about the job," he said. She could see the confusion and even a little fear in his eyes. "It's just a . . . solution . . . for us to stay together."

She slowly set her glass on the small table between them, certain he could see her hand shaking. She would not blow, she told herself. She would not have a temper tantrum or crying jag or otherwise mortify herself. She would leave with her dignity intact.

"We're not a problem that requires a *solution*," she said softly as she stood. "I've decided to go home. To-morrow." The word was out before she could swallow it back. Not waiting to see his reaction, she rose and walked toward the house.

Of course he would come to her. She knew he would. But he didn't appear for over an hour. Enough time for the ache to turn into a black hole of pain and the tears that she'd fought for days to flow freely. By the time he stood silently in the doorway, she'd finished packing and washed her face.

He stayed there a long time, watching her zip the bag and flip it on a chair before he spoke.

"I really screwed that up, didn't I?"

She smiled a little and shrugged. "I guess the tendency to speak before thinking is contagious. You'll go back to your normal, deliberate self when I'm gone."

He glanced at the suitcase on the chair. "You're serious, aren't you?"

"Yes, Dane. I'm serious." She pushed a wayward curl from her eyes and looked at him. "I've been thinking about it for a while. You know that I have to go home."

He leaned against the doorjamb and ran both

hands through his hair, a heavy sigh clearly communicating his frustration.

"I'm really sorry, Ava. You deserve moonlight and flowers and far more romantic words."

"Romantic words?" She laughed bitterly and turned to face the windows. "Not for a job offer, honey. I'm sure you lure your best employees with a fat paycheck and a no-fault contract." She stared at the rising moon through the shutters. "One that you can get out of at a moment's notice."

A small grunt registered the hit. "I just want you to stay. I wanted a compelling reason to keep you from going back to the restaurant, back to your family, back to your life."

Had he lost his mind? Didn't he know that he was compelling enough?

"What happened to you?" She turned to him with fire in her eyes. "You were so smart. You got it. You got *me*. You understood exactly what made me tick, and how to make me happy. Deeply happy. Down-to-the-bone happy. Why would you even make a suggestion like that?"

As he closed the space between them, he reached for her, but she pulled her shoulders back and stepped farther away, as far back as she could go.

"I'm scared, Ava," he whispered.

"Of what?"

"That I won't know how to love you. The way you deserve to be loved. The way I want to love you." His voice cracked a little, squeezing her heart. "I just have no idea how to promise what you . . . what you want."

How could she convince him that it could last forever? She couldn't. Maybe it just *couldn't* last forever.

Their inevitable parting scared her so much that she had to make it happen on her own terms.

She shook her head. "Well, I have no idea how to live that way. Temporary. As an employee. As a long-term guest. Never sure when the clock will run out on your affections."

"Cassie and Marco lived together," he said defensively. "That worked."

She put her hands on her hips and stared at him. "Cassie has a tattoo on her chest, Dane. We may get along great, but we're different girls. I'm no free spirit tumbleweed who makes love during a job interview." She stopped for a second and fought back a bitter laugh. "Well, maybe I did and didn't realize it."

In one swift move, he was in front of her, his arms trapping her. "I hate that you have that sound in your voice. That pain. I hate it." He squeezed her, pulling her closer so that every inch of his body touched every inch of hers. "I never, ever wanted to hurt you." His lips crushed hers, the kiss frantic and solid and demanding. With a will of its own, her body responded.

When he pulled away, his voice was hoarse, solemn. "Listen to me." He put his finger on her lips and looked straight into her eyes. "I love you, Ava Rose Santori. I *love* you."

The words stunned her. They shot through her like a poison arrow, breaking her heart in a million pieces never to be repaired.

"I love you too, Dane Erikson," she whispered. "And I know I'll love you forever."

She could see the tears in his eyes. "I don't know how to promise that."

She longed to teach him. To be part of his family,

his life, his world. She could teach him all about for-ever, but it was fruitless. He didn't want to learn.

"That's a shame," she whispered as she touched his cheek. "That's a loss."

She put her arms around his neck and kissed him again. Pulling him toward the bed, she tumbled onto him. Wordlessly, breathlessly, they undressed and began to make love. Not the possessed and impas-sioned explorations of each other that they usually enjoyed. This time they made love face-to-face, heart to heart, body to body. As she rocked with a climax, her legs wrapped around him until she thought they would break, Ava cried out his name over and over, kissing him and letting the tears mingle between their mouths. She knew she'd never love like this again.

He couldn't get out of bed. He heard her showering but didn't go in the bathroom and join her, like he used to. He tried to ignore the sounds she made in the kitchen, the soft murmur of her voice on the phone, making arrangements with the airlines, call-ing Cassie and Marco to say good-bye and promising to see them in Boston in just a few weeks, for Christ-mas.

He had no plan, no strategy, no scheme. Just a helpless, hopeless ache because the inevitable had ar-rived. The rogue wave had swallowed him whole and left him drowning in its foam.

She came into the room, dressed in a crisp white blouse and pressed blue jeans. Her hair was pulled off her face in a gold clip, all neat and refined. Back to Boston. Back to the hundred years of Santori's Ris-torante in the North End. He had such a strong mental image of the place, he could easily imagine her there. Among the brown bricks and cobblestones. In the snow, now that it was early December.

He leaned up on his elbows, staring at her while she slipped on her watch. What words could he use to convince her to stay? What promises could he make that would get her to unclip that hair and unbutton that blouse and come back to bed and forget everything but this moment?

None. No promises. Nothing he could be sure of keeping, anyway.

"I'm taking an eleven-o'clock flight to San Juan. It's got a long layover, but there's a direct connection to Logan that will get me home tonight."

He glanced at the clock on the nightstand. Two hours. He had two hours. He threw back the sheet and saw her gaze travel over his naked body. Then she turned back to the dresser and busied herself with earrings.

"I'll take you to the airport," he said quietly.

After he showered and dressed, he found her on the veranda, looking out at the mountains of St. Martin.

She didn't turn at the sound of his footsteps.

"Tell everyone I said good-bye," she finally said. "Especially Marj. And Claire. And all the cooks. Your whole . . . family."

He heard her voice break on the last word and felt his heart dance with a little hope. He came up behind her and slowly wrapped his arms around her stomach, feeling her instantly tighten. He tucked her head under his chin, where she fit so perfectly, and gazed out at the sea. The breeze lifted a curl that had escaped her clip, tickling his face.

"The northern wind," he whispered. "Odin is not happy."

"Neither am I," she responded and turned to look up at him, tears threatening. "Let's go."

The wind increased as they made their way to the airport, bringing heavy clouds and the first splatter of raindrops.

"Maybe you should wait and take a later flight," he suggested while they drove around the little terminal looking for a parking spot.

"No. I'll be fine."

He pulled into a slot and threw the gearshift into park with a jolt.

"But I won't," he said roughly, staring ahead, watching the fat drops of rain burst on the windshield. "I won't be fine."

He waited for her response. Hadn't she learned that her impetuous actions were foolish? This was a prime example. He turned to tell her, but she had opened the door and stepped out into the rain. He could only follow.

The pounding in his head matched the thump of his heart as they went through the motions of getting her ticket. *Don't do this, Ava. Don't do this.*

But he didn't say it. They waited at the airport's only gate, surrounded by the happy faces of relaxed tourists, tanned and mellow from their week in paradise and reluctant to leave. *Don't do this, Ava.* He just couldn't say it. They sat in metal seats together, holding hands.

"You don't have to wait," she said. "With the rain, it could be delayed."

"I want to wait."

From the desk, a woman announced the boarding

of flight twenty-one to San Juan. Two dozen reluctant passengers started their walk across the runway, through the steady downpour to the waiting twin-engine turboprop.

They stood and she slipped her purse on her shoulder.

"I hate this part," she said with a nervous laugh. "Don't draw it out."

He touched her cheek, lingering one last time on her dimple and smiling into the depths of the olive black eyes he'd come to love. "Bon voyage, princess."

She turned and walked through the glass door to the runway.

God had a hand in giving her the window seat that faced the terminal. No, it must have been Satan, because it hurt like hell to see him there. He'd come out to stand behind the metal rail, the rain soaking his blond hair to a dark brown. With both hands on the railing, he stared at her plane. Maybe the rain mixed with his tears, she thought with an ache that squeezed her heart.

Maybe he's going to come running madly across the runway, demanding they turn off those damn propellers because the woman he wanted to marry was on that plane. Wasn't that what she wanted? Wasn't all this quiet drama just her way of getting him to say the words she longed to hear? *Please, Ava, stay and be my wife and love me forever.* She ached at the admission, but it was true. That's what she wanted. Hell, she wanted the Culinary Operations job too, she thought with a wry smile. But more than that, she wanted forever. And she wouldn't settle for less.

Run, Dane. Now. The tears burned and fell down her cheeks. *Now, honey, now. Run to me.*

But he gripped the railing and stared, soaked and still.

As the wheels rumbled over the cracked concrete and the engines screamed to announce takeoff, Ava kept her gaze locked on him. His T-shirt had turned to a wet rag clinging to his body. She could see the water dripping off his hair. He never moved.

I love you, Dane Erikson. Forever.

Farther and farther they taxied, and she watched his sad figure grow smaller in the distance until she could see him no more. Then they lifted into the wet, gray clouds and she imagined him standing in the rain a long, long time.

20

Ava stood on her toes to see over the heads blocking her view of the arriving passengers from Miami. At two o'clock in the afternoon of Christmas Eve, Logan was crammed with anxious travelers and impatient relatives greeting them. No one was more anxious or impatient than the three Santoris who'd waited five years for this moment. Ava squeezed her mother's arm through a thick parka sleeve and grinned.

"Don't worry, Mama. I know they made the flight. Cassie called from Miami."

"I'm not worried, honey. I'm just happy." Mama looked from Ava to Dominic as he, too, peered into the darkness of the jetway beyond each passenger. "This day has been a long time coming."

Then they saw him. Tall and imposing like his father, his arm slung around Cassie, they came strolling out of the darkened hallway wearing wide, matching smiles.

"There he is!" Mama called out. "Marco! Cassie!"

In a flash, they found each other and Maggie

threw her arms around Marco and Dominic hugged them both. Ava folded Cassie in her own arms and kissed her cheek. When they parted, Ava's gaze drifted beyond the tiny woman, and she cursed herself for looking.

"It's just us, luv," Cassie whispered in her ear. "Sorry."

"Of course," she said casually and smiled into the knowing green eyes. "Welcome to Boston, Cass."

Marco reached down and swooped his sister into a bear hug.

"Avel Navel, you brat." He kissed her on the cheek. "We missed you down there."

She backed away and winked at him. "We missed you up here." He looked so much stronger. His face was no longer hollow but handsome again, and the teasing spark that lit his eyes had returned. "Let's get you home, Marco Polo."

Dominic pronounced it the best Christmas Eve dinner in Santori history. They closed the restaurant and ate in Mama and Dominic's spacious apartment, the dining room, living room, and kitchen bursting with the joy of reunion. The entire clan gathered for the traditional meal of seafood and pasta.

While Ava and Grandma Rose made Marco's favorite *baccalà* and calamari, the little white-haired woman wiped a steady stream of tears, muttering her mantra of "if only Mike were here, if only Mike could see this." The fact that her husband had died three years earlier without ever seeing Marco again pained her, but Ava just kissed her wrinkled cheek and assured her that Grandpa Mike was watching from heaven.

Three generations of Santoris hovered around

Marco like he was a visiting dignitary. Laughter escalated with the homemade wine and the courses continued for hours as they lingered and ate and argued
and celebrated the extraordinary moment in their
family history. As dinner ended, Ava's gaze traveled
over Dominic's brother John and his whole family,
Aunt Anna and Uncle Frank, all of the cousins, Mia
and Nick, Tony and Mary Rose, and a few extra babies from the next generation. How she adored her
passionate, raucous, argumentative, lovable family.
She tried to imagine Dane in this room and how his
sculpted, Nordic magnificence would stand out among
this crowd. But, somehow, she knew he would have fit
right in. The knowledge stabbed at her, and she looked
around for the comfort of Cassie.

Grandma and Aunt Anna announced that cannolis
and coffee would be served in ten minutes, so Ava
slipped into the back of the apartment and found
Cassie sitting on the floor with baby Christina, her
cousin Nicky's one-year-old daughter. Cassie cooed
and the baby giggled.

"Getting a little practice in?" Ava asked as she
came into the room.

Cassie swooped up the crawling child, who tried
to escape with drooling determination. "Oh, isn't she
a darling wee thing? She followed me to the bathroom and I had to stop and discuss life with her. Now
I think I want a girl."

The baby tugged at the bedspread, trying to pull
herself up. Cassie lifted her into a gentle stand.
"There you go, little luv."

Ava sat on the corner of the bed and ruffled
Christina's wispy brown waves. "So, what do you
think of the mad Santori clan?"

Cassie leaned back on her hands and crossed her legs in front of her. "Loud. Funny. Absolutely wonderful. Reminds me of the wild and wooly Sebrings I left down under."

"Think you'll stay for a while?" Ava ventured.

"Definitely. At least until Marco's one hundred percent, and probably until the baby's born." Christina plopped back down on her diaper and Cassie pulled the little bundle into her arms. "We've picked January twenty-first as a wedding day. It's enough time to pull something together, but not so long that I'll be the size of a house." She tightened her blouse over a now noticeable rise in her stomach. "Think you can help me organize a small wedding in a few weeks?"

Ava laughed. "Italians who own a restaurant? Are you kidding? We can do a wedding in our sleep. But don't count on small."

"That's okay. I think my folks will come up from Sydney, maybe my two brothers too. I don't have a sister, Ava." She looked up expectantly. "I was hoping you'd take on the maid of honor job for me."

A warm rush spread through Ava, and she slipped from the bed to join Cassie on the floor. "Oh, Cass," she said as they embraced. "You have a sister now."

Little Christina tried to get in the middle of the hug. They tickled her and Ava decided she couldn't contain her curiosity any longer.

"And what about the best man?" she asked cautiously. "Who gets to walk me back down the aisle after you say 'I do' to my brother?"

Cassie kissed a brown curl and helped Christina up on wobbly legs. "He said he didn't think he could get away."

Ava's stomach dropped and she avoided Cassie's

gaze. "Oh. You mean Dane? Well, of course not. He's so busy. And this is your high season, right?"

"I don't think that's the reason, Ava."

Ava's heart pounded faster as she waited for the explanation.

"He's . . . he's . . . not really doing so well," Cassie said softly.

"What is . . . what do . . . what's wrong with him?"

Cassie shrugged. "He took your leaving quite hard. I must say, I've never seen him in such a state."

A tendril of satisfaction, a flicker of hope, and a warm rush of sympathy collided in her heart.

"How about you?" Cassie asked. "Have you put your pirate days behind you yet?"

Ava dropped her head and closed her eyes for a moment. Pirate days. What a lovely way to think of her time with the heart-stopping sailor and his magnificent ships. "I'm all right."

Cassie cleared her throat in an obvious demand for the truth.

Ava stared at the ceiling. "Okay. Not all right. I'm a mess."

"That makes two of you, then," Cassie said as she lifted the baby onto her lap. "Because he's a royal disaster."

"He's only called twice." She knew the exact day and hour of each call but didn't tell that to Cassie. "He says he wants to stay . . . in touch. He sounded fine. A little distant, but really fine."

Cassie shook her head. "If he sounded fine, he deserves an acting award. I've never seen him like this, Ava. He just works and works, all day and all night. If he's not working, which is rare, he comes over and spends his only spare time with Marco. I can't remember hearing him laugh. He's so . . . preoccupied. So sad and dark."

"He has a big job in putting things back in order," Ava offered. "Six employees involved in drug running, Maurice Arnot at the center of it, and quite a few damning headlines about the company. It'll be months before Utopia is what it once was."

"Oh, yeah. But that's not what's eating away at him."

"Cassie," Ava sighed. "He had every opportunity. I was not opposed to the idea of staying in St. Barts. I love him. But . . ." She swallowed against the familiar lump that started to form in her throat. "I don't want a temporary arrangement. And he couldn't promise anything else."

"All I know is that the man is dying, Ava." Cassie looked pointedly at her friend. "Just dying."

The thought of his misery hurt even more than the constant ache that had become part of her everyday existence. "He's been through a lot."

Cassie nodded. "Yes, he has. He lost his ship. He lost all those men. And then he lost the first woman I think he ever loved."

The words cut her. "What should I do?"

"Go to him. Live with him. Be his woman."

Ava closed her eyes against tears she could no longer fight. "No. I want the whole deal, Cassie. I want to marry him and spend the rest of my life with him. I love him too much to be happy with anything else."

The baby squawked in Cassie's face, pulling at her necklace, demanding attention. "Well, to answer your question, I think Marco will ask your father to be his best man. So, Dominic will walk you down the aisle."

Ava knew her sad smile gave away her true feelings. "Might be his only chance."

The sun broke through and made a valiant effort to melt the snow that had accumulated on the sidewalks and streets of the North End. But for most of the day on January 21, Ava only got the weather report from Mia, who periodically left her post in the kitchen to check the skies. Determined to supervise the feast, Ava had the kitchen in high gear by the time she looked at her watch and realized she'd have to get Cassie over to her apartment in less than half an hour if they were to have enough time to get ready for this wedding.

Ava took one last taste of the marinara sauce and looked around for her cousin. "Mia!" she called. "Where are you?"

The kitchen doors swung open and Mia nearly skipped in, hurriedly pulling her long honey-colored hair back into the required ponytail. "Sorry, Ava. I didn't know you were looking for me. How's the marinara? I worked so hard on it."

"It's perfect. Really. Dominic will be proud of you. It will be the hit of the wedding."

"Hey, I learned from you, Ave," Mia said earnestly.

"Don't tell your uncle." Ava winked at her cousin and took a quick look around the kitchen. Several cooks were busy at the stoves, and the pastry chef hid behind a three-tier white wedding cake. "I've been buried in this kitchen since dawn. I want to go get Cassie and her gown, and get back to my place to take a bath, and have lots of time to make my new sister a beautiful bride."

Mia glanced toward the dining room doors. "Don't

forget the maid of honor, Ave. You're going to be a knockout in that dress you picked. You look fabulous in red."

"I don't know what got into me, choosing a dress like that." Ava grinned at the thought of the slinky red dress that had what Cassie called "maximum cleavage." Six months ago she wouldn't have considered wearing a dress that revealing. She started to untie her apron. "Let's go upstairs and get Cassie."

"Oh, she's in the dining room," Mia said, a tiny smile curling at her lips. "She and Marco just got back from the airport."

"The airport?" Ava's hands froze on her apron strings. Cassie's family had arrived yesterday afternoon, and they weren't expecting anyone else. "What were they doing at the airport?"

"They picked up their boss from St. Barts. He's out there with them now." Mia broke into a full grin. "You failed to mention he was a gorgeous hunk of blond."

Ava felt the blood drain from her head. Dane. He'd come to her. *He'd come to her.*

She covered her mouth with her hand as she stared at Mia, speechless. She ignored her cousin's giggle and let the rush of joy and warmth and complete confusion wash over her.

"He's here?" The words strangled in her throat.

Mia nodded. "There's one handsome man waiting for you out there. He's politely making small talk but seems to be looking around an awful lot."

A nervous laugh escaped Ava's lips. "Oh ... oh my God. I can't believe this ..." Her hands flew to her hair and down her stained apron. "I better ... I ... do I look okay?"

Mia leaned against a stainless steel counter and crossed her arms as she scrutinized her cousin. "I'd say you look dazed, Ave. Dazed and . . . maybe a little in love?"

She shot her cousin a deep, infectious grin. "More than a little, Mia."

She heard his laugh as soon as she opened the door. Like music, like angels singing, she thought, wallowing in the beauty of the sound. She saw him from the back, his broad shoulders blocking the light of the winter sun pouring through the front window, his hand comfortably on Marco's shoulder. They stood in a small group, Marco, Maggie and Dominic, Cassie and her two brothers and her parents. And Dane.

"Oh, here's Ava now," she heard Mama say.

He turned instantly. Backlit from the window, she could hardly see his face in the shadows. She could see his hair had been cut neatly and noticed that he looked oddly out of place in a sweater and long pants, a leather jacket hooked in his finger and hung over his shoulder. The knock of her heart and a rush of blood through her veins were the only sounds she heard. He moved toward her and out of the shadow, and she could see his warm blue eyes and an even warmer smile. She had no doubt, no doubt at all, why he was there.

"I hear there's going to be a wedding tonight," he said softly, reaching for her before she could even exhale. "I didn't want to miss it."

She nearly got his name out, but he pulled her into his arms before she could speak and his mouth came down on hers and covered it with a long, soulful kiss that left her dizzy and breathless.

His lips moved to her ear. His breath, warm with promise, tickled her, sending sparks of anticipation and joy right down to her toes. "I can't live another day without you, baby."

"Good lord, you're more nervous than I am," Cassie teased as she tucked a wayward tendril of Ava's hair into an uncooperative knot.

Ava shook her head hard and the curl fell down. "Damn!" Her gaze moved from her own face in the mirror to Cassie. "I think I want it down, Cass. Do you mind?"

"I don't care if you wear a bathing cap, for goodness' sakes. Just finish and help me button this contraption." She turned to show Ava the open back of her wedding gown.

With shaking fingers, Ava started working on the silk loops of Cassie's dress. Eventually she attached them all to a coordinating button, then took every pin out of her hair and shook her mass of curls into long waves that fell over the bare skin revealed by her off-the-shoulder dress.

Stepping back to the full-length mirror in her bedroom, she did a little twirl to let the red silk dance around her body. She ran her hands along the magnificent lines of the dress, turning to the side to appreciate the way it hugged her body. She'd never thought of herself as sexy, she thought as she studied the deeply cut bodice and gave the strapless bra a final tug to accentuate the rise of her breasts against the red. Never thought of herself as quite this beautiful. But that was before Dane.

Cassie's bright eyes twinkled behind Ava's reflection. "Hey, make room for the bride, luv." They stood side by side, drinking in the result of their hard work.

"Hmmm . . ." Cassie cocked her head in the mirror. "An angel and a devil, wouldn't you say?"

In her glorious white gown and a lace veil that gently fell over golden curls, Cassie indeed looked heavenly. With black hair spilling to the edges of the fitted scarlet silk, Ava looked anything but angelic.

"You are truly a divine bride, Cass."

"Thanks. And Dane's going to drop dead when you walk in that church, luv."

Ava's throaty laugh was the only response. She looked into Cassie's eyes in the mirror and raised a questioning eyebrow.

"Did you, uh, talk to him recently?"

Cassie looked away and plucked at the white lace of her long sleeve. "I did not."

Ava squinted at her. "Do not lie to me. You are about to legally become my sister, Cassie Sebring Santori."

"Ooh. I like the sound of that." Cassie giggled but couldn't avoid Ava's pointed stare. "I really didn't talk to him. But Marco may have had a little chat with him."

"And said . . . ?" Ava prompted.

"Who knows what men say to each other, luv? He probably gave Dane the same advice Dane has given him for years."

"And that would be?"

"Find your way," Cassie said simply, and then winked. "Evidently, he found his way right to you."

Ava flushed, remembering the words he'd whispered in her ear earlier, after a long and meaningful kiss in front of her whole family.

There had been no time for more than a few lin-

gering gazes before they had to run upstairs and
gather Cassie's dress and take off for Ava's apartment. But tonight, at the wedding, they would talk.
And after, she would bring him here. A shiver of anticipation ran through her at the thought. The phone
rang and Ava answered it, then smiled at Cassie.
"The limo's here."

It was time to marry Marco and Cassie.

The bells of the 125-year-old Italian church on Prince
Street pealed a joyous welcome as the white limou-
sine approached. Ava pulled her wrap around her
shoulders and lifted her delicate bouquet and Cassie's
from the opposite seat.

"This is it, sweetie. Are you ready?"

Cassie rubbed her tummy, easily concealed under
several layers of silk and lace. "We both are."

"Then let's get the three of you married." Ava
smiled as the driver opened their door, and they gingerly stepped onto the sidewalk.

An icy wind lifted Cassie's veil and Ava took her
hand and guided the newest member of the Santori
family up the stairs of St. Leonard's. The church
where her own parents were married and where
Grandma Rose and Grandpa Mike were married.
Where family traditions lived on. The thought warmed
her against the bitter temperatures as the limo driver
hurried to open the heavy mahogany door for the
ladies in red and white.

The small crowd in the back gasped and fussed
over the bride, and after many kisses, Cassie's brothers escorted the last of the remaining guests to their
seats. Cassie's father, a redheaded Aussie who obviously gave Cassie her green eyes and sassy attitude,

put his arms around both of them. "Everyone's ready. When the music starts, you can go, Ava. Then I'll take my little girl to her groom."

The opening notes of Beethoven's "Ode to Joy" reverberated through the church. Ava took a deep breath and reached over and pressed her cheek against Cassie's.

Cassie whispered into her ear, *"Non ti spagnare."* Ava had to laugh a little at the Australian accent butchering the high Italian.

"I'm not. Don't you be, either."

Cassie glowed, anything but afraid. Ava blew a kiss to Cassie, then nodded to an usher who opened the door for her.

At the back of the darkened church, she took a deep breath and looked up to the altar. She could see Dane, resplendent in a black tuxedo, standing next to Dominic. Marco beamed from the center. Ava drank in the sight of the three men she loved most in the whole world. Her gaze moved to Dane and she began her long, slow walk. Dimly aware of flickering candles and the attention of two hundred people and vaguely conscious of the dramatic music, Ava squeezed the handle of her spray of white roses. Her attention never strayed from the aquamarine eyes that shone with love and certainty. When she reached the three stone steps to the altar, she climbed them slowly, then turned and sighed with the rest of the congregation as Cassie entered the church and began her wedding march to Marco.

Then they said their vows and made their promises. *To love, honor, and cherish.* Over the bowed heads of the bride and groom, Dane watched her, his expression serious.

In sickness and in health. Their gazes remained locked as though a magnetic force refused to let either one of them look away.

For richer or poorer. Sparks flew from his blue-green eyes, and his mouth curled in the slightest smile.

Until death do us part. The sound of her own heart drowned out Cassie's voice repeating the words of the priest.

"I pronounce you husband and wife."

The guests broke into applause that echoed through the enormous church, but Ava and Dane just looked at each other. His lips moved ever so slightly with a silent message. *I love you.* She heard it as loud as if he had shouted it to the whole church.

The first two notes of Mendelssohn's wedding march burst from the organ as Cassie and Marco turned to start their happy stroll back down the aisle as a married couple. Ava glanced at Dominic expectantly, remembering how they'd rehearsed their own departure.

But Dane took her father's arm and whispered something in his ear.

Dominic flashed his black eyes at Ava in mock surprise, then smiled at Dane, put a hand on his back and gently nudged him toward her. As she slipped her fingers into the curve of his arm, he leaned his face close to hers.

"I hope you were paying attention," he whispered.

They took the first few steps down to the aisle. "I was a little distracted."

"Did you hear the part about love, honor, and cherish?"

"I think so."

They made their way slowly down the aisle, their

heads leaning toward each other as the dramatic and glorious notes of the wedding song rang in their ears.

"And you memorized the last line, right?" he asked as they reached the back of the church. A tender, heartbreaking smile broke over his face as he turned her to face him. "Till death do us part, Ava."

The crowd swelled around them, emptying the church, moving toward the bride and groom. They stood like stones in the river as people glided past the two lovers who were unaware of anything but each other.

"Till death do us part," she repeated. She took a breath to add something, but he put one finger over her lips.

"Don't give me a speech, Ava. I love you, and I want to marry you and share my life with you, and make you the happiest woman in the world. *Forever.* Just say yes."

"Oh, Dane, I love you. Yes! I—"

"Shh." He pulled her closer, and his arms felt so strong and sure around her. "I want to kiss my bride."

Epilogue

The relentless July sun beat hard on the docks of St. Barts, the heat and humidity relieved only by the steady breeze that blew the ladies' summer dresses and filled the sails of the massive ships resting in the Caribbean waters.

Dane gazed at the mix of islanders, the different shades of skin and hair, the vivid clothes, the brilliant blue of the water and the sky. A hush had fallen over the crowd, broken only by the soft words of the priest and a few whimpers from young Dominic Bartholomew Santori. Nico, as they called him, had evidently resigned himself to the fact that he'd been dunked and blessed and held by his godmother, instead of the familiar woman who brought him into the world.

Dane watched his wife soothe the baby, her fingers stroking the creamy cheeks, her body swaying in a slow rhythm that women seemed to be born to do. As always, he needed to touch her. He put his hand on Ava's back, and she looked up at him. The glow from their weeks on a honeymoon in Italy still burnished her silky complexion. The fire that lit her eyes glowed as hot as ever.

She had to be thinking, as he was, of the day they had met on these docks. Of the sorrow and tragedy that brought them together. Of the joy and sense of wholeness that they now shared. He marveled at the journey they'd been on together and the adventure they were just beginning.

She looked so natural holding the baby, its tufts of black hair matching her own. Baby Nico, at less than two months old, had yet to really smile, so Dane was left to wonder whether his godson had inherited the trademark Santori dimple.

He would know as they watched him grow and gave him the gift of cousins, even though Cassie and Marco had decided to settle in Boston. Marco had moved naturally into Ava's old job and Cassie seemed thrilled with the ever-present Santori clan to help raise their child. The Caribbean christening was timed to let them say good-bye to all the Utopians and arrange their new life in the States. Something told Dane that Marco and Cassie would come back to the islands. As soon as Marco had healed completely, as soon as he could sail again.

Dane and Ava had already planned to have another home in Boston so they could be certain their own children, although raised in the Caribbean, would know the tradition and roots of their century-old Italian family. And even spend some time in New York with the Eriksons, he thought with a wry smile. His parents. Ava's latest project.

Dane ran his hand over the bare skin of her back, loving the feel of her, loving the strength and determination and fiery impulsive nature that made her so passionate. The wind blew her hair and lifted the edge of little Nico's christening gown. As it did, Ava looked up at him.

"The southern wind," he whispered to his wife.

"Don't tell me: Odin is happy."

"I don't know." He smiled. "But I am."

Author's Note

TROPICAL GETAWAY is based on a real-life event. In November of 1998, the *S/V Fantome*, part of the famous Windjammer Barefoot Cruise fleet, had disembarked its passengers in Belize at the first signs of Hurricane Mitch. Thirty-one men stayed on board to chart a path in the opposite direction and make a hasty retreat, which is standard procedure for sailing vessels. Unfortunately, Hurricane Mitch changed its course, defying meteorologists as it turned south. The hurricane headed straight for the *Fantome*, and the ship and its crew were lost.

Attorneys immediately began to circle, looking for blood and retribution. They accused the company of deliberately navigating the ship to its certain death, and promised the grieving families million-dollar settlements. Eventually the unfounded lawsuits were dropped and the little cruise company could finally try to heal from its gaping wound.

The story of the *Fantome* haunted me as much as its name, which is French for "ghost." I was especially moved by the love story of the *Fantome*'s captain who died and never married the sweet British girl who worked as a housekeeper on board the ship.

From the devastating loss of *Fantome*, I was inspired to write *Tropical Getaway*. In fiction, there is love, hope, and answers. My own real-life experience of losing my home in Hurricane Andrew in 1992 added to my ability to describe the results of such devastation. More than anything, I pray that the thirty-one souls lost on the *Fantome* are at peace and that their loved ones have found comfort. My story is completely fictional. My characters are from my imagination. My ending, more than anything, is far happier than reality.

Dear Reader:

Welcome to the exciting world of *Bon Voyage* romances!

Have you ever longed to sail on a luxury ship in the Caribbean, with the wind blowing through your hair, and a steel band playing a tropical beat on deck as you dance with a dangerously attractive man? Or to meander the misty emerald hills of Ireland as a handsome stranger whispers sweet nothings in your ear in a delightful brogue? Or to sit at a tiny table for two in a Roman plaza at dusk, gazing into the eyes of a tall, dark, mysterious man as a singer croons a plaintive Italian love song?

Everyone loves traveling to romantic, exotic destinations—even if only in their imagination—and *Bon Voyage* will take you away to the lands of all your fantasies. Sexy modern English dukes, romantic evenings in Paris, the sun-drenched coast of Greece . . . Love knows no bounds, so we're expanding the world of romance, bringing you irresistible contemporary love stories from all over the world.

Turn the page to get a taste of our next romance, *The Last Bride in Ballymuir* by Dorien Kelly, where Miss Kylie "Soon-to-Be-a-Saint" O'Shea gets involved with a dangerous stranger who awakens her dreams and desires. And in July, look for *That's Amore* by Carol Grace, where newly divorced Anne Marie Jackson innocently becomes entangled with international jewel thieves, and a sexy Italian detective suspects her of being an accomplice—her calm, predictable life has never been so exciting!

So happy reading . . . and *bon voyage!*

Micki Nuding
Senior Editor

**Pocket Star Books
Proudly Presents**

The Last Bride in Ballymuir

Dorien Kelly

**Coming soon from
Pocket Star Books**

**Turn the page for a preview of
Dorien Kelly's contemporary
romantic novel. . . .**

Bon Voyage!

> *"A little always tastes good."*
> —*Irish Proverb*

Ballymuir, Ireland

Each Sunday morning when she slipped through the plain doors of St. Brendan's Church, Kylie carried a guilty little secret with her: she liked going to mass not only for what she got out of it, but for being seen. Her father hadn't been much of a church-goer. Perhaps he stayed home out of fear of a lightning bolt striking straight to his heart, but more likely because sitting still for an hour and more was inconceivable to Johnny O'Shea. As was the concept of a Higher Authority.

Kylie was not her father; she believed. Each Sunday was a reaffirmation of the way she tried to live her life—*tried* being the operative word. Last night, for instance, she'd had far too many uncomfortable and inappropriate thoughts about Michael Kilbride. And today, as she settled early in a pew, she fought not to crane her neck like a spectator at the Bally-muir Races.

How she wanted him to be there. Coming in with his sister Vi, as he would, there'd be no missing him. Between her height and her flame red hair, Vi stood no more chance of being inconspicuous than Kylie did of being bold. And Michael was no man to be easily lost in a crowd, either. Even one packed into tiny St. Brendan's. Kylie shifted as subtly as she could to increase the range of her peripheral vision.

Breege Flaherty, who had sat next to her, reached over and patted her hand. "All morning you've been as nervous as an ewe come mating season. Whatever's the problem?"

"No problem, none at all," she assured her friend, secretly amused and appalled at how close Breege had struck to the truth.

Widowed Breege was Kylie's closest neighbor, both in proximity and in her heart. When the rest of the town had turned from Kylie after her father's arrest for fraud, Breege had remained steadfast. The fact that her dearest friend was eighty-two years old didn't seem odd in the least.

"If you've no problem, then slide down, dear. You've left people waiting in the aisle."

Embarrassed, Kylie glanced back up and found herself looking straight into Michael Kilbride's unforgettable green eyes. Her eyes did a low, lazy loop as she took in exactly how splendid this man was. He was wearing nothing grand, just dark trousers and a thick fisherman's knit sweater. Ah, but he wore it well. She'd not mind looking at him till time spun to a stop.

Breege's subtle nudge called Kylie back to her surroundings.

She tugged her gaze away from Michael. Right behind him stood his sister looking none too pleased to be biding her time in the aisle. Kylie hastily moved closer to Breege, making room for the two Kilbrides. After giving what she hoped passed for a polite smile rather than the half-hysterical grin she felt painting its way across her face, she focused on the service about to begin. For a few brief minutes she even succeeded.

But inches away sat Michael Kilbride, seeming almost oblivious to her presence. The less he noticed her, the more she did him. Or so it seemed to Kylie, who had begun to hear only his deep voice as he sang, his steady responses. A crowd of hundreds and she had reduced it to one. Not once, though, did he glance her way. By neither word nor gesture was he anything other than impersonal. In fact, his disregard seemed to wave itself like a flag of challenge.

Lately, she had fixed upon the idea of committing an act so wild and unexpected that for a short while it would lift the weight of respectability from her. And for that short while, she could sink her teeth into life—not be proper on the exterior, ready to shatter inside, Miss Kylie Soon-to-Be-a-Saint O'Shea.

Here and now—in the middle of church—she'd

like to shake Michael Kilbride by his broad shoulders and hiss, *"Have you forgotten me already? Did that kiss mean nothing to you?"* Sanity kept her in her seat. It was a blessing, too, considering Vi Kilbride's watchful gaze was upon her almost as much as hers was on Michael.

By the end of mass Kylie had herself firmly convinced that the man didn't even recognize her. And though she told herself she should be relieved, that he was far too rough and masculine for her to handle, she was sure her heart would break.

When Breege stopped to chat with a group of friends, Kylie kept her head down. She didn't know where Michael Kilbride was, and didn't want to. She'd not embarrass herself further. At least now her humiliation was a private thing. When Breege announced that she'd be staying in town for supper with Mrs. McCafferty, relieved, Kylie turned heel and fled.

The miles to Kylie O'Shea's couldn't have seemed longer. Michael immediately learned that it was one thing to commandeer Vi's car, but another to drive it. He was thankful that this time of year he stood little chance of running into a poor sod of a tourist who'd strayed to the wrong side of the road. It was struggle enough to keep true to the curves and hills without hopelessly grinding the car's gears.

Rounding the last torturous bend before the little track to Kylie's home, for the first time he asked himself what exactly he was doing. He owed her an apology, perhaps two. That much was certain. Yet he wasn't truly sorry for the kiss—shocked that he'd done it, and a bit mystified, too. But sorry? No, he was too selfish to feel regret. All he could bear to give was an excuse. The honest truth was that the sight of her took away his good sense and what few words he'd ever been able to string together. And he expected this meeting to be no different.

As she had been the day before, Kylie was at work in her field. Knowing no one else would come their way, Michael parked the car in the middle of the track and climbed out. Since his Sunday best and his everyday were one and the same, he didn't hesitate before joining her.

She had changed from the simple blue dress she'd worn to church. The oversized sweater he'd seen yesterday hung to her fingertips. Her long, slender legs were now covered by khaki colored pants tucked into muddied black wellies. Her hair, though, was the same as it had been in the too-close confines of St. Brendan's. She wore it pulled back from her face in a neatly woven style he vaguely recalled the girls saying was a French braid all those years ago.

Whatever the name, he'd sat through mass with his fingers burning to loosen the strands of the plait, to feel its silken length. Because he knew he wasn't beyond temptation—he'd proven that well enough the night before—he'd pretended that Kylie O'Shea wasn't there at all. And hurt her by it, he knew.

"Hello," he said.

She murmured a greeting in reply but never stopped working. He had wondered whether she would make this easy on him. Now he had his answer.

"Fine day to finish clearing the field," he offered as he fell in step next to her.

She spared him a chilly glance from under her lashes.

Filling her arms with jagged rocks, she stalked off to the fence and began setting in her load. Torn between frustration and the sure knowledge he was getting a warmer reception than he deserved, Michael stood and watched her for a moment.

Then with a shake of his head, he bent down and jimmied a large rock free of the earth. Using hands and occasionally the foot, he rolled it in a zig-zagging path to the fence. And all the while he considered his next move. Honesty seemed the only way out.

She still stood at the low line of fence, scowling at it as if by sheer force of will she could make it grow. Michael moved behind her, wanting to rest his hands on her slender shoulders but not daring to touch her. Not deserving to.

"I'm sorry."

She swung round to face him. A hot flame danced in those cool blue eyes, making him realize that his sister wasn't alone in the ranks of warrior.

"Sorry for what?"

Jamming his hands deep into his pockets he muttered, "For kissing you. It was wrong of me . . . stupid. I should have warned you . . . or something."

"Kissing me? You're sorry for that? There's nothing else you've done that you think might be worth an apology?"

A recitation of that list would stretch long past sunset, not that the woman in front of him looked inclined to let him slip in a word.

"Well, I'll admit the kiss was unexpected," she said. "And not invited, either. But I want you to take a look at me."

As though he'd be able to look away from such shimmering beauty.

She held her hands out to her sides. "I might seem a child to some, but I'm twenty-four years old and capable of knowing when I want to be kissed. And equally capable of telling a man to stop. Not that I stopped you last night. And not that I'll need to worry about stopping you, with you all but offering to send an engraved announcement before you try again."

She moved close enough that if he took his hands from his pockets he could haul her up against him. Tempting, so tempting.

"What amazes me, Michael Kilbride, and makes me doubt for my sanity, is that I'm beginning to think you've had less experience with the opposite sex than I have. Though looking at you, I can't imagine how that could be true."

He didn't think she'd like the answer, so he gave her none.

"Now, will I be getting that apology for the way you acted this morning?" The rueful shake of her head was something he was sure she'd practiced on her students time and again. "Not so much as a neighborly nod or hello."

Michael had promised himself that he'd give her the truth. Slipping his hands from his pockets, he stepped closer yet. He cupped her hand—so small— in his palm.

"For this morning, I'm truly sorry," he said, savoring the feel of her cool skin. The fact that it was a bit work-roughened somehow made her seem all the more appealing. "I'm not much good at social matters."

He turned her hand so that, palm upward, it still rested within his. She didn't fight him, just gazed at him through cautious eyes. It astounded him— humbled him—that she would welcome his touch. With his free hand he pushed back the heavy wool of her sweater until the inside of her wrist was exposed.

"Don't think that I ignored you, Kylie O'Shea, because you filled my morning, not whatever words Father Cready was offering up."

With one fingertip he traced the slender blue veins beneath her translucent white skin. The intimacy of it made him swallow hard and hesitate before speaking again. But it didn't make him stop touching her. Never that.

"So think I'm a boorish sod, but never, ever think that I didn't notice you."

Kylie couldn't look away from the long finger so intimately stroking her skin. This was no kiss, she thought. But it might as well have been, for the quicksilver thrill his touch sent chasing through her. She imagined that caress traveling further, up to the sensitive skin at the inside of her elbow and to the upper curves of her breasts.

Kylie tugged her hand from Michael's. She drew in a ragged breath and met his eyes. He hadn't meant to, but he'd shaken her. She didn't want him to know exactly how much.

"You are a man to seize the moment, aren't you?"

He gave her a crooked smile. "Are you looking for another apology?"

Not for his touch, she wasn't. Fussing with the lopsided hem of her sweater she answered, "No more than I was last night."

His smile was wry and teasing all at once. "Good, because the well was running dry. I've given you more apologies this morning than I've managed to force out in my entire life."

Still breathless, she stepped away and set back to work.

"So how long are you in Ballymuir?" she asked, though not certain she really wanted to know.

"I'm not sure. I'm thinking of settling here," he said, sounding almost startled at his own words.

Kylie's first thought was that she couldn't have wished on a star and done better.

"Truly?" she stammered. She scrambled for some inane question to mask the confusing sense of elation and something much darker that whispered across her skin, leaving the downy hairs at the back of her neck dancing in its wake. "And you're moving from where?"

Michael paused. "I've family in Kilkenny."

"Ah. Well, if you need help finding a place or settling in, just let me know." The words slipped out, and how Kylie wanted to swallow them back. Glancing at Michael, she wondered whether it was her imagination or if he truly was inching closer to his car. She felt half-ready to run, herself.

"I expect I'll be staying with Vi," he said. "At least till I'm more sure about things."

"I see." Kylie gathered up a few more rocks and

tossed them onto the pile. She'd do well to stop the personal questions now, she knew. Before she found her thoughts too far down a path she knew she shouldn't take.

When clouds blew in to cover the sun and a chill rain began to spit from the sky, Kylie gave up on field clearing for the day. She turned to Michael. "Would you like to come inside for a while? I started some bread just before you—*the bread!*"

Forgetting manners, Michael, everything but her two precious loaves of bread no doubt blackened to cinders, she flew to her house. When she reached the oven door, she already knew it was too late. Grabbing a potholder she pulled out the loaves and dropped the pans on the stove top where they landed with a metallic clank. Though she wasn't one for swearing, she tried on one of her father's favorites for size.

Low laughter rolled from the doorway. She turned to see Michael framed in the entry, and experienced a mixture of embarrassment and pleasure.

"I've never heard anything more halfhearted in my life. If you're going to use talk like that, you've got to give the words power. Like this—" Loud enough to ring in the rafters, he launched the same profane phrase she had. "Now you try it."

A hot crimson blush climbed her face. "I couldn't. I've scarcely thought words like that, let alone used them."

He laughed. "I'd noticed. But this would be our secret. Here in the privacy of your home, no one need know what you're saying. Though I don't suppose you should get so accustomed to those words that they slip out while you're teaching the young ones."

"You can't imagine what I've heard from a few of those eleven-year-old boys when they think no adult's listening."

Moving out of the doorway and closing the door behind him, he grinned. "Oh, I can imagine, all right. I was about that age when I had a bar of soap for supper one night after Vi told Mum what she'd heard me saying. I belched bubbles for a fortnight."

"You did not," Kylie replied, laughing in spite of herself.

"A day, then. But my first point's the same. Relax in your own home, Kylie. It's one of the few places on earth you're free to be as you really are."

Kylie looked down at the burnt loaves. Michael had homed in on her personal sorrow: not allowing herself even that bit of freedom. She couldn't afford it, any more than she could more flour for bread. And for the lack of both, she wanted to hate her father, but knew she was more to blame.

It had been her choice to accept the job at Gaelscoil Pearse. "The next worst thing to being a nun" the other teaching students had sniped when she'd told them where she was going. True, the school held a very conservative philosophy and expected its teachers to be above reproach.

To Kylie, it had seemed a perfect fit, especially since the school paid better than any other in the area. She didn't mind wearing her skirts below her knees and was certain she wouldn't enjoy the local nightclub, anyway. As she'd focused on the struggle to repay her father's endless debts, she'd scarcely thought about what she might be missing. And being able to stay close to Breege was worth almost any sacrifice. But lately . . .

She cut off that thought, too.

Looking back at Michael, she saw a passing expression on his face that seemed to echo her emptiness. Burdened with her own regret, she had no time to wonder why he should look that way. It was enough to find the composure to gloss over the moment. She stepped away from the stove and toward the hearth where two bricks of peat still glowed, their scent competing with that of the well-cooked bread.

"I can hardly offer you the bread." She paused to tug her damp woolen sweater over her head and smooth down the worn cotton shirt she wore beneath. "Are you wanting some tea, though? Wouldn't take more than a minute to get the kettle going."

At his answering silence, she turned to face him. Just looking at him, feeling the odd, intense current that seemed to envelop them both, sent a shiver through her. Gooseflesh raised on her arms and she rubbed at it.

"What I'm wanting has nothing to do with food," he said in a voice so quiet and low that she had to strain to hear it over the pounding of her heart. "What I'm wanting is to come to you and undo each of the buttons on your shirt till I find what waits for me beneath. Then I'm wanting to put my mouth against your skin and learn the feel of you till I know you so well that you're part of me."

More words than she'd yet had from him. Small wonder he saved them up, what he could do with them. She didn't look away from his green eyes. Mesmerized, she didn't blink, couldn't have if she wanted to.

"But since all that would surely call for an apology, I'll be leaving now." As he walked out the door, he called back over his shoulder, "Though if you like, you can consider it your engraved announcement for our next time together."

Their next time. Kylie flopped into the worn armchair she'd been so fiercely gripping. *Their next time.* Her heart had scarcely survived this one.